# MURDER ON THE GOLD COAST

4-26-06

# MURDER ON THE GOLD COAST

## A MATTHEW ALEXANDER MYSTERY

For: Dr. John Hope Franklin,
It was a pleasure seeing you
again in Cincinnati at the
Distinguished Historian Lecture.
I look forward to seeing you in
N.C. this summer. I hope you
enjoy the book. Barbara Fleming

## BARBARA FLEMING

*Silver Maple Publications • Yellow Springs, Ohio*

SILVER MAPLE PUBLICATIONS

Printed in the United States of America

The Text of this book is composed in
Georgia

Cover Art Design by
Silver Maple Publications, Yellow Springs, Ohio

Book Design and Composition by
Tod Tyslan

Fleming, Barbara
Murder on the Gold Coast / by Barbara Fleming.

Fleming, Barbara,
Murder on the Gold Coast / Barbara Fleming.
p. cm. — (A Matthew Alexander mystery)
LCCN 2004195396
ISBN 0-9708970-1-4

1. Alexander, Matthew (Fictitious character)—Fiction.
2. Detectives—Washington (D.C.)—Fiction.
3. Murder—Investigation—Washington (D.C.)—Fiction.
4. Washington (D.C.)—Fiction.
5. Mystery fiction.
I. Title.

PS3606.L459M87 2005          813'.6
QBI04-700612

Published by
Silver Maple Publications
Yellow Springs, Ohio

*Dedicated, with love,
to my Husband.*

# MURDER ON THE GOLD COAST

# PRIMARY CHARACTERS

**DISTRICT OF COLUMBIA POLICE DEPARTMENT (DCPD)**
Administrative Office
**Jefferson Carter**: Chief of Police

Fourth District Headquarters
**Lloyd Cullison**: Commander

Homicide Division
**Henry Bryant**: Captain
**Matthew Alexander (Matt)**: Detective Lieutenant
**James Jackson (Jake):** Detective Sergeant
**Sam Johnson**: Supervisor, Forensics Laboratory
**Carl Davis**: Detective Lieutenant
Vice, Prostitution, & Illegal Gambling Division

**DISTRICT OF COLUMBIA MEDICAL EXAMINER'S OFFICE**
**Stephen Mitchell, M.D.**: Deputy Medical Examiner

**DISTRICT OF COLUMBIA PROSECUTING ATTORNEY'S OFFICE**
**Edward Davenport**: Chief Prosecuting Attorney

**BOWMAN FAMILY**
**Walter Bowman, J.D.**: Supervisor, District of Columbia
Reclamation Land Agency (DCRLA)
**Helen Bowman**: Wife
**Angela Bowman:** Daughter

**WATERSON FAMILY**
**Harold William Waterson, Sr.**: Managing Partner,
Waterson, Sullivan & Loew Corporation
**Felicia Waterson:** Wife
**Harold William Waterson, Jr.**: Son
**Martha Waterson**: Maternal Aunt of Harold William Waterson, Sr.

**MARTIN FAMILY**
**Thomas Martin, M.D.**: Physician & Real Estate Speculator
**Claudia Martin**: Wife & District of Columbia Socialite

**WASHINGTON FAMILY**
**Gary Washington**: Estranged husband of Angela Bowman
**Frederick Douglass Washington**: Maternal Uncle of
Gary Washington

**MATTHEW ALEXANDER'S FAMILY**
**Carla Alexander, Ph.D.**: Wife and Clinical Psychologist
**Jennifer Elizabeth Alexander**: Three-Year-Old Daughter
**Robert Matthew Alexander**: One-Year-Old Son

# CHAPTER 1

"Answer me! Who's out there?"

The silence was both ominous and confusing because he knew someone had entered the house. Grabbing his hat and coat from the sofa, he called out again, his voice more shrill than before. Still, there was no reply. He stood motionless, his body frozen in place and stared into the hallway for what seemed an eternity before walking across the room. When he reached the darkened hallway, he saw a vague figure standing in the shadows near the basement door to his left. As he stepped across the threshold to get a better look, two rapidly executed gunshots exploded into his chest. For a brief time, he was suspended between the brutal horror of his certain death and the dreaded eternity that quickly engulfed him, all the while refusing to believe he had been shot as his mind raced against death in a futile effort to know why. Why would anyone want to kill him?

He wasn't ready for death, but it came anyway. It came without warning, without asking his opinion or begging his pardon. It hadn't come softly, little by little, as he expected it to...as he hoped it would. Instead, death came loud and undignified, like a thundering explosion which blasted into his chest and ripped the life out of his body.

He smelled the acrid stench as the bullets slammed into his heart and wrenched his body into a spasm of excruciating pain. He tried to scream, but the effort died somewhere between his lungs and throat as warm blood filled his mouth instead. He fought hard to stay alive to no avail, producing only a useless gurgling noise as his body hung in the air, desperately clinging to the last seconds of life that remained. Then he died a standing death of exquisite agony that he wouldn't have wished on his worst enemy. The force of the bullets that exploded into his chest threw his body back into the family room, where he performed a macabre pirouette, left arm suspended in mid air, right hand clutching the bloody wounds in his chest. When his body fell to the floor like the dead weight it was, his raincoat landed over his face and upper body, and his hat came to rest under the table where the telephone sat.

\*\*\*\*\*\*\*\*\*\*

Georgia Avenue hummed with midnight traffic as an unmarked police car sped north on rain-slicked tires, its siren screaming. The squad car raced past the ultra-modern Walter Reed Army Hospital as it loomed large over the surrounding community of row houses and store fronts. Without warning, the driver negotiated a sliding left onto Alaska Avenue, flying past the Dominican seminary on the north and the wide expanse of neatly manicured hospital grounds on the south side of the avenue. His tires having scarcely touched the wet pavement of Alaska, the driver executed a screeching right onto Sixteenth Street hurtling toward that exclusive residential enclave on the Maryland border known locally and enviously as the Gold Coast.

"Turn the siren off, Jake, and get the lead out of your foot long enough to tell me what happened at the scene?"

"I already told you everything I know, partner," Jake replied in a resonant voice reminiscent of deep southern roots despite twenty-five years separation from a culture and pace of life that clung to him as if he'd never left. His face knitted itself into a sudden scowl as he continued, "I can't stand the way Lloyd Cullison runs Homicide, man. He couldn't care less when those poor slobs in Shaw or Anacostia are wasted, but he pulls out all the stops for a murder on the Gold Coast. When you're dead you're done, it doesn't matter a rat's rump who you are or where you live."

Matt sensed that Jake was working himself up to a full-blown tirade against Fourth District Headquarters that would probably include an exhaustive litany of prior racist injustices, both imagined and real. He changed the subject.

"Did Lloyd assign Captain Bryant to the case, too?"

"Yeah, man. That butt-kissing Uncle Tom ought to be at the scene by now." Refusing to be sidetracked from his pet peeve, Jake resumed his harangue against the Homicide Division's Commander.

"I'm not trying to tell you how to run your business, partner;

but I wouldn't let Lloyd Cullison break my back with work. You been working like a dog on the open case backlog for weeks; but instead of giving you a break, he calls you out at midnight in the cold and rain on another homicide case."

"No sweat, man. I can handle it."

"By the way, partner, Carla looked real pissed when she opened the door just now. My call didn't interrupt anything important did it?" Jake knew that he was treading on sensitive ground, "But what the hell," he thought. "When you're married to a fox like Carla Channing, you ought to be able to take the heat."

In Jake's humble estimation, Carla Channing-Alexander was a stunning woman who took his breath away just by looking at her. There were no two ways about it, a woman as beautiful and sexy as Carla got herself commented on no matter who she was married to. Any fool could understand that, and Matthew Alexander was nobody's fool.

"You old dog," Matt replied laughing. "It sounds like your love jones has come down on you hard. Have you and Flo made up yet?"

"Does a chicken have lips? I'm still in the dog house, man. I've been sleeping in the guest room so long, I forget why I was sent there in the first place. You know Flo, Matt. There's no reasoning with her when she gets in one of her funky moods."

"I know the feeling. There's nothing I dread more than Carla going silent and refusing to talk. Run the particulars of the call by me again, Jake, just to be sure I got all the details."

"Sure, only there's not much to tell. Commander Cullison called me at eleven fifteen. He said a call had come into Homicide at ten-thirty tonight reporting a body on Floribunda Lane in the Gold Coast and that the third shift dispatcher had already ordered all available units and a rescue squad ambulance to the scene. He said he was assigning you and Captain Bryant to supervise the investigation. You know what that means...you do all the work and Bryant does all the butt-kissing and double-dealing behind your back. Cullison called the Captain before he called me, so Bryant should be at the scene by now."

"I used to date a girl named who lives on Floribunda, Jake. We went together for a year when I was a senior at Howard. I wanted to marry her, but her father wasn't about to let that happen."

" Yeah, man. I know the type."

"I didn't have much to offer her and she wasn't ready to break with her old man on my account. Her father gave her a hell of a lot more than I could, and he made it clear that she couldn't have it both ways."

"Did she break your engagement?"

"No, I did. It wasn't official anyway because I couldn't afford to buy her a ring. Floribunda's coming up on the left. What's the address?" Jake took a small notebook from his pocket and passed it to his partner.

"You sure this is the address Cullison gave you?"

"Yeah, I'm sure. If there's a mistake, Cullison made it, not me. What's wrong?"

"1637 is Angela Bowman's address. They're the family I was just talking about. Damn! You think Angela's father has been killed in his own house?"

"We'll soon find out," Jake said as he made a sharp right onto Floribunda. He pulled in behind a row of at least five squad cars that were already parked facing west on Floribunda. The street in front of the house was being used by the rescue squad ambulance and and several other unmarked vehicles. Both officers opened their doors at the same time with, Matt emerging last because of the time it took to maneuver his tall frame from the economy-sized squad car. Ignoring the lightly misting rain, both men took their time in sizing up the impressive exterior of the large Georgian-styled residence at 1637 Floribunda Lane before they entered the house.

The residence's facade consisted of a triangular pediment that sheltered a rectangular portico, which abutted the length of the facade. There were two sets of French doors framed by open shutters, one on either side of the entrance. The porch light consisted of a large brass coach lantern supported by four chained swags centered over the entrance. The roof-level pediment was supported by six twenty-five foot columns evenly spaced the length of the portico, three on either side of the entrance. The main entrance itself was an elaborate affair of large paneled double doors framed by vertically-grooved pilasters with a huge leaded glass fanlight overhead. The deep frontage of the house was contained by boxwood privets which framed groupings of immense blue spruce firs growing on opposite sides of the lawn, which was split by a flagstone walk leading to the front steps.

Matt's inspection of the property told him that the well-ordered residence arrayed before him was a far cry from the unstable, mainly poor homes that bred most murders in the District of Columbia. He thought about how the wealth and stability of the Gold Coast community itself presented such a stark contrast when compared to the disorder and chaos that accompanied most homicides in the District.

Shifting his attention from the Bowman residence to the houses surrounding it, Matt discerned that the 1600 block of Floribunda was unusually long due to the way the street curved to the northwest as it moved down its gently sloping embankment toward Rock Creek. It struck him for the first time that the Creek's physical presence was insignificant when weighed against the social disparity attached to its innocent meandering through the District. For people like him who grew up in the District, Rock Creek was the dividing line symbolizing the distance between the Haves and the Have-Nots, the winners and the losers. He thought about how the directions "East" and "West" of the park had always symbolized more than mere topography in the District by denoting the social gulf between the desirables and the undesirables. For most white District residents, an address west of Rock Creek Park was infinitely more desirable, all things being equal, than one east of the park, where one was likely to find an unsavory mix of ethnicity and poverty. Although white gentrification of what had typically been slum areas in the District was fast changing that equation, including his own neighborhood of LeDroit Park.

While Jake continued talking to an officer standing on the portico, Matt pulled the collar of his aged all-weather coat tighter to ward off the bone-chilling cold before he jogged around the corner of the block to the service alley in the rear, which lay parallel to Floribunda and perpendicular to both Sixteenth and Seventeenth Streets. He systematically scanned the rear of all the residences in the block looking for the Bowman residence. It wasn't hard to find because the back of the house was as meticulously cared for as the front. Matt was peeved that Henry Bryant hadn't secured the area around the house before now. As he turned to leave, he was struck by how nearly perfect the Bowman house was. There was even a small gazebo on the east side of the lawn. Built of trellised hardwood, it had a conical roof covered in hardwood shingles that had turned slate gray with age. He finished his inspection and returned to the front of the residence just as the door was being opened for Jake.

Similarly, curious neighbors inspected the two detectives with unabashed interest before they entered the Bowman residence. Reticent ones watched from the protection of curtained windows while the more audacious among them gaped from open windows and front porches despite the damp penetrating cold of a late November night. What the affluent residents of the Gold Coast saw were two African-American males, one young, handsome, athletic but too dark-skinned for comfort; the other middle-aged, brown-skinned, and not so handsome with a prominent gut running to fat. They were both tall, the younger man over six feet two inches in height.

# CHAPTER II

A uniformed officer opened the front door just as Matt and Jake stepped onto the porch.

"The Captain just asked me about you two. We been here since eleven. What took you so long?" Officer Lewis asked.

"We got here as fast as we could," Jake replied. " The Commander didn't call us until eleven fifteen. It's barely midnight, which is damned good time considering we pushed eighty all the way over here."

"Where are the others?" Matt asked.

"Captain Bryant and Foster are downstairs. That's where the victim is, and where the homicide happened too, I guess. Coleman is guarding the family upstairs."

"Where upstairs?"

"The master bedroom. Can you believe just three people live in this joint? It's big enough to sleep the Redskins' defensive line with room to spare."

From where he was standing just inside the front double door, Matt looked around the first floor of 1637 Floribunda Lane. He could see the staircase leading to the second floor straight ahead, as well as two large arched entrys midway between the stairs and the front doors on either side of the sizeable foyer. The opening on the left led into a formal dining room while the one on the right led into the Bowmans' elaborately furnished living room. A short corridor extended around the left side of the staircase and led to the kitchen and lower level of the house. Matt's one visit to the Bowman residence had been several years earlier before he married Carla, but his memory of the house was still vivid. He wasn't as impressed the second time around.

"Damn, partner, you weren't exaggerating when you said this place was laid. My mama, may she rest in peace, worked for white folk down in Mississippi all her life, but none of the homes she worked in was as fine as this one. Are the Bowmans rich or what?"

"No, they're not rich, but I guess there's some truth to the notion that living well is the best revenge." The Lieutenant's attention was called back to the business at hand by the appearance of Captain Henry Bryant from downstairs.

"So what's the story, Bryant?" Matt asked as Captain Bryant walked from the living room into the foyer.

"Incredible!" Bryant replied. "I'll give you three guesses as to who the stiff is downstairs?"

"Give us a break, Bryant! What went down here?" Matt demanded to know.

Determined to hold on to the suspense of the moment a while longer, Captain Bryant blocked their access to the basement while he took his time in identifying the deceased.

"The victim appears to be a male Caucasian approximately fifty years old. The deceased has dark brown hair, hazel eyes, weighs approximately two hundred pounds, give or take a few, and stood about six feet tall. Death was caused by two gunshots to the upper chest inflicted from close range. From the size of the wounds and the amount of bleeding, I estimate the murder weapon to be a large caliber handgun, probably a thirty-eight. The corpse isn't cold yet, but he's deader than a doornail, no doubt about it."

"What you mean `appears to be a Caucasian male, Bryant? Either the stiff is white or it ain't," Jake insisted.

"Well, maybe he's white or maybe he's not," Bryant cagily replied. "Only his mama knows for sure."

"Get out of the way, Bryant. You're wasting our time with this bullshit," Matt insisted.

Bryant continued to block their access to the kitchen and lower level of the house. He was obviously enjoying himself as he replied, "Brace yourselves, gentlemen. The stiff has tentatively been identified as the real estate developer, Harold William Waterson, Sr."

Both detectives were stunned, Matt even more so because he expected the body to be Walter Bowman's.

"You know damned well Waterson isn't white, Bryant," Matt shot back.

"You could have fooled me, Alexander. That's one of the palest bodies I've ever seen, and I've seen hundreds of 'em."

"I'll be damned!" Jake exclaimed. "The crap has hit the fan for real this time. Who's the shooter, Captain?"

 Bryant began to recite the facts he had uncovered so far as he led the new arrivals down the basement stairs.

"The call came in to headquarters at ten-thirty tonight reporting a homicide at 1637 Floribunda Lane. I got over here shortly before eleven, and the entire block was already filled with prowl cars from the surrounding vicinity. Lewis came with me. Officers Foster and Coleman got here just before we did. It was just my luck to get caught putting in some overtime at the office when the call came in. I grabbed Lewis, the goddamned prick, as he was on his way home. You wouldn't believe how much hell he raised about putting in a couple of hours overtime. Just wait until the son-of-a-bitch needs a favor from me."

"Get to the point, Bryant!" Matt insisted..

"Give me a break, Alexander! That stiff isn't going anywhere. Anyway, Foster and Coleman were the first to arrive at the scene. They said that Walter Bowman opened the door for them. Lucky for Bowman, he had the good sense to lay the shotgun he was carrying on the floor before he opened the door. Otherwise there would have been hell to pay if Foster and Coleman had found themselves staring down the barrels of a twenty-five gauge shotgun. Coleman said that the wife and daughter were standing in the foyer with Walter Bowman and that the daughter was crying hysterically."

Captain Bryant stopped talking as they approached the corpse, which lay in the middle of the basement family room. Jake was the first to examine the curiously positioned body where it lay in the middle of the floor, totally oblivious to the morbid interest it generated there. Jake's professional detachment gave way to unabashed curiosity as he gawked like a mesmerized school boy at a Saturday horror double-feature. Unlike his partner's unrestrained display, Matt's approach was more detached and measured. He was as interested in the physical environment where the homicide occurred as he was in Waterson's corpse.

The body lay on its back with the face staring up at the family room ceiling. The eyes were open, showing the brief but agonizing struggle for life that transpired before death. There was a strained terror about the eyes that made the officers uncomfortable, although they would never admit as much to each other. The open mouth was permanently twisted into a grimace with pools of dried blood encrusted in the corners. The corpse was clean shaven, but the pale skin had turned ashen with a sallow yellow tint. The right leg was twisted under the left one, and the left arm lay in a fencer's pose above the head. The right arm lay close to the body, while the right hand was covered in the victim's own blood and curled into a limp fist. The stench from the release of the sphincter and bladder muscles was tolerable; but it would get much worse as the night wore on, as each of the officers well knew.

The dead man was dressed in a custom-made grey pin-stripped suit, expensive Italian leather oxfords, and a French-cuffed shirt with his initials on the pocket. Harold Waterson had been a handsome man, although his corpse gave little indication of that fact now. His raincoat was lying some distance away and showed a large bloodstain on the back. Noting that most of the blood loss had been confined to the clothing Waterson was wearing, Matt was troubled by bloodstains on the raincoat so far from the body. Captain Bryant confirmed Matt's guess that the raincoat belonged to the deceased.

"Why is the raincoat over here?" Matt asked Bryant as he moved the coat with his foot to see if there was blood on the carpet underneath. Using Matt's question as a cue, Captain Bryant resumed his recitation of events leading up to their arrival.

"According to Walter Bowman, the raincoat was covering the face and upper torso of the victim when he discovered the body. He says he had to remove it to get a closer look at the face and feel for a pulse on the carotid artery. We searched the basement and the backyard for prowlers, but we didn't find anyone down here or anywhere else in the house either. Just between you and me and the fencepost, Alexander, I would have been surprised if we had found anyone. If this isn't an inside job, I'll eat my hat. The rescue-squad arrived just before we got here. The paramedics tried to revive him, but he had been dead too long for that. We searched the grounds around the house, too, but we didn't find any evidence of prowlers."

"Why haven't you cordoned off the alley behind the house, Bryant?"

"My hands have been full since I got here, Alexander! That

was the next thing on my list," Bryant complained.

"The daughter was so hysterical when we got here, I told the mother to take her upstairs until she calmed down. I stationed Coleman upstairs to watch them in case they tried anything, but I haven't gotten around to talking to either the mother or the daughter, yet."

"I'm still waiting to find out who iced Waterson, Bryant," Matt said.

"The way the story goes, Walter Bowman and his wife were upstairs when he heard the daughter screaming like a banshee down in the basement. That was around ten fifteen tonight. Bowman claims he was upstairs in his study watching television when he heard the screams. He ran downstairs to see what was going on; and as he was going down the stairs, Angela Bowman was coming up. He says they met in the hall off the kitchen and that he almost ran her over. He also said she was hysterical and damned near incoherent, but she did manage to tell him that Waterson had been shot. She said she didn't know who had shot him.

Bowman says he rushed downstairs, where he found the deceased laying where he is now with his raincoat on top of him. He removed the raincoat to feel for a pulse. He didn't find one, so he assumed that Waterson was dead even though the body was still warm to the touch. Then, Bowman says it occurred to him that whoever killed Waterson might still be lurking in the basement, so he ran back upstairs to get his pistol from the desk drawer in his study. Get this, Alexander, he says the pistol wasn't in the desk drawer where he usually keeps it, so he got his hunting rifle from the closet in his study along with a box of cartridges. He says he loaded the rifle, put several cartridges in his pocket, and called the police from the master bedroom where his wife and daughter were. Bowman placed the call around ten-thirty and you know the rest. By the way, Alexander, I called Commander Cullison to bring him up to date on the situation, here."

"I figured you had, Bryant," Matt replied indifferently. He knew from past experience that Henry Bryant was absolutely unscrupulous when it came to covering his own back. And, while Bryant wasn't difficult to work with, Matt also knew that the Captain would have no qualms about leaving him in the lurch at the slightest provocation if he detected any risk to himself. All the men under Bryant's command knew that when the going got rough, it was every man for himself because they were on their own. Henry Bryant didn't have a rebellious bone in his body. He deferred to Commander Cullison in cases that were clearly within his power to resolve as Captain of the Homicide Special Investigations Division. Every officer who worked for Bryant was painfully aware that Commander Cullison was running Homicide in addition to Fourth District Headquarters. Homicide investigators resented being housed at District Headquarters because it meant that they had to be sensitive to the politics and protocol that went with the turf, while officers in free-standing precincts had more freedom in the performance of their duties or lack thereof. And while Lloyd Cullison was responsible for the administrative supervision of all precincts and divisions under his command, his authority did not include day-to-day management of the Homicide Division. However, with Henry Bryant at the helm, Commander Cullison met no resistance on that score. Unlike Captain Bryant, Lieutenant Matthew Alexander was more than able to hold his own with Commander Cullison, but it invariably cost him more than he was willing to admit. Lloyd Cullison detested strong-willed subordinates.

"Have you found the murder weapon yet, Bryant?"

"No, but I'll give you ten to one that he was shot with Walter Bowman's missing pistol. I haven't had time to get a thorough search underway. If it's here, we'll find it."

"Captain Bryant is right, Matt. Waterson looks as white as they come," Jake insisted.

"I don't care how white he looked, Jake, he was black. But, rumor has it that his father was white."

"Did Walter Bowman give you any idea what Harold Waterson was doing in his basement in the first place, Bryant?"

"He swears he doesn't know what he was doing here, or who killed him for that matter."

"We all know better than that," Jake interrupted.

"When I pressed Bowman, he told me that he was a lawyer and that he knew his rights. He said he wasn't going to stand for any police harassment of him or his family, so I left it at that."

Matt stooped over the corpse to get a firsthand look at the bullet wounds in Waterson's chest.

"After Bowman finished telling his story, I sent him back upstairs. I went upstairs myself to question the mother and daughter just before you got here, but the daughter was still crying hysterically. Coleman thinks she might go off the deep end any minute. The mother didn't look too good either. I kept the rifle and the cartridges down here. They're over there on the bar."

All three men looked toward the bar at the same time where they saw Sergeant Foster standing behind the bar watching them. Foster had a well-known aversion to hard work. He usually got away with doing very little simply by staying out of everyone's way and keeping his mouth shut as he was doing now.

Having inspected the corpse as much as he dared before the medical examiner arrived, Matt turned his attention to the basement of the Bowman residence. The family room where he was standing and where the body lay occupied roughly one-fourth of the lower level of the house. Like the first floor, the basement was partitioned by a central corridor that extended the entire length of the lower level of the house. The corridor ceiling held three old-fashioned fixtures which gave off very little light, leaving most of the hallway in shadow. The basement stairs, which they had just descended, shared the north wall of the house with a door which opened onto steps leading up to the back porch and a landing leading into the backyard. Lieutenant Alexander looked through the one window pane situated high in the door and noted how dimly lit the landing outside the basement entrance of the Bowman residence was.

Four rooms lay opposite the massive family room in the basement, their doors open and lights on. The first door was very near the basement door and led into a bathroom. The second and third doors were midway down the hall. One room opened into a spacious recreation room with exercise equipment, while the next revealed a spacious bedroom furnished in beautiful Scandinavian teak with a queen-sized platform bed. The last door sat opposite the basement entrance to the house at the Southern end of the house and led into a utility room that held, among other things, an upright freezer. Matt asked Captain Bryant if the lights had been on when they first inspected the basement. Bryant explained that the only lights they found on were those in the hallway and the family room. The other lights were turned on as they searched the basement for intruders.

Matt saw that none of the rooms was physically disturbed and dismissed the idea of a struggle, concluding that Waterson had, in all probability, been too surprised to mount a defense. Like Bryant, he doubted Walter Bowman's claim that none of his family was involved. But if an intruder was responsible, he felt that the basement door could very easily have provided entry and exit with no one upstairs being the wiser. Not wanting to waste any more time before the medical examiner arrived, Matt donned a pair of plastic gloves and went back to the body to examine it more closely. The Homicide Division's forensic expert, Sam Johnson, routinely gave detectives hell for turf intrusions, which Matt just as routinely ignored.

After looking the body over, Matt gingerly perused the

refrigerator, stove and cupboards being careful not to disturb surfaces where prints were likely to be found. He left a thorough search of the family room to Jake and moved into the corridor.

Matt was especially interested in the area of the corridor near the basement door. Using his flashlight, he closely examined the space from the basement door to the family room, looking for any sign that the body may have been moved after Waterson was killed. The dark brown tile in front of the basement door had several pairs of dried footprints superimposed on each other. Matt made careful measurements of the faint but discernible impressions, which Sam would photograph later. Several of the prints were made by high heels. When he asked Bryant whether he or the other officers had used the basement door to go outside, Bryant swore that they hadn't. According to the Captain, the officers who searched the grounds had been out front and simply walked around the house without using the basement door.

Looking through the windows in the basement door, Matt again observed that the rear of 1637 Floribunda Lane was enclosed by a five-foot wrought iron fence interrupted by a two-car garage in the northwest corner of the property. A gate adjacent to the garage opened onto the service alley and provided the only access other than the garage door to the rear of the residence. When he had cased the back of the house earlier, Matt noted three entrances to the property: the back door, a solarium on the west side of the house and a screened porch on the east side of the property. The basement door made four rear entrances to the house in addition to three in the front if the French doors were included...far too many. Matt returned to the first floor of the house.

As he stood on the threshold of the Bowman's living room, Matt recalled the time seven years ago when he had met Angela Bowman's father for the first time. The meeting had been a disaster. Walter Bowman hadn't minced his words when he let

Matt know how little he thought of him and his intentions toward his only child, Angela. Matt remembered the bitter humiliation he felt as Walter Bowman insulted him and his family because they were poor, and lived on the wrong side of the tracks out in Southeast D.C. He felt his resentment surge again; but he reminded himself that the incident, though painful, was part of the past best buried and forgotten. Actually, Walter Bowman had done him a favor seven years ago. If he hadn't stopped him from marrying Angela, Matt would never have met Carla when he did, so at one level he was grateful that Walter Bowman had thwarted his intentions toward his daughter. But his humiliation at the hands of Walter Bowman had been devastating at the time, so his resentment was real. He didn't know how he would react to seeing Walter Bowman again. He certainly didn't look forward to interrogating him.

Waiting for Bowman to come down, the young detective looked around the scene of his personal humiliation seven years earlier. The living room was elegant and beautiful, but cold as a stage set. As impressive as the Bowman residence was on the surface, it couldn't hide the smell of death that permeated the lower level of the house. Everything was as it should be from where Matt stood in the living room. The physical arrangement, was undisturbed but there was no doubt in his mind that the psychology of the house had been altered. The corpse downstairs changed everything-the relationship of the Bowmans to each other, to their friends and neighbors, and most importantly, to the authorities. They were suspect; and whether or not one of them had killed Harold Waterson, they would certainly feel the impact of the investigation most strongly.

# CHAPTER III

Looking through the French doors in the Bowmans' living room, Matt thought about death and dying and how easy it is for one person to take another's life. He dismissed the popular hype about killers being deranged and dangerous and not fit to live among the rest of society. He had believed that too, once; but seeing so many people killed in so many ridiculous ways by so many "sane" people had stripped him of the common misconceptions about who can and cannot kill. Society did an adequate job of socializing most of its citizens against violence. Unfortunately, some people got less conditioning than they needed while others who knew better intentionally defied the legal and moral prohibitions against murder. Either way, men continued to kill each other despite civilized society's best efforts to stop them. Feeling as he did often made Matt wonder what was the point of it all? He knew he could never become immune to murder despite the fact that he accepted its often grotesque reality.

Homicide investigations were not without their personal hazards, too. Some had a disturbing malevolence that pulled on the investigating officer with a peculiar emotional intensity, almost as if he were an accessory to the crime itself. Matt had felt that malevolence, so he lacked enthusiasm for reconstructing the circumstances of a violent death despite the fact that it was his stock and trade. He was as adept as the other detectives at feigning indifference to the violence and personal tragedy homicides left in their wake. But, policemen are human too; and like most people, he sometimes felt the urge to walk away from the brutality and ugliness and pretend that it didn't exist.

Unlike most people who register the details of a particular homicide only in passing, he was required to involve himself in the smallest detail of the killing until it permeated his unconscious, saturated his senses, and clung to him like a bad odor. He kept searching for that immunity that the older officers told him would come with time, but he knew he would never get used to the wanton destruction of human life.

Being a sports enthusiast, Matt strongly believed in the rules of fair play, which for him amounted to never kicking a man when he's down and never hesitating to give an opponent a second chance. Harold Waterson never stood a chance against the cunning of his cold-blooded assassin. The victim's vulnerability bothered Matt more than he was prepared to admit. Accidental death robbed an individual of life, but it did so impartially with malice toward none or all depending on your point of view. On the other hand, to kill deliberately, stealthily without warning implied a callous disregard for the victim that reduced the killer to the level of a self-appointed executioner.

Harold Waterson had been a wealthy businessman. He was certain to have made some enemies, but probably no more than other businessmen like himself who were still alive. Was he so different from his contemporaries that his deviance might account for his death? Matt didn't think so. His experience in the homicide division told him that it was unlikely that the circumstances of Waterson's life would be so exotic as to inevitably point to his death. Men died similar deaths for different reasons; but the common link in their collective demise was their encounter, however brief or sustained, with their assassin. For Matt, the solution to Harold Waterson's homicide lay in establishing the fatal link between the victim and the killer. Where that could be done, motive could be established, and coupled with means and opportunity, a suspect was born.

At that moment, Matt turned to find Officer Lewis entering the living room with Walter Bowman in tow. Bowman, looking pinched and drained, tried his best to rise to the occasion; but what Matt saw was a emotionally exhausted man struggling to maintain a facade of poise and indifference in the onslaught of damning events for him and his family.

Standing only five-feet-six-inches tall, Walter Bowman had never cut an imposing figure, despite his opinion to the contrary. The Lieutenant noted that the resemblance between father and daughter was striking, but where Angela Bowman's eyes were soft and luminous, her father's were guarded, penetrating, and distrusting. He wore his sparse straight hair in a comb-over parted low on the right side and brushed over the balding crown of his head. Bowman's face was thin and angular with a nondescript jaw that was clean shaven with the exception of a small neatly-trimmed mustache over well-defined lips, which had yet to reveal his fear and apprehension. His pale skin contrasted with black hair that showed no perceptible hint of gray despite his age which Matt guessed to be at least sixty-five. Walter Bowman looked deceptively young in spite of his receding hairline. He could easily have passed for a much younger man. However, his mannerisms placed him squarely among the geriatric set in that they were slow, cautious, and deliberate.

When Walter Bowman returned Matt's appraisal, he saw a dark-skinned young man tall and fit enough to play college basketball and handsome enough to be a male model. He recalled his daughter's infatuation with Matthew Alexander and had the decency to be ashamed for how rudely and angrily he had responded to their engagement seven years earlier. The young detective standing in his living room wore his thick black hair, which framed his face attractively, in a short natural style. He was clean-shaven with the exception of well-trimmed mustache over beautifully-formed lips. He stood facing the French doors that led onto the porch as he watched the rain fall through dark luminous eyes framed by stylish wire-rimmed spectacles.

Being very light-skinned, Walter Bowman had little appreciation for the aesthetics of black beauty, having disdained its value most of his life. However, he had often yearned for a pair of ample well-formed lips rather than the meager, almost nonexistent pair God via his parents had bestowed on him. He had to admit that many African Americans, more often than not, had full beautiful lips that he sorely envied. When he first entered his living room, Walter Bowman's apprehension had visibly eased when he discerned that the police detective who was going to question him was Matthew Alexander. The strain in Bowman's voice echoed the pressure he was under as he spoke for the first time:

"Matthew Alexander! You don't know how relieved I am to see a friendly face. Now that you're here, maybe you can convince the rest of these officers that we didn't kill Harold Waterson."

Matt ignored Walter Bowman's eagerly outstretched hand.

"I'm here to investigate a murder, Mr. Bowman, not to exonerate you. If you need someone to plead your case, I suggest you hire a defense attorney."

"Don't get me wrong, young man, I'm not asking you to do us any favors because none of us killed Harold Waterson. I'm as anxious as you are to find out who did kill him. I still can't believe someone had the nerve to kill him in my house."

"I'm relieved to hear you say that, Mr. Bowman, because I

intend to use the full force of the homicide division to bring Waterson's killer to justice, regardless of who it is."

"I wouldn't have it any other way," Bowman insisted as if his opinion mattered.

The doorbell's sudden rings called Officer Lewis away from his position in the foyer just outside the living room, where he was eavesdropping on what promised to be an exciting confrontation between Lieutenant Alexander and Walter Bowman. When he opened the door, he found Sam Johnson, the homicide division's forensic specialist and the crew from the medical examiner's officer waiting outside. Sam, a meticulous little man, entered first carrying his familiar menagerie of photographic and forensic equipment. With Sam being so slight, the equipment, from the sheer size and profusion of it, might have been carrying him. However, Sam was as strong and agile as he was diminutive; and invariably emerged from the bowels of his equipment looking as natty as a country club regular or a street corner pimp, depending on where you go to get hustled.

Dr. Stephen Mitchell, the deputy medical examiner, followed Sam into the house looking as usual like a holdover from the Free Speech Movement of the late Sixties. Dr. Mitchell's appearance was a throw-back to the height of the "Movement" days...a middle-aged hippie forced to pay his establishment dues. He compensated for his enforced servitude by getting high whenever time permitted, which earned him the reputation for smoking more reefer than the law allows, although he did refrain in the presence of his more conventional law-abiding colleagues.

The word was that the deputy medical examiner had been one of those wealthy white kids who blamed the system for allowing them to grow up comfortably in affluent suburbs. If his present appearance was any indication, he still had problems reconciling his freedom from material want with the plight of the less fortunate. Typical of many caught in this dilemma, he lacked the courage to resolve it satisfactorily one way or the other. Since he was the best forensic pathologist in the medical examiner's office under the influence or not, the powers that be tolerated his flagrant disregard for their more mundane professional and social amenities as long as he didn't light up in the office. He refused to cut his long brown hair, wearing it in a pony tail instead. He was as apt to appear in the office unshaven as shaven. He wore tennis shoes daily and bought his clothes from God knows what thrift shop. He had been through two wives, the latter of whom changed from earth mother to barracuda during their divorce proceedings, excising a substantial portion of his income before the transformation was complete. During the divorce proceedings, Dr. Mitchell petitioned the court to allow him to adopt his wife since it was obvious that she intended to become a lifelong drain on his finances. Unfortunately, the judge found little merit in his request and awarded his wife joint custody of their two children, the house, the car, alimony and child support.

As improbable as it may have seemed, Stephen Mitchell survived the devastation of his second divorce by smoking even more reefer than usual. Since he was far exceeding the level that allowed him to do quality work, he took a month's leave of absence from his duties at the medical examiner's office ostensibly to recuperate from the emotional strain of his divorce. That was over a year ago and, to all appearances, Dr. Stephen Mitchell was back to normal, which for him meant a thoroughly good buzz to end the day.

Dr. Mitchell was followed by two attendants carrying the portable gurney and other death-related paraphernalia. The two attendants were the antithesis of each other in every respect. One was old, the other young. While the older attendant was small in stature, the younger one stood over six feet tall. The older man was the essence of bourgeois respectability from the waves in his salt and pepper hair to his polished white shoes. On the other hand, the younger attendant had a seedy, "frayed-around-the-edges" look indicating that he had walked on the wild side on more than one occasion. His disheveled appearance, however, did not detract from his virile good looks. The younger attendant exuded a smug air of self-satisfaction that had its basis in the fact that he was young, strong, handsome, and well aware of all three. As for the older attendant, it was to be expected that he compensated for conspicuous deficits in all three areas with years of on-the-job experience and a keen sense of dedication to his duties.

Back in the living room, Matt and Walter Bowman had battled to a stand-off on the question of favoritism, with the Lieutenant insisting that he wouldn't show any and Bowman equally insistent that he didn't need any. Chagrined at having to leave such a promising confrontation just when it was getting "hot," Officer Lewis contained his curiosity long enough to inform the Lieutenant that the men from the medical examiner's office were waiting in the foyer. Before Lewis could finish, Sam Johnson walked into the living room and demanded to know "where the stiff was if it wasn't too much trouble".

"I don't lug this shit around for my health, you know."

"Keep your shirt on, Sam," the Lieutenant replied as he walked into the foyer and acknowledged the presence of Stephen Mitchell with a handshake.

"How's it going, Steve?"

"I can't complain. How are things with you, Matt?"

"A lot more hectic than I like, and this homicide isn't helping any. How are the kids?"

"They're fine, but I don't get to see them as much as I'd like to. How is your family?"

"They're great. The baby is growing like a weed. We've got a real treat for you tonight, Steve."

"Oh no! It's not another hatchet job is it?" Stephen Mitchell replied, alluding to a gruesome case that had created quite a sensation in the local press two years ago.

"No, nothing like that. As a matter of fact, the corpse is in pretty good condition considering that he was shot at close range with a large caliber handgun. Prepare yourself for a shock." The sound of several pairs of feet descending the stairs to the basement brought Jake and Captain Bryant out of the family room into the corridor. Their curiosity whetted by Lieutenant Alexander's allusion to the corpse's identity, the new arrivals quickly arranged themselves around the body so they could get as good a view as possible. Arrayed around the deceased as they were, they resembled a misbegotten football huddle whose lifeless quarterback had called his last play.

"Good grief! That's Harold Waterson, isn't it?" Dr. Mitchell asked.

"Who the hell shot him?" Sam Johnson demanded to know.

"That's the one question we can't answer, Sam," Matt replied.

"How long has he been dead?" Stephen Mitchell asked.

"As far as we know," Captain Bryant replied, "he was killed before ten-thirty tonight. That's when the call came into Fourth District Headquarters. Walter Bowman, he's the owner of the house, reported the homicide. He claims his daughter found the body. She was hysterical when we arrived, so we haven't talked to her yet."

"Who is Harold Waterson?" asked the younger attendant of the older one.

"Only the richest black man in the District. He was so rich he might as well have been white. That's how rich he was. Umph! Umph! Umph! Whoever would have thought? Shot down like a mangy dog, and his money can't help him one bit now."

Having satisfied his curiosity as to the corpse's identity, Sam Johnson darted into the basement corridor to unload his equipment. Barking orders to his two criminalists, Lois and Ruby, Sam worked fast as he prepared for the more-often-than-not fruitless task of collecting and preserving evidence against the onslaught of his well-intentioned but destructive colleagues. Having taken care of first things first, Sam pulled himself up to his full height in anticipation of the inevitable running battle that was bound to ensue between him and the other officers at the scene until he finished his work.

Sam's appreciation for the hazards of collecting evidence was apparent as he shouted into the family room, "Hey, you clowns! Get away from that stiff! You're not supposed to touch anything on that corpse until I photograph it! Give me a break will you! How do you expect me to make an accurate record if you ass-holes start moving the body around!"

Ignoring Sam's demands, Stephen Mitchell squatted near the corpse's torso, where he confirmed Bryant's assessment that Waterson had been shot from close range with a large caliber revolver. He noted the profusion of blood on the front of the shirt and guessed that a major artery had been hit, probably the aorta. He saw that the corpse's eyes were open and fixed on the ceiling almost as if Harold Waterson couldn't believe he was dead. Regrettably, he was as dead as they came. The sallow color and awkward position of the body confirmed the fact. The Deputy Medical Examiner noted the two wounds in the center of Waterson's chest where the bullets had found their mark. His cursory examination complete, Steve Mitchell walked over to where Matt and Jake were standing near the bar.

Intrigued by the untimely demise of a mainstay of the District's business community under such unexpected circumstances, Steve asked, "What gives here, Matt? I see Waterson's corpse lying there; but I still can't believe he's dead. What was he doing here anyway?"

"I haven't the faintest, Steve. Hopefully, the Bowmans can enlighten us, considering he was killed in their basement."

"His number was up," Jake insisted. "When your number is up, you have to meet the Man upstairs whether you're ready or not. Old Waterson picked a fine place to die, if you ask me. This house is a mansion compared to most of the dives we pull stiffs out of."

"This house is small potatoes compared to what Waterson was used to, Jake. He was a multi-millionaire several times over. He lived in an estate off Reservoir Road. I remember reading somewhere that aside from his residence here, the Watersons owned a co-op apartment in New York City and a farm in Warren, Virginia," Matt replied.

"His money can't help him worth a damn now," Jake added.

"He must have known the Bowman family, Matt," Steve reasoned.

"Not to hear Walter Bowman tell it, Steve. The lie he told me and Henry Bryant is that he barely knew Waterson and that he had no idea what the deceased was doing in his basement tonight."

"That is bizarre," Steve replied. "The newspapers are going to have a field day with this homicide."

"If you think the *Post* and the *Star* are going to exploit what happened," said Jake, "wait until you get a load of that publicity hound Lloyd Cullison. He's probably practicing up for his television appearances right now."

Both Matt and Dr. Mitchell laughed at Jake's description of the Commander because it rang so true. Lloyd Cullison was an ambitious man who enthusiastically pursued his share of media coverage. Waterson's homicide was certain to stir up a good deal of hype; and, with Lloyd being Lloyd, it was guaranteed that he would get his share of the media coverage, even if it meant competing with the corpse for air time.

As Sam Johnson positioned his lights at strategic points around the body and began taking pictures, Matt watched the corpse being photographed in all its indignity. He considered the irony of Waterson's death...a pillar of the District's wealthy business and social community lying in an absurd heap in the middle of the room being inspected and photographed like he didn't have a dime. Jake was right. No amount of money can get you off the hook with the grim reaper. When he arrives he expects the ultimate payoff, and he never settles for less.

Sam finished taking pictures of the body and directed his attention to the rest of the family room where the crime occurred. Jake, meanwhile, grew impatient waiting for Sam to finish. They couldn't begin to take the room apart until Sam lifted the prints, and Sam couldn't lift the prints until he finished taking the photographs.

"Shake a leg, Sam. We have to start looking for the murder weapon sometime tonight," Matt insisted.

"I'm working as fast as I can, Alexander. You clowns don't make my work any easier, you know. You destroy the goddamned evidence before I can get to it, and then you have the nerve to get pissed when I take too long trying to piece it back together again. You can't have it both ways, Lieutenant. Either I do a thorough job or a quick job. In this business, you can't do both."

Matt considered pushing the matter, but decided against it. Sam was too damned particular to suit him; but he worked at his own pace, as every detective in the homicide division well knew. As far as Matt was concerned, Sam Johnson was a fastidious little fart, but he knew his job better than anyone on the force; and he didn't mind letting you know that he knew it. Besides that, he was a hell-raising little bastard who wouldn't hesitate to jump in your chest if you pissed him off.

Leaving Sam to his own devices, Matt shifted his attention to the family room, which unlike the first floor, was decorated with ultra-modern furniture. The overhead lighting was supplied by a system of track lights that ran the length of the ceiling on either side of the family room. A large plush sectional sofa sat against the east wall of the house, facing the corridor. The corpse lay just inside open pocket doors that separated the family room from the corridor. Two large chairs, with a telephone table between them, were placed against the south wall to the left of where the victim lay sprawled in the middle of the family room. The victim's all weather, short-brimmed hat lay under the telephone table. The matching raincoat, which Matt had examined earlier, was lying beneath the coffee table in front of the sofa. The northeast corner of the family room housed a large oak bar which encircled a spacious kitchenette, while floor-to-ceiling wall units flanked the pocket doors.

Sam finished taking pictures, disposed of his photographic equipment, and began dusting for prints. As soon as Sam had completed photographing the corpse, Dr. Mitchell began the first stage of the post mortem. Examining the corpse as it lay, he started by taking the body temperature; examining the eyes, nose and mouth; and testing the joints for flexibility. After the older attendant had drawn an outline of the body's position onto the carpet, Dr. Mitchell straightened the legs and arms. He noted the skin color and examined the head for contusions and lacerations. The Deputy Medical Examiner talked into a portable tape recorder as he conducted the examination, while the older attendant wrote the information being softly relayed onto a standard form attached to a clip board he held. The presence of the tape recorder indicated that Stephen Mitchell appreciated the risk of human error in recording facts. However, the speed and dexterity of the older attendant led you to believe that if a mistake were made, it was as likely to be the tape recorder as the older attendant.

Feeling less apprehensive now that things were moving along at a faster pace, Jake asked Matt where he wanted them to begin the search for the murder weapon.

"You and Bryant can start down here in the family room as soon Sam finishes lifting prints," Matt replied between taking notes from the information Stephen Mitchell was giving to his attendant. He also warned Steve Mitchell not to remove the corpse through the basement entrance because Sam and his criminalists hadn't processed the area yet.

When Dr. Mitchell finished his preliminary examination, Matt walked over to the body and instructed the morgue attendants to empty Waterson's pockets into a large plastic bag. They also placed Waterson's raincoat into another bag along with his hat and shoes. All of the corpse's clothing would come to his office after analysis and eventually find their way to the District Prosecutor's office once an indictment was handed down. Matt stayed in the family room long enough to see the attendants put Waterson's corpse into a body bag and lift it onto the portable gurney. He thought about how something as cold and silent as a corpse had the power to reach out from the grave, in a manner of speaking, to leave its mark in a tangle of investigative legalese and official documentation simply by dying a violent death.

The body disposed of, Matt went back upstairs after reminding Jake to inform him when gun was found. Steve Mitchell preceded Matt up the stairs with the morgue attendants close on his heels as they struggled to negotiate the narrow stairway with a six-foot corpse on a gurney. For his part, Dr. Mitchell was pleased that the preliminary post-mortem had been wrapped up so neatly. From his experience, it could have been worse...a lot worse.

Matt had heard several descriptions of Angela Bowman's emotional condition, none of them good. He decided to settle the question by going upstairs to the parents' bedroom to see for himself. Officer Coleman was stationed outside the door to the master bedroom. Matt opened the door just wide enough to look inside. He saw Helen Bowman sitting on the side of the king-sized bed trying to comfort her daughter, who was lying prostrate in the middle of the bed. He had seen enough suffering to know that hers was genuine, so he want downstairs without disturbing mother or daughter.

# CHAPTER IV

Matt returned to the living room, where he found Walter Bowman seated on the edge of one of a pair of plush peach-colored velvet sofas. Bowman sat on the one that faced the French doors where Matt was standing. Still holding his notebook and pen, Matt walked over to the fireplace situated between the sofas, and facing Bowman said, "Before you answer any questions, Mr. Bowman, I want to make it clear that you aren't under arrest. Someone shot and killed a man in your basement tonight. In order for me to find out who killed him and why, I need to know everything that happened. If you and your family had nothing to do with Waterson's death, establishing what actually happened will clear all of you...if you're telling the truth."

"Angela is too upset to be questioned. She needs a sedative to calm her down."

"Do you know a doctor who'll come to the house to treat her? Otherwise, I'll call the paramedics back and they can take her to the hospital."

"Tom Martin, our next door neighbor, is a doctor. I'd like to have him look at her now, if you don't mind."

"I know Tom Martin. As a matter of fact, Officer Lewis can go over to his house to get him now," Matt suggested, looking toward the staircase in the foyer, where Lewis had one arm draped over the bannister and one foot propped on the bottom stair as if he hadn't a care in the world. Hearing his name called, Lewis snapped to attention and hustled his lanky frame into the living room, where he was instructed to fetch Dr. Martin.

After Lewis left, Walter Bowman literally squirmed in his seat, dreading the qestions he was powerless to escape. Matt began by very quietly asking:

"What happened here tonight, Mr. Bowman?"

Walter Bowman's reply was a nervous staccato recitation of the facts he had given Captain Bryant earlier. The Lieutenant listened patiently, finding no essential difference in either time or sequence to the earlier account.

"Did you hear the gunshots?"

"No, I didn't hear anything until Angela screamed."

"Harold Waterson was killed with a large caliber handgun, probably a thirty-eight. You must have heard something; a thirty-eight makes a loud report."

"I didn't hear anything from downstairs until I heard Angela screaming like she was being attacked. I might have dozed off while I was watching TV, but I know gunshot would have woke me up."

"Where was your wife when you heard Angela's screams?"

"She was asleep. Helen's normally in bed by nine every night."

"Isn't nine o'clock early to go to bed for the night?"

"Not for Helen. She's suffered from insomnia for years. She takes sleeping pills, and they usually knock her out cold. She's always asleep by ten o'clock ."

"You said," the Lieutenant corrected, "that she was awake when you went back upstairs to get your gun."

"That's because Angela ran up to our bedroom and woke her

up after she passed me in the hall."

"Was your wife's bedroom door open when you ran downstairs."

"No, it wasn't. I usually watch television in my study until eleven-thirty. The sound of the television bothers Helen, so she always closes the bedroom door."

"If you didn't actually see her asleep in the bedroom when Angela screamed, how do you know she was in there? For that matter, how do you know where she was then?"

"Well, I can't swear that she was asleep, but that's her usual routine. She was in the bedroom when Angela ran upstairs, so she must have been in there when I ran downstairs."

"Is there another way to get to the second floor from the basement?"

"No, there isn't," Walter Bowman shouted angrily. "This house has only one basement staircase. Helen was in our bedroom asleep, and you can't prove otherwise."

Ignoring Walter Bowman's temporary indignation, Matt continued his line of questioning:

"What make of handgun do you own, Mr. Bowman?"

"Army issue Smith & Wesson thirty-eight caliber revolver."

"Since you claim that your revolver wasn't in the desk drawer where you usually keep it, can you tell me the last time you saw it there?"

"That's hard to say. I've always kept it in the bottom drawer of my desk. Helen and Angela have never gone near that gun, and they both told me they hadn't seen the gun when I asked them about it after I found the body. I don"t keep the gun loaded, but there were several bullets in the drawer with the gun, and they're missing too. My revolver is more of a souvenir from my old Army days than anything else. I usually oil and clean it about once a year, but I don't remember when I saw it last."

"You must have some idea. When was the last time you cleaned it?"

"I swear I don't remember."

Matt wasn't convinced, but he decided not to pursue the question of the missing gun for the time being.

"What was your relationship to the dead man, Mr. Bowman?"

"I barely knew Harold Waterson. He was at the Martins' cocktail party tonight, but his wife wasn't with him. He came alone. I remember them attending a garden party the Martins gave last spring. But, to answer your question, I didn't know him personally. His social contacts were almost exclusively white, so it's not likely that we would have had much in common. You know his wife is white. As far as that goes, he may as well have been white. Everyone knows that he preferred them to us. He would have passed if he could have gotten away with it, but there are too many people in the District who knew him when he was growing up in Warren, Virginia, barefoot and raggedy-assed. He was as poor as dirt back then. But, you'd never know where he came from by the way he lorded it over us ordinary black folks."

"So Waterson was a snob. So what? That still doesn't explain how someone you barely know is murdered in your house without your knowledge. If you didn't know Waterson, some other member of your family must have know him very well."

"I don't care what you believe," Walter bowman angrily shouted. "I know better than anyone how well I knew Harold Waterson, and I'm telling you that I hardly knew the man...I certainly didn't know him well enough for him to pay me a visit."

"Why was he invited to the Martins' cocktail party?"

"You'll have to ask Claudia Martin about that. The party was a fundraiser for a charity organization she's involved with at the moment. Everyone knows what a shameless social climber Claudia is. She has enough nerve to invite the President to one of her parties if she thought he would come."

Matt noted Walter Bowman's hostility toward Claudia Martin and filed it away for future reference.

"Since you claim that you didn't know Harold Waterson personally, are you aware of whether your wife or daughter knew him personally?"

"Certainly not! Neither of them knew him any better than I did."

"Come off it, Bowman. Are you seriously asking me to believe that a perfect stranger walks into your house and is blown away without anyone in your family being involved. Man, you have got to be joking. Waterson wasn't a second story man. He didn't come here to rob the place. Somebody let him into this house, Bowman, and that person had to be a member of your family...if you didn't do it yourself."

Walter Bowman was too frustrated to reply. It occurred to Matt that Walter Bowman probably knew very little about his wife's or daughter's personal affairs outside the confines of his own house. If one of them knew Harold Waterson on a personal level, it was not likely that Bowman would be privy to that fact. However, finding out about it might be ample motive for murder, especially if the victim was involved with Bowman's wife. Matt looked up to find Officer Lewis entering the living room, followed by Dr. Thomas Martin.

Dr. Thomas Martin complied with the peculiar summons without question, but it was apparent that his curiosity was bursting at the seams beneath his air of professional detachment. Dr. Martin carried his medical bag in one hand and lit cigarette in the other. Walter Bowman disliked his friend Tom's habit of chain smoking cigarettes almost as much as he disliked Tom's wife, Claudia. Neither Bowman nor his wife smoked. He out of choice, she out of compliance with his wishes.

As out-going as he was likeable, Tom Martin overcame the tension in the air by acknowledging Matt and Walter Bowman with handshakes, extinguishing his cigarette in an expensive crystal bowl on the coffee table, and ensconcing his ample girth on the matching sofa across from Walter Bowman before speaking, "The young officer over there told me Angela was sick, Walter. What seems to be the problem?" Matt quickly spoke up before Walter Bowman could answer.

"It's not life threatening, Tom. She needs a sedative."

"I think I can manage that given my current state of inebriation. Claudia had another of her infamous cocktail parties tonight, Matthew. Once I get several drinks under my belt, my attention span is limited to staying on my feet and keeping my hands to myself. Most of the ladies don't seem to mind my attention, but their husbands are another matter altogether. By the way, did someone call an ambulance over here, earlier, Walter? I thought I heard a siren about an hour ago."

Again Matt replied to Tom Martin's question. "The ambulance wasn't for Angela, Tom. Someone was murdered in the Bowman's basement tonight."

Tom gasped as his large body propelled itself to the edge of the sofa. "Murdered! My God! Was it Helen!?"

"No, it wasn't," Matt answered. "The homicide victim wasn't a member of the Bowman family. As a matter of fact, Mr. Bowman claims to have scarcely known the victim," he continued with undisguised cynicism.

"Who was he?" Tom asked.

Matt thought about Tom's question before replying.

"I'm not at liberty to divulge the victim's identity. What time did your party start, Tom, and how many people were there?"

"It started around seven. Offhand, I'd say there were about fifty people. I can't be certain, but Claudia can tell you exactly how many were there. Most of them left around ten o'clock. A few die-hard drinkers stayed and the party moved down into the basement recreation room. That's where I was when the officer over there came to get me."

Matt walked from the living room into the foyer, where he sent Officer Lewis downstairs to get Jake. Then he shouted upstairs for Officer Coleman to show Tom Martin to the master bedroom and stay with him until he finished treating Angela Bowman. He also cautioned Tom against discussing the homicide with the Bowman women.

"Your wish is my command," Tom affably replied as he puffed up the stairs like a locomotive on a steep incline. Jake appeared in the foyer in time to catch a glimpse of the rotund figure trudging up the stairs.

"Wasn't that Doc Martin?"

"Yes, he's giving Angela Bowman a sedative. Tom and his wife live next door, Jake. They gave a cocktail party tonight, and I'll give you three guesses as to who was there."

"Harold Waterson."

"The one and only. Walter and Helen Bowman were there, too."

"What time did Waterson leave the Martins' party?"

"I didn't go into that with Tom, yet."

"How many people were at the party?"

"At least fifty according to Tom."

"Jesus! Do we have to question fifty people?"

"Let's hope not, man," Matt replied more optimistically than he actually felt.

"This case is beginning to shape up like another Cairo Club," Jake insisted, referring to the murder of the owner of what had been the District's most popular night spot three years earlier. In that case, the only thing more numerous than the Cairo Club's devotees was the list of potential murder suspects in attendance the night the club's owner was killed. It seemed that the owner had spent most of his spare time cultivating a respectable list of enemies on both sides of the law. There were just fifty people at the Martins' cocktail party, but what with reputation, social position, and ego to protect, Jake correctly guessed that they would have considerably more at stake that the Cairo Club regulars.

"Did you find the gun yet?" Matt asked.

"Not yet, man. We only just got started looking. Sam Johnson is taking his own sweet time lifting prints downstairs."

"Be sure to check the basement windows, Jake. They're too small for anyone full size to use for entry or exit, but they could have been used to get rid of the gun. Tell Sam to make sure he dusts those windows before he finishes downstairs."

"Knowing Sam, he's probably done them already. He doesn't miss much."

"I asked Walter Bowman about his missing revolver. He swears he doesn't remember when he saw it last, but it's a sure bet that the Bowman gun was the one that was used to kill Waterson."

"I'd lay odds on it," Jake agreed.

"Listen, Jake. I want you to leave the searching to Bryant and Foster for now. I need you to go over to the Martins' and get a list of everyone present at the cocktail party tonight from Claudia Martin, Tom's wife."

"Sure thing. Where do the Martins' live?"

"Next door. Be careful, Jake; she's a real choice morsel," Matt replied laughing.

"Nothing I can't handle," said Jake with a grin. "If she's ready, I'm willing and able."

"Not if Tom Martin has anything to say about it," Matt replied as he returned to the living room where he found Walter Bowman absorbed in his own thoughts. He resumed his interrogation by asking Walter Bowman to recount everything he did during the day prior to Waterson's homicide.

"Do you want to know everything I did all day long?" Bowman asked incredulously.

"I don't need to know what you did from one moment to the next, Mr. Bowman, and I doubt if you could remember at that level of detail even if you wanted to. What I need is an accurate record of your movements yesterday including any trips away from the house."

Walter Bowman recounted his movements with some detail including a trip to the nursery to buy mulch for the shrubbery and perennial flower beds, and a trip to the shopping center north of his house. He informed Matt that his wife, Helen, had already left the house when he returned from his shopping trip at five o'clock and that his daughter left shortly thereafter. He concluded by stating that he and his wife left for the Martins' cocktail party at seven and stayed until nine. He insisted that his daughter was still out when they returned from the cocktail party because he didn't see her car out front where she always parked and he didn't hear any sounds from her apartment in the basement of the house.

"Did you make or receive any telephone calls yesterday?"

"No, I didn't make any calls, and no one called me."

At that point, Tom Martin reappeared from upstairs.

"How is Angela," her father asked.

"She's very upset, Walter. I sedated her with an injection; and I also left some pills with Helen for Angela to take when she comes around. She should sleep soundly for the next eight hours. Helen doesn't look well either, so I advised her to take one of the same pills every six hours until she feels better. Angela's emotional condition is unstable right now, but she'll be okay. She shouldn't be subjected to any more stress until she's had time to recover."

"When can I question her?" Matt asked.

"That depends on how you intend to question her," Tom Martin replied.

"I don't intend to use a rubber hose, if that's what you're worried about," Matt shot back.

"What I meant," Tom patiently explained, "is that precautions should be taken not to subject her to any additional stress. Nervous collapses brought on by trauma can have long-term consequences. However, when and where you question her is a matter for you and her father to decide, Matthew."

Satisfied that he had properly discharged his duties, Tom Martin rose from the sofa, collected his medical bag, and headed for the door.

"Since I've sedated Angela, and since you won't tell me who's been killed, I'm going home. Nice seeing you again, Matthew. It's a pity it couldn't have been under better circumstances. I suppose it's all in a night's work for you, though. Don't worry, Walter, I'm confident our energetic young detective here will straighten this mess out for you. Good night gentlemen."

Matt checked his watch, which showed the time to be two-ten A.M. Anxious to get as much done as possible, he decided to speed up the tempo of his questions to Walter Bowman.

"Where do you work, Mr. Bowman?"

"At the District of Columbia Reclamation Land Agency."

"How long have you been there?"

"I've worked for the District government since I finished law school, but I've been with the DCRLA just for the past five years."

"What's your position there?"

"I'm supervising attorney for the legal department. We review specifications for constructing or rehabilitating District government property before requests-for-proposals are released to the public. Then we review all the bids we receive to make sure they meet the specifications in the original project solicitation."

"Did you know that Harold Waterson was a real estate developer?"

"Of course I knew he was a principal partner with Waterson, Sulivan and Loew Development Corporation."

"I find it intriguing that you and Waterson were in the same line of business, so to speak, Mr. Bowman. I'm sure you must have dealt with the dead man's construction company all the time."

"Waterson's firm regularly submitted bids for DCRLA

construction projects just like a lot of other developers, but I never had any reason to conduct business with him face-to-face. Any problems that arise in the course of a bid submission are usually worked out with the firm's architects and engineers. It's rare that the construction firm's partners would be brought into such transactions by my office."

"Didn't Waterson's firm get the contract for the Anacostia Riverfront Development Project last year?"

"Yes, that contract went to Waterson's firm."

"And, wasn't there a big stink over the fact that a black firm didn't get the contract even though they submitted a lower bid?"

"It's no secret that the bid submitted by Smith, Jones and Reynolds was rejected. Their firm was too small and inexperienced to build the large scale residential and commercial development project the bid specifications required. They didn't have much of a track record when they submitted on the Anacostia Riverfront Development Project. The DCRLA reserves the right to reject low bidders if they fail to meet our other requirements."

"If I remember correctly, the difference in the bids was roughly ten million dollars."

"It was ten million, two hundred thousand to be precise."

"Well, well. The plot thickens, Mr. Bowman."

"Since you are reminiscing, Matthew, let me remind you that Smith, Jones, and Reynolds appealed the award to an impartial review board where our selection process was totally vindicated. I don't have anything to hide on that score."

"I prefer to think that the jury is still out, Mr. Bowman. There's no telling what time and a little patient digging will unearth"

"You'll be wasting your time digging around in my department. I run my office strictly by the book. I'd be a fool if I didn't."

Matt was unconvinced; but he also realized that if Walter

Bowman had taken a kickback from Waterson, it was damned foolish for him to have killed the man in his own house. However, he may not have had a choice. Either way, Bowman was smart enough to have covered his tracks at the DCRLA. Matt believed him when he said his books were in order. If Waterson had given Bowman a payoff, it was going to be damned difficult if not impossible to trace. Harold Waterson was no novice to the construction game.

"How long have you known Tom Martin, Mr. Bowman?"

"Tom and I have been neighbors for twenty-five years. We bought this house around the same time he and his first wife bought the house next door, but I've known Tom practically all my life. He and I grew up together in Georgetown when the houses over there weren't worth a dime."

"How well did Tom know Harold Waterson?"

"A lot better than I did. Tom invests in real estate, too. He wasn't big time like Harold Waterson, but he owns a lot of rental property in the District and in Prince Georges County."

"That will be all for now, Mr. Bowman. You'll be required to sign a written statement confirming what you've told me tonight. If your memory returns and you remember the last time you saw your gun, let me know. I'm sure I'll find the information useful."

"I would appreciate it if you didn't disturb Angela, Matthew. She's been through enough tonight."

"I can wait until tomorrow to question Angela, but I have to talk to your wife tonight. I'll send for her when I'm ready."

Jake returned from the Martins' as Walter Bowman walked up the stairs to the second floor of his house. Sam Johnson also chose that moment to appear in the foyer from downstairs. He addressed his question to Matt.

"I've finished lifting prints downstairs. What do you want me to do about the rest of the house?"

"Test all of the Bowmans' hands for powder residue, Sam,

and don't forget to get elimination prints from them. After that, do all the windows and doors on the first and second floors. Start with the kitchen and bathrooms."

"That's a tall order, Alexander. I'll do as much as I can tonight; but the windows will have to wait until tomorrow."

"Should we search the grounds, again?" Jake asked.

"There's no point in searching in the dark, Jake. Be sure to secure the back of the house, but the yard can wait until tomorrow. Did you get a copy of the Martins' guest list?"

"Yeah, here it is," Jake replied as he passed the neatly copied list to Matt who glanced at it only briefly before folding it in half and inserting it into his notebook.

After Jake left for the basement, Matt asked Officer Lewis to bring Helen Bowman down for questioning. Meanwhile, Sam Johnson gingerly deposited his equipment on the Oriental rug in the foyer taking only what he needed to start lifting prints from the kitchen and the first floor powder room.

Unlike her husband, Helen Bowman made a deliberate, measured descent down the stairs as if each step were bringing her closer to something she dreaded. She was calm, but her composure was a fragile thing, as delicate as a windchime in a thunderstorm. When she reached the bottom of the stairs, she stopped and stared at Sam's equipment, but said nothing. She continued into the living room and unknowingly took the same seat her husband had occupied earlier. She waited for the Lieutenant to speak first.

Matt remembered Helen Bowman as a quiet reserved woman who left the impression that she tolerated your presence because it was the polite thing to do. Personally, she wasn't easy to figure, appearing remote and unapproachable to those who didn't know her well, including Matt. The few times he had been in her presence when he was dating Angela, he got the impression that it was okay with her if he stayed and equally as satisfactory if he left; but in either case she didn't put herself out to get to know him any better. Helen Bowman was quiet to the point of introversion. Matt also recalled that her indifference changed to genuine concern when she interacted with her daughter, Angela. It was apparent to anyone who know the Bowmans well that Helen Bowman adored her daughter.

At least two inches taller than her husband, Helen Bowman wore no make-up for her session with Matt. She obviously hadn't tried to camouflage her grief over Harold Waterson's, death which showed most perceptibly around her eyes. Distressed or not, she was a lovely woman. Her stylishly cut short black hair was peppered with gray, and her copper skin reminded the Lieutenant of tropical sunsets. Though not as pretty as her daughter, Helen Bowman was a striking woman whose forlorn disposition enhanced rather than diminished her appeal, to Matt anyway. Angela Bowman resembled her father more than her mother, but Matt decided that she got her figure from her mother, who was built like a woman half her age. Helen Bowman wore a navy velour lounging outfit, and Matt found himself wondering if she worked out to keep herself in shape. He decided that she didn't because he couldn't picture Helen Bowman working up a sweat in a gym.

"I'm sorry to take you away from your daughter, Mrs. Bowman, but there are some questions I need to ask you about the murder in your basement tonight."

"I still can't believe that Harold Waterson was shot dead in my home. It's like a horrible nightmare, Matthew. It keeps repeating over and over again in my head, but it just doesn't seem real."

"Tell me what happened this evening, Mrs. Bowman."

"There's not much I can tell you. Walter and I got back from Claudia Martin's cocktail party around nine o'clock. Angela wasn't home. I went to bed soon after we got back. I must have fallen asleep about ten o'clock. Walter was in his study as usual. He watches the eleven o'clock news in there every night. The door to my bedroom was closed, so I didn't hear anything until Angela burst into the room and threw herself across the bed. She was hysterical. When I asked her what had happened, she couldn't tell me at first because she was crying so hard. She scared me so badly, I started shaking myself. I thought something had happened to Walter. I didn't realize what had happened until Walter came tearing up the stairs after his gun. When he told me that Harold Waterson had been shot dead in our basement, I almost became hysterical myself. Walter couldn't find his handgun, so he loaded his shotgun, came into the bedroom, locked the door and called the police. We waited in the bedroom with Walter pointing the gun at the door until the police came. We all went downstairs when the police arrived, but Angela was still very upset. I brought her back upstairs to my bedroom so she could lie down. Tom Martin gave her a sedative about thirty minutes ago."

"I understand that Harold Waterson was at Claudia Martin's cocktail party, tonight."

"Yes, he was there."

"Were you personally acquainted with the deceased, Mrs. Bowman?"

Helen Bowman had been looking directly at Matt before the question. Afterwards, her eyes shifted from his face to the fingers of her left hand where she nervously twisted her wedding rings. She took longer to answer the question than she should have.

"I had met him before tonight if that's what you mean, but I didn't know him personally. Walter didn't either."

"Where had you met him before?"

"At various receptions and social functions around the District. You see people in passing and you know them well enough to speak, but not much better than that."

"Your husband said that Angela didn't attend the Martins' party tonight. Is that true?"

"Yes, that's right. She left to go over to a friend's house earlier in the evening."

"Did you or your husband speak to Waterson at the Martins' tonight?"

"Yes, we spoke to him briefly. He is...or was a very popular man, Matthew. Most of the people at the party made a point of speaking to him."

"Do you remember whether Waterson was still at the party when you and your husband left?"

"I can't be sure, but I think he was. Walter and I were some of the first to leave."

"Do you know who let Waterson into your house, Mrs. Bowman?"

"No, I don't. I still can't believe that he was killed in our basement. It doesn't make any sense. We barely knew him."

"Let me see if I have this straight? You were not personally acquainted with the deceased, and you don't know what he was doing in your basement or who let him in. Am I correct?"

"Yes, that's right."

"I'm sure it won't surprise you to learn that your husband says essentially the same thing."

"No, it doesn't surprise me because it's the truth."

"The way I see it, Mrs. Bowman, one of you had to let Waterson in unless he had his own key. He wasn't a cat burglar."

"None of us knew Harold Waterson personally. But, even if we did, what possible reason would we have had for killing him in our own home? You know us, Matthew, so you must know that we're not capable of murdering anyone."

"He was killed in your basement, Mrs. Bowman, so you, your husband, and Angela are our prime suspects. There's no getting around that fact. When did you first learn that your husband's revolver was missing?"

"Tonight was the first I knew about it."

"Do you remember the last time you saw it in that desk drawer?"

"No, I don't. I'm afraid of guns. As a matter of fact, I've never touched the gun; and I'm certain Angela hasn't either."

"Had the gun ever disappeared before?"

"Not to my knowledge."

"What do you think happened to it?"

"I have no idea. What happens to Walter's things are his business, not mine. I..." Helen Bowman stopped short, instantly regretting her words.

"You were saying, Mrs. Bowman."

"I was saying that I don't know what happened to the gun, Matthew."

"Did you hear any gunshots from the basement, before Angela burst into your room?"

"No, I didn't."

"Your husband says he didn't hear any shots either; but if Waterson was shot with a thirty-eight, as we suspect, there is no way anyone inside or outside this house could have missed hearing shots from a gun that size."

"I didn't hear anything until Angela burst into my bedroom and woke me up."

"How would you explain the fact that Harold Waterson was killed in your basement, tonight, Mrs. Bowman?"

"If I could explain it, I could probably have anticipated it; and if I could have anticipated it, Matthew, I wouldn't have allowed it to happen...at least not in my home."

Her reply stopped Matt cold. He thought he knew Helen Bowman, but did he? She appeared to be a bored middle-class housewife trapped in a marriage she detested, but was she so transparent? The longer he questioned Helen Bowman, the more he realized that he was dealing with a woman of subtle complexities. She wore a carefully constructed persona of polite indifference and modest intelligence. However, Matt suspected that she was a good deal more intelligent than she let on, and a good deal less docile, too.

"Tell me how you spent your day, Mrs. Bowman."

"I left the house at four o'clock to attend my sorority meeting at Howard University. The meeting lasted until five-thirty. I got back home at six. When I got back Walter told me that Angela had left for a friend's while I was out. I went up to my room to rest a while before I got ready for Claudia Martin's cocktail party, and we left for the Martins at seven. We were the first to arrive at the party."

"Your husband said Angela left the house around five. Do you know where she went?"

"No, I don't. Angela has a lot of friends, and I don't normally pry into her personal life."

"The last I heard, Angela was married and living in southeast. How long has she been back home, Mrs. Bowman?"

"Almost a year and a half, now. She moved back in August a year ago when she and Gary separated."

"I presume Gary is her estranged husband?"

"Yes, his name is Gary Washington."

"I don't know him. Is he from the District?"

"No. He grew up in Prince Georges County. Neither one of us knew that Angela was dating Gary until after they were married. Angela was afraid to bring him home because she knew her father would disapprove. Walter behaved very badly when he found out they were married. I had never seen him so disappointed. Of course, Gary wasn't the kind of man I would have chosen for Angela either, but he had a steady job; and it was obvious that he loved her. They found an apartment on Good Hope Road in Southeast. Walter refused to give her a dime. He still doesn't know it, but I gave Angela and Gary the money to furnish their apartment."

"I enjoyed seeing my daughter start a life of her own. I looked forward to having grandchildren, too, but I should have known better. Walter didn't rest until he had broken them up. Angela is our only child, and you know how over-protective

Walter is. As far as he is concerned, no man is good enough for her. He claims that he does it for her own good, but it's more for his benefit than hers. Angela can't deal with her father's disapproval for very long. She doesn't have the strength to break away from him, and he won't let her go."

"Walter never acknowledged the fact that Gary was Angela's husband. He absolutely refused to allow Gary to visit us here, and he refused to go to their apartment. Angela stuck it out for a year and a half, but I honestly didn't expect her to last that long. I begged her not to leave Gary, but it was useless. Walter degraded Gary every chance he got. Angela couldn't stand his harping on her marriage any longer, so she left Gary a year ago and moved back home. Walter had all the furniture I bought for them moved into the basement; and that's where she lives now...downstairs in her father's house. Gary still refuses to give her a divorce. I don't blame him because she has no grounds for it other than the fact that her father disapproved of her husband. Walter made Angela file for a legal separation. After two years of living apart from Gary, she'll be eligible for an uncontested divorce; and Walter will have accomplished what he set out to do."

"Has Gary tried to see her since she moved back here?"

"Yes, more times that I can count. He's crazy about Angela. He was good to her, too. He did everything he could to talk her out of leaving him. I talked to her myself until I saw that she had made up her mind and there was nothing I could do to convince her to stay with Gary. He came to the house several times, but Walter ran him away. He telephoned so much that Walter had our number changed and unlisted. It got so bad that Walter took out a restraining order on Gary to keep him from coming to the house to see Angela, who is still his wife. He hasn't been around for several months now, so I guess he finally got the message."

Matt listened to Helen Bowman's story without comment. He knew from personal experience that Walter Bowman was very close to his daughter, but he hadn't realized just how neurotically possessive he was until now. When he and Angela broke up seven years ago, he blamed her as much as her father. He was still convinced that she liked to have her cake and eat it too. But, Helen Bowman's story made it plain that Angela didn't have the strength or the will to fight her father's interference in her personal life.

"Did you make or receive any telephone calls yesterday, Mrs. Bowman?"

Helen Bowman hesitated for a second before replying, "No, Matthew. I didn't make any calls yesterday; and no one called me."

"Do you know what time Angela returned home last night?"

"She wasn't here when we got back from the Martins' party around nine. Her car wasn't parked out front, and Walter checked the basement just to be sure."

Matt checked his watch again and saw that it was three-thirty in the morning.

"That's all for now, Mrs. Bowman. You'll be required to come down to headquarters in a day or two to sign a formal statement based on what you've told me here tonight. It's just routine procedure, nothing to worry about."

Helen Bowman rose from the corner of the sofa and started walking out of the living room when she suddenly stopped as if she had just remembered something important.

"How is your family, Matthew? I heard that you married Carla Channing not long after you and Angela broke up."

"Yes, that's right. Carla and I have been married for almost five years, now. I have a daughter, three, and a son sixteen months old."

"You probably didn't know this at the time you were dating Angela, but of all the young men she brought to the house, I liked you the best. I sensed that you were different from the others. You seemed to be more sure of yourself. I'll never forget the way you stood up to Walter the night Angela brought you home to meet us. I still regret not fighting Walter when he came between you and Angela. You were strong enough to protect her from him. The only reason I've stayed with Walter all these years is because of Angela. I haven't been much of a match for him over the years, Matthew, but I tried. I may as well have left him years ago; because in spite of all my efforts, Walter has finally won." With that, Helen Bowman turned and left the room.

Matt was surprised to hear Helen Bowman's revelation. At the time he was dating Angela, her mother had never given him the slightest indication that she knew he existed let alone liked him. He was still mulling over her statement when Jake came up to tell him that they had completed a thorough search of the basement and still hadn't found the murder weapon.

"Waterson's next of kin have to be notified about his death, Jake. We need to get them to identify the body as soon as possible. I'm sure Lloyd will brief Chief Carter first thing in the morning, if he hasn't already. So we need a positive ID from a family member by morning. Bryant, Foster, and Lewis can search the rest of the house. You and I need to get over to the Waterson residence."

"What about Waterson's car, man? His key rings have a set of Mercedes-Benz keys on it; and there's a white 450 SL parked out front. Must be his car."

"More than likely. We'll look through it as soon as we leave. I'll tell Bryant to put in a request to have it towed to the impound lot. That will give us time to search it more thoroughly in the morning. If you get there first, be sure to have Sam dust it for prints." Matt grabbed his all-weather coat from the sofa before going downstairs to talk to Captain Bryant. He emerged from the basement five minutes later carrying the plastic bags with Waterson's personal effects. Jake was waiting for him in front of the house.

After they left 1637 Floribunda Lane, Matt took a moment to savor the cold night air, which he inhaled several times in quick succession. He had barely begun to reconstruct the events that led up to Harold Waterson's homicide, but he already sensed that the case wouldn't be an easy one. It was unfortunate that he knew the Bowmans as well as he did...especially Angela. He could ask to be taken off the case, but he knew he wouldn't. And, he was damned if Commander Lloyd Cullison or anyone else would force him to step down without a hell of a fight from him. He could be impartial and he would be impartial, but it wasn't going to be easy to develop a case against someone he had once loved. But he was no stranger to difficulty. He had cut his teeth on hard times. Besides that, he had been in the storm too long to worry about getting rained on at this stage of the game. He was in for the count.

# CHAPTER V

Once outside, Matt used the dead man's keys to open the Mercedes 450 SL parked in front of the house. He placed the contents of the glove compartment into a plastic bag. Satisfied that there was little more of interest inside the car, Matt locked the doors and opened the trunk, which contained nothing aside from the requisite spare tire, jack, and lug wrench. After closing the trunk, he walked over to where Jake was standing beside their car. Matt climbed into the passenger seat.

"Find anything interesting?"

"I didn't expect to find Walter Bowman's gun," Matt explained as Jake swerved away from the curb and made an unexpected U-turn onto Floribunda that pointed them in the direction of Sixteenth Street. He made a right on Sixteenth Street and sped south for several minutes.

"Well, partner, who killed him?"

"The only thing I know for certain is that he didn't kill himself. From what I've learned so far, all the Bowmans had opportunity and means too if Walter Bowman's thirty-eight is the murder weapon. The problem is motive. Why was he shot in their basement? It seems that Walter and Helen Bowman had gotten their lies straight before we got there. They both concealed as much as they admitted, and they both claim they didn't know what Harold Waterson was doing in their house. They also denied hearing the shot. I find their story very hard to swallow, but I'm reserving judgement until I talk to Angela tomorrow."

"I'll lay odds that by the time you question her, she'll tell the same story as her parents, man."

"Maybe so, Jake, but I'll cross that bridge when I get there. I'll find the killer; but the tough part is going to be getting enough solid evidence for a conviction, especially if we don't find the murder weapon. I don't think the killing was premeditated, but my gut tells me that whoever shot Waterson covered their tracks pretty thoroughly. Do you know where we can get some hot coffee at this hour?"

"Yeah. There's an all night carry-out at Georgia and Kennedy."

"Let's run by there before we go over to the Waterson place."

"Don't you think you ought to check in with Cullison before you lay the bad news on Waterson's old lady, man?"

"What's the big deal? You know I have to get a positive ID on the corpse as soon as possible after the homicide. I can't call Lloyd to clear every move I make on this case before I make it, man. I'm going over to the Waterson house now, case closed."

Changing the subject, Matt continued, "Remind me not to put in any more overtime on Saturdays, Jake."

"Man, you don't listen to a thing I say. I've told you before that it's crazy to work yourself into the ground for Cullison. The more you do, the more he gives you to do. He likes to see us working like slaves."

"Give me a break, man."

"Okay, it's your funeral, not mine. But, don't say I didn't warn you."

"What did you think of Claudia Martin?" Matt asked as he took her guest list from his pocket.

"She's more than a notion, Man. I wasn't over there two minutes before that broad had me eating out of her hand. She's not bad to look at either."

"Carla says women can't stand Claudia Martin because they disappear into the woodwork when Claudia's around. Their husbands gravitate to Claudia like flies to honey."

"You can say that again," Jake agreed. "She has a habit of standing real close when she talks to you, made me nervous as a cat, man. I feel sorry for poor old Doc Martin."

"Don't let Tom's appearance fool you, Jake. Claudia isn't smart enough to pull the wool over Tom's eyes. He's a cunning operator when it comes to looking out for himself. Claudia isn't about to mess over Tom or his money."

"How much is he worth?"

"A bundle, from what I hear. Walter Bowman told me tonight that Tom has extensive real estate holdings in the District and Prince Georges County."

"You'd never know it to look at him, man. Doc Martin always looks like forty miles of bad road. He ought to use some of that money to fix himself up; but as short and fat as he is, it would probably be a total waste of time and money. He looks a lot older than his wife."

"He's only about five years older than Claudia. She takes good care of herself with Tom's money. Claudia is Tom's second wife. His first wife died about ten years ago. Dig this, man," Matt continued laughing, "Claudia was married when she and Tom became engaged. After his first wife died, Tom was the most eligible catch on the Gold Coast. Women were pursuing him from as far away as Chicago and New York. Claudia had to move fast to beat the competition, so she reeled Tom in before her divorce became final. The word is that she and Tom bought a divorce from her former husband, Jim Gregory. She saddled Jim with a mountain of debt and dropped him like a hot potato when Tom came along.

"Tom's motives weren't pure either. It seems that the only thing Tom's money hasn't been able to buy him is entree into Gold Coast society. The word is that Tom's mother ran a gin joint and cat house over in Georgetown in the thirties and forties; and that she used her earnings to send Tom to college and medical school. If you ask me, the money was well earned and spent if she had the good sense to educate her son with it. Anyway, the "Light-Brights" have never forgiven Tom for being the son of a madam. Claudia's family boasts about tracing their roots back to before the civil war, man. They claim to have never been slaves either, but I'm not buying that. Both her father and grandfather were medical doctors. They were furious when she married Tom, but Claudia didn't give a damn how they felt about him. She does exactly as she pleases, and it pleased her to marry Tom's money. Claudia knows anybody who claims to be somebody on the Gold Coast, so she and Tom seem to have struck a good bargain."

"Did Claudia's ex-husband marry again?"

"Yes, and his new wife hates Claudia with a passion. It seems that Claudia and Jim remained the best of friends after their divorce. You can't be indifferent to Claudia, man. You either love her or you hate her."

"I can see why," Jake replied. "I went over there to question her; and before I knew what was happening, she was asking the questions. It was like I was in a daze, man. I didn't snap out of it until she asked me who had been killed. I caught myself before I answered, but she almost had me. She's a bona fide pistol."

"That's putting it mildly, Jake. Claudia's guest list reads like the who's who of District society," Matt said as he scanned the list. "I'm impressed, man. There's the former mayor of the District, the current mayor, the AME Bishop, the District congresswoman, the President of Howard University, the

President of the University of the District of Columbia, the Under Secretary of State for African Affairs, the Director of the African Art Museum, the Director of the African-American History Museum, the Director of the Museum of American History, a whole slew of diplomats, and of course Hal Waterson and his wife, only she wasn't there. It'll be interesting to find out why she stayed away. Looks like Claudia pulled out all the stops for this party. I wonder why?"

"I'm not impressed by the people on that list, man. They're just like everybody else. I don't see what's so special about them."

"You're wrong, Jake. They're not like everybody else, otherwise everybody else would have been invited to the party too."

"They step into their pants one leg at a time just like I do," Jake stubbornly insisted.

"I'm not denying that they're human, Jake. But they are different. Some of these people are at the top of their game, and they caught hell getting there too. Most people, black or white, never approach the level of power they have. They're not the brightest people around. The geniuses usually retreat to academia where they bore students to death with long-winded lectures from dog-eared notes. But, the people on this list are smart. They weren't afraid to go after what they wanted with everything they had. They worked hard for their careers. They're the best at what they do, you have to give them credit for that."

"They aren't any smarter than you or me, man. They just happened to be in the right place at the right time."

"That's just it, Jake. Being in the right place at the right time isn't accidental. It takes drive and ambition. You have to plan, strategize, wait, pay your dues, and stick it out when you'd rather give up. It takes a lot of guts to play the game on their level, man. Besides that, they influence our lives a lot more than you realize."

"I'm still not impressed," Jake replied as he pulled into the parking lot of the all night carry-out on the corner of George and Kennedy Avenues, where he took his partner's order and disappeared into the carry-out.

Matt closed his eyes as he waited for his partner's return, but he couldn't rest for thinking about the confused tangle of facts or lies that he had learned from Walter and Helen Bowman. Whenever he investigated a homicide, he felt compelled to work things out mentally from every possible angle. It was helpful, but emotionally draining. The more difficult the case, the more he thought about it. The Waterson homicide intrigued him because it was out of synch and out of context. It didn't make sense that a slight acquaintance could end up murdered in your house for no apparent reason. Something had brought Waterson to the Bowman residence. Some chance circumstance initiated a chain of events that climaxed with his murder. Matt held to his original assumption that the killer's motives would be found among the usual reasons that one person gives for taking another's life—passion, greed, jealously, revenge, hatred or some other intense drive to strike out at the victim. Motives were more or less predictable, so Matt found them less intriguing than the other circumstances surrounding a violent death. What interested him more was the sequence of events, movements, and communication between the deceased and the killer prior to the homicide.

Matt was fascinated not by the fact that Waterson had been killed, but why he died at the precise moment that he did. Why hadn't he been killed sooner or later? What had occurred Saturday after Waterson left Claudia Martin's cocktail party that presented the precise psychological moment for the killer to strike? For him, the events leading up to Waterson's homicide took on the aspect of a pre-death ritual where the pivotal suspects either consciously or unwittingly played their parts as if they had been choreographed to perform the movements that ended with the victim's death. Once the chain of events was set in motion, all the players performed on cue and the victim moved among them oblivious to the fate that waited for him at the end of the performance. If the Bowmans were telling the truth, Harold Waterson shouldn't have been in their basement, yet he was there. Obviously, the scenario had played itself out to a chilling conclusion.

"Where do the Watersons' live?" Jake asked as he opened the door and passed Matt the coffee.

"After giving Jake the address, Matt noticed that the rain had finally stopped, leaving a penetrating November cold that permeated everything with its dampness. The past week had set a record for rain in the District. The downpour had slackened off early Friday morning, but storm drains in low-lying areas of the city had over-flowed into the streets for several days and Rock Creek was still flooding its banks. Jake complained about the dampness and chill as he continued his drive to the Watersons, but Jake complained about everything. He drove his usual break neck speed while his partner sipped hot coffee and kept his own counsel.

For his part, Matt thought how rarely his work in the homicide division took him to the high rent district where they found themselves headed tonight. District homicides were typically confined to low-rent areas of the city rife with poverty, violence, and crime, communities where the residents are all too familiar with crime in all its manifestations. Because violence invades the lives of the urban poor with relentless indifference, Matt was aware of the hazards of being poor in a hostile urban environment. He found that the people most vulnerable to crime are often powerless to escape its tentacles. Distances in the District of Columbia are not far, but the urban poor live light years away from the order and predictability of communities like the Gold Coast. As secure as life appeared to be on the Gold Coast, Harold Waterson had been murdered anyway. Obviously, someone had no respect for wealthy communities.

"What time is it?" Jake asked.

"Three-fifty," Matt replied with a yawn. He had finished his first cup of coffee and was halfway through the second before he felt his stamina limp back.

"Man, I'm too old to be keeping these late hours," Jake commented as he made the narrow right turn from Beach Drive onto Tilden on his way to God's country west of Rock Creek Park. With Pierce Mill on the right, he crossed the small bridge that forded the creek and began the deceptively steep climb Tilden requires before it intersects with Connecticut Avenue. When he arrived at Nebraska Avenue, he continued south past the sprawling expanse of American University's campus on the right, and the University's large parking lot on the left.

The American University Park community took little notice of the squad car that sped through its street at such a God forsaken hour of the morning. Matt knew it was a safe bet that at three-fifty in the morning, all the District's movers and shakers were tucked up safely in snug beds from A.U. Park to the Pallisades and from Spring Valley to Georgetown. Criminal activity east of the park rarely caught the attention of the District's power brokers, but this particular crime would be deliciously scrutinized by the inhabitants of God's country down to its last salacious detail.

Matt considered Harold Waterson's life...a half-breed, a renegade who moved among the moneyed white elite as if he belonged. He appropriated their prized possessions, a beautiful wife, wealth, property, with all the cunning, guile, and charm of the genuine article. He cultivated them as equals until they discovered his terrible secret that wasn't a secret after all. But, how were they to know when he looked more white than some of them with his hazel eyes and blond wife? The earth moved when they discovered the deception they had played on themselves. What did it mean to be white when a black person could have a blond child and the money you'd kill for? It didn't fit into the world they had come to trust, so they contented themselves knowing he wasn't the genuine article after all.

He was tainted, cursed... but he lived among them and socialized among them and they didn't seem to mind. They kept waiting for signs of his curse to surface, but he had as much poise and self-assurance as they. Of course, he tried harder. He couldn't let his guard down and they could. They had never seen him drunk or offensive, but that was because he couldn't risk letting his black jigaboo out of the bag. They didn't mind letting their hair down because their jigaboos were white. However, the black jigaboo had finally jumped. Hal Waterson had been shot down east of the park. It was a vindication of sorts, because blood will tell, especially black blood. The taint was in him all along. He did a masterful of disguising it, but it was bound to come out in the end. They would rest easier knowing that he hadn't been killed west of the park.

Matt looked through Hal Waterson's personal effects. The expensive brown leather wallet contained the dead man's driver's license, a variety of credit cards, plus several hundred dollars in cash. The matching appointment book contained no reference to the Bowmans or the Martins' cocktail party. Hal Waterson had made two appointments on Saturday, one at two P.M., and one at five P.M., both at his downtown office. He made a note to check with Watersons' secretary to see if she knew whom he had met at those times on the day he died.

"What was that address again?" Jake asked as he made a left onto Foxhall Road. Matt repeated it.

"We'll never find it in the dark," Jake confidently asserted as he navigated the winding curves of Foxhall Road. "Which way should I turn on Reservoir Road, man?"

"Right," Matt answered at the same time as Jake made a left at the intersection of Foxhall and Reservoir Roads. Jake corrected his mistake by making a swerving U-turn in the middle of Reservoir Road. The patrol car was inching its way down Reservoir when Jake spotted the address on the left side of the street. He drove up to the house through a pair of ten-foot stone pillars and followed a semi-circular driveway illuminated by wrought-iron lamp posts placed at regular intervals around its circumference. Halfway around the driveway, Jake stopped the car under an impressive well-lit portico that abutted an immense Tudor-styled stone mansion with mullioned windows and white trim. Matt got out of the car first, walked up the portico steps and stood under a highly polished brass coach lantern with chained swags as he pressed the doorbell. Jake followed close on his heels. After eight rings on the doorbell in as many minutes, a crusty old female voice full of sleep and suspicion demanded to know who they were and what they wanted. Matt shouted their bona fides through the door and demanded to see Mrs. Waterson immediately.

"How do I know you're who you say you are. I won't disturb her just on your say so."

"I told you before that I'm Lieutenant Alexander and this is Sergeant Jackson. Burglars don't ring doorbells, madam."

"You could very well be burglars and probably are. I won't wake her up until you show me proof that you're who you say you are."

"Give me your badge, Jake," Matt demanded as prepared to slip the two badges through the mail slot in the front door.

"You can call Fourth District Headquarters if you're not satisfied with our badges," he shouted through the door.

"I hope she doesn't set the dogs on us," Jake said mockingly.

"Dogs don't scare me so long as I have my forty-five," Matt replied. They waited five minutes more on the porch and decided that an indefinite wait would pass more comfortably inside their car where they could keep warm.

"Can you believe the size of this house?" Jake asked. "It looks like Waterson left some serious worldly possessions behind, partner. One thing's for damned sure, you can't take it with you. We all crawled into this world naked, and we all go out of it into a six-foot hole in the ground. The Bible says that in my Father's house there are many mansions; but having one on earth is no guarantee of getting one in heaven."

"If there is a heaven," Matt added. "Old Waterson had it so good here on earth, he shouldn't mind any discomfort he's suffering now. He was lucky for as long as it lasted, Jake. Most of us catch hell here and there, too."

Nearly fifteen minutes passed before the front door slowly opened. The figure they saw in the lighted doorway was an old white woman in a white night cap and a pink chenille bathrobe that looked as ancient as she did. When they walked up to the door, they saw that she was holding a very large, vicious German shepherd on a short leash.

"Didn't I tell you the dogs would be next!" Jake insisted. "I'll cover you, man" he volunteered backing down the portico steps.

"There's no need for that, Jake," Matt said with an air of confidence that instantly evaporated when the German shepherd started snarling and baring its fangs. Matt stayed put and addressed his question to the old woman.

"Is Mrs. Waterson ready to see us?"

"Yes, I am," a younger voice replied as a taller figure stepped into the open doorway beside the old woman.

"Take Max away, Aunt Martha," she told the old woman. She called the two detectives by name and invited them inside, looking at their identification to make sure she got their names right. "I'm sorry we had to keep you waiting, but crime in the District is so bad, you really can't be too careful."

Felicia Waterson's hospitality was strained...as if she were trying to hold onto the sanity and civility of the moment as long as she could. She escorted them into an immense anteroom where she returned their badges and offered them seats. They both sat facing her across the larger foyer. She sat erect, poised nervously on the edge of her chair. As anxious as she appeared to be, she didn't rush them. She allowed them time to become accustomed to her and the house.

Matt saw that Felicia Waterson was a lovely woman. She was a least five-feet-eight-inches tall, her height accentuated by a scrupulously erect carriage. She wore her medium length blond hair brushed away from her brow, where it fell in loose waves to the top of her shoulders. Her skin was pale and her cheeks were flushed, whether normally or from anxiety at their presence, Matt couldn't tell. Her large blue eyes were troubled and restless under faint brows set in a square-shaped face with cheekbones reminiscent of a high-fashion model past her prime. She wore a pale blue dressing gown that matched her eyes; and she exuded an aura of delicate perfection that reminded Matt of a religious painting. She gave him the impression of someone who existed beyond the ugliness and cruelty of everyday life. She looked as if none of these things had ever touched her or ever could. There was something disturbing about her, though...a discrepant note that left him wondering.

"What brings you to my house at this hour, Lieutenant Alexander?"

"Bad news I'm sorry to say, Mrs. Waterson. I regret to..."

Felicia Waterson's composure swiftly evaporated as she succumbed to an intense surge of anxiety, "Oh my God! Has something happened to my son?"

"No, it's not your son, Mrs. Waterson. It's your husband. We have reason to believe he's been killed."

Her anxiety turned to instant terror as she screamed hysterically, "Killed! Hal killed! I don't believe you! He can't be dead! He's upstairs asleep in his bed!" she frantically protested as if saying it would make it so. She gripped the arms of her chair and tried to stand as sobs racked her body.

"Please stay seated, Mrs. Waterson," Matt urged as he helped her back into her chair.

"Jake, get the old lady out here quick!" he called to his partner while silently praying that Felicia Waterson wouldn't break down completely.

"If you don't leave the dog in the kitchen, I won't be responsible for the consequences," Jake warned Aunt Martha as she very nearly knocked him down trying to get to Felicia Waterson.

"Aunt Martha," Felicia cried like a wounded child, "he says Hal is dead! Tell him it's not true! Tell him that Hal is upstairs in his bed. Tell him, Aunt Martha!" she sobbed hysterically before burying her face into the old lady's abdomen.

Aunt Martha reeled backwards when she heard the news. For a moment, Matt feared she would collapse from the shock; and what he didn't need was another hysterical woman on his hands. Shaking like a leaf, Aunt Martha allowed Matt to assist her to a chair, but it was obvious that she was as grief-stricken as Felicia Waterson. Tears were running down her cheeks when Matt first realized that Aunt Martha wasn't white. She was light-skinned to be sure, but clearly African-American. He helped her into the chair Jake had vacated. Unlike Felicia Waterson, Aunt Martha resigned herself to the truth of what they said.

"How did he die?" she asked.

"He was shot to death."

Both women screamed out at the same time.

"We took this wallet and appointment book off a man killed about six hours ago at 1637 Floribunda Lane in northwest Washington." Matt shows both items to Aunt Martha, who was reluctant to look at them.

"It's Hal's wallet!" she cried out. He's not upstairs in his bedroom, Felicia. I told you he wasn't there when I woke you up. It's him they've found dead," she sobbed. "My poor child is dead." She held the wallet and appointment book close to her body as she rocked back and forth and sobbed.

"Help me, Aunt Martha!" Felicia cried stretching out her hand to the old lady.

Her cries went unaided because Aunt Martha was consumed by her own grief. The Lieutenant waited several minutes during which time he tried to comfort them as best he could. Jake, clearly uncomfortable with female grief, kept his distance near the kitchen door. After Aunt Martha calmed down, Matt informed her that someone in the family had to identify the body.

"I can't go!" Felicia Waterson screamed.

"There's no need for you to go, Mrs. Waterson," Matt hastily assured her. He turned to Aunt Martha and asked her if there were other family members present in the house.

"Their son, William, is here. He lives in the guest house out back. He's too young for such a dreadful job, his own father. I'll go with you to identify my poor child."

"No, Aunt Martha! Don't leave me!" Felicia Waterson cried out.

Aunt Martha assured her that she wouldn't leave her alone.

"If you don't go, the son has to," Matt insisted. "Someone has to identify the remains, and the sooner the better for everyone concerned."

"I'll call the boy," Aunt Martha said.

Matt helped her out of her chair and over to the telephone near the staircase. She placed the call to William Waterson, but she didn't say why she wanted to see him. Matt guessed that she preferred that they tell the son about his father's death. Then Aunt Martha went over to Felicia Waterson and tried to comfort her. She stroked her hair and told her not to worry because everything will be all right.

"The Lord will see us through this. Come up to your bed and lie down. Everything will be all right. I'll call Dr. Jacobson as soon as you lie down. He'll come over and give you something to calm your nerves. I'll take care of everything. Don't you worry. Aunt Martha will take care of everything."

She took Felicia Waterson by the hand and led her up the

sweep of stairs at the rear of the anteroom. The two detectives watched in silence. After they left, Matt was the first to speak, "I'd give a year's salary not to do what I just did, Jake."

"Somebody had to do it, man; and better you than me. She took it real bad, though. She must have really loved him."

"Maybe she did, and maybe she didn't. Did you hear the old lady say that she had just checked in HIS bedroom? If they slept in separate bedrooms, I wonder just how much love there was between them? Grief is a funny thing, Jake. I've seen people go off the deep end over someone they couldn't stand the site of alive. Death takes people like that sometimes."

"If you truly hate somebody, you ought not to care one way or the other when they die."

"It's guilt mostly. They wish they had been nicer to the deceased or they sometimes realize that they didn't hate them after all...when it's too late to do anything about it."

The detectives waited in the anteroom for at least fifteen minutes before they heard the German shepherd barking from the kitchen. They both looked in the direction of the kitchen as young Waterson emerged. Harold Waterson's son stood over six feet tall and bore a striking resemblance to his dead father. He was thin and fit and wore a gray and burgundy designer sweatsuit. He was surprised to find them there and didn't mince words in demanding to know who they were and what they wanted. Matt identified himself and Jake.

"You say you're policemen. So, what do you want with us?"

"We're here to inform you that your father has been killed, Mr. Waterson."

William Waterson stopped dead in his tracks as the color drained from his face and he struggled mightily to maintain his composure in front of the detectives.

"How was he killed?" he asked in a voice nearly devoid of emotion.

"He was shot to death around ten o'clock last night," the

71

Lieutenant replied.

"Who shot him?" he demanded to know.

"We don't know yet, Mr. Waterson. We took this wallet and appointment book off a body at 1637 Floribunda Lane about six hours ago. The driver's license identifies the deceased as Harold Waterson, Sr." Matt showed the dead man's possessions to his son who clearly didn't want to look at them.

"We've informed both your mother and your aunt about your father's death. Both of them took the news very hard. Your Aunt Martha took Mrs. Waterson upstairs to her bed."

"Martha is not my aunt; she's his aunt."

"Whoever she's kin to, Mr. Waterson, we need to have someone in your family identify the body, preferably the next of kin, as soon as possible. Now, neither YOUR mother or HIS aunt is in any condition to do it, so that leaves you, HIS son."

Young Waterson looked grim at the prospect of identifying his father's corpse, but he offered no resistance.

"If it has to be done, I suppose I'll have to do it," he said. "Where did you say he was killed?"

"At 1637 Floribunda Lane off Sixteenth Street in Northwest."

"Whose house is it, and what was he doing there?'

"We don't know what he was doing there, yet; but the house belongs to the Walter Bowman family. Apparently your father attended a cocktail party at the house next door to 1637 earlier in the evening."

"Why don't you know who killed him? If he was shot in this Bowman family's house, it's obvious that one of them must have shot him. Why haven't you arrested them?"

"We don't have a clear picture of what happened to your father from the time he left the cocktail party until he was killed. We can't arrest anyone until we substantiate the details surrounding his death."

"The hell you can't. Who was in the house when he was killed?!"

"We don't know yet; and I'm not at liberty to discuss the particulars of the case with you, Mr. Waterson."

"You have one hell of a nerve, Lieutenant Alexander! I have a right to know who killed my father!"

"And I have a duty to protect innocent people! I can't deliver a suspect on a silver platter to satisfy you! We have procedures to be followed in a homicide investigation, Mr. Waterson," Matt shouted.

"I won't stand to be treated like this! If you won't tell me what happened to my father, I'll go over your head. My father knows the mayor and the chief of police."

"Your father is dead, Mr. Waterson. How can I tell you who killed him when I don't know myself. All I know for certain is that he was killed by two gunshot wounds to the chest, and the autopsy report may change all that. By the way, where were you five hours ago, Mr. Waterson."

Young Waterson had been angry but when he realized the implications of Matt's question he became furious.

"Do you have the nerve to suggest I killed my father!?"

"Nothing of the kind, but it's standard procedure to ask the whereabouts of anyone with a close connection to the deceased at the time of death. We have to know where you were and what you were doing."

"I shouldn't dignify that question with an answer; but if you must know, I was home all evening."

"Is there anyone who can verify that?"

"I don't need anyone to verify where I was. I told you I was home all evening and that's all the verification you need. You're way out of line insinuating that I shot my own father. You have no right to harass me like this, considering my father has been killed."

"I'm relieved to see that your father's death concerns you, Mr. Waterson. You gave the impression earlier that you couldn't care less."

"Of course I care that my father has been killed. Why shouldn't I care? Anyway, I don't have to justify my feelings to the likes of you."

"I didn't ask for a justification of your feelings Mr. Waterson, just an explanation of your whereabouts at the time your father died."

"I refuse to answer any more of your insulting questions," Lieutenant."

"Calm down, Mr. Waterson," Jake interceded in an attempt to cool the air. "Lieutenant Alexander's questions were just routine, that's all. You're upset, so you took them the wrong way. We didn't come here to accuse you of shooting your father. All we want you to do is to come down to the morgue with us to identify his remains. It's been a long night for us, so why don't we leave the questions for later and get the identification over with for now?"

"That's fine with me," Matt said, realizing that he had let William Waterson get to him. He didn't like young Waterson. He was arrogant and seemed to be indifferent to his father's death. But, personal feelings aside, Matt recognized that he had a job to do and sparring with young Waterson wasn't going to get it done.

Apparently, Jake's words were effective in cooling the air. William Waterson seemed to accept the truce for the time being.

"I'll be ready to go as soon as I check on my mother." After he disappeared up the stairs, Jake turned his anger on his partner.

"Man, don't you know better than to rumble with him like that. All he has to do is get the right person to put the word on you downtown and you'll be out on your ass."

"His attitude really pissed me off, Jake."

"I know how you feel, man. He got next to me, too, but you don't know who he knows. A call to the right person, and the first thing you know you're busted and back out on a beat. I know

Chief Carter from way back, Matt. If he has to choose, it won't be you, man. You can make book on it."

"That callous son-of-a-bitch rubbed me the wrong way, man."

"Doesn't matter which way he rubs you, Matt. He's not worth a rap downtown. It would suit him right down to the ground to see you reprimanded or fired."

"He won't get the satisfaction," Matt insisted.

"Man, did you see how calmly he took it when you told him that his father had been killed. I've seen people more upset when their dog died. You'd think he'd have the decency to pretend to care even if he didn't," Jake reasoned.

"Not him. He couldn't care less what the likes of us think about him. He's cold, man...doesn't seem to have much human feeling."

"Did you see the color of his hair, Matt? It's blond."

"Tell me about it."

"But, regardless of how he felt about his father, man, he didn't have the opportunity to kill him, considering where he died. I'm still putting my money on the Bowmans."

"As far as I'm concerned, the jury is still out on who killed Waterson. I agree that the Bowmans are the most likely suspects, but there are still a lot of questions that haven't been answered," Matt replied.

"Maybe he was shot accidentally," Jake suggested.

"No way, man. If he was shot accidentally, why would the Bowmans cover it up? Both Walter and Helen Bowman claim they don't know who shot him. It could have been a crime of passion I suppose, but whose passion? Neither one of the Bowmans admits to having any personal involvement with Waterson."

"The way I see it," Jake replied, "at least one of the Bowmans will be indicted, maybe more. The evidence is against them, man."

Matt agreed with Jake's assessment. The Bowmans were the most likely suspects. Circumstances were overwhelmingly arrayed against them...their house, their gun, and their motives when he finally uncovered them. Matt's attention was diverted from the hapless Bowmans when young Waterson, an eminently more deserving suspect in the detective's biased opinion, returned from upstairs. The young man's resemblance to his dead father was eerie. His hair was honey blond rather than dark brown, but he had the same hazel eyes, was roughly the same height, and had the same good looks. His face was lean and angular with a strong nose and chin while his teeth and lips completed the picture of the all-American youth whose tawny complexion hinted of days spent at leisure.

William Waterson seemed less confident after the trip upstairs. He hadn't expected his mother to break down the way she had. He looked confused, almost frightened...nothing like the arrogant young man who had battled Matt to a stand-off moments earlier.

The ride back to Reservoir Road from D.C. General Hospital's morgue was quiet. Young Waterson sat alone in the back seat, withdrawn and motionless. He had believed his nerve would carry him through the identification; it hadn't. He was tough, so he thought, callous enough to look into his dead father's face without feeling or remorse; he was wrong. When he saw his father's body...so cold, and pale, and lifeless, he felt everything. He was swept by emotion he hadn't known since childhood, when his father was everything to him. He experienced feelings he had forgotten years ago, feelings that had no place in his life now. He recalled the good times he had purged from his memory because they didn't fit the cruel, unfaithful father who had caused his mother so much pain. He was determined not to mourn that father, but his resolve swiftly evaporated in the face of his father's cold body, and he was swept to the depth of his being by waves of bitter anguish and the darkest despair. He howled bitter, useless tears for the father he thought he hated.

Matt was surprised at young Waterson's reaction to his father's corpse. A half-hour ago he would have given odds that the arrogant young man would identify the body without a twinge of remorse, and he would have lost. Young Waterson's bluff was called at the morgue. He walked up to his father's body and nearly fainted. Steve Mitchell kept him on his feet long enough to make the identification. When the Deputy Medical Examiner asked whether the corpse was his father, he was too devastated to speak, nodding his agreement instead. Matt decided right then and there that young Waterson wouldn't sell him any more woof tickets. It was obvious that the young man wasn't as heartless as he pretended to be, but why the charade? Why did he feign indifference to his father's death when he really cared? Matt didn't understand; but then neither did the young man whose father lay dead. He was more confused than anyone.

When they finally arrived at the house on Reservoir Road, Matt followed the young man into the house and thought what a waste it was for him to have realized that he really loved his father now that it was too late for both of them. The time and love lost between father and son would never be recovered. There would be no understanding or forgiving between them now. Any chance they may have had was gone forever with two well-placed bullets. Everything was finished between them before it really began. Matt watched as William Waterson mounted the stairs to his mother's room.

Matt followed him into the house on a hunch that Aunt Martha would still be up. He thought about the old lady as they drove to and from the morgue. He needed to know where she fit in. She claimed to be the aunt of the deceased, but the son didn't admit being related to her. That was peculiar; either she was a relative or she wasn't. He wondered just what her position was in the Waterson household, so he walked across the foyer and looked into the kitchen hoping to find Aunt Martha. Luck was with him. She was in the kitchen trying to make coffee, but making a mess instead. She had spilled more coffee around the pot than she got inside. Her hands trembled as she tried to pour water into the drip coffee maker. She spilled the water too. She didn't hear Matt come into the kitchen. He called several times before she turned around. Tears were streaming down her lined cheeks. When she saw him, she broke down into sobs. She walked over to the kitchen table and sat down. She cried into a large white handkerchief, and it took several minutes for the sobs to subside. Matt gave her time to compose herself by cleaning up the mess she had made on the counter. Then he poured the rest of the water into the coffee pot and plugged it into the outlet on the stove.

Aunt Martha looked very frail and frightened. She had removed her nightcap. Her hair was completely white. She looked like she had aged twenty years since she opened the door for them. Matt sat across the table from her. He expressed his condolences again and asked how Mrs. Waterson was doing. Aunt Martha said that the doctor had been there and gone, and that he had given Felicia Waterson a sedative. She told him she refused the medicine the doctor offered her.

"She's resting now, poor child. Of all the awful things to happen. Who would have thought?" she murmured rocking her self back and forth. "He was a good man; and he didn't mean anybody any harm. He was so good to me and his family. Why would anyone kill Hal?"

"I don't know, but I intend to find out who killed him. You can help me, you know. Can you tell me anything you think might help me find his killer."

"It's a punishment from God," she said with resignation. "He took him to punish me for my transgressions."

"What transgressions?"

"The money, I took the money when God wanted her to have it."

"What money?"

"The money his father gave him before he died."

"Who was his father?"

"Mr. William Harper of Warren, Virginia. I worked for the Harpers for thirty-five years. I was their housekeeper. It wasn't generally known that Mr. Harper was Hal's father, though people in Warren did suspect as much. But, Mr. Harper never denied fathering the boy to me, he knew better. Mr. Harper was the richest white man in Warren. He owned the only bank in town. He was a kind man and a gentleman too, even if he did get my baby sister in a family way. I should never have taken her up there to work, but work was so hard to come by in those days. Working in a fine home for a respectable family was a good job back then, the best a decent young colored woman could hope to find. So I took her to work for them. She wasn't there a year before he got her in a family way. She didn't want to tell me who did it; but I got it out of her, I most certainly did. I faced him down with it too; made him own up to his handiwork, indeed I did. Mr. Harper was a gentleman, or he never would have owned up to fathering the child. But he knew she hadn't been touched by another man before I brought her into the house. My baby sister didn't lie on him either. The child came into this world looking like Mr. William Harper spit him out, every inch of him a Harper. I never said a word to Mrs. Harper. I didn't try to blackmail him either, but I let him know what his responsibilities were by that child. He took care of the boy, too. He doubled my salary and slipped me bonuses for Christmas and my birthday." Aunt Martha seemed to be talking as much for her benefit as Matt's, but he listened attentively.

"He was a fine baby, weighed nearly nine pounds when he was born. My sister named him Harold William after his father and our father. Pour soul, she never did recover from birthing him. She died when he was fourteen months old. She'd never been strong, and giving birth to a big strapping baby like that killed her. She pleasured in him while she lived though," the old lady said, smiling for the first time. "Her eyes would dance with joy when she held him. Toward the end, she was so weak she could hardly lift her head from the pillow; but she insisted that he come to play with her everyday. He was a big active baby, and we feared to put him in her bed; but she cried so hard we had to. He would crawl all over her and pull her hair, but she'd only smile and kiss him. She dearly loved that baby, poor child. Mr. Harper mourned her when she died, too. He was a real gentleman, even came to her funeral. The colored folks in Warren talked about that for years, still do as far as I know. Their talk didn't bother me; and it couldn't bother her, she was dead. After she died, I took the baby and raised him like he was my own child. I would take him to the house occasionally when Mrs. Harper was away. Mr. Harper didn't have any children by his wife, so he was genuinely fond of Hal," she said as the sobbing started again. "It's a pity that both of his parents loved him, but he had neither mother nor father his entire life. I loved him like a mother; but it wasn't the same...no one can replace your own mother."

"What about the money?"

"Mrs. Harper never let on to me that she knew about Hal, although I suspected she did. All the Watersons were fair-skinned people back then, but Hal was the only one of us who could pass for white. Mrs. Harper would give me odd looks every so often, and she asked about the boy more often than she should have, but no more than that. When Hal was eighteen or nineteen years old, Mr. William Harper was taken low sick. He knew he was dying; and he wanted to provide for the boy before he passed. He didn't trust leaving him money in his will, so he transferred some stocks, bonds, and property to me before he died. Mrs. Harper never knew anything about it. He put me in touch with an investment broker who sold the stocks and bonds he gave me and reinvested the money with me as Hal's guardian. Mr. Harper destroyed his old will and made out a new one a week before he died. He left everything to Mrs. Harper except a large tract of land in Warren that he left to me. You'd think that would have been enough for her, indeed you would. When she found out that he had left me the land, she nearly died herself. She wanted it all for herself, every dime.

She sued me to get the land back, said I'd used undue influence on Mr. Harper when he was down low sick. She sued me after I slaved in her house for thirty-five years. I did work for her that she wouldn't do for herself. I nursed her when she was sick, consoled her when she was troubled, cheered her up when her spirits were low, and she sued me. I had to come all the way to Washington D.C. to get a lawyer to represent me. None of the lawyers in Warren would take my case. We were in court for two years, but I won. She had the nerve to spit on me after the trial was over. I didn't say anything at the time, but I made a special trip to her house to let her know just what I thought of her. She wasn't quality like Mr. Harper, no where near his caliber. He was a gentleman through and through. I sold off some of the land to get money to send Hal to college; but I never touched the money that was invested. Mr. Harper told me to make out a will saying Hal couldn't get the money until he was thirty years old, and that's what I did. When he came of age, I turned his money over to him. That's the way his father wanted it."

"How much money was there?"

"Mr. William Harper gave me stocks and bonds worth two hundred and fifty thousand dollars. When Hal got the reinvested stocks and bonds, they were worth over two million dollars. That was twenty-two years ago, just before he married Felicia. His money can't help him now, poor child. God is punishing me for taking that money. We were never meant to have it."

"You shouldn't blame yourself. You had nothing to do with

the homicide. You simply did what you thought was best for your nephew, what anyone would have done under the circumstances."

"Lord knows he would have been better off without that money. It didn't bring him anything but grief," she whispered to herself. Matt got up from the table and poured coffee for both of them. The hot coffee no longer interested Aunt Martha, but Matt was glad to get his. He drank several sips before his next question.

"When we talked to your nephew's son, he said you were his father's aunt; but that you weren't any kin to him. What did he mean by that?"

The old lady looked thoroughly disgusted. "He said that did he? Well, well. I never thought I'd live to see the day he would disown his own family; but I was wrong. He can't help the way he was raised, though. His mother is the reason he's the way he is. She didn't teach him to love his father's people. We weren't good enough for her, being colored and all. But her people were as poor as most coloreds. She didn't have a dime when Hal married her. To hear her tell it, she did him a favor because she's white. White is as white does, I always say. She always made a difference between her people and his people. She can't do enough for her folks. She even had the nerve to try to keep our people from visiting Hal, but I put a stop to that nonsense, quick. As long as I live in this house, my people will always be welcome here," she insisted.

Matt wondered how much longer she would live there, now that her nephew was dead.

"Felicia turned William against his father's people. She convinced the child that he's white like her. I told her time and again that she was raising the child for heartbreak; but she didn't pay me any mind, indeed she didn't. She flies into a rage if anyone says that child is colored, taught him to do the same. She made him feel that he was better than colored people, taught him to be ashamed of what he is. After that, he began to despise his father's people, his father too, if you ask me. It broke my heart to see him like that. William lost respect for his father. He talked ugly to him, said any cruel thing that came into his head. Hal took it because he understood what ailed the child. It was a sad thing to see because he used to love his father so much when he was a boy. He loved his Aunt Martha, too, indeed he did. He preferred me to his own mother. She didn't like it one bit, tried to get Hal to send me away; but he wouldn't hear of such a thing. Hal let her get away with a lot; but he wouldn't stand for her to abuse me. She soon learned to grin and bear Aunt Martha, indeed she did. She was jealous of William's affection for his Aunt Martha, couldn't bear to think that he loved Hal's people as much as hers, so she turned the child against us. She wouldn't let him visit Hal's folks in Warren, and she didn't want them to come here either."

Matt poured himself another cup of coffee.

"Hal loved his people; and why shouldn't he? He grew up among us, and we were good to him. We all loved and cared for him. She tried to destroy his feelings for us, and that's where she made her mistake," the old lady said with satisfaction. "She didn't realize how much Hal's family meant to him. He had neither mother nor father, sister or brother; and she expected him to turn his back on us for her and her family. Why, Hal was closer to his cousins than most are to their brothers and sisters. He loved them, his aunts and uncles, too. She couldn't turn him against us; we were his people, his roots. He wouldn't have abandoned us for her or anybody else. What she did was to turn him against her. She didn't know that despising us meant that she despised him too. We were that close. She drove Hal away from her, but she kept the boy under her spell, indeed she did. I have often believed that she used the boy to spite Hal. He's a troubled child, so miserable; and it's all her doing. She loves him well enough; but she didn't love him enough to put her feelings aside and do what was best for him."

"How did your nephew and his wife get along, Aunt Martha?"

"They were miserable. This isn't a happy home, God knows it isn't. She made his life hell; and when he went on the outside for some affection and peace of mind, she hated him for it. She drove him out there, indeed she did. She wouldn't try to make him happy; and she wouldn't let him go." Aunt Martha's cup of coffee sat untouched. Matt offered to refresh it, but she refused.

"How long had they been having problems?"

"The Lord only knows," she replied shaking her head. "Things have been bad between them for a long time, but it got a whole lot worse this past year. It got to the point where they would argue almost every night. I heard them from my bedroom down the hall. She regularly accused him of seeing other women. He denied it, of course; but it got to the point where he couldn't stand the arguing every night. Last month, he moved out of their bedroom into one of the guest rooms. You'd think that she would have been satisfied the way she harangued him all night long. But, after he moved out she began crying herself to sleep. Felicia is the kind of woman who would bite off her nose to spite her face."

"Why didn't they get a divorce if they were so unhappy?"

"He did ask her for a divorce several years ago; but she wouldn't agree, wanted to have her cake and eat it too. She couldn't stand the idea of him being happy with someone else. Hal didn't leave on account of the boy. His son meant everything to him," she said as the tears and rocking started again.

"What time did your nephew leave home on Saturday?"

Aunt Martha was lost in her own thoughts, so she didn't respond right away.

Matt was on the verge of repeating the question when she replied, "Hal took me to the Farmer's Market in Bethesda yesterday morning. He took me every Saturday morning because he knew how much I like fresh vegetables. He was thoughtful like that. We left here at nine o'clock and we got back at eleven. We had breakfast in the little cafeteria at the market. I certainly did look forward to my Saturdays with Hal. Most young people don't want to be bothered with an old lady like me. But my Hal always had time for me, no matter how busy he was. He always had time for his Aunt Martha."

"What did he do after you got back from the market?"

"He left as soon as he brought the groceries into the house. He told me he was going to his office in downtown Washington."

"How long was he gone?"

"He didn't come back home after he left," she sobbed. "That was the last time I saw him alive. He kissed his Aunt Martha goodbye before he left, indeed he did."

"Did he call home after he left, yesterday?"

"He didn't call me."

"Did anyone call him yesterday?"

"Yes, a woman called him around one o'clock in the afternoon. She asked to speak to Hal, but she didn't tell me her name. When I told her he wasn't home, she hung up."

"Did he get any more calls?"

"None that I answered."

"Did you notice anything different or unusual about your nephew during the past week?"

"He did seem to have something on his mind. He had a lot of pressure on him from work and home too, if the truth be known. Lately, he seemed to be under more pressure than usual. I didn't pry; but I could tell that something was bothering him, something important. He just wasn't himself."

"How did he act? What did he do to make you feel that he wasn't himself?"

"He was moody and withdrawn. I made his breakfast every morning. For the past two weeks, he seemed preoccupied; and he wasn't much interested in talking. I just let him be, though. I decided that he'd work out, whatever it was that was bothering him."

"How did your nephew get along with his wife and son over the past two weeks?"

"Whenever William and Hal talked to each other, they ended up arguing and shouting. I don't recall them arguing lately, but Hal and Felicia had a terrible fight last Friday night. Felicia hadn't been herself all day Friday. I could tell she had something on her mind. She started the fight as soon as Hal walked through the front door Friday evening. They argued something fierce, said mean, vicious things to each other...hurtful things you can't take back once they've been said. That night I prayed for them both. I prayed for God to help them to see their way out of their misery. The devil danced in this house Friday night. When married people say the kind of things they said to each other, the devil jumps for joy. So, I prayed extra hard for them and the boy. I asked God to heal this pitiful family, to help them understand that families are supposed to love each other. I asked him to lift the hate from their hearts so they could cherish each other again. It's a terrible thing to see a family tear each other apart the way they've been doing so I prayed for them, indeed I did."

"What was the fight about?"

"The same thing they usually argue about. She accused him of going with another woman. He denied it, but she wouldn't let up. She kept at him until he lost his temper. Then, he told her that he would see whoever he pleased since she didn't want to be a wife to him. They fought like cats and dogs. She finally threatened him, told him he had to give up the black bitch or else."

"Or else what?"

"She didn't say."

"Did she mention the woman's name?"

"No more than to call her a black bitch. She couldn't bear to think of him going with another woman. The very idea made her furious. She drove him to it; then she hated him for it. He couldn't stay, and he couldn't leave. He had to go outside his own home to find some peace of mind, indeed he did."

"Did he ever mention the woman to you?"

"Indeed he did not! If he had, I would not have hesitated to give him a piece of my mind. I don't condone that sort of behavior. I'm a Christian woman, and I raised Hal in the church. He knew better than to do what he did, but she drove him to it. He couldn't find love and peace of mind in his own home, poor child, so he went looking for it on the outside. I understood why he did it, but understanding don't make it right. What he did was wrong in the sight of God and the church."

"Your nephew made two appointments at his downtown office on Saturday afternoon. Did he happen to tell you who he was meeting?"

"No, he didn't say anything about it to me."

"Did he ever discuss his business with you?"

"Sometimes he would tell me about problems he was having at work. I pretended to know what he was talking about, but all that construction talk didn't mean anything to me."

"Did he ever mention the Anacostia Riverfront Development Project to you?"

"No, not that I recall."

Changing the subject, Matt asked: "Did Mrs. Waterson leave the house, yesterday?"

"She went shopping yesterday afternoon with some friends of hers."

"What time did she get back?"

"Around seven o'clock. I had dinner ready when she returned, but she said she had already eaten. She went on up to her room."

"What did she do for the rest of the evening?"

"She stayed upstairs most of the evening. I put dinner away

and cleaned up the kitchen. Then I went up to my bedroom. I go to bed early, around eight o'clock most nights."

"What did William Waterson do yesterday?"

"He came over to the house after we left for the Farmer's Market. I saw him going into the back door of the house as Hal was backing out of the garage. He usually stayed away when his father was home."

"How long has he lived in the guest cottage?"

"He moved out there when he came home from boarding school. Hal and William argued all the time about him going to college. Hal wanted him to study architecture or engineering so he could run the firm when he retired, but William told him he wasn't interested in the construction business. He didn't want to do anything, but lay out there in that guest house smoking marijuana cigarettes. He doesn't even have the decency to hide them from his parents and me, leaves them out in the open like they're regular cigarettes. He enrolled in college back in September, but I don't think he goes to classes. I see his no-account friends going in and out of the guest house any time of the day or night. You'd think he was working somewhere the way he entertains over there. I can't keep food in the kitchen for him taking it over there to cook for his friends. He takes all the best cuts of meat, lives high off the hog, indeed he does."

"Did you see William Waterson after you returned from the market on Saturday?"

"No. I didn't see him after that."

Matt could see that Aunt Martha was tired, weary from her long journey. She had brought her nephew from rural Warren to a wealthy estate on Reservoir Road in the District of Columbia, and now he was dead. She blamed herself, but it was no fault of hers. Choices were made, actions taken, events set in motion across the time bridge that separated the colored section of Warren from the impressive residence west of the park where they now sat...events that climaxed in her nephew's murder. No man is an island, and Aunt Martha couldn't protect him when he needed it most. She wanted the best for him, and she got it or so it seemed. She wasn't all-knowing. She couldn't have predicted where his money would take him if it took him anywhere at all. He was dead now. The child she loved like her own. The child she worked for, schemed for, all out of love, she thought. No matter now, he was gone before his time; and a bone-weary old woman was left to mourn him.

Matt helped Aunt Martha up the stairs before letting himself out. Jake was asleep under the wheel of the car. The sun was rising over the house whey they drove out of the driveway.

"What time is it?" Jake asked.

"Quarter to six," Matt replied before closing his eyes. Jake got him home without incident. Later, Matt would be unable to recall saying goodby to Jake, climbing his front steps, unlocking the door, finding his way to the bedroom that he and his wife shared, undressing in his closet, or collapsing onto his side of the bed before drifting into a comatose sleep.

# CHAPTER VI

Matt was sleeping soundly when his wife, Carla, entered their bedroom late Sunday morning. She hated to wake him up, but his commander, Lloyd Cullison, had sounded very edgy when he had called fifteen minutes earlier. She sat on Matt's side of the bed, and nibbled his earlobe as she softly whispered:

"Wake up, sleeping beauty."

Matt stirred and turned his head over. She nibbled his other earlobe. He turned over again but remained asleep. Beginning at the center of his forehead, she planted a series of soft kisses down the side of his face, against his ear, and across the nape of his neck. That woke him up and his groping on her side of the bed left no doubt about what was on his mind. He turned over to find his wife leaning over him, one arm on either side of his chest. Her scent, a mixture of boudoir from her perfume, nursery from the baby's powder, and kitchen from the pot roast she was cooking for dinner, was pleasing. She aroused a familiar surge of desire that he responded to by pulling her into his arms. She momentarily succumbed to his caresses. Unfortunately, the pot roast on the stove, the pressing call from Lloyd Cullison, and the children playing downstairs alone, dampened her mood.

"Lloyd Cullison wants you to call him, Matthew."

He released her abruptly as the sound of his Commander's name unleashed a flood of images from the night before.

"Damn! Why did you have to mention him, Carla?"

"Because he was very nasty when he called, especially when I wouldn't put him through to you." Carla attempted to rise from their bed but was restrained by her husband's firm grip on her wrist.

"Don't go yet," he begged. "Sit here for a minute so I can feast my eyes on what I'm missing right now."

"Duty calls, Matthew. You need to call Lloyd Cullison right away and the children are downstairs by themselves," she answered as she tried to rise a second time.

"The children can wait a few minutes more," he said maintaining a firm grip on her wrist. "Did Lloyd say what was on his mind?"

"No, he didn't tell me anything. He simply ordered me to tell you to call him immediately. He insisted on speaking to you personally, but I lied and said you were in the shower. What on earth happened last night?"

"God! What didn't happen last night," Matt wearily replied.

Carla gave him a consoling kiss.

"Let me get the children squared away. After that I'll make you a strong cup of coffee and you can tell me about it, okay?" He released her hand.

"Hand me the telephone before you leave, Carla. I need to call Lloyd before he wets his pants."

As Carla got up to to leave the room, Matt was unable to resist the urge to stroke her shapely behind.

Dialing Lloyd Cullison's number, Matt questioned his sanity in having joined the District police force in the first place. Nights like the one he had just experienced were common enough to convince him that the aggravation wasn't worth the effort. Lloyd

Cullison answered his office telephone after just one ring.

"This is Matt Alexander returning your call, Lloyd."

"It's about time you called me back, Lieutenant. I left word with your wife at least thirty minutes ago. I spoke to Chief Carter earlier, and the shit has hit the fan downtown over the Waterson homicide. The *Washington Star* got a scoop from some loose-lipped son-of-a-bitch in the medical examiner's office. They're running the story in the afternoon edition of today's paper. Chief Carter is pissed because his PR people won't have time to schedule a press conference before the story breaks. He wants you and me in his office by one this afternoon.

"What time is it now?"

"Twelve-fifteen."

"I can't get downtown before one-thirty at the earliest."

"I don't think you heard me correctly, Lieutenant," Lloyd shot back in his most intimidating voice. Chief Carter expects us in his office by one P.M."

"I heard you the first time!" Matt angrily shouted. "Neither you or Chief Carter stayed up until six A.M. this morning. I said I would be there by one-thirty."

"Suit yourself, Alexander; but if I were you, I'd watch my step. I don't like the way you took it upon yourself to visit Mrs. Waterson at four A.M. You should have consulted me on the identity of the victim before you notified his next of kin."

"That's precisely why I went ahead," Matt thought to himself, "I didn't want your goddamned advice."

"There are some other things I need to clear up with you, hotshot. Be in my office at eight tomorrow morning, and not a goddamned second later. I warn you that I won't be responsible for the consequences with Chief Carter if you're late for his meeting today," Lloyd shouted before slamming the receiver down.

Matt was usually more sensitive to his Commander's need to assert his authority. But, Lloyd's call had caught him at a bad time. And, while there was no love lost between them, Matt appreciated the difficulties Lloyd daily faced in supervising a division where the majority of his line, supervisory, and administrative officers were black. Being white, Lloyd was caught on the horns of the racial dilemma whenever he disciplined a black officer or promoted a white one. Matt knew that most of the African-American line officers failed to appreciate the complexities involved in making the administrative decisions Lloyd was routinely required to make, but his empathy for Lloyd Cullison's administrative dilemma didn't blind him to his commander's intolerance for opinions and attitudes different from his own.

The Commander of Fourth District Headquarters had a mind like a steel trap. He was as strong-willed and bull-headed as they came; but he also tried to be fair to the men under his command, which didn't come naturally considering the time and place that spawned Lloyd Cullison. He was born and reared in the South Carolina of fifty years ago. His cultural niche was the old South of race superiority and bigotry toward anyone different. The genteel South of ante-bellum mansions and courtly manners didn't figure in Lloyd's world. He sprang from a family of hard-scrabble farmers who struggled from year to year just to survive. He worked his family's fields in the scorching South Carolina heat along with the other day laborers...if they were lucky enough to be able to hire them that year. Lloyd Cullison was a fighter, too. He had weathered hard times and reversals without resorting to the false security of racial bigotry and hatred. He preferred his own kind, true enough; but he also allowed those who were different room to be different. While Lloyd figured there was space enough to give everybody some elbow room, he had absolutely no qualms about pushing people around if it suited his purposes.

Unlike Jake, Matt wasn't overly concerned with Lloyd's feelings one way or the other. His primary concern was how Lloyd behaved. Matt knew he couldn't change Lloyd's attitudes anymore than Lloyd could change his. The fact of the matter was that he didn't care whether Lloyd changed his attitudes or not so long as he dealt him a fair hand. Behavior could be observed and measured, feelings could not. Lloyd's feelings were Lloyd's problem and Matt refused to internalize them to the extent that Jake had. He couldn't control how Lloyd or anyone else felt about him; but if they crossed him on his turf, they were in for the count because he refused to go down without a fight. He was determined to let Lloyd and any other comers know that making a move on him would cost them. He wasn't naive enough to think that he could win all his fights, but he was damned if he would surrender without giving it his best shot.

Matt had reached a point in his life where he understood that the mere existence of intolerance and bigotry didn't diminish him as a person. His route to self-awareness had been long, slow, and often painful; but he learned to accept himself for what he was and more importantly, who he could be. Unlike Jake, Matt had eventually learned that what matters is not the name people call you but the name you answer to. He didn't need strokes from outsiders who might or might not wish him well. Some saw his indifference to their opinions as arrogance, but that didn't bother him. He listened to the people who mattered in his life, the people who cared about him and were genuinely interested in his well-being. He didn't see Lloyd Cullison as an enemy, but he also didn't trust the Commander to look after his best interests. Lieutenant Matthew Alexander was the only one who could do that to his satisfaction. The telephone rang just as he got out of bed.

"Are you up yet?" Jake wanted to know.

"Barely."

"Cullison called me about a half-hour ago to get the lowdown on what happened last night. I told him that you were going to fill him in today, but he wanted to get the details from me anyway. I don't know why he didn't call you in the first place."

"Lloyd's cunning that way, Jake. It's my guess he wanted to get your version before he talked to me."

"I'll never understand that joker. What time do you want me to pick you up?"

"Don't bother. I talked to Lloyd just before you called. Chief Carter wants Lloyd and me in his office at one o'clock this afternoon. I'll take my own car."

"The Chief and Cullison...there's not a dime's worth of difference between them when it comes to covering their behinds and taking credit for someone else's work."

"It's called ambition, Jake."

"Treachery is what I call it, man. What do you want me to do, today?"

"I haven't talked to Bryant, yet, so I don't know how much they got done after we left last night. I told Bryant to call me as soon as they found the gun. He hasn't called yet. The first thing you should do is get Sam to dust the Mercedes for prints. Help Bryant inside the house if he didn't finish searching it last night. That should cover things until I arrive."

"Why does the Chief want to see you and Cullison so soon?"

"The *Washington Star* is going to break the news on Waterson's homicide in their Sunday edition."

"Oh yeah? I didn't see anything about the killing in the *Post*."

"The *Post* goes to print around midnight, so they wouldn't have had time to print anything even if they had gotten the scoop. I don't get the *Star* so round up a copy for me. Some creep in the medical examiner's office leaked the story, and I'm making it my business to find out who it was. Chief Carter is worried because his press conference won't beat the paper to the streets. I guess Lloyd and I will have to brief him."

"What the does Cullison know about it other than what he's been told?" Jake insisted.

"Do I detect a note of disrespect in your voice, Jake?"

"Cullison is always ready to step in and take the credit for someone else's work!"

"It goes with the territory, Jake," Matt replied yawning. "I need to place a call to Bryant before I leave the house, man, so I'll see you at the Bowman house when I get there."

Matt's conversation with Henry Bryant confirmed his hunch that the weapon hadn't been found. Bryant insisted that their search so far had been thorough, but they hadn't come up with anything remotely resembling a thirty-eight caliber Smith & Wesson revolver.

During his cold shower, Matt wondered about Walter Bowman's revolver and where it could be. He was beginning to doubt whether it was the gun that was used to kill Waterson. The fact that Bowman's thirty-eight was missing was too much of a coincidence to suit him. At the same time, he didn't want to be sidetracked by a red herring. The fact that all three of the Bowmans were in the house when Waterson was killed was also too much of a coincidence to suit him, but he was convinced that the Bowmans could clear up much of the confusion and uncertainty surrounding Waterson's murder.

Carla brought his cup of coffee into the bathroom as he was stepping out of the shower. She placed it on the shelf under the medicine cabinet. Then, she sat on top of the clothes hamper and watched as her husband dried his lean body.

"Do you mind if I feast my eyes for a while?" she asked. "Turn about is fair play, you know."

"Be my guest," he replied dropping the towel rather than draping it around his waist as he usually did between a shower and a shave. "What's mine is yours," he generously offered.

"Have you no shame?" she asked laughing.

"None!" he emphatically answered, lathering the handsome face she loved so madly, although it hadn't always been so.

They had first met when he enrolled in an abnormal psychology course she was teaching at Howard University seven years earlier. He had been on the District police force for two years at the time and needed the course as an in-service education requirement for the promotion he was already pursuing with single-minded determination. She had completed her doctorate in clinical psychology the previous spring, and began teaching part-time in the Howard University Psychology department that fall. She handled her lectures well in spite of her inexperience until he began giving her a hard time. He wasn't disruptive, but he consistently challenged every important point she made with his brand of clear, concise logic that left her scrambling for a comeback. It got to the point where she dreaded teaching the course because of his impertinence which was, more often than not, right on the mark. To make matters worse, she found herself attracted to the smart-assed policeman who was making her life miserable.

Her lectures began to suffer because of his presence in her class. Never one to allow a situation to get the best of her, Carla finally requested a conference with him to see if they couldn't call a truce. The upshot of the meeting was that he agreed to stop questioning her in class if she would agree to go out with him. Dr. Carla Channing's professionalism was insulted, but her instincts told her that Matthew Alexander was the most exciting man she'd ever met. He was tall, damned good looking, and totally self-assured. More importantly, he wasn't threatened by her credentials.

As accustomed as she was to controlling her own life, Carla became aware of a pleasant willingness to let her guard down when she was with him. She was confused by her feelings since she had worked so hard to assert her independence and establish her career. She didn't discuss her lack of hesitation in allowing him to control the pace of their relationship with her female colleagues for fear that her liberated sisters in the halls of academe would have been horrified at her breach of faith. She had agreed to go out with him on the condition that he stop harassing her during her class. However, the real reason was a lot more basic than that. She was turned on by his dark sensitively arched brows, his beautiful lips, his rich brown skin, and the undeniable sexuality of his tall, athletic body. He told her on their first date that he intended to marry her. And, while she was shocked by his audacity, she knew that she probably would marry him. He aced her course with the highest score in the class, and she married him a year later.

That was six years ago; and while they had gone through their share of ups and downs, she was satisfied...more than satisfied, she was happy. She thrived on her marriage and her family; and while her career had suffered from the hiatus she took after the birth of their first child, she didn't feel that the setback was permanent. She taught part-time until her second child was born, then she abandoned teaching altogether in favor of working as a consulting clinical psychologist at the local community mental health center. She was slowly working her way back to full-time employment, but she wasn't in a hurry. All things considered, she was dangerously content for a feminist career woman. Ignoring her husband's exhibitionism, Carla asked:

"What happened last night, Matthew?"

"Harold Waterson was killed."

"Waterson, the wealthy developer?"

"The one and only."

"You've hooked a big one this time, honey. Who killed him?"

"We don't know...yet."

"Where was he killed?"

"That's the crazy part, Carla. He was found shot to death in the basement of Angela Bowman's parents' home."

"What!" Carla exclaimed rising from the clothes hamper in shock. "I don't believe it! What was he doing there?"

"That's even more crazy. Angela's parents say they don't know what he was doing in their basement. As a matter of fact, they say they barely knew him, and they both deny any personal dealings with him."

"What does Angela say?"

"Nothing, so far. Apparently, she was the one who found Waterson's body lying in the basement after he had been shot...if what her father says is true. She went into hysterics from the shock, so I wasn't able to question her last night."

"How convenient for her," Carla replied, the old enmity for Angela apparent in her voice.

"She wasn't faking, Carla. She really went to pieces last night."

"Give me a break, Matthew. Even a blind man can see that the hysterics were staged for your benefit."

"Give her a break, Carla. You're accusing her of murder simply because you don't like her."

"I certainly wouldn't put it past her. But, for the sake of argument, who do you think killed him?"

"I have no idea who killed him because I'm still not certain what happened last night."

"You must have an opinion about what happened," Carla insisted.

"Opinions are dangerous luxuries in a homicide investigation, Carla. Facts are more objective and conclusive; and right now, I simply don't have enough facts to make an educated guess."

"You wouldn't tell me even if you had all the facts and knew exactly who killed him. I don't know why you have to be so damned professional with me, Matthew. You know I won't discuss what you tell me with anyone else."

"It's not that I don't trust you, baby. You know I do. But, I'm not God, Carla. Even after we've pieced together all the facts in a homicide investigation, we're never one hundred percent sure we've covered all the bases. There's always the possibility that we may have overlooked an important piece of evidence that could be crucial to the case, and witnesses have been known to deliberately lie to cover their tracks. I can't say who I think may have killed Waterson without prejudicing my ability to deal objectively with that person later on."

"Where were Angela's parents when she found the body?"

Matt gave Carla a brief summary of what had transpired the night before.

"So, all three of them were in the house when Waterson was shot?"

"It looks that way. The parents attended a cocktail party at Tom and Claudia Martin's Saturday night. They say they left there around nine; and Walter Bowman placed the call to Fourth District Headquarters reporting the homicide at ten-thirty last night."

"At Tom and Claudia Martin's! This is too good to be true! Are the Martins mixed-up in the murder, too?"

"I don't think so," Matt replied with more conviction than he felt. "The Bowmans both say that Angela wasn't home when they returned from the Martins'. Walter Bowman said he heard Angela screaming from the basement around ten-fifteen. If what the Bowmans say is true, and it may very well not be, Waterson was shot after he left the Martins' party and before Angela found his body at ten-fifteen, which doesn't leave much time. The Bowmans said Waterson was still at the party when they left. That should be easy enough to verify. Did you know that Angela was living at home, Carla?"

"I remember someone mentioning that she and her husband had split up, but I didn't know that she had moved back to her parents' house. It figures, though. She's very close to them...too close if you ask me. They really spoiled her, Matthew. When we were in high school, she got an MG midget for her sixteenth birthday. Of course, we were all green with envy because all the guys started giving her the rush. Angela Bowman always had the best of everything."

"Do you know the guy she married? His name is Gary Washington."

"No, I don't know him, but I understand her father hates him with a passion. I guess he's not good enough for her."

"Neither was I. It appears that no one is good enough for Walter Bowman's daughter."

Matt completed his personal grooming and walked into the bedroom to finish dressing. He opened the blinds at the window to admit more light.

"My God, Matthew! Don't stand in front of the windows naked. What will the neighbors think?"

"Anything they like, which they do anyway."

"You're incorrigible. If you really upheld the law, you'd arrest yourself on a charge of indecent exposure."

"I didn't raise the blinds, Carla; I only opened them to get more light. Indecent exposure probably wouldn't stick. Why don't I go for something serious like ravishing my sexy wife."

"If you touch me, I'll scream."

"You scream every night. The children have gotten used to it by now. I'm pressed for time right now. otherwise you'd be screaming your lungs out and enjoying every minute of it."

"Seriously, Matthew. How could someone other than the Bowmans have killed Harold Waterson?"

"Anything's possible; but, you're right, it's unlikely considering where he was found."

"Maybe someone else forced him into their basement at gunpoint," Carla imaginatively suggested.

"That's not very likely considering that people were going into and out of the Martins' party most of the night. Someone could have had the drop on him, but it would have been damned risky."

"Maybe he was having an affair with Claudia Martin and Tom found out about it, shot him, and dragged him over to the Bowman's basement."

"Pure melodrama, Carla, and not very good melodrama either. This is the last pair of clean socks I have left. Didn't Mrs. Taylor wash on Friday?"

"She didn't come on Friday. She asked me if she could come on Monday instead. She'll wash your clothes tomorrow."

"Why didn't you wash on Friday if you knew she couldn't come?"

"Honey, you know how much I hate to wash."

"What will I do for socks tomorrow morning, Carla?"

"You're so helpless. I'll wash you a pair today."

"Don't fill the washer to wash one pair of socks, Carla."

"You don't expect me to wash dirty socks by hand, do you?"

"Don't bother to wash them at all if you have to use the washer. I'll wash my socks myself when I get home tonight."

"On no, love. I'll wash them for you," Carla insisted, knowing full well that she intended to use the washer.

As much as Matt loved Carla, he had been appalled by her lack of home-making skills after they were married. She couldn't cook, she couldn't clean house two cents worth, and she detested washing dirty clothes...said they smelled. She preferred eating on paper plates to washing dirty dishes and was at a total loss when it came to preparing a meal more complicated than hamburgers and french fries. He taught her as much as he knew about cooking; and he was a terrible cook. After six months of awful meals and dirty clothes, they hired Mrs. Taylor to clean house.

When Matt had asked Carla why she hadn't learned to do any housework, she matter-of-factly replied that she hadn't needed to do any before they were married. She said her mother had never worked out of the home and her father refused to eat anyone's cooking but her mother's. Of the three Channing sisters, Carla claimed that she cooked better than either Phyllis or Cassie, if that could be believed. Portia Channing later confirmed the fact that Arthur Channing wouldn't eat his daughters' cooking. He maintained that they were terrible cooks; she insisted that they wouldn't get any better without practice. They were both right. Arthur Channing's position was that he worked hard to provide for his family, and the least he could expect was a decently cooked meal after he got home from a hard day at the office. He would accept no less. If his wife was unable to cook, for whatever reason, he went over to his mother's to eat.

Carla's cooking had improved over the years. Unfortunately, Mrs. Taylor's weekly visits had lessened her incentive to become more adept at cleaning and washing. Carla was still sensitive about her cooking, especially when her father was around, but she had summoned enough confidence to invite her family and Matt's mother to Thanksgiving dinner later that week...which wasn't to say that she hadn't had misgivings after she'd extended the invitations. The previous Thursday, she had panicked and offered Mrs. Taylor a day's pay for three hours of work on Thanksgiving morning helping her to cook the dinner, but Mrs. Taylor had declined in favor of spending the holiday at home with her own family. Carla's resolve had flagged temporarily. However, with her husband's encouragement, she had rebounded to the point where she was determined to go through with the dinner anyway.

"I've got a meeting downtown at one-thirty, Carla. Will you make me a sandwich before I leave?"

"Will you be home for dinner?"

"Probably not."

"I don't know why I bother to cook, Matthew! You're never home to eat when the meal is ready. It's always 'I'll eat later or I'll grab a sandwich out.' What was the point in my learning to cook if I have to eat all my meals alone?"

"You don't have to eat alone. The children can eat with you."

"The children would just as soon eat peanut butter and jelly as pot roast. I wouldn't have cooked the damned pot roast if I had known you wouldn't be here for dinner." He smiled and grabbed her around the waist before leaving.

"Don't be angry, baby. You know you can cook for me anytime," he whispered as he kissed her on the mouth and throat.

"I was referring to food, not sex. Don't think you can sweet talk your way around me again, Matthew. I'm going to stop cooking meals for you because you don't appreciate them anyway."

"Please, baby, don't ever stop cooking for me. Yours is the best there is; I've never had better," he insisted pressing her body very close to his.

"I told you I wasn't referring to sex, you maniac," she replied laughing. "Let me go," she protested, pretending to be angry.

"What do I need with food, Carla, when you satisfy me more than I can say," he murmured, backing her against the door as he gave her a profoundly satisfying kiss that left her pleasantly disoriented.

"Where are the children?" he asked releasing her abruptly.

"They're downstairs playing in the breakfast room."

"Hurry up with my sandwich, Carla. I don't want to be any later than I already am." He checked the time as he went downstairs. He had just twenty minutes to get to the Chief's office. His daughter, Jenny, heard her father coming down the stairs and ran into the foyer to greet him. He scooped her up and continued into the breakfast room without breaking his stride. He put her down to pick his son up but Jenny was back in his lap as soon as he sat down. He played with them until Carla finished his sandwich.

"What time will you be home, Matthew," she asked trying to cover her disappointment.

"That's hard to say, Carla, but I'll try to get home early tonight," he responded more sincerely than realistically.

"I'll wait up for you. I feel as if I haven't spent any time with you in days."

Matt left his house on Fourth Street at one o'clock Sunday afternoon.

# CHAPTER VII

Matt left LeDroit Park by way of Sixth Street to Constitution Avenue. Once downtown, he parked illegally on Third Street and ran the distance from his car to the front entrance of the Municipal Building arriving at one twenty-eight. The foyer of the building was protected by a malevolent-looking old guard who inspected the young detective from head to toe before grudgingly allowing him to enter the building. The old guard kept a sharp eye on Matt's retreating form until he disappeared into the stairwell.

Unwilling to stake his remaining two minutes on the caprice of ancient elevators, he took the stairs two at a time until he reached the third floor, where he arrived at Chief Carter's office no worse for wear than if he had been on a leisurely Sunday stroll. When he opened the door to the Chief's suite of offices, he found Marge Smith, the Chief's seductive secretary, and Larry Murray, his sycophantic Public Relations Director, in the outer office. Marge was sitting at her desk, while Larry Murray was sitting on top of it with his head very close to hers in animated conversation. They both looked up as he walked in. Murray eased himself off the desk as Marge's attitude shifted chameleon-like from conspiratorial to ultra-professional.

"Matthew Alexander to see Chief Carter."

"Is he expecting you?" Marge asked, knowing full well that he was.

"I wouldn't be here otherwise."

Marge took her time announcing him over the inter-com. Larry Murray stood off to the side waiting to be acknowledged first, but Matt refused to give him the satisfaction. Like most of the detectives who dealt with Murray, Matt disliked him on principle and wouldn't willingly give him the time of day. It didn't take long for officers new to the homicide division to learn that Larry Murray was an apple-polisher who fawned over his superiors and high-handed everyone else. Dressed to the teeth in a three-piece suit, he looked more like a model for a mens' haberdashery than the Public Relations Director of the District police department. Sensing a snub in the air, Murray broke the ice.

"Well, if it isn't Matthew Alexander. I can't remember the last time I saw you downtown."

"Everybody can't hang around the Chief's office dressed in three-piece suits, Murray. Somebody has to do the work that you take credit for in your press conferences."

Before Larry Murray could reply, Marge got up to show Matt into Chief Hendrick's office. She wore a black knit dress that left no question about what lay underneath. For the benefit of those simple souls who failed to give her body the undivided attention it deserved, Marge generously iced the cake with a hypnotic prance that usually made the chief's visitors forget why they were there. Larry Murray seemed duly appreciative, but Matt's mind was on other things at the moment.

When he entered the inner office, he found a grim Chief, a sullen Commander, and a poker-faced stenographer who was as conspicuously lacking in natural assets as Marge was well-endowed. He recalled the middle-aged stenographer from a visit to the chief's office two years ago. She performed her duties as assiduously then as now, giving him no more than a perfunctory glance as he walked into the room. It was obvious that Marge Smith was little more than window dressing, the nitty-gritty office work being delegated to the matronly foot-soldier who sat furiously scribbling short hand notes onto her pad.

Matt's first visit to Chief Hendrick's office had been two years earlier, when he and several fellow officers attended a small reception the Chief held to celebrate their promotions to the rank of Lieutenant. None of the men knew what to expect, but the Chief soon put them at ease. He seemed to take a genuine interest in each officer who was there, asking them about their career plans with the force. Matt decided that Jefferson Carter would make a good drinking buddy if he weren't Chief of Police. All things considered, Matt thought it unlikely that he would receive as enthusiastic a welcome today in light of Waterson's homicide and the fact that Lloyd had preceded him by thirty minutes.

"What the hell!" he thought. "I give them a hundred and fifty percent everyday. If they want more than that, they'll have to get it from someone else."

With that thought in mind, Matt walked over to the Chief's immense mahogany desk and thrust his hand across in a gesture symbolizing both respect and defiance. Chief Carter rose and shook his hand. He dispelled Matt's doubts by greeting him cordially, and offering him one of two brown leather wing chairs in front of his desk. Lloyd occupied the other chair. The stenographer was seated, unobtrusively, at a round conference table near the windows. Chief Carter got right to the point by asking Matt for a detailed account of the Waterson homicide. Matt gave a concise though complete report, covering each aspect of the case he had investigated so far. The Chief listened thoughtfully and waited until Matt finished speaking before asking:

"What do you think happened to the gun, Lieutenant?"

"That's a good question. When I talked to Captain Bryant this morning, he said they still hadn't found it; and they searched most of the house thoroughly, last night. Bryant is going to finish searching the house, today; and I'm going over to supervise a search of the grounds and surrounding neighborhood. But, I've got a feeling that if it isn't found on the Bowman's property, we'll be searching for a needle in a haystack."

"It'll be harder for the District Prosecutor to build a good case without the murder weapon," the Chief insisted.

Lloyd didn't agree, "If the prosecutor's office can demonstrate that the slugs found in Waterson's chest came from a thirty-eight revolver the same model as Bowman's gun, he can get a conviction."

"Maybe," the Chief replied, "but I'll rest a hell of a lot easier if you could find the murder weapon."

"We all will," Matt agreed.

"Here's a preliminary report on the post mortem, Lieutenant," the Chief said handing him a thin blue folder. "They haven't finished the specimen tests yet, but they recovered both bullets and sent them over to the forensics lab at Fourth District. One of the bullets hit Waterson's aorta; he didn't stand a chance after that. The report says that with wounds like that, death occurs immediately. The report says he died between nine and ten-thirty last night. How does that set with your facts, Lieutenant?"

"Walter Bowman claims he found the body at ten-fifteen last night, so the medical examiner's time looks okay so far."

"They specifically asked that the preliminary report be kept out of circulation until they finish the specimen tests and issue their final report on the post mortem. This looks like a clear cut case of murder to me. How do you read it, Lieutenant?"

"It's definitely a homicide, Chief. The fact that there were three people in the house when Waterson was killed complicates things, so we have to be careful in building our case against them. At this point, I wouldn't want to hazard a guess as to which one of them may have pulled the trigger."

"Maybe they didn't conspire to kill him," Lloyd suggested. "But they may have conspired to cover the tracks of whoever did kill him by getting rid of the gun."

"It's possible," Matt agreed. "But, I prefer to wait until I have more facts before I draw any conclusions."

"Was the daughter really hysterical or just faking it?" the Chief asked.

"She wasn't faking. Tom Martin came over to the house and gave her a tranquilizer last night. He said her condition was serious. I agreed not to question her last night, but I let her father know that we have to question her today. Dr. Martin didn't think it was a good idea to question her at all until she has had time to recover."

Chief Carter looked skeptical.

"You should have questioned her anyway," Lloyd insisted. "By holding off, you've given her and her parents time to put their heads together. You can bet they've got their lies straight by now."

"That's what makes it a horse race, Lloyd," Matt fired back. "I get paid to figure out who's lying and who isn't."

Lloyd inwardly bristled at Matt's impudence in front of Chief Carter's. He had a come-back on the tip of his tongue; but not knowing how the Chief would respond to hostile repartee between him and his chief investigating officer on the case, Lloyd decided to let it ride. He kept cool as his anger rose and subsided, but he mentally added another debit to Lieutenant Matthew Alexander's balance sheet, which already included a long list of public affronts to his authority. Lloyd could add the list up any time, but he preferred to wait until the arrogant smart-assed lieutenant needed something from him.

For his part, Chief Carter only looked and listened. He would have enjoyed the power play between Cullison and Alexander if it had been anyone but Harold Waterson on a slab in the medical Examiner's refrigerator. He hadn't received any calls from the "powers that be" so far, but he knew that when they started the calls would be hot and heavy with unqualified demands that Waterson's killer be brought to justice. Most of the calls would be from people who were accustomed to calling the shots. When they said "jump," the only clarification allowed was "how high." The kind of people who didn't mind paying the cost to be the boss. They were generous if they liked you and vicious if they didn't, and you had to deliver on cue if you wanted to stay in their good graces. Jefferson Carter had been Chief of Police long enough to know that if he didn't satisfy their demands, he might as well pack it in.

Since his tenure in office, no one with as much money and solid connections as Waterson had been killed in the District. Certainly, it was the first time such a crime had occurred on the Gold Coast where the mayor lived...practically in his back yard. To put it succinctly, the Chief's knew better than anyone that he was on the hot seat. Very soon, there could be enormous pressure to indict one or all three of the Bowmans.

Chief Carter was accustomed to the pressures of office, but the Waterson homicide had him worried. The next few days would demand the nerve of a wire walker and the finesse of a con artist. He would have to convince his money and power constituency that the department was moving against the killer with all its resources, while, at the same time, assuring the public at-large that they were not rushing to judgement to satisfy the power-elite's lust for retribution. He would have to find the middle ground between a death sentence on the one hand and a reprieve on the other, as he attempted to convince all his constituents that serving their interests was the first item on his agenda. It wouldn't be easy, so Chief Carter was pleased to see that Matthew Alexander had been assigned to the case.

He had recognized Matthew Alexander's potential two years ago when he was promoted to Lieutenant. During the promotion ceremony, the Chief had been impressed by the fact that Matthew Alexander was at least ten years younger than the youngest of the remaining six candidates. He recalled asking him whether he thought his youth would be a hindrance in his new position. The Lieutenant replied that while he didn't under-estimate the importance of experience, he didn't think that it compensated for a lack of aptitude for the job. Chief Carter had discerned a degree of over-confidence in the young man's reply, most of which he attributed to youthful optimism. But, more importantly, he perceived a level of determination and intelli-gence rare in a young officer. The Lieutenant's reply had a certain poignancy for the Chief in light of his own ascent to the top job on the force. It had been a difficult climb where past experience and political savvy had counted for everything. Chief Carter didn't denigrate the merit of aptitude or intelligence; but for his money, political savvy went a hell of a lot further than either one.

The Chief of Police was an interesting study in that he lacked the traditional career assets like height, good looks, family connection, or money. But what he lacked in these areas was balanced by a rare political intuition that was at best astute; and at worst, downright cunning. Jefferson Carter had nine lives, and he made a point of always landing of his feet. His rise to the top had demanded a sharp wit and a keen sense of timing considering his liabilities: he was short, no more than five feet nine in his dress boots with the two inch heels; he was stocky, but not fat, adhering to a strict food regimen which excluded most of the food he loved; he wasn't handsome, but he was hardly ugly with close-cropped hair that defied description and a clean shaven face that was both wholesomely reassuring and remarkably ordinary.

Chief Carter quickly learned that his failure to stand out in a crowd was both a blessing and a curse. It hurt him to the extent that his name didn't automatically crop up when his superiors were casting around for someone to fill a higher-level vacancy. However, existing below the threshold of name recognition helped him to the extent that he was not automatically blamed when circumstances or events went awry. Chief Carter had developed a talent for maneuvering in the seams of the system until he was ready to present himself and his credentials for approval. At that point, most of the ambitious young Turks who joined the force with him had burned themselves out through over-exposure or misadventure or both. However, where others failed, Jefferson Carter prevailed through a combination of savvy, perfect timing, and a total lack of glamour. He was as ordinary as a pair of old slippers, and he liked it that way.

Whichever way he cut it, the Chief recognized the potential for disaster that loomed in Waterson's homicide. And though he didn't ordinarily look on the down side, he could almost feel the storm clouds gather over his head. He knew that it would take all of his finesse and then some to keep the Waterson homicide investigation from exploding in his face.

"Have you questioned any of the people who attended the party, yet?" the Chief asked.

"I haven't had time," Matt replied.

"What about the Martins?" They invited Waterson to the party last night."

"I talked to Tom Martin briefly before he sedated Angela Bowman last night. Of course, he denies being involved in any way. I'll go into more detail when I question him and his wife today."

"We need to know the names and addresses of everyone who attended the cocktail party as well as their relationship to the deceased," Lloyd said after a lengthy silence.

"We already have that information," Matt assured him as he

passed Claudia Martin's guest list to Chief Carter. "As you can see, sir, these guests won't welcome any notoriety that connects them with the homicide."

"Good grief!" the chief moaned. "Every hot shot in the District of Columbia is on this list! Holy Moses ! What a mess!" he cried as the storm clouds grew blacker and heavier.

Unable to restrain his curiosity, Lloyd leaned over the Chief's desk to get a firsthand look at the guest list.

"I'll be damned," he added. "This case is full of surprises."

"I need a copy of this list," the Chief continued as he thrust the list in the direction of his stenographer, who hustled over to get it.

"The mayor...Of all the bad luck! Listen you two. You have got to handle these people with kid gloves. I don't want you to make any exceptions for them but there will be hell to pay if I get any flack from the people on this list, especially the mayor. If your people can't handle this, Cullison, I need to know it straight up. I won't have them putting me on front street."

"What an old fart," Lloyd thought "trying to cover his own butt as usual." He said, "You don't have to worry about that, Chief. There won't be any strong-arm tactics by my men. We'll be so discreet, you'll think we're all charm school graduates."

The Chief wasn't amused.

"Let's hope you're right for your sake. What's your opinion of this case so far, Commander?"

"From where I stand, either one or all three of the Bowmans are involved in the homicide. That gun has got to be somewhere; and I intend to find it. Alexander here has the right approach, but he lacks the necessary experience to bring the investigation to a speedy conclusion," Lloyd concluded, getting his own back in the progress.

"Quick is not always better," the Chief admonished. "I want this case sewn up so tight it will never come back to haunt me. The evidence has got to be there to support the indictment."

"Covering his butt again," Lloyd thought.

The chief continued, "There's going to be a hell of a lot of pressure on me to deliver Waterson's killer, but I can field the pressure as long as you give me the solid investigation I need to send the case to the prosecutor's office for an indictment. We don't have much time because the longer it takes us to solve the crime, the more likely we are to come up short. The evidence you gather will have to be strong enough to stand up in court, Cullison. In a case like this, getting a conviction is as important as the indictment. I won't stand for shoddy facts and insupportable evidence. You have to work fast, but you have to bring home the bacon, too. Do I make myself clear?"

"You don't have to worry about the Homicide Division, Chief," Lloyd replied. "My men will wrap this case up in no time."

Matt thought: "If Lloyd keeps this up, I'm going to be sick."

"What do you intend to do if you don't find the gun, Lieutenant?"

"If it comes to that, I'll weigh the evidence and make recommendations to Commander Cullison with respect to our options."

"How, may I ask, are you going to decide which one of them to arrest if the girl sticks to the story her parents told you and you don't find the weapon."

"I'll decide on the arrest, Chief," Lloyd interrupted, "but I won't make a move in that direction until I confer with you."

"Make damned sure that you don't," the Chief warned. "How you handle this case is going to reflect on the reputation of the entire force, Cullison. There'll be hell to pay if the Waterson investigation is bungled. But, if you give me the shooter, I'll personally see to it that the Fourth District Homicide Division is commended for their efforts on this case. I guess that about covers it for now," the Chief concluded rising from his chair.

"My press conference is scheduled for four today. I'd give

anything not to face that pack. I'll call you tonight for an update on the case. You have to stay on top of this situation, Commander; I'm depending on you to keep me informed."

Chief Carter thanked both men for coming and told them to send Larry Murray in on their way out. The Chief's stenographer returned the guest list to Matt before they left.

Lloyd Cullison was unable to resist another lecherous look at Marge Smith in the outer office. Waiting for the elevator he said with a smirk, "That Marge is a knockout. She can do my typing anytime."

Matt didn't comment.

"What is it with you and the Chief, Alexander? The two of you seem pretty chummy to me?"

"I don't know what you're talking about, Lloyd. We'll have to light a fire under Sam to get him moving on the bullets, the prints, and the powder tests."

Lloyd realized that Matt was evading the question, so he pressed him again.

"Are you and the Chief related or something, Alexander?" he asked in an attempt to understand why Chief Carter hadn't upbraided Matt up for being late.

"You know better than that, Lloyd."

"Since when do I 'know' anything, Alexander? I thought you had the market cornered on brains. What I know for certain is that you had a lot of nerve showing up at that meeting at one-thirty instead of one o'clock when you were supposed to be there."

"If it's any comfort to you, Lloyd, I don't know the Chief personally. I met him a couple of years ago when he had that reception for the officers who made Lieutenant. You were there, remember?"

Lloyd quickly changed the subject.

"What's the fastest route to the Bowman house? I want to be there when you start the search today to make sure it gets done right."

"You're welcome to supervise the search yourself, Lloyd. I can use my time to get on with questioning Angela Bowman and the Martins."

"I didn't say I wanted to supervise the search," Lloyd countered. "I simply want to be there to make sure you do it right."

"That's your prerogative," Matt angrily replied.

"You're damned right it is!" Lloyd shot back. "It's my prerogative and my responsibility and don't you forget it. You work for me, hot shot; and you should bear that in mind more often than you do! You still haven't answered my question."

"Take Sixteenth Street north to Floribunda and make a left on Floribunda."

"I'll see you there, Alexander, unless you stop by home to take another nap," Lloyd quipped as they parted in front of the municipal building.

Determined to reach the Bowman residence before Lloyd, Matt decided to take Rock Creek Parkway. It was a good deal longer than the route Lloyd was taking, but there would be fewer lights and much less traffic going north on Sunday. If he pushed it, he could beat Lloyd by four or five minutes, not to mention the satisfaction he would get from asking his commander what took him so long. As he drove west on Constitution toward the White House, Matt felt good knowing that Chief Carter was satisfied with his handling of the investigation so far.

Lloyd was another matter, but he could deal with Lloyd. The two of them had an unspoken agreement. Lloyd didn't encroach on his space; and he didn't undermine Lloyd's authority to the black officers at Fourth District Headquarters . They both benefitted from the understanding. Both men recognized that good morale at the Fourth was damned good PR for Lloyd downtown. It decreased racial tensions and insulated Lloyd from the kinds of confrontations that could weaken his control over his men.

For his part, Lloyd was nobody's fool. He knew from experience that the situation at the Fourth could have been a good deal more volatile and unstable than it was. The Second District Commander had experienced a situation close to mutiny in one of his precincts last year and almost got the sack from Chief Carter because of it. Lloyd didn't like Lieutenant Matthew Alexander...he was too mouthy and arrogant to suit him; but given his rapport with the other officers at the Fourth, he knew he was better off with him than without him.

Driving down Constitution, Matt noted that Sunday had arrived, like a good omen, in a blaze of sunlight and color compared to the wet dreariness of the past week. The temperature was unseasonably warm. The mall was filled with pedestrians and bicyclists who couldn't resist taking advantage of possibly the last warm weather before winter. Seeing scores of small children out with their parents made Matt question why he wasn't doing the same. He did make time for his family, but it wasn't enough time and he didn't delude himself into thinking that it was. Lately, he was beginning to wonder why he was driving himself so hard.

When he joined the force nine years ago, he had given himself twelve years to reach Captain's rank. So far he was on schedule. He had three more years to go, at the end of which time he was confident that he would get his promotion. But they would be three years filled with long hours and back-breaking investigations. His son would be four years old by then, and his daughter would be seven. The closer he got, the more he wondered whether it was worth the valuable time lost with Carla and the children, not to mention the small pleasures that were regularly postponed...placed on indefinite hold until the great day arrived. He had always believed that his ambition and drive were assets that he used to reach his goals. Lately, he was beginning to question the legitimacy of his goals.

The irony of his success in the homicide division so far

wasn't lost on Matt. He was painfully aware that his absorption in running the career race left precious little time to appreciate the things that meant the most to him. He told himself that he was doing it for Carla and the kids, but he found that even he wasn't buying that anymore. His career had become a vicious circle where the more successful he became, the more time he had to spend on the job...and away from his family.

Apprehensions aside, it was impossible to be glum in such weather. An airy canopy of pale blue, the sky held a smattering of fluffy white clouds while the sun bathed the District with a gently intoxicating glow confirming Matt's belief that the District of Columbia is a great city to call home...maybe the best in the world. Bypassing the Washington Monument on its eastern flank, his route took him around the northern edge of the tidal basin where the dormant cherry blossoms patiently waited for spring to display their fuzzy pink blooms. Across the basin, sunlight danced off the dome of the Jefferson Memorial from its snug niche in East Potomac Park. Matt continued along the south side of the mall, skirting the entire length of the sun-dappled reflecting pool as he approached the Lincoln Memorial, where the seated figure of Abraham Lincoln revealed glimpses of its solemn grandeur amidst stately marble columns. His attention was distracted by light bouncing off the gigantic mounts guarding the entrance to Memorial Bridge and Arlington National cemetery beyond.

Circumventing the Lincoln Memorial, he drove under the Theodore Roosevelt Bridge, where he sped toward the massive Kennedy Center with its enormous cantilevered balconies and delicate gold columnar supports. He opened his windows to admit the brisk breeze that periodically whipped piles of dead leaves into dancing twisters. Driving past the Watergate Complex with its crescent-shaped buildings and battlement-like balconies, he felt a creeping sense of relaxation in spite of the ensuing investigation. Noting the Georgetown waterfront on the left, he followed the Parkway's snake-like route under the Whitehurst Freeway and Pennsylvania Avenue, both of which were straining under the weight of Sunday traffic moving into and out of Georgetown.

Sunlight streamed through bare stands of trees and splintered into a thousand fragments as it bounced from the surface of the road. The air held a refreshing coolness that enveloped Matt long enough to make him forget the Waterson homicide. After last night, the drive was a reprieve and he wanted to hold onto the pleasure of it as long as he could. The Parkway's natural order and stability were stark contrast to the man-made chaos that waited for him at the end of the drive. The peace and quiet were enticing as the many cul-de-sacs, play, and rest areas invited him to stop and linger in a world temporarily undisturbed by violence. Rather than succumb to its pleasure, he continued north as the Parkway wound under the embassies and mansions of Massachusetts Avenue.

As he turned onto Floribunda, Matt saw that the 1600 block had been inundated with a score of police cars that were still coming. The officers who had already arrived were milling about in front of the Bowman residence. Jake was standing on the front porch when Matt passed the house looking for an empty parking space which he found on the north side of Floribunda very close to Seventeenth Street. He was pleased that he didn't see Lloyd's car anywhere about. As he walked the distance from his car to the house, he noticed the unabashed interest shown by the Bowmans' neighbors on both sides of Floribunda. Many were sitting or standing on their porches, some were standing in their yards, and still others who didn't care to expose their curiosity to public scrutiny were observing from the protection of their curtained windows.

When he arrived in front of the house, he noticed that several officers were reading the article on Waterson's homicide in the Washington Star. He borrowed the paper from one of the officers and began reading the account which was prominently featured on the front page under a picture of the deceased. The headline read: PROMINENT LOCAL DEVELOPER KILLED.

"On Saturday night, November 23rd, the District police were called to 1637 Floribunda Lane to investigate a reported homicide. The victim has been identified as Harold William Waterson, Sr., the well-known land developer. Waterson was a principal partner with Waterson, Sullivan, and Loew Development Corporation. The *Washington Star* has learned that the victim was shot twice in the chest with a large caliber handgun from close range. The deceased resided at 40078 Reservoir Road with his wife Felicia Waterson and his only child, Harold William Waterson, Jr. The family could not be reached for comment. The office of the Chief of Police has also refused to comment on the homicide, saying that a statement would be issued to the press later today. Harold William Waterson, Sr., was a controlling partner of one of the largest real estate development firms in the area, with headquarters in Foggy Bottom. Two years ago, the DCRLA awarded the contract for the Anacostia Riverfront Development Project to Waterson, Sullivan and Loew, Inc. The award precipitated a lawsuit by Reynolds, Smith and Robinson, a local black architectural design and engineering firm, which claimed discrimination in the selection process. The Reynolds et al. bid was nearly ten million dollars less than the Waterson et. al. bid. The case was settled in arbitration where an impartial panel upheld the DCRLA in their selection of Waterson, Sullivan and Loew to develop and build the project."

"The house where the victim was killed, 1637 Floribunda Lane, is situated in the exclusive Gold Coast area of the District of Columbia, noted for its large, well-kept homes. 1637 Floribunda Lane is the residence of Walter and Helen Bowman. Walter Bowman is employed by the District of Columbia city government as General Counsel in the D.C. Reclamation Land Agency (DCRLA), Office of Contract Compliance and Review. The *Washington Star* has also learned that the victim is estimated to have died between nine and ten-thirty P.M. on the night of November 23rd. The cause of death has been attributed to two gunshots fired into the victims's chest from close range. The body was found in the basement of the Bowman residence at 1637 Floribunda Lane. Neither Walter or Helen Bowman could be reached for comment. Fourth District Headquarters Commander Lloyd Cullison refused to comment on whether either of the Bowmans have been arrested or charged with the homicide."

Matt finished reading the article just as Lloyd turned onto Floribunda from Sixteenth Street. He returned the paper to its owner and walked over to where Jake was standing on the porch.

"What the hell is going on, Jake?"

"Damned if I know, man. As near as I can tell, Cullison ordered these officers in to help search for the gun, but there are too many of them. They'll spend more time falling over themselves than looking for the gun. Lloyd Cullison doesn't know his ass from a hole in the ground when it comes to a homicide investigation," Jake concluded.

"Cool it, man," Matt warned. "You never know who's listening in a crowd like this."

"I couldn't care less," Jake insisted with more bravado then he actually felt. "Look at him making Holt move so he won't have to look for a parking space like everybody else." Matt turned to find Lloyd maneuvering into what had been Sergeant Holt's space and had to laugh. The humor of the situation was lost on Jake.

"Look at is this way, Jake. You'll be able to do that too, when you make commander."

"Commander, my ass! I'll never get another promotion as long as I'm working for that racist."

"Tell you what, Jake. When I get promoted to captain, I'll promote you to commander," the Lieutenant laughed.

"I'm going to hold you to that promise, man," Jake laughed in spite of himself. "Yes sir, that's one promise I won't let you forget."

"Heah come de boss," Jake whispered as Lloyd walked over to where they were standing.

"What took you so long, Lloyd?" the Lieutenant asked. "I got here ten minutes ago."

"That means you should have organized these officers and started the search ten minutes ago, Alexander. So, what the hell are you waiting for?"

"I didn't want to steal your thunder, Lloyd. I figured that with so many officers here, you must have something spectacular in mind."

"Keep it up, Alexander, and you'll be giving your smart-assed spiel to a disciplinary review board."

Sensing that he was riding Lloyd's last nerve, the Lieutenant decided to back off.

"Seriously Lloyd, how do you suggest that we organize the search?" Lloyd was more skeptical than flattered by the question, but the need to assert his authority took hold as he launched into his search strategy.

"Have the metal detectors arrived, yet?"

"The ones from the Fourth are already here," Jake answered as he pointed to where they were lying on the porch near the French doors.

"I requested more from Second and Third District," Lloyd replied. "They ought to be here by now. Assign half the men to the alley behind Floribunda and the rest to the yards of the surrounding houses unless the owners object. The men assigned to the alley should search everything back there including the garbage cans. Start at opposite ends of the street and work toward the middle of the block. I'll supervise the search inside the house. Select five officers and send them inside, Alexander. I'll call Second and Third District Headquarters to see what's holding up the other detectors." Lloyd picked up two metal detectors from the porch before he went inside.

"Yes sir, Mr. boss man, sir," Jake muttered under his breath after Lloyd went inside the house.

"Give him a break," Matt said laughing. "It's not a bad strategy, Jake."

Matt had to shout several times to get the officers' attention. After they assembled, he directed five men to go inside the house. Anxious to get on with questioning Angela Bowman, he left Jake to supervise the men working outside.

# CHAPTER VIII

When Matt entered the Bowman house, he saw that the five officers he had sent inside earlier were systematically taking the first floor apart with Lloyd Cullison supervising the whole affair from the foyer.

"How are things moving outside?" Lloyd asked.

"Okay so far. I left Jake in charge. The other metal detectors still haven't arrived."

"They should get here any time, now. I just talked to Commander Peterson at the Second, and he's seeing to it personally."

"The sooner, the better," Matt replied. "I have a lot of ground to cover today interrogating witnesses, and I'd like to get on with it."

"I think I'll assign another detective to this case, Alexander. You look like you could use the help."

"I can handle it, Lloyd. The primary witness list is limited right now. I'll finish questioning all of them today, by tomorrow morning at the latest. Then, if you still feel the investigation ought to be expanded to include the Martins' party, I'll be glad to get some help. Right now, I've got everything under control."

"I'll be the judge of that!" Lloyd shouted.

"Look, man! You do whatever you have to! In the meantime, I have a job to do!" Matt shouted back.

The flush from Lloyd's neck and face caused his carefully groomed hair and heavy brows to look even blacker than usual as his face knitted itself into a tight knot of rage.

Feigning indifference to Lloyd's anger, Matt walked over to Captain Henry Bryant, who stood quivering at the foot of the stairs waiting for Lloyd to explode any second. Henry Bryant was a cautious man. He didn't invite trouble like Matt Alexander, and he certainly didn't appreciate being caught in the middle of an explosive situation that could backfire on him if he were asked to take sides. Bryant squirmed like it was him on the hot seat instead of his young lieutenant.

"I've got to question Angela Bowman, Bryant. Where's the best place to go for some privacy?"

"The commander wants them to take the basement apart after they finish up here," Bryant nervously replied his eyes shifting from Lloyd to Matt as he spoke. "I guess the best place to go right now is upstairs, but they'll be up there before long."

"Where's Angela Bowman?"

"She's in her parents' bedroom."

"Have any of the Bowmans been downstairs, today?"

"The mother came down and made breakfast around ten o'clock. She took it back upstairs. Later on, Walter Bowman went down into the basement of get the daughter a change of clothes. I escorted him down there and back to make sure that was all he did. I checked upstairs thirty minutes ago, and they're all present and accounted for."

"I think I'll use the father's study. Has Sam dusted it for prints, Yet?"

"He went through all the upstairs' rooms with a fine tooth comb this morning. He's up in the attic now."

Lloyd had abandoned stewing in his own juices to more active supervision of the first floor search, which is not to say that he had dismissed the altercation with Matt as trivial. Far from it. Lloyd Cullison's time-tested method of dealing with the Matthew Alexanders of the world could be summed up succinctly...he didn't get mad, he simply got even at the first available opportunity.

Followed by Captain Bryant, Matt mounted the sweeping staircase, which rose into a spacious second floor alcove furnished as a sitting room. A wide corridor ran the length of the second floor of the house from east to west with rooms on both the north and south sides of the house. The alcove was situated in the center of the corridor. Matt's inspection of the second floor revealed a huge master bedroom suite where the Bowmans were currently quarantined in additioned to three spacious guest bedrooms with their own baths, and a large study. He also found a powder room which must have come in handy for Coleman as he guarded the master bedroom from his current station.

Matt lingered in the corridor to get a feel for the second floor layout. He walked to the east end of the corridor past the master bedroom, opened the door facing him and found a walk-in storage and linen closet. The matching door at the west end of the corridor revealed stairs to the attic and to the lower levels of the house. He inspected all the guest bedrooms which shared the north side of the corridor along with the alcove and the powder room. The master bedroom and the study were situated on the north side of the corridor, the master bedroom in the northwest corner of the house and the study in the northeast corner.

Looking through the window in the alcove, Matt noted the increased level of police activity in the service alley and the Bowmans' backyard. He stood for a moment and watched the methodical movements of the officers as they searched the alley, their divergent search patterns united by sunlight reflecting off the metal housings of the detectors they carried. Bringing his attention back to the second floor, he concluded that the Bowmans had spent a small fortune furnishing their home...with the exception of the study, which was totally out of step with the rest of the house: its shabbiness was conspicuous. Matt found it ironic that Walter Bowman had gone to such great expense in every room of his house except the one that he reserved for his personal use. It was strange, considering that Bowman probably spent more time in his study than in any other room of his home.

Light streaming through open drapes at the study's south-facing windows showed the study to be in good order, considering the search and print-taking that had occurred earlier. Captain Bryant stood in the corridor just outside the door as Matt gave the study and its adjoining bathroom the once over. Satisfied that the room suited his needs, Matt asked Officer Coleman to fetch Angela Bowman from the master bedroom for questioning and Bryant returned downstairs.

The last time Matt remembered seeing Angela Bowman was over two years ago at the ten- year reunion of Carla's high school graduation. He and Carla had spoken to Angela only briefly, but he recalled how little she had changed from the time he dated her. Angela Bowman had the kind of looks that bowled you over. He though he had a fatal fascination for her until her father convinced him otherwise. Meeting Carla immediately after the break-up had cured his infatuation with Angela. Even so, he appreciated a beautiful woman, and Angela Bowman was an incredibly beautiful woman. The sound of moving bodies in the corridor drew Matt's attention to the door as his elusive witness appeared for the first time in the flesh. She looked both exhausted and groggy as she walked over to the corner of the sofa nearest the desk and sat down. She curled her legs under her body very tightly and pulled a long drag on her cigarette before speaking.

"Hello, Matthew, it's good to see you again." Her voice was low and uncertain.

"It's good to see you too, Angela. How do you feel?"

"Okay, I guess. I'm still sleepy from the tranquilizer Tom gave me last night. Pass me that dish with the paper clips in it, will you? Daddy won't allow ashtrays anywhere in the house but the basement."

He passed her the dish after he emptied the paper clips onto the desk blotter. She thanked him and lit another cigarette from the one she was smoking. She took quick nervous puffs like a beginner, but Matt knew her to be a heavy smoker. She seemed to be using the cigarettes to calm her nerves.

Angela's eyes were still puffy from the previous night's hysterics, but she looked beautiful anyway. Her pale creamy skin contrasted with raven black curls cut short in a style that made her look ten years younger than her thirty years. She appeared calm enough, but the tremor in her right hand where she held the lit cigarette made him wonder how long her composure would last. Angela wore a pair of brown wool slacks, a beige turtle-neck sweater, and black slippers. He was surprised at how small she looked, but then he recalled how she always wore three-inch heels to make herself look taller. Determined to take advantage of every minute, he got right to the point speaking firmly but calmly from where he sat at the desk.

"You already know Harold Waterson was murdered in your basement last night Angela. I talked to both of your parents last night, and they gave me their versions of what happened. I don't know whether they've coached you or not, but I don't care either. I'm going to find out who killed Harold Waterson. The best thing for you to do is to tell me the truth. Do you understand what I'm saying?"

"Yes, I do," she softly replied.

"Good. Why don't you begin by telling me how you spent the day on Saturday."

Angela's story coincided with the explanations her parents gave up to the time she left home, which she estimated to be about five-thirty Saturday afternoon.

"Where did you go after you left the house?"

"I visited a friend. We went out to dinner later."

"Were you driving your car?"

"Yes, I was."

"Who was the friend you were with, Angela?"

"Just a friend, Matthew. You don't know him."

"Don't play games with me, Angela. Harold Waterson was killed in your basement last night, and one of you will probably be arrested for his murder. Now, who were you out with last night?"

"My husband, Gary Washington."

"Where does he live?"

"On Goodhope Road inSsoutheast."

"Where did you have dinner last night."

"At the Ethiopian Restaurant on Fourteenth and Gallatin."

"What time did you get to the restaurant and what time did you leave?"

"We got there around seven and we left about eight-thirty."

"Where did you go when you left the restaurant?"

"We took my car to the restaurant because Gary didn't want to lose his space in the parking lot at his building. After we left the restaurant, I drove back to Southeast to drop Gary off at his apartment. Then, I drove home."

"Did you stop anywhere on the way home?"

"No, I drove straight home."

"What time did you get home?"

"Around nine-thirty," she replied, her hand visibly shaking as she pulled a long drag from her cigarette.

"What happened after you got home last night?"

"I parked my car in front of the house. As I was getting out of my car, I noticed a white Mercedes sports car parked several cars away. It looked like Hal's car. Then, I saw Hal come out of the Martins' house. I tried to get inside our house before he saw me, but I wasn't fast enough. He called to me to wait up. He said he wanted to talk to me. He had been drinking. I may as well tell you now because it's bound to come out sooner or later. Hal and I had been seeing each other for over a year. I decided to break it off about a month ago."

"Is that what he wanted to talk to you about?"

"Yes, he refused to accept it. Hal was putting a lot of pressure on me to move to New York City. His company has an office up there. He had arranged a job and an apartment for me, but I wasn't about to move to New York."

"Why was it so important for you move to New York?"

"I don't know. It all started a month ago. The only explanation he gave me was that he felt that our 'arrangement' would be easier for both of us if I moved to New York."

"How did you handle your 'arrangement' here in the District?" Matt inquired as politely as possible under the circumstances.

"Hal's company was leasing two apartments at a downtown condominium. One was used by the firm's New York partner and their out-of-town clients, and the other was reserved for his personal use. We met there once a week, usually on Fridays after work."

"You said the affair had been going on for a year?"

"Yes, since last October."

"How long had you known Hal Waterson?"

"About a year. I started seeing him soon after we met."

"How did you meet him?"

"At a fundraiser for Youth Shelter at his house on Reservoir Road. Claudia invited me to attend the fund raiser with her. Anyway, Hal called me a couple of weeks after the party at his house and asked me to have lunch with him. He said he wanted to talk to me about working for his firm over lunch, but once I got there, he made it clear what he wanted. At the time, I was flattered that he was interested in me. He could be very charming you know. He had a way about him that could convince you go along with his program, and he was very persuasive. I started seeing him, but I gradually realized that he didn't love me. He just wanted to control me. I don't know why I thought it would be any different. I was going to stop seeing him anyway. I was tired of him telling me what to do. Do I shock you, Matthew?"

"No, Angela, you don't. How many people besides you and Harold Waterson knew about your affair?"

"The only person I told about it was Claudia Martin. I don't know who Hal told."

"When did you tell Claudia?"

"Several months ago."

"Why did you want to end the affair?"

"I had wanted to do it for a long time, but I didn't get the courage to actually tell him until four weeks ago. Hal was very considerate when I first started seeing him, but lately, he had begun to treat me as if he owned me. What I wanted didn't matter, he was only interested in what he wanted."

Matt was leery of Angela's version of the affair. if she was telling the truth, their relationship had soured for her, but not for Waterson when affairs of the heart usually worked themselves out the other way around.

"Did you receive money from Waterson?"

"No. He wanted to give me money, but it made me feel so dirty. He kept insisting, but I refused to take any money from him.

"Exactly when did you tell him you wanted to end the affair?"

"Four weeks ago this past Friday. I wasn't about to leave the District to move to New York City, and I told him so. He was furious. He wouldn't take no for an answer. That's why he insisted on speaking to me last night. I knew we would be conspicuous standing in front of my parents' house, so I took him around back to the basement entrance that I use so we could talk without being seen."

"Had he ever been to your house before?"

"No. Last night was his first time."

"And his last," Matt thought to himself. "What time did you take Waterson into the basement, Angela?"

"It was right after I parked out front, so it must have been around ten o'clock, but I'm not certain. The telephone rang almost as soon as we got inside the house. We only talked a couple of minutes before I got up to answer it. It was a woman from Claudia's party. She said that Tom and Claudia had run out of ice, and she asked if I could bring some over."

"This is the first time I've heard about a telephone call, Angela. What time did you receive the call?"

"We had just begun to talk when the telephone rang. Hal was angry at the interruption, but I took the ice over anyway. I suppose I was trying to stall for time. He was in a very nasty mood."

"Are you saying that Waterson was alive when you left to take the ice over to the Martins?"

"Yes, he was sitting on the sofa when I left," she replied fighting tears. "When I came back, he was lying in the middle of the floor with his raincoat over his face. I knew he was dead by the way his body was twisted. It was horrible. I didn't kill him, Matthew, and I don't know who did." She insisted as she sobbed into a handful of tissues.

"Stay calm, Angela, Getting upset again isn't going to help us get through this any faster." She did make an effort to control the sobbing, but tears continued to stream down her cheeks and her hands shook violently as she tried to take another cigarette from the pack. Matt went into the bathroom to get her some more tissues.

"Where does your father keep his liquor? You need a drink."

"Downstairs in the bar off the dining room."

"Stay where you are and try to relax. I'll ask Officer Coleman to make you a drink. What would you like?"

"Bourbon."

"Coming up," he replied a little too lightheartedly as he stepped out into the corridor. Some of the search activity had moved to the second floor which is where Matt found Henry Bryant standing in the corridor outside the master bedroom talking to Officer Coleman.

"Any luck yet, Bryant?"

"Nope. If you ask me, the Commander is wasting his time. I don't believe the gun is anywhere in the house. They would be crazy to leave it here waiting to be found. I told him I searched the basement from top to bottom last night, but he wouldn't take my word for it. He's down there now."

"They probably did get rid of the gun, but a lot depends on when Waterson was killed. Walter Bowman made the call into Headquarters at ten-thirty P.M. If Waterson was killed after ten o'clock it's not likely that the Bowmans would have had the time to get rid of it. It's bound to be in the vicinity if not in the house. If they're lying and he was killed earlier, there's no telling where the weapon could be by now. One thing's for certain, though. Walter Bowman made the call after he got rid of the gun if he's guilty."

"How can you be so sure, Alexander?"

"Because he had no way of predicting how soon the squad cars would arrive. For all he knew one could have been the next street over when he made the call. Waiting until after he made the call would have been too risky."

"Yeah, I see what you mean."

"Angela Bowman is getting hysterical again, Bryant. She needs a drink to calm her nerves. The liquor is downstairs in the bar. Do me a favor and pour her a bourbon and water on ice and bring it upstairs right away."

"Do I look like your servant, Alexander? What's the Commander going to think about me walking around with a drink, on duty?"

"Tell Lloyd who it's for, who ordered it, and to go to hell!"

"You tell him yourself, man. What kind of ass-hole do you take me for anyway."

"Do me a favor, Bryant, and make the drink. Lloyd shouldn't care one way or the other."

Matt back upstairs before Bryant could refuse. Angela was lighting another cigarette when he returned.

"How do you feel?"

"Better. The shock of finding Hal like that was more than I could handle."

"I know what you mean. I saw him too. Did you see anyone outside last night when you delivered the ice?"

"No, I didn't see anybody."

"Did you notice anyone on Floribunda when you and Waterson were talking out front?"

"No. I distinctly remember looking around and I didn't see anybody on the street, but it was dark."

"Who let you in over to the Martins?"

"The back door wasn't locked. I left the ice on the counter and turned to leave because I knew Hal would be furious if I stayed too long. But Claudia came into the kitchen while I was there. We chatted for a moment or two, and she offered me a drink. I refused the drink and was about to leave when she talked me into helping her arrange some serving trays with food, but that didn't take long. I couldn't have been gone any longer than ten minutes...but Hal was dead when I got back."

"Think hard, Angela. Did you see anyone in the service alley or the back yard on your way back from the Martins?"

"No. I didn't see anyone. It was raining and I had my umbrella over my head, but I really wasn't looking to see anything out of the ordinary, Matthew. I certainly didn't expect Hal to be murdered between the time I left and the time I got back."

"Did you notice anything unusual when you got back to the house?"

"I don't know." she insisted. "Everything was so confused after that." Her voice started to crack again.

"Think, Angela!"

"Oh God! I am trying to think!" she cried out.

They were interrupted by Henry Bryant, who entered the study to give Angela her drink. She took several quick sips of the drink, after which she took a long drag on her cigarette.

"Was anything in the basement disturbed? Did you notice anything different from the way you left it?"

"Now that I think about it, the basement door was locked when I got back. I remember closing it when I left to go over to Claudia's, but I left the lock off. When I got back I had to use my door key to get in."

"Are you certain the door wasn't locked when you left?"

"I remember thinking that I would only be gone a couple of minutes, so I just pulled it close, but I didn't slam it the way you have to do to activate the lock. Daddy put a spring lock on the door because I forget to lock it sometimes. It's a real nuisance because I have to remember to carry my key to take the garbage out. I've gotten into the habit of taking my key every time I leave the house."

"Tell me what happened after you let yourself into the basement."

"I put my umbrella into the stand near the door, and I hung my raincoat in the closet under the stairs. I recall that there was a strange smell in the air like something burning, but I assumed that Hal had been smoking. He smoked a lot. Nothing seemed disturbed out in the hall. Then I went into the family room and saw his body lying on the floor in front of the coffee table. I knew he was dead from the way he was sprawled...it was so unnatural. When I saw the blood on the front of his shirt, I panicked and started screaming. I think I could have handled it if it weren't for the blood. There was so much of it, all over the front of his shirt. I remember that his hand was bloody too. I couldn't see his face because it was covered by his raincoat." Angela's body shuddered as she drained the last of her drink.

"I've told you all I know, Matthew. Do I have to go on with this?"

"What did you do after you found the body?"

"I started screaming and running for the stairs at the same time. I fell going up the stairs. That made me panic even more. I didn't know my parents had returned from the Martins' party, but Daddy came running down the stairs after he heard me scream."

"Who do you think killed him, Angela?"

"I don't know who killed him. He probably let someone in the door while I was over to Claudia's."

"Someone like who?"

"I don't know, but he must have let someone in! I didn't kill him and I know my parents didn't do it!"

"How do you know they didn't if you were over to the Martins at the time he was killed.?"

"What possible reason would they have for killing Hal Waterson?"

"That's what I'd like to know. Both of your parents were in the house while you were at the Martins. They had opportunity and means to kill him too, if your father's revolver is the murder weapon. Did they know about your affair with him?"

"No! I'm certain that neither one of them knew. Claudia Martin was the only person I told about the affair."

"It's possible that Claudia could have told one or both of your parents what you told her."

"Claudia is a friend of mine. She would never do anything like that."

"Not even if she thought it was in your best interest?"

"No. She would never tell them anything like that. Besides, if she had told them, I know Daddy would have said something to me about it."

"How well did your parents know Harold Waterson?"

"They didn't know him very well at all."

"It's funny that you should say that because your father's work kept him in regular contact with Waterson's firm."

"Hal never mentioned knowing my father to me."

"All the same, there may have been times when he had to talk to your father about business."

"Hal Waterson didn't know my father. I'll swear to that."

"The only person who can swear to that is your father, since Waterson is no longer with us."

Angela lit another cigarette.

"Did your estranged husband know about you and Waterson?"

"Yes. I forgot I told Gary about Hal when I decided to break off with him."

"Why did you confide in someone you were planning to divorce? You are planning to divorce him aren't you?"

"I suppose so...Oh, I don't know what I'm going to do, Matt. Everything is so confused right now. Over the past year, I've felt like I'm being pulled apart. My life became very complicated after I moved back home. When I was married to Gary, I was free to come and go as I pleased. Ever since I moved back home, everyone's been putting pressure on me to do what they want...not what I want. Gary isn't like Daddy or Hal. He doesn't pressure me to be what he wants me to be. He accepts me as I am. Hal Waterson couldn't force me to move to New York City, so he gets himself killed in my parents' house."

"I'm sure Waterson didn't arrange his murder to inconvenience you. If it were up to him, I'm positive he'd still be alive. You've changed, Angela."

"I've finally realized that my life belongs to me. I've spent most of my life trying to please my father. That's mostly why I left Gary. I don't know whether I love him or not, but I wasn't in turmoil when we were together."

"Did you know that your father's gun is missing?"

"Yes, he told us about it last night before the police arrived."

"When was the last time you saw that gun, Angela?"

"I haven't seen it in years."

"Since your fahter's gun is missing, the working assumption is that it's the murder weapon used to kill Waterson. So, if you know anything at all about the whereabouts of that gun, the smart thing to do is to tell me right now."

"I swear I don't know anything about it, Matthew."

"Your father says he didn't know the gun was missing until last night. Can you back him up on that?"

"No, I can't."

"Tell me what happened after you found Waterson's body."

"Like I said, I started screaming and running for the stairs. I was so scared I slipped on the bottom stair and fell. I got up and started running up the stairs again. Then I ran into Daddy who was running downstairs to see what was going on. He almost knocked me down in the kitchen. He grabbed me and kept asking what was wrong. I guess I managed to tell him what had happened to Hal. Then, I ran upstairs to my parents' bedroom."

"Where was your mother?"

"In bed asleep."

"What did she do after you ran into the room?"

"She got very upset."

"She didn't go downstairs?"

"No, she didn't. Daddy came back upstairs soon afterwards. He got his rifle from the study, locked the bedroom door, and called the police."

"According to what you've told me, Angela, you were the last person to see Harold Waterson alive." Matt could see the fear in

BARBARA FLEMING

her eyes after he spoke. Up to now, she had been preoccupied with the emotional trauma of finding the body, but his statement made her realize just how vulnerable she was.

"I'm tired, Matthew. Do I have to answer any more questions?"

"No, I think I've covered everything for now." He helped her get up and watched as she walked back to her parents' bedroom. After she went in, Walter Bowman appeared.

"We're like prisoners in our own home! How much longer is this going to last?" he asked Matt.

"You're damned lucky you haven't been arrested and taken to a holding cell downtown," Matt replied, checking Walter Bowman in his tracks. "The Fourth District Commander is supervising the search. Why don't you ask him how long he'll be?"

Matt left Bowman standing in the second floor corridor. On his way downstairs, he met Lloyd in the foyer. The five officers assigned to the Commander had finished searching the basement, but Lloyd's mood left no doubt that they hadn't found the gun.

"You're just in time, Lloyd. Walter Bowman says he wants to speak to you about the inconvenience you're creating for him and his family."

"Inconvenience is it? I ought to arrest his butt right now and save us the inconvenience of searching his damned house," Lloyd snapped as he started up the stairs with a look that made Matt feel sorry for Walter Bowman.

Matt left the Bowman residence at three-thirty P.M. He stood on the front porch for a moment and watched as most of the officers assigned to searching Floribunda drifted back onto the sidewalk in front of the house. Matt walked over to where Jake was standing.

"You find the gun, man?"

"Are you kidding? Just spinning our wheels, partner...

spinning our wheels."

"What's the score with the men in the alley?"

"Just about finished, too; but it's the same story...no gun."

"Lloyd told Chief Carter that he was going to find that gun if it took him a week, Jake. It looks like he'll have to make good on his promise."

"What's the word on Angela Bowman? Did you question her yet?"

"Just finished. My hunch was right. She did let him into the house last night. If she's telling the truth, Waterson was killed between ten and ten-fifteen last night."

"That's cutting it pretty close isn't it?"

"It's possible. She says she got a call from someone at the Martins' party almost immediately after she took him inside, so she alleges. The woman who called wanted to borrow some ice and asked Angela to bring it over. She says she left shortly after ten and that she was gone no more than ten minutes. When she got back around ten-fifteen, Waterson had been killed."

"Maybe the shooter got her out of the basement so they could ice him."

"Maybe, but the tight time line makes it hard to see how someone from outside the house could have lured Angela out of the basement, killed Hal Waterson, and gotten clean away in fifteen minutes or less."

"Maybe they knew when she was coming back."

"Too many 'maybe's,'" Jake.

"What was he doing in the Bowmans' basement?"

"She says they were having an affair."

"That figures," Jake replied. "Was he knocking off a piece in her parents' basement last night?"

"She says they met once a week for that at a downtown condo that belonged to his firm. She wanted out of the affair, so she says. She also says he'd been drinking heavily last night, and she didn't want him to make a scene on the street in front of her house. So she took him into the basement where they could talk."

"Where was she the earlier part of the night?"

"Out with her estranged husband, Gary Washington?"

"Did he bring her home?"

"She says she drove home alone."

"I wonder how he figures in all of this, partner. Did he know about her affair with Waterson?"

"She says she told him about it the same time she quit Waterson. But, if he is as crazy about her as everyone says he is, he may have known before then."

"Do you want me to pick him up?"

"Yeah. Take him over to the Fourth. I'll be at Headquarters no later than five o'clock. I also want you to check everyone connected with the case so far for priors."

# CHAPTER IX

Claudia Martin opened her front door. She wore an embroidered red caftan that gave her an exotic, seductive appeal that was wholly intended.

"It's about time you got here, Matthew. I was beginning to feel neglected," she pouted before giving him one of her disarming smiles.

"Come in and tell me everything," she urged linking her arm through his as she walked him toward her sparsely furnished living room.

Matt noted that the layout of the Martin house was similar to the Bowmans' in that it featured a split foyer with a central staircase leading to the second floor; but that's where the similarity stopped. Claudia's furniture was ultra-modern from the pale gray velvet sectional sofa in the living room to the Scandinavian-designed rosewood furnishings in the dining room. The Martins' living room occupied the entire east flank of the first floor. It was an immense room. An ebony grand piano sat at the north end of the room while the sectional sofa, arranged pit-style, sat at the south end. The floor was covered in charcoal gray carpeting that looked almost black against the white walls. The house was sleek and uncluttered, minimal color, clean lines, and classic shapes, much like Claudia herself. Dressed in red as she was, Claudia looked strangely intense against the muted backdrop of gray, white, and black, as if she had been staged like one of the African masks that were strategically placed around the living room for maximum effect.

Claudia sat in one of two white leather wing chairs flanking her mirrored floor-to-ceiling fireplace and motioned for Matt to take the other chair. Matt guessed her age to be forty-five, but she looked ten years younger. She wore her shoulder-length red hair in a loose page-boy parted in the middle, framing an oval-shaped face. Her make-up, if she wore any, was undetectable, revealing superb skin with a smattering of freckles across her nose and cheeks. Claudia Martin was not a beautiful woman, but she was unquestionably alluring. She could exercise considerable charm when she chose to, and she was an expert at optimizing her assets from her intriguing almond-shaped eyes to her beautiful hands which lay calmly in her lap.

Her charming reception didn't deceive Matt. He sensed her determination to control his interrogation. Claudia Martin wasn't the type to be bullied into saying anything she didn't want to say, and he knew that she wouldn't cave in to threats either. He decided that whatever information he got from her would depend more on his ability to manipulate than to intimidate. Claudia would be more inclined to trade something she knew for something he knew, but he would have to be careful with her because how much information she gave him would depend on his ability to make her believe that she was getting as good as she gave. It wouldn't be easy, considering the fact that he didn't intend to tell her anymore than she knew already.

"Is Tom at home?"

"Yes, but he's taking a shower just now."

"I suppose you know that Harold Waterson was killed in the

Bowmans' basement last night, Claudia."

"As a matter of fact, I just finished reading the article in the paper."

"Was that the first you knew about the homicide?"

"Well, Tom told me someone had been killed over there last night, but he said you wouldn't tell him who it was. I didn't know it was Hal Waterson until I read the *Star* today."

"You managed to suppress your curiosity a long time, considering all the police activity next door."

"I try not to concern myself with things that aren't my business, Matthew. It's as much as I can do to keep up with things that do concern me."

"Weren't you even remotely interested in who was killed last night?"

"Barely, dear. I believe in leaving well enough alone, if you know what I mean."

"What are your feelings about the homicide?"

"I'm shocked and horrified, of course."

"Why? You knew Hal Waterson and Angela Bowman were having an affair."

"How do you know what I knew?" she angrily demanded.

"Angela Bowman says you were the only person she told about the affair."

"Angela isn't known for speaking the gospel, Matthew, so, I'd advise you to take what she says with a grain of salt. And even if she did tell me, which I'm not admitting for a second, who's to say that I took it in? I'd have to be a computer to store all the gossip I hear. I don't know anything about a sexual liaison between Angela Bowman and Hal Waterson. Anyone who says otherwise can't prove it by me. Besides, love affairs don't usually lead to murder you know. If they did, you'd have more homicides than you could imagine."

"This one did lead to murder, Claudia. As a matter of fact, Angela Bowman claims that you were responsible for bringing the two of them together."

"If you're referring to Felicia Waterson's fundraiser, there were dozens of people there besides Hal Waterson. I hope you're not implying that I contrived to have them meet."

"Nothing of the kind, Claudia. I'm just trying to establish the fact that you were aware of Angela's affair with the deceased."

"I know that Angela knew Hal Waterson. Where's the harm in that?"

Taking Claudia's guest list from his notebook, Matt tried another tack with her.

"Why were the Watersons invited to your party last night, Claudia?"

"The cocktail party was a fundraiser for Youth Shelter, a non-profit organization that provides social services and housing for teen-age runaways here in the District. Felicia Waterson and I are members of the Youth Shelter Advisory Board. It's customary to invite all board members and administrative staff of the organization to its fundraisers. That's why the Watersons were invited."

"Did Mrs. Waterson attend the party?"

"No, she didn't."

"Don't you find it odd that he came without her? After all, she was the board member, not him."

"He said she wasn't feeling well and that she insisted he come in her place. There was nothing odd about it."

"How long have you known the Watersons?"

"Felicia Waterson joined the board of Youth Shelter two years ago. She serves as board president and co-chairs the fundraising committee with me. I had met her before she joined the board, but I've gotten to know her infinitely better since she became co-chair of my committee."

"Since you have gotten to know her so well, how did the two of you get along?"

"Felicia's not the type of person you like. I think worship

more adequately describes the relationship she prefers. But, we got along fine, after I let her know that I didn't intend to fetch and carry for her."

"How long have you been on the board of Youth Shelter?"

"Five years. I'm vice-president of the board, too."

"Did you socialize with the Watersons often?"

"My contacts with Hal and Felicia Waterson were limited to activities involving Youth Shelter. Otherwise, I rarely saw them."

"What time did Waterson arrive at your house last night?"

"I can't say for certain. The party started at seven, but I think he came around eight or eight-thirty."

"What time did he leave?"

"About ten. Both Tom and I saw him to the door when he left."

"How do you know the exact time he left, Claudia?"

"I looked at my watch. What time was he killed?"

"We don't know yet, but it looks like you and Tom were the last people to see him alive," Matt lied.

"I don't like the sound of that, Matthew. Hal Waterson was killed at the Bowmans', not over here. As a matter of fact, I don't see why you're wasting your time questioning me when it's the Bowmans you ought to be investigating. They know a hell of a lot more about who killed Hal Waterson than I do."

"I have questioned all of the Bowmans."

"Well then, why haven't you arrested one of them? You know that Walter Bowman killed him…he probably found out about Hal Waterson's affair with Angela and killed him out of spite."

"Why don't you leave the guesswork to me, Claudia? Did you notice anything unusual about Waterson while he was at your party?"

"He was as high as a kite, but I wouldn't call that unusual considering the fact that most of the people there had had one too many. His speech was a bit slurred; but other than that, his behavior wasn't unusual at all."

"Did you notice him having a heated discussion with either Walter or Helen bowman or anyone else for that matter?'

"No, I didn't see him arguing with anyone last night. I think all the guests made a point of speaking to him before he left. Some were more obvious than others, but I don't recall anyone making a nuisance of themselves, but you may want to ask Tom. I was busy making sure everything was going smoothly, so I probably I missed a lot that went on during the party."

"Do you remember seeing either one of the Bowmans speak to Hal Waterson last night?"

"No, I don't. But that doesn't mean that they didn't speak to him. People were moving in and out of all the rooms on the first floor, and it was practically impossible to keep up with who was in what room with whom. He was here in the living room most of the time, but I do recall seeing him in the den where the bar is before he left."

"Where were the Bowmans?"

"Walter stayed in the den for the most part, and I'm almost certain that Helen was in the living room the entire time they were here. She wasn't circulating at all, but that's not unusual for her."

"I understand you ran out of ice last night."

"Who told you that? Tom bought plenty of ice for the party."

"Do you remember Angela coming over here last night?"

"Yes, but she didn't stay. She helped me to arrange some snacks on a tray out in the kitchen and then she left."

"Didn't she tell you she had brought some ice over?"

"Why would she do that? I told you we didn't ask her for any ice."

"Do you have any idea how long she had been in the kitchen before you walked in?"

"No, because I didn't open the door for her."

"How long did she stay?"

"No more than ten minutes, maybe less."

"What time was it when she left?"

"I didn't look at my watch, but it couldn't have been any later than a quarter past ten."

"Why did you ask Angela to help you with the food, Claudia? Didn't you hire the maid to do that?"

"It was a large party, Matthew. You can't expect one person to stay on top of everything. Why is Angela's visit so important? Hal Waterson was killed over there, not here."

"Angela says she got a call from someone at your party asking her to bring some ice over because you had run out. The caller was a woman who said you told her to call."

"That's a dirty lie! I didn't ask anyone to call Angela last night! The bartender was serving the drinks, and he never mentioned running out of ice to me."

"So, you deny asking someone to call her for ice."

"Yes, I deny it! But why would she lie about something like that...it doesn't make sense."

"It makes sense if someone were trying to get Angela out of the Bowman house."

"Are you saying that Hal Waterson was killed while Angela Bowman was over here?"

"It looks that way."

"I don't believe you! She couldn't have been over here any longer than ten minutes. How can you be certain that he died during that ten minutes?"

"We're not certain, but everything is pointing toward the fifteen minutes after Hal Waterson left your party."

"I don't believe anyone from my party called Angela. It's just a lie Walter Bowman made up to drag me and Tom into this mess! We didn't have anything to do with Hal Waterson's death, and I'll be damned if you can prove otherwise, Matthew Alexander," Claudia shouted as she angrily gripped the arms of her chair.

"Calm down, Claudia. No one's accusing you or Tom of anything."

"Whose word do you have other than Angela's that someone from my party actually called her?"

"I can't discuss that with you, Claudia, but I will need the names and addresses of your maid and bartender." All things considered, Matt had doubts about Angela's story too, but he wasn't going to dismiss the story just on Claudia's denial before he talked to other witnesses at the party.

"Did Felicia Waterson know her husband was having an affair with Angela Bowman?"

Recognizing the trap that had been laid for her, Claudia cunningly replied, "If I didn't know about the affair, how would I know whether anyone else knew?"

"Come off it, Claudia! You probably know as much about what went on as Angela Bowman!"

"Prove it!" she defiantly challenged. "Talk is cheap. It's one thing for you to say that I knew, but proving it is another matter altogether. You don't scare me."

"I'm not trying to scare you, Claudia. From where I stand, Angela Bowman is the prime suspect in our investigation even though she swears she didn't kill Waterson. There's a chance that she didn't kill him, if she's telling the truth. Harold Waterson is dead, and the dead tell no tales. All I'm trying to do is to find out what really happened last night. If you give me a hard time, you'll increase Angela's chances of being indicted. It's up to you."

Matt sensed that Claudia was genuinely fond of Angela Bowman, and he hoped his little speech would soften her up long enough to get some credible information from her.

For her part, Claudia was moved by what he said about Angela, but she decided that two could play the same game.

"Angela didn't kill Hal Waterson. The person you ought to arrest and indict is that idiot father of hers."

"That's your opinion, Claudia, for all it's worth, unless you personally saw him pull the trigger. I need facts, not useless opinions."

"The article in the paper said that he was shot to death. Did you know that Walter Bowman owns a gun?" she asked.

"Yes, we know about his revolver."

"Was Walter's gun used to kill him?"

"We don't know."

"Where was the body found?"

"In the family room in the Bowmans' basement."

"Why was he there?"

"You know the answer to that question as well as I do."

"Angela. She lived in the basement, so anyone down there would be visiting her."

"It's my turn, now," Matt insisted. "Did you know that Angela and Waterson were having an affair?"

"Yes, she told me several months ago."

"Can you be more specific about when she told you?"

"It was at our annual Christmas fundraiser last December. She said that they had been seeing each other since they met at Felicia's fundraiser in September. She also told me when they were meeting and where...that sort of thing. I was concerned, but I figured she's a big girl. I don't volunteer advice unless I'm asked, and she didn't ask for any."

"Has she mentioned their relationship to you since that time?"

"About a month ago she told me that Hal wanted her to move to New York City to work in his business there, but she wasn't going. That's all she said."

"Did you tell anyone about their affair?"

Claudia considered the question before replying, "No, I never told anyone. I don't blab friends' confidences around town."

"Did anyone ever ask you about their affair?"

"No, never."

Changing the subject Matt asked: "What do you think of Angela's relationship with her father, Claudia?"

"Very unhealthy for her. He broke up her marriage, you know. Although, I have often wondered just how much Angela cared about Gary if she allowed Walter to break them up. It may be that she simply used Walter to get out of a bad marriage. Angela's been known to take the easy way out before, but I'm not telling you anything you don't already know, Matthew. This is ancient history for you, isn't it?"

Matt didn't respond, so Claudia continued:

"I can't stand Walter Bowman. He's arrogant, selfish, and he doesn't give a damn about anyone but himself. Oh, he spreads it on real thick about how much he loves his daughter, but he can't stand the thought of her leaving home for good. He claims that the men she chooses aren't good enough for her when, what he really means is that they aren't good enough for him. Walter treated Gary like dirt. He didn't rest until he had broken them up. But Angela went along with his program, so fundamentally, she's no better than he is."

"Her mother says that Angela can't stand her father's disapproval, and that's why she left her husband."

"I don't buy that for a minute. Angela had her own reason for leaving Gary. Walter simply provided the means for her to do it without assuming total responsibility herself. If you ask me, Helen is no better than Angela when it comes to Walter. He treats them both like they were children. Personally, I like Helen and Angela, but I can't stand the way they allow Walter to manipulate them. I've told Angela so, too. She's spineless when it comes to her father, and he knows it. I detest Walter Bowman more than anyone I know."

"A woman after my own heart," Matt thought, deciding then and there that Claudia Martin possessed one redeeming quality after all.

"He gives the impression that you aren't his favorite person either, Claudia."

"Score one for me, Matthew. I'd have some serious doubts about myself if Walter liked me. He's never liked the fact that Angela and I are friends. He thinks I'm a bad influence on her, if you can believe that. Hal Waterson's murder last night ought to open his eyes on that score," she smugly replied.

"Did you know that Angela is seeing Gary Washington again?"

"No, I didn't know it, but I'm not surprised. She needed someone to get Hal Waterson off her case. Do you think Gary killed him?"

Matt ignored her question.

"Do you know Gary Washington, personally?"

"Yes, I know him. Angela brought him over a couple of times when they were living together in Southeast."

"What do you think of him?"

"He's younger than she is and damned good looking. I don't blame Angela, I would have married him, too; and to hell with what anyone else thought, especially Walter. It was obvious that Gary was crazy about Angela. He worshiped the ground she walked on. Isn't it ironic that you're investigating Hal Waterson's death? I would have given anything to see the look on Walter's face when you showed up last night. Sometimes I believe that there is justice in the world after all," Claudia laughed.

"Why didn't Helen Bowman stop her husband from interfering in Angela's marriage?"

"You must be joking, Matthew! Helen's just as spineless as Angela when it comes to Walter. Sometimes I think he has the two of them mesmerized, the little pipsqueak. If I were married to him, I'd give him hell for breakfast, lunch, and dinner. It's simply appalling the way he dominates and controls them. It would be funny if it weren't so pathetic. Helen hates his guts, you know, but she doesn't have the nerve to admit to herself, let alone anyone else. Helen doesn't need Walter; she's got her own money that her father left her when he died five years ago. She told me so herself. Walter tried to talk her into letting him invest it for her; but she absolutely refused. I have to give her credit for having that much sense. Have you talked to Helen, yet?"

"Yes, I have."

"What does she have to say?"

"She says she doesn't know who killed Waterson or why."

"Does she? That's very interesting, Matthew. Who did Walter accuse of killing him, me?"

"Not quite," Matt laughed. "He says he doesn't know anything about the homicide either."

"That's bullshit. Somebody over there killed him."

"I have my own ideas on the subject, Claudia."

"I need a drink. What would you like?"

"Nothing, thanks. I'm on duty."

"There's a fresh pot of coffee in the kitchen. Can I interest you in a cup?"

Matt refused the coffee too.

"What type of person is Felicia Waterson, Claudia?"

Claudia thought for a minute before replying, "She tries very hard to show concern about the poor and their problems, but there's always that distance of hers. Now that I think about it, I don't believe she's as cold as she is out of touch with the realities of living outside her own world over there in Georgetown. She prefers not to deal with realities like child molestation and teen-age prostitution, the kind of problems that are par for the course at Youth Shelter. Felicia can be very charming to you or me personally, but give her a group of runaways who have been living on the streets and she'll wilt right before your eyes. She's simply not up to it."

"Were the Watersons very close?"

"I don't know anything about their personal relationship.

Felicia didn't confide in me. I saw her more often than him, but we're not bosom buddies by any stretch of the imagination. She's very stand-offish, even with the white board members. Personality traits are usually consistent, so I wouldn't expect her to be a warm affectionate wife. But, who knows, she may have worshipped the ground he walked on."

"Do you know their son?"

"No, I've never met him. But, a board member who knows the family says he's a spoiled brat who can do no wrong as far as Felicia is concerned. The same board member told me that he terrorized half a dozen prep schools from Virginia to Massachusetts. She also said that Hal Waterson didn't get along with his son, especially after the boy came home to attend college."

"Who is this board member?"

"Marjorie Rhoades."

"Do you have her address and telephone number?"

"Yes, but don't tell her that I put you on to her. She's very particular about who knows her telephone number."

"Don't worry, I won't mention your name. Why do you think Waterson was putting pressure on Angela to move to New York?"

"It's obvious, isn't it? Someone was putting pressure on him to give her up...probably Felicia. He wanted to have his cake and eat it too, typical male behavior if you ask me."

"Do you have any reason to suspect that Felicia Waterson knew that her husband was having an affair with Angela Bowman?"

Claudia's almond-shaped eyes narrowed sharply as a hint of malice crossed her face ever so swiftly. If Matt had blinked, he would have missed it. As it was, he suspected that she was being less than candid when she replied, "No, I don't. Just call it woman's intuition. Really, Matthew, who do you think was putting the squeeze on him if it wasn't Felicia?"

"You never know, Claudia. This case is full of surprises."

"That's putting it mildly. I'm sorry Hal Waterson was killed, but, I'd give anything to be a fly on the wall when Felicia explains where he died to the Foxhall Road crowd. That's a real hoot...killed in Walter Bowman's house. I call that just retribution; and it couldn't have happened to a more deserving reprobate than Walter, even at the risk of involving Helen and Angela."

"Either Angela or Helen Bowman is as likely to have killed Waterson as Walter Bowman, Claudia. For that matter, either you or Tom might have killed him."

Matt had finally laid his cards on the table and true to form, Claudia seized the challenge without a moment's hesitation. All of her senses snapped to attention; and in her urgency to defend home and hearth, self and mate, she rose from her perch on the edge of her chair like a blazing phoenix rising up through the flames of indignation and false accusation, ready for the kill.

"You're not dealing with a couple of idiots, Matthew Alexander! Your case isn't nearly as hot as it will get if you try to drag Tom and me into this mess! We weren't born yesterday! Try to pin this murder on us, and there will be hell to pay!"

"Since you protest your innocence so strongly, Claudia, maybe you can tell me where Tom was while Angela was in your kitchen last night?"

"How do I know where he was!? This is a big house, and Tom is free to come and go as he pleases without informing me of his whereabouts. He could have been anywhere, including the toilet. But, that's beside the point. I know damned well that he wasn't next door killing Hal Waterson."

"It seems to me that if you don't know where he was, you also don't know where he wasn't."

"You're right, Matthew. I can't prove he was here; but you can't prove he was over there, either, so that makes us even. But, why question me about Tom's movements when you can ask him for yourself?"

"I'll do just that," Matt replied before crossing the living room to the intercom on the wall near the foyer.

"You can come down, now, Tom. I think you've heard enough."

Tom Martin gasped in surprise, gave a high-pitched nervous laugh, and tried to recover his composure as he sheepishly replied, "I see you peeped our hold card, Matthew," over the intercom.

Claudia's composure faltered briefly, but she quickly recovered to the extent of denying that she knew the intercom was on.

"I don't miss much, Claudia. The fact that Hal Waterson was killed in the Bowmans' basement doesn't automatically prove that one of them is the killer. If Angela Bowman is telling the truth about the call she got from your party, that opens up a whole new realm of possibilities with respect to who had opportunity to kill Waterson. Either you or Tom could have watched Waterson after he left your house, saw him stop Angela Bowman in front of her house, saw her take him into the basement, and then asked someone to place the call. Under those circumstances, getting Angela over here between ten and ten-fifteen would explain a lot."

"You're only guessing because you don't have a shred of proof that we did anything of the kind. Anyway, why would Tom or I want to kill Hal Waterson? It's absurd."

"Murder is often absurd, Claudia, and its always a crime."

"Explain to me, if you can, how we could have killed Hal Waterson when we don't even own a gun?"

Tom Martin quietly entered the living room and kept his head down as he walked over to the sofa.

"I should have known that we couldn't fool you, Matthew," he sheepishly grinned in an unsuccessful attempt to recover his composure. "I can explain about the intercom. The only reason I had it on was..."

"Skip the explanation, Tom. Why you were listening isn't important because lies can be woven only so tightly before they begin to unravel."

"I don't have any reason to lie," Tom protested. "I didn't have anything to do with Hal Waterson's death."

Tom looked even fatter than usual as his ample body sank into the plush sofa. His buttocks disappeared into the back of the cushion while his stomach perched on the front like an unwelcome guest. Tom's usual affability disappeared as he struggled to come back from the humiliation of being caught eavesdropping. He felt foolish and looked the part, too.

"Did you speak to Hal Waterson when he was at your party last night, Tom?"

"Yes, I spoke to him shortly after he arrived."

"What did you talk about?"

"Nothing in particular. You know what conversation is like at a party. What we talked about can't be that important, can it?"

"What you said could be crucial considering the fact that you and Claudia were two of the last people to see him alive."

"I don't remember exactly what I said to him, Matthew. I'd been drinking at least a couple of hours before he arrived."

"Did you see Waterson having a heated conversation with anyone while he was here?"

"I saw him talking to several people, but none of them seemed to be arguing with him."

"Tell me what you did after Waterson left your party, Tom."

"Nothing much...oh yes, I remember that I went downstairs to get some extra bottles of liquor and mixer from the bar down there."

"Does your basement have an outside entrance like the Bowmans' basement?"

"Yes. There's a door that leads out into the backyard."

"Did you go out the basement door while you were down there?"

"Absolutely not. I had no reason to use that door last night. I collected the extra bottles of liquor and brought them upstairs to the bar in the den just like I said."

"Did you see Angela Bowman when she was over here last night?"

"No. I didn't know she had been here until I heard you ask Claudia how long she stayed."

"Did you ask anyone to call Angela to ask for ice?"

"No! I bought four twenty-five pound bags of ice for the party. We didn't run out of ice. You can ask the bartender if you don't believe me."

"How well did you know Hal Waterson, Tom?"

Tom looked at Claudia before he answered, but she was as sober as a judge and just as inscrutable. She returned Tom's gaze intently until he replied that he knew Hal Waterson only through his wife's charity work.

"Did you ever have any business dealing with Waterson? You're both in real estate."

Claudia fixed her attention on Tom once more as he nervously protested, "No, I never did, Matthew. He's way out of my league."

"I understand that you have sizeable real estate holdings in the District and in Prince Georges County."

"I do own some property, but I wouldn't describe my holdings as sizeable. They aren't that extensive."

"Waterson's primary business interests were in developing and selling real estate weren't they?"

"Yes, I believe so."

"How long have you invested in real estate in the District, Tom?"

"Twenty-five years."

"And during that time you've never had any business dealings with one of the largest developers in the city?"

"No, I never have," Tom nervously replied.

"You're wasting your time with us, Matthew. You should be questioning the Bowmans about their dealings with Hal Waterson," Claudia insisted.

"That's right," Tom chimed in. "It's ridiculous to believe Claudia and I are involved in his murder. That call could have been made by anyone from anywhere, if there really was a call."

"Tom, why did you say 'who is he?' when I told you someone had been killed at the Bowmans' last night?"

Tom was incredulous. "Did I say that?"

"Yes, you did. How did you know the victim was a `he' and not a `she'?"

"I didn't know!" Tom shouted while thrusting his body forward.

Tom's stomach lost its forward perch on the cushion as it dropped over the edge and strained mightily against the buttons of his custom-made, snug-fitting shirt. Matt fully expected the corpulent mass to explode from its buttoned restraint any second.

"I don't know why I said 'he'. It had to be force of habit, Matthew. Everyone assumes male gender until we know otherwise," he insisted.

"You could just as logically asked whether the corpse was male or female," Matt insisted, "but you didn't."

Claudia had watched the discussion between the two men with growing alarm before she interrupted.

"I don't believe Tom said 'who is he'."

"I know for a fact that he did, Claudia. I wrote it down in my notebook at the time." He flipped to the page where he made the entry.

"Did you tape the conversation without Tom's knowledge?"

"That wasn't necessary, Claudia. Walter Bowman was there when he said it."

"Everyone's recall is subject to error, Matthew, and I think you made a mistake when you heard Tom refer to the body as 'he'. The difference between 'she' and 'he' is ever so slight, especially when a person is upset by something as dreadful as a murder in his best friend's house. Isn't that so. Tom?"

"Yes, that's right, now that I think about it I don't remember saying 'he', Matthew. You must have misunderstood what I said."

"You've got a hell of a nerve tying to hustle me, Claudia! I ought to run both of you in for lying about the facts in a murder investigation!" Matt angrily threatened.

"We're not under oath," Claudia shouted, just as angrily.

"You're lying through your teeth," Matt shouted back looking first at Claudia and then at Tom, who preferred looking at his shoes to facing the detective's ire.

"You're trying it implicate us in a murder!" Claudia screamed. "What the hell do you expect us to do, thank you!?"

"If you try to hustle me again, I'll arrest both of you...right now!"

"Let's calm down," Tom pleaded. "We want to cooperate, Matthew, but you have us at a disadvantage. We have to protect ourselves. Who wouldn't under the circumstances?"

"If you're innocent, how can the truth hurt you?"

"Whose truth?" Claudia insisted. "When you're in court, truth is a damned good lawyer and the money to pay him and whoever else is on the take. I'll be damned if you stick us with Waterson's murder."

"You will be arrested, indicted, and convicted if you're guilty! You have my word on that, Claudia!"

For once Claudia was at a loss for words, but the looks she gave Matt was worth a thousand vulgar ones. Tom sat trance-like daring not to speak for fear of complicating an already bad situation.

"I need the names, addresses, and telephone numbers of the maid and bartender who were here last night," Matt said to Claudia as he prepared to leave.

Claudia swept out of the living room in a huff of indignation. "I'll be in touch, Tom."

Tom didn't reply. His eyes followed Matt into the foyer, but his thoughts were paralyzed with fear. Taking Claudia's lead, he had gone along with her decision to tough it out with Detective Lieutenant Matthew Alexander, but it was clear to Tom that Claudia's strategy had seriously eroded their position with the DCPD Homicide Division.

For his part, Matt was certain that Tom and Claudia were hiding something. He waited for Claudia in the foyer. Several minutes later, she stormed out of her kitchen and thrust the slip of paper she was carrying under his nose and slammed the door after he left.

Matt left the Martins satisfied with the day's offerings so far. The information he got from Angela Bowman, Tom, and Claudia Martin went a long way toward making sense of what happened last night...if a murder ever made sense. He was satisfied with the progress he had made in the case, but he still had a long way to go. Floribunda Lane remained inundated with police cars. Since there were very few officers in sight, Matt guessed that Lloyd had broadened the search to adjacent alleys, and streets. More importantly, it meant that the gun was still missing; and the farther afield they searched, the less likely they were to find it. Failing to produce a murder weapon would dilute the strength of their case, as Chief Carter had pointed out earlier. Matt decided that the gun was going to be a thorn in his side one way or the other. He debated whether to go directly to his officer or to the Watersons'. Tired of confronting witnesses, he decided to give himself a break by tying up loose-ends in his office.

# (HAPTER X

The ride from Floribunda Lane to Fourth District Headquarters on Georgia Avenue took less than ten minutes. Matt stopped at the fast-food restaurant across the street from Headquarters and ordered a dinner of hamburgers and French fries, although he would have vastly preferred Carla's pot roast. Waiting in line at the carry-out, he guessed that if he had a nickel for every hamburger Fourth District officers had bought there, he could retire from the force a rich man. The wait in line took more time than the ride across town.

While he waited for his order, Matt wondered how long Lloyd would search for the gun. Lloyd had to look long enough to make good on his promise to Chief Carter, but he would have to stop before he made himself look foolish. Matt was certain that Lloyd's personal supervision of the search would be over at the end of the day, gun or no gun. However, with or without a weapon, one of the Bowmans was certain to be charged with the homicide. From what Matt had learned today, it would most likely be Angela. While her motive was still murky, she had the clearest link to the deceased; and she had also admitted being the last person to see him alive with the exception of the killer, if they weren't one and the same.

Matt was almost certain Lloyd would go for an arrest on Monday, which would leave him very little time to sort out the facts that had surfaced so far. He was also certain that if Angela didn't kill Waterson, her best chance lay in his ability to go beyond the facts as they presented themselves, to disregard the obvious conclusions, and to ferret out the obscure motives of the real killer...assuming of course that Angela Bowman was innocent. The question of her guilt worried him more than he was consciously willing to admit; but when weighed against Lloyd's inclination to rush to judgement, she would need an advocate desperately and for better or worse, he was the best she had for the time being.

On the way to his second-floor office, Matt noted that the level of activity in the first floor area reserved for the public reflected business as usual. From the number of people waiting in the bail line, he guessed that the lower-level holding cells were filled to capacity as usual on the week-end. The neighborhood surrounding Fourth District Headquarters was primarily working class residential with almost no bars or night spots. The bulk of their weekend detainees consisted of the overflow from downtown. Their holding cells were cramped most week-ends, but the Fourth District's accommodations were the best the city had to offer its criminal element.

Fourth District was the last regional Headquarters to be constructed in the series of four serving the city of Washington, D.C. The building was seven years old and had cost roughly ten million dollars to construct. An ultra-modern structure of steel, tinted glass, and polished granite, it rose three stories above the ground and descended one below. The first floor administrative offices were shared by the Fourth District, the DCPD Homicide Division, the forensics laboratory, the Fifteenth Precinct, and two departments out of the Chief of Police's office: Recruitment and Community Relations. The building's best feature was a large conference hall situated on the east side of the first floor opposite the administrative offices where city-wide administrative staff meetings and in-service training classes were routinely scheduled. Daily briefings and detail assignments were also issued from the hall prior to the beginning of each shift.

The open space in front of the main desk was the only area of the building unrestricted to the general public. The front desk sat on the left as you entered the building through bullet-proof glass doors facing Georgia Avenue. The public area extended from the Georgia Avenue entrance to the steel-reinforced, electronically operated door marked "RESTRICTED" that opened onto the main north-south corridor, where Matt was now standing. The building had one small elevator, so the central stairway accommodated more than its share of foot traffic from officers coming and going during shift changes.

Second floor office space was reserved for detectives and those officers assigned to office-based detail. Some offices had double occupancy, but most housed four or more detectives. The third floor held another conference room, lockers, and a lounge-gym combination that was open to all staff. Matt noted that the building was quiet compared to its usual din. He was pleased that most of the second-shift officers were out of the building already because going up the stairs could be downright hazardous during a shift change when everyone was coming down. He hadn't been in his office long enough to sit down behind his desk when Carl Davis walked in from across the hall.

"Matthew Alexlander, my man! What's going down these days?" Davis asked as he stepped inside Matt's office.

"Homicide is going down, Davis."

"You can say that again, Jack. I heard about it on the car radio, read about it in the newspaper, and saw a report on television before I left home today. Looks like you're on the hot seat this time, Lieutenant."

"I'll manage, Davis. I always have."

"I hate to rain on your parade, Jack, but this is the type of case where even if you win you lose. It's going to be a real ball-buster, but better you than me, Lieutenant."

"Your compassion overwhelms me, Davis."

"You'll need a hell of a lot more than compassion if you don't solve this case PDQ. You'll need nine lives, and you don't look like a cat to me." Carl Davis laughed as he lounged against the door jamb, looking more disreputable than the low-life characters he was supposed to keep off the streets.

"I'm not worried, Davis."

"I'm worried enough for both of us, Alexander."

"Give me a break, man, and save your energy for your own cases. The last I heard, hookers are still peddling it from one end of the District to the other."

"What can I say, Jack? Vice is like death and taxes, it's not going anywhere. Do-Gooders carry on about saving junkies and prostitutes from themselves, but they love it out there. I don't hurt myself cleaning up the streets because you can't keep the ones who like it away...they wallow in it. The first lesson you learn working vice is that corrupt people create vice, not the other way round. Sure, some innocent people get caught up in it, but what's to stop them from walking away. It's a free country, Jack."

"As much as I'd like to shoot the breeze, Davis, I have a hell of a lot of work to do. You'll have to catch me later, man."

"Hey! No problem, Jack. I'll be on my merry way because you're going to need all the time you can get to solve the Waterson homicide."

After Carl Davis left, Matt considered the irony of the son of the most prominent minister in the District of Columbia working vice as a profession. Davis not only worked it, he enjoyed it. Davis' affinity for street life had spawned countless rumors to the effect that: He was pimping prostitutes out of a sleaze joint downtown; he was in the employ of the local mob; he was romantically involved with the most notorious hooker on Fourteenth Street; or that he was a dealer, a pusher, a junkie, or all three. Matt dismissed the gossip for what it was, concluding that the rumors weren't based on fact as much as they were on Davis' affinity for District low-life. Most of the officers who worked with Carl Davis didn't know what he was capable of because they didn't really know him. He was an enigma. Matt had known him for seven years, but he would be hard pressed to make a definitive statement about Davis' character one way or the other.

Davis was obviously intelligent and well-educated, but his personality was murky at best. Despite his lackluster spiel on deterring vice, he had been known to crack down on street crime with a vengeance, but his pursuit record was inconsistent. Davis could be relentless in running what he called "dregs" to ground. On the other hand, he could also show exceptional tolerance in allowing them to ply their trade. His ambivalence was tolerated because he had a camaraderie with the District's pimps, prostitutes, and junkies that none of the other officers remotely approached. He could get information out of them when no one else could. He was so sympatico, in fact, that it was sometimes questionable as to where his loyalties lay. Davis was an outsider inside both systems. He wasn't completely trusted by the dregs or his fellow officers. As a consequence, he would periodically feel the need to demonstrate his loyalty to the legitimate system. Then all hell would break loose on the streets, and the smart dregs went underground until Davis finished paying his establishment dues.

Carl Davis looked a good deal younger than his forty years, and dressed like a man half his age. Many of the female rookies beat a path to his door. Some cooled when they discovered that he was married, but others didn't care. The rule against romantic fraternization among the officers got lip service and little more than that from Lloyd, who saw no point in creating problems for himself as long as the officers were on separate details. Davis' conquests were dropped as easily as they were acquired, with few adverse consequences to himself. For all his boyish charm and looks, Carl Davis had a mean streak that was as formidable as it was unselective when he was angry. Consequently, he rarely had trouble with his women.

After Carl Davis left, Matt closed the heat vent and opened the windows. The cool air was refreshing as it circulated through the over-heated office. After two and a half hours of steady work, he heard footsteps coming toward the office. Jake walked in and collapsed into his chair.

"Did Lloyd find the gun?"

"Heck no! We must have searched all the way from Floribunda to the Maryland line. I don't remember when I've worked so hard, man."

"It figures, and Lloyd was so certain that he would find it. Now, I'll have to take the flack because he came up empty-handed."

"He was pretty damned sore when we didn't find it," Jake admitted.

"Did you locate Gary Washington?"

"Yeah. He's downstairs in Interrogation Room A."

"Where did you find him?"

"At his mother's place on Alabama Avenue. I went to his apartment on Good Hope Road first, but he wasn't there. I got his mother's address from the building superintendent."

"What did he do when you showed up at his mother's house?"

"Nothing. I told him he was wanted for questioning in connection with the Waterson homicide. He came peaceably."

"What time did you leave Floribunda?"

"I told Cullison you wanted me to fetch Gary Washington from southeast, so he let me go about six-thirty. I'll bet a fat man they're still searching."

"It's too dark. I'm sure they've thrown in the towel by now."

"You know how stubborn Cullison can be once he sets his mind on something, man. The Bowmans must be a bunch of magicians. That gun has disappeared into thin air."

"I know what you mean," Matt agreed. "Did Lloyd search the house thoroughly?"

"We searched it until we were blue in the face, but he didn't find a damned thing connected with the homicide. We raked through the mulch Bowman put around the trees and shrubs yesterday, checked holes in the ground, looked down the sewer opening on the sidewalk, searched the garages and cars in the service alley, picked through garbage for the entire neighborhood and still came up empty-handed."

"Did you search the woods near Rock Creek?"

"We searched most of the woods along Seventeenth Street before I left."

"Well, I guess Lloyd shot his wad today, Jake."

Jake laughed out loud, "Man, you can say that again. That was the hardest I've ever seen that racist work. He definitely earned his money, today."

"If Waterson was really shot between ten and ten-fifteen, that leaves just fifteen minutes for the killer to get rid of the gun. Not much time is it? How long do you think it would take to run from the Bowman house to Rock Creek and back again, Jake?"

"I suppose if you were in good shape, and kept up a steady pace all the way there and back, you could do it in seven or eight minutes, ten at the outside. There's a steep winding path from Seventeenth Street down to the creek bed, Matt. It was as slippery as hell today, so I know it would have been murder getting down there last night. If someone tried it, they must have been sure-footed as a mountain goat, especially in the dark."

"Not if they had a flashlight."

Jake was unconvinced. "I can't see anybody in a hurry

running all the way down to the creek, man."

"That gun has to be somewhere, Jake. How many pairs of rubber hip boots do we have?"

"How the hell would I know? Cullison hasn't give me any time off to go fishing lately. What do you need with rubber hip boots?"

"I want to search the area of the creek near the path."

"Count me out, Matt. You know I can't swim."

"You're not likely to drown in Rock Creek," Matt laughed. "Find out how many pairs of boots we have, Jake. I want ten men in that area of the creek by nine-thirty tomorrow morning. Rock Creek was high and moving fast yesterday, so if the gun was thrown in, it's probably in the Chesapeake by now; but there's a remote chance that it might have lodged between the rocks on the creek bed. We may as well check out the possibility since you've already searched the woods. Did you run the computer check on the priors, yet?"

"Damn, Matt! It slipped my mind. I'll start it now."

"Here's the list of suspects' names and addresses. Run a gun registration check while you're on the terminal, Jake. It'll be interesting to see what turns up." The telephone rang as Jake was leaving the room.

"For you, Matt. It's Cullison."

"Now what?"

Jake's curiosity kept him in the office until Matt rang off.

"What did he want this time?"

"To see me in his office. I thought I had seen the last of him today."

"Cullison's just like a bad penny, he keeps turning up when you least expect it," Jake replied referring to Lloyd's unannounced excursions through the second and third floors of the building.

"He had better be quick about it because I have a ton of work to finish before I leave tonight."

Lloyd was sitting at his desk with a pensive look on his face when Matt entered his first floor office. He gave Matt a short status report on the search, which confirmed Jake's account but in much kinder terms. Matt brought Lloyd up to date on what he had learned from Angela Bowman and the Martins'. Lloyd was quick to point out that they were on the cutting edge of time. Matt agreed, but insisted that the homicide division was moving as fast as possible under the circumstances. He informed Lloyd that Gary Washington was downstairs waiting to be questioned and that he was going to interrogate the rest of the immediate circle of witnesses on Monday. Lloyd remained apprehensive in spite of Matt's assurances that the investigation was moving well.

They left Lloyd's office together. Lloyd left the building on his way home. Matt continued downstairs to the interrogation rooms. The lower-level holding cells occupied most of the space downstairs. The rest of the underground space was divided between the large forensics laboratory, the property and storage room, the line-up room, and three interrogation rooms. Matt acknowledged the duty officer outside the holding cells before he entered the room marked "A".

Gary Washington sat facing the door at the large square table in the middle of the room. From the look on his face, it was obvious that he was prepared for the worst. Matt's first impression of Gary Washington was that he was expensively dressed and looked too young for Angela Bowman. Gary was wearing the latest in trend-setting mens' wear: designer jeans, a white crew neck sweater, an expensive brown leather bomber jacket, and a pair of loafers that cost a small fortune. Gary was handsome in an over-done, self-absorbed fashion...the type who never went anywhere unless he was looking his best. Matt imagined him going from one mirror to the next, compulsively checking his appearance and combing his hair, which was cut short and worn in the latest style...relaxed and brushed away from the forehead in waves. Gary wore a heavy gold chain around his neck, a diamond pinkie ring on his left hand, and an expensive watch, all of which made Matt wonder just what he did for a living. His lean face was clean shaven; and his smooth brown skin was accentuated by a pair of gold-rimmed tinted glasses that couldn't have been prescription-shades made him look cool while glasses would have added a sour note of imperfection. Gary Washington stood when Matt entered the room. They shook hands across the table. Matt introduced himself and sat down opposite Gary. Gary removed his shades.

Being as clothes conscious has he was, the first thing Gary noticed about Lieutenant Matthew Alexander was his clothes which consisted of an old camel-colored jacket that couldn't be cashmere and a pair of good wool gabardine slacks. The jacket didn't do anything for the slacks in Gary's opinion, and his shirt and tie weren't worth mentioning. Gary also noticed that he was at least six-feet-two-inches tall, weighed well over two hundred pounds and seemed to be in excellent physical condition. He was dark-skinned with high cheekbones, black hair, and a strong angular face with a neatly trimmed mustache over well-formed lips. His short natural hair style, though well-cut, was hopelessly out-of-date; and his wire-rimmed glasses didn't do anything for his looks. Gary decided that while he wasn't bad looking, Lieutenant Matthew Alexander lacked style. Clothes aside, however, Gary was very uneasy in his presence because he sensed that Matthew Alexander wasn't the type to back down in a fight. He looked like he wouldn't mind kicking your butt if it needed to be done. Gary's heightened anxiety level wasn't helped any by Matt's relaxed demeanor and his six-inch height advantage.

Matt pushed his chair away from the table, rested his left ankle on his right knee, massaged it thoughtfully, and began questioning Gary Washington by taking him through the usual procedural questions about his background. He was surprised to learn that Gary was just twenty-five years old…five years younger than Angela. He completed the background information and moved on to Gary's relationship with his estranged wife.

Gary explained the sequence of events surrounding his marriage and separation from Angela Bowman. And while he didn't add anything to what Matt had previously learned from other sources, his explanation was important because it pointed out how emotionally devastating the separation had been for him. Gary's hatred of Walter Bowman was evident as he repeatedly stressed the role that Bowman had played in breaking up his marriage.

"When was the last time you saw Angela Bowman?" Gary hesitated before answering:

"I saw her last night."

"Have you been seeing her regularly?"

"She called me about a month ago and asked if she could come over and talk to me."

"About what?"

"About us getting back together."

"Did she tell you about a relationship she was having with another man?"

"Yeah, she mentioned it."

"Who was the person she mentioned?"

"Harold Waterson, that dude who was killed over there last night?"

"What did Angela tell you about him?"

"She said the dude was giving her a hard time; and she wanted him out of her life. She told him to back off but he kept bothering her."

"What was he doing to Angela that annoyed her so much?"

"Calling her all the time and putting pressure on her to take a job in New York."

"Did she say why he was doing these things?"

"Yeah, she said she had been seeing the dude. But that didn't make any difference to me, man. She's still my wife, and I love her. You get married for better or worse. I didn't like it but I didn't hold it against her either. Angela was very confused when we split up. I mean...you know...he took advantage of her when she was vulnerable; otherwise, she never would have gotten involved with him. It wasn't her fault, man."

Matt thought back to Claudia's description of Gary's devotion to Angela and decided she was right on the money.

"Did Angela visit you at your apartment in Southeast, yesterday?"

"Yeah. She came over to my place around six o'clock yesterday evening."

"How long did she stay?"

"She was there about an hour before we went out to dinner."

"Where did you go to dinner?" Gary described a similar sequence of events as Angela up to the time she dropped him off at his apartment after dinner.

"Did you ever meet Angela's lover?" Matt asked to see if Gary would grab the bait.

"No! I never met the creep; and he wasn't her lover, man!"

"They weren't kissing cousins, Washington. But for the sake of argument, how would you describe the relationship she had with him?"

"I told you before, man. She made a mistake when she got involved with that Waterson dude. She didn't want to have anything more to do with him."

Playing a hunch, Matt leaned across the table and shouted into Gary's face, "Look Washington! Don't lie to me! You had better come clean about Waterson, or I'll come down on you like a ton of bricks! I'm talking about murder, you jive-ass chump! You saw Waterson recently, and I want to know where and when!" Matt shouted as he leaned across the table in Gary's face.

Gary was visibly shaken, but he stuck by his statement that

he had never met Waterson.

"Do you own a gun, Washington?"

"No, I don't."

"Does your wife own a gun?"

"Hell no, man! Why would Angela need a gun?"

"To kill Waterson, for starters."

"That's a lie!" Gary shouted. Angela didn't kill the motherfucker, but I should have!"

"Watch what you say, Washington unless you mean it!"

"Angela didn't kill him, man! I know she didn't do it!"

"Maybe you killed him for her."

"I didn't kill him! I already told you that!"

"Why should I believe you, Washington? He was going with your wife. Most men would have killed him for a lot less. Are you any different from most men?"

"That's a dirty lie! She wasn't sleeping with him!"

"That's right. She wasn't sleeping with him, she was having sex with him; but let's get back to what you and Angela did after she dropped you off at your place in Southeast."

"I waited until she drove off, then I went up to my apartment."

"Did anyone see you go up to your apartment?"

"No. I didn't see anyone in the lobby when I went up."

Matt's feelers went out as he instantly recognized something less than the truth.

"I don't believe you went up to your apartment, Washington. I think you followed Angela home to make sure she didn't meet Harold Waterson last night. Isn't that so, Washington?"

"I did follow her in my car," Gary reluctantly admitted, "but it was only to make sure she got home safely. I followed her to Sixteenth and Floribunda. After I saw her turn onto Floribunda, I drove back to Southeast."

"It's a pity you didn't stay longer, Washington. Angela met Harold Waterson in front of her house last night right after she parked her car. But I'm sure you saw the two of them with your own eyes."

"I didn't see anybody, man. I told you I made a right on Floribunda after she turned left. I drove over to Fourteenth Street, and then I drove south to Columbia Road. I stopped to get gas at the filling station on the corner of Columbia Road and Eighteenth and I was home by ten-thirty." Matt was interrupted by a knock on the door. He got up to see who it was.

"What's up, Jake?"

"Gary Washington's uncle is in our office," Jake whispered. "He came into the building raising holy hell, wanting to know where his nephew was being held and whether he's been arrested. He cooled off when I explained that we were only questioning him, but now he's demanding to talk to his nephew and to see you, Matt. He's a feisty little guy," Jake grinned. "He can't be over five-feet-three-inches tall and a hundred and twenty pounds soaking wet, but to see him throw his weight around you'd think he was Muhammad Ali."

"Just what I don't need, Jake...an irate relative. Is Sam still in the lab? If he is, tell him not to leave until I finish questioning Gary Washington. I want Washington's picture and fingerprints before he leaves. Tell the uncle to hold his horses. I'll talk to him after I finish with the nephew."

"Did anyone see you in your apartment building after ten-thirty last night, Washington?"

"I already told you I don't remember seeing anybody in the lobby when I got back."

"You lied before, you're probably lying now."

"I'm not lying this time. I really did get back at ten-thirty."

"That doesn't mean a thing if it can't be verified by witnesses."

"Why do I need witnesses? I'm telling you the truth, man."

"Telling me isn't good enough, Washington. You have to prove that you were back in Southeast by ten-thirty. If you can't prove it, you had better find yourself a damned good lawyer, because Harold Waterson was killed between ten and ten-thirty last night. You've already admitted being in the vicinity at ten o'clock. That means that you're in serious trouble if you can't verify your whereabouts last night."

"I didn't kill him!" Gary shouted.

"Don't waste your time trying to convince me, Washington. If you're indicted, what I think won't matter; you'll have to convince a judge and jury you didn't kill him."

"Look man! I told you I didn't kill the dude. I can see that you're trying to set me up, but I'm not going to be railroaded into prison. I'll be damned if I take the fall for killing Waterson when I didn't do it."

"Suppose Angela did it, would you take the fall for her?"

"Hell no! I'm not going to prison for anybody."

Matt was surprised to see Gary's instincts for self-preservation temporarily overcome his devotion to Angela.

"Angela didn't kill him either! I know she didn't!"

"You know a damned sight more than I do, Washington. For all I know the two of you conspired to kill him. I'm going to release you for the time being, but don't try to skip town. You'll be watched until we make an arrest in this case."

"Why should I leave town? I don't have any reason to run."

"So you say. I don't have anymore questions for now, but I want to get a photograph and fingerprints from you before you leave."

"Why do you need my fingerprints? I haven't been arrested."

"I need it for my records. If you have any problems with that, I can arrest you and get them."

Gary looked scared, but he agreed to the lesser of the two evils.

Sam Johnson was livid at having to stay to process Gary, but he became enraged when Matt said the picture had to be developed and delivered to his office before Sam left for the night. Matt ignored Sam's string of choice curses that were reserved for such occasions, leaving him and Gary Washington in the forensics lab. He bought a cup of coffee from the vending machine on the first floor, needing the reinforcement before he faced Gary's uncle. When he got back to his office, he found Jake sitting quietly behind his desk as the uncle harangued him with a fiery sermon on the plight of black men in the criminal justice system. Jake was mesmerized by the uncle's strident cadences as they rhythmically rose and subsided with the speaker's desire to emphasize or modulate his points. Gary's uncle was so immersed in his own oratory that he didn't hear Matt enter the office. Jake interrupted his diatribe, but before he could make the introductions, Gary's uncle made himself known to the young detective who didn't look much older than his nephew.

"The name is Washington, Frederick Douglass Washington. You know who Frederick Douglass, was don't you?"

Before Matt could respond, Fred Washington answered his own question, "Frederick Douglass was one of the greatest men that ever lived, black or white. He went from being a slave to the greatest orator in nineteenth century America, and I was named after him."

"What can I do for you, Mr. Washington?"

Matt detected the stale odor of cheap liquor. Apparently, Frederick Douglass Washington was on intimate terms with the bottle.

"You can start by explaining why you've arrested my nephew."

Fred Washington knew that his nephew hadn't been arrested. Jake had taken some pains to explain that he hadn't been arrested. He asked the question anyway to put Matt on the defensive and to give himself a better bargaining position as his nephew's advocate. He moved the chair he was sitting in away from Jake's desk to the side of Matt's. The smell of day-old liquor was over-powering, but there was little that could be done since Jake had already opened the windows in spite of himself. Fred Washington perched on the edge of his chair like a sprinter waiting for the starting gun...ready to refute Matt's reply regardless of what it happened to be.

"Your nephew hasn't been arrested, Mr. Washington. He should be released any minute. He was brought in for questioning because he spent most of Saturday night with Angela Bowman and because she was the last person to see the dead man alive. I assume you know that Harold Waterson was killed in the Bowman house."

"Yes. I read about it in the paper. But, Gary can't be involved because her father never let him set foot in his house. You're barking up the wrong tree, Lieutenant."

"As I said, Mr. Washington, we haven't arrested your nephew. We questioned him in connection with the investigation because he may be a material witness, an accessory to murder, or a murderer. It's my job to find out which."

"Or, he may be innocent," Fred Washington insisted. "I know my nephew, Lieutenant. He couldn't kill anybody. But it's what you know that worries me. What evidence do you have on Gary other than the fact that he was out with his wife before the man was killed?"

"I can't discuss the investigation with you, Mr. Washington. I told you why your nephew was brought in for questioning, and I also told you that he's been released. I can't give you any more information than that, and I don't have any more time either."

"How could Gary kill him? He doesn't even own a gun."

"The Bowmans own a gun, Mr. Washington. It wouldn't have been difficult for Angela to pass the gun to Gary."

"Listen, Lieutenant, you know that a black man doesn't stand a chance against a homicide rap. If he's indicted, he'll be convicted...no questions asked. Man, I been there. You got to give him a break. He didn't kill Waterson."

Matt interrupted Fred Washington as Jake got up to leave, "Did you round up the hip boots yet, Jake?"

"Yeah. We have twelve pairs downstairs in the property room."

"Good. I have an eight o'clock meeting with Lloyd in the morning, but I should be ready to go no later than eight-thirty. If not, you can get started without me. I'll talk to Bryant about assigning some rookies and patrol officers to the detail before I leave tonight. Do you need a ride home, Mr. Washington?" he asked in an attempt to get rid of Gary Washington's uncle.

"No, I don't. My cab is out front and I'm still on duty."

After Jake left, Fred Washington took a moment to regroup as he lit a cigarette from a scruffy match book. Matt used the lull in the conversation to give Gary's uncle the once over. It was obvious that Gary didn't develop his taste in clothes at his uncle's knee. The latter was wearing a greasy khaki cap, Army surplus shirt and pants, a worn navy blue nylon insulated ski jacket with a fur-trimmed hood, and a pair of ancient combat boots that hadn't been polished since they saw active duty. As seedy as he was, and reeking of liquor as he did, there was something about Frederick Douglass Washington that said he would be reckoned with or know the reason why not. There were no excuses or apologies in his body language.

Matt refused a cigarette from his pack, but he watched intently as Fred Washington inhaled the warm smoke in thoughtful puffs. There was a strong family resemblance between Gary and his uncle. They could easily be father and son. They were both dark and lean with fine features and prominent facial bone structures, the kind sculptors used as models. Gary was taller, at least five-feet-ten-inches, while his uncle was no more than five-feet-five-inches tall. Unlike his nephew, Fred Washington wore a mustache and a Vandyke beard that was more gray than black, giving a discordant note to an otherwise youthful appearance. His eyes, however, looked old and worried as he resumed speaking.

"I was in prison once, for more years than I care to remember. It was pure hell, the most brutal, degrading experience you can imagine. When preachers talk about going to hell, I laugh because I've already been there. There wasn't any fire in prison, but all the decency inside me shriveled up and died...until I was nothing but a filthy, disgusting animal just like the rest of them in there. That's why I drink, Lieutenant. They throw you in a cell; then they strip away all your humanity, all of your dignity, and all of your manhood like you were nothing more than a filthy piece of stinking garbage. The very thing that makes you human and makes you a man, they destroy right off the bat. They rape you, Lieutenant Alexander. Not just your body either. They rape your mind and your spirit.

"I can't describe what it's really like. You have to experience it firsthand to see what it does to men. They cage you up like a pack of wild dogs so you can tear at each other's throats and genitals until the wildest and maddest ones come out on top, head of the pack. In prison, things like honor, reason, and compassion don't matter worth a damn. They have no meaning in a cage. I can look at you, Lieutenant Alexander, and tell that you are a reasonable man. You've met my nephew, so you must know that he couldn't survive in that kind of environment for very long. I'm strong and it destroyed me. I was never the same again after they let me out. Gary's weak. All he knows is looking good and pretty women. He has no knowledge of himself and where he ought to be going. Did he tell you that he has two children?"

"No, he didn't mention it."

"He has four-year-old twin boys. The smartest little fellows I've ever seen, but they get their brains from their mother, not Gary. He was supposed to marry their mother, but he married Angela Bowman instead. He doesn't give the boys mother a penny for their support, either. As a matter of fact, he didn't even want them to visit his apartment, said they might break some of his 'things'. I almost kicked him in the ass when he told me that, but it's not his fault that he's a fool. We live in a world where it's easier for a black man to be a fool than it is for him to be a man.

"I was a fool for more years than I care to remember. I left my wife and family in North Carolina when I came up to D.C. twenty-five years ago. I was going to send for them, but after I got up here, the bright lights and fast women turned my head. I never did send for them...hardly ever sent them any money either. I was too busy being a big shot in the big city. Then I got caught selling drugs, and I went down for seven years at Lorton. I wanted to make it up to them after I got out, but twelve years is a long time...too long. It was too late. All of my children were grown by then. My wife didn't want me back, and my children didn't want any part of me either. I keep warning Gary not to make the same mistake I did, but he won't listen to me.

"After Angela left him, he all but crawled on his hands and knees to get her back. Angela and her father had Gary put under a peace bond to get him to leave her alone. It would be funny if it weren't so pathetic. His sons' mother would marry him today and treat him like a king, but she's not good enough for him. He only wants the best out of life. That's what he had the nerve to tell me when he knows he grew up on welfare out in the projects in Suitland, Maryland. He's so dumb, he wouldn't recognize 'best' if it slapped him down in the middle of the street and ran over his black ass."

Anxious to finish his work and go home, Matt asked, "What's your point, Mr. Washington?"

"My point is that Gary is vulnerable. He's black and he doesn't have any money to speak of. That adds up to prime jail bait, Lieutenant. From the inside of a prison, you'd think this country was predominantly black instead of white. Gary didn't kill Waterson, not even for Angela. He doesn't have the guts to kill, but I do. One of the first things you learn in prison is that there's almost nothing too depraved for you to do and live with yourself afterwards. I can't tell you how to handle your investigation, Lieutenant, but give him a break. Once the judicial system sinks its teeth into his ass, it's all over. You may be the only hope he has."

"I appreciate your concerns, Mr. Washington, but you don't have to worry about your nephew being railroaded. My job is to make sure that Waterson's murderer is brought to justice. If Gary Washington is innocent, he won't be indicted or prosecuted."

"But is it ever as simple as that? Suppose you don't find out who killed Waterson. Where will Gary be then?"

"That's not likely to happen. But even if it did, Gary's chances of being indicted won't be any greater than the other suspects' chances. It all depends on the evidence, Mr. Washington."

"Waterson was a very important man, Lieutenant. Someone is gonna have to take the rap for killing him. Isn't the District Prosecutor white?"

"Yes."

"You can see right there that Gary will be more vulnerable than the other suspects."

"I don't agree with you, Mr. Washington. The District Prosecutor is very careful when he brings down an indictment in this city. Politics cut both ways in the District."

"I wish I could be as optimistic as you, Lieutenant, but I've had firsthand experience with the District's criminal justice system. I know how heavy-handed it is in dealing out justice to black men. You damned if you do and damned if you don't. The only way to beat the system is to steer clear of it altogether. You don't stand a chance otherwise."

"Being part of that system, I can't say that I agree with you, but I do understand your concerns. As I said before, I'll give Gary Washington the same consideration as the other suspects, no more and no less. I can't give you any more assurance than that, and I can't give you any more time either, Mr. Washington. I have a lot of work to finish tonight. Gary's free, and I sincerely hope he stays that way."

Matt rose and shook Fred Washington's hand. Fred Washington wasn't finished, but he realized that if the Lieutenant was through, there was no point in pressing him any further. And though he was far from satisfied, he also sensed that the young detective standing before him was the strongest ally he'd find anywhere in the judicial system outside the public defender's office. He was obliged to take him at his word in spite of his gut instinct to plead his nephew's case further.

"I want to thank you for the time you've spent hearing me out, Lieutenant. I take you to be a man of your word, so I believe you'll give my nephew a square deal. I only hope that you find the real killer before the case goes to the Prosecutor's office. That's Gary's only chance to beat this rap."

After Fred Washington left, Matt walked over to the windows and stood for several minutes watching the traffic rushing both ways on Georgia Avenue. The cold night air was tinged with gasoline fumes and the hint of much colder weather to come. The traffic's noise reflected his feelings about the homicide investigation so far...discordant sounds from several directions all trying to get some place other than where he wanted them to go. He thought how much simpler life would be if Harold Waterson hadn't been killed, but he had been killed and life went on. He reminded himself that it was still early yet, Waterson hadn't been dead twenty-four hours. However, he wasn't consoled by the thought. He had precious little time to complete his investigation, Lloyd Cullison would make certain of that. He went back to his desk and called the captain of the Fifteenth Precinct to request five men for his work detail on Monday morning. The captain offered some token resistance more out of form than necessity, but finally agreed to select and detail the men to Jake by eight-thirty A.M. the next day. After that, Matt worked steadily until eleven-thirty P.M.

On the way home, he stopped by the Ethiopian restaurant at Fourteenth and Gallatin with the photograph of Gary Washington that Sam Johnson had grudgingly left on his desk at nine o'clock. He was admitted by the restaurant's manager despite the fact that the place had been closed for two hours. Two of the waiters who still remained recognized Gary Washington as the person who had accompanied that "beautiful young lady" on Saturday night. They couldn't pinpoint their exact times of arrival or departure, but their estimates were close enough to satisfy Matt that Gary and Angela had been there. He got the names and telephone numbers of the waiters before he left.

When he arrived at home, he found Carla asleep in the living room with a fire dying in the fireplace. He placed his briefcase on the parson's bench in the hall and continued upstairs to check on his son and daughter, who were sleeping soundly, she with her teddy bear; and he with his thumb in his mouth. He dislodged his son's thumb before he went to his bedroom, where he undressed and changed to his favorite kimono bathrobe. He went downstairs and placed a large log on the fireplace grate. Then he stoked the embers until the log blazed.

"What time is it?" Carla asked sleepily from the sofa across the room.

"Twelve-thirty."

"It's about time you got home. I'm beginning to feel like a single parent, Matthew."

"I'll make it up to you, baby. The rest of this week is going to be hell, too, but after this case breaks, I'm going to spend more time with you and the kids, I promise."

"Promises, promises. All I get is promises."

"You know I'd be here if it were up to me, Carla."

"Would you? Sometimes, I wonder what you would do if you had to choose between your family and your job. I ought to call your bluff to see just how much the children and I really mean to you."

"Lighten up, Carla," he coaxed sitting down beside her on the sofa. "You know I wouldn't be away so much if I didn't have to."

"You're so caught up in your work, I think you forget about me and the children most of the time, Matthew."

"That's not true, baby," he insisted pulling her into his arms. "You're my first priority." He kissed her neck and throat.

"You don't fool me for a second, Lieutenant Matthew Alexander," she softly murmured, snuggling into his arms and returning his kisses more passionately than he had expected. She wasn't as angry as she pretended to be. She pulled away when he started stroking her hips and thighs.

"That was lovely," she whispered.

"There's much more," he assured her, loosening the belt on his robe.

"I want you to fill me in on what happened today, honey," she replied rising from the sofa. "Now that I think about it, your job does have some advantages after all. Would you like a drink?" Momentarily distracted by the firelight shining through the gauzy film of Carla's black negligee, he didn't hear the question. She asked him again.

"Uh...yes, I would. Make it a double Maker's Mark on ice."

"I'll make it a single. I don't want you to get sleepy too soon. You can have a double after you deliver."

"You drive a hard bargain, lady, but I'm game if you are," he languidly replied, the strain of the day already beginning to recede. Carla put his favorite Sarah Vaughan CD, "Brazilian Romance" on the stereo. Stretching, his arms across the back of the sofa, Matt basked in the soft warmth of the fire's glow as he listened to its gentle hissing against the background of mellow sound of Sarah's lush voice. Carla gave him his drink before curling up next to him on the sofa.

"You wouldn't believe the number of people who called today, all wanting to get the inside scoop on the Waterson homicide. Daddy went off the deep end when I told him I didn't know anything about it. He says he's concerned because Walter Bowman is one of his fraternity brothers, but if you ask me, he was just being nosy like everyone else. Now, start at the beginning and tell me everything that happened, today."

He obliged her to the extent of giving her a sketchy outline of what happened. He didn't go into any details, but Carla was persistent.

"As much as I prefer to believe that Angela shot him, Matthew, I can't see murder as a solution to a bad affair, especially since she was the one who wanted out. It would make more sense if he had shot her. Of course, she may be lying about who wanted to end the affair."

"I don't think so, Carla. Both her husband and Claudia Martin confirm the fact that Angela told them Waterson wanted her to move to New York."

"Do you think Angela's husband shot him?"

"He's crazy about Angela, so I suppose he could have shot Waterson in a fit of jealousy. But if Walter Bowman's gun is the murder weapon, why would Angela have helped her husband kill her lover in her parents' home with her father's gun? It doesn't make much sense, but few murders do. Angela's not that good either, but maybe Gary thought so."

"Good in what way, I'd like to know?"

"Come on, baby," he replied laughing. "That was over long before we ever met. That's ancient history, now," he insisted kissing the soft spot in her throat.

"I had no idea you and Angela had been so intimate."

"Give me a break, Carla," he pleaded instantly regretting his allusion to that old relationship. "That was years ago."

"I don't want to talk about you and Angela anymore, if you don't mind."

"Neither do I," he agreed kissing her face and lips. Carla refused to be sidetracked.

"If Angela or Gary Washington didn't kill Waterson, that still leaves her parents, Matthew."

"It's hard for me to believe that Helen Bowman shot him, Carla. It's out of character for her to get emotionally involved to the point of actually killing someone. Her emotions are so controlled."

"The repressed ones are the type who will turn on you," Carla insisted. "They're unpredictable."

"Maybe, but why would Helen Bowman kill Waterson for having an affair with her thirty-year old hardly chaste daughter? That's a poor motive for murder," he concluded as he finished his drink and turned his attention to her shapely thigh.

"Stop it, Matthew! You're distracting me, and you haven't answered all of my questions, yet. I think Angela's father killed Harold Waterson. He probably shot him to keep him from taking Angela to New York City."

"He wasn't taking her to Timbuktu, Carla. New York is only a three-hour drive from D.C. Why kill the man when Angela had already decided she wasn't going? This case always gets back to motive. I don't know why Waterson was killed; and so far, no one has given me what I consider to be a credible motive."

"You're assuming that people have rational motives for murder, Matthew. I don't assume that at all. The more I think about it, killing Harold Waterson was an exceptionally irrational thing to do, considering where he was found. It wouldn't surprise me a bit if the person who killed him turns out to have a serious emotional problem."

"We all have emotional problems, Carla. It comes with the territory."

"What did Claudia and Tom have to say?"

"Claudia did most of the talking, as usual. She's a bona fide bitch. She ought to carry a broom around with her and be done with it."

Carla laughed. "Did she give you a hard time?"

"Nothing I couldn't handle," he insisted. "I wasn't entirely satisfied with Claudia and Tom's explanations, but I still haven't questioned the maid and bartender who served their party Saturday night."

"You don't think the Martins are involved in the murder do you?"

"I don't know, Carla. There was something about the way Tom and Claudia behaved that made me uneasy. I have a couple of hunches...nothing solid, but I wouldn't be surprised if the Martins aren't as pure as they pretend to be."

"What about...," she said before being abruptly stopped by a passionate kiss. "You're interrupting my concentration," she whispered when he let her up for air.

"You're destroying mine," he huskily replied as he slipped the flimsy negligee off her shoulders and pushed her back on the sofa. Returning her husband's passionate caresses, Carla decided that there was a time and a place for everything, and now was not the time for talk. The only sound in the living room was made by the fire's embers as they softly cracked and hissed and cast an orange-red glow on the couple making passionate love on the sofa."

# CHAPTER XI

Rain fell hard and cold Monday morning, making the previous week's downpours look like intermittent showers by comparison. The sun had packed the city's upbeat mood and gone on vacation behind a heavy blanket of gloomy gray clouds. The District retreated from its weekend optimism, closed in on itself, and hunkered down to wait for the rain to disappear. Anyone who didn't have to go out stayed in. Those who couldn't avoid the weather dressed wet, psyched themselves up, and took to the streets. The heavy downpour discouraged most foot traffic with the exception of those die-hard joggers who ran in all but the worst weather. Matthew Alexander could be counted among the latter.

Matt left his house in LeDroit Park at seven o'clock. After running several blocks he was soaked to the bone, but he found it invigorating after his groggy night's sleep. He ran west on Florida Avenue past the Howard Theater where legendary black entertainers had once strutted their stuff for the home crowd. It was an old relic now, little more than a poignant reminder of the good times for those who cared to remember. He turned north at the Southern Cafeteria on the corner of Florida and Georgia Avenues, where the traffic crawled at a snail's pace inching up the gradual incline Georgia Avenue presented as it skirted Howard University. Matt continued running north past seething motorists unable to go forward or retreat. He passed faces blurred with disgust and considered himself lucky.

Matt's alma mater, Howard University, sprawled off to his right as he continued jogging up the deceptive rise Georgia Avenue took as it skirted the west boundary of the campus. He passed the University's former inn as he ran past the large main campus on his left followed by the Bannecker Science and Math Magnet High School farther up the hill on his right. The old D.C. Teachers' College, the College of Architecture and the College of Engineering on Howard's campus, all perched high above him on his right before the climb leveled off at Fairmont Street. Traffic around the University was heavy as students searched for non-existent parking spots.

Keeping to his usual route, Matt took Columbia Road east to Rock Creek Church Road, where he made a detour through the grounds of Old Soldiers Home, the best part of the run. Emerging from the grounds of the Home, he continued south on First Street until he reached McMillan Reservoir, the eastern boundary of Howard University's campus. He ran around the southern flank of the reservoir to Fourth Street and from there to LeDroit Part and home.

After a quick shower and change of clothes, he left for his eight o'clock meeting with Lloyd, which had been postponed without his knowledge. Pissed, he left Fourth District Headquarters for Floribunda and Seventeenth, near the Bowman residence and very close to Rock Creek, where Jake was supposed to have a contingent of five men waiting to search the creek bed. When Matt arrived, he found Jake sitting in his car stewing while the other officers stood outside protected from the downpour by their slickers and hip boots.

Jake resented the weather and the detail and couldn't wait to let his partner know just how ridiculous the whole thing was. He seriously doubted they would find the gun, but he was certain they would get soaked down to their underwear looking for it. Jake didn't look forward to the prospect of getting drenched in fifty-degree weather on a hunch, and he didn't see why he and the other officers had to suffer because his partner was a rate buster. After Matt parked, Jake walked over to his car and thrust the slicker and hip boots through the window.

"Here, Matt! I saved these especially for you."

"You're too good to me, Jake."

"Hey, no sweat, man. I knew you wouldn't want us in that damned creek without you. If it's good enough for your men, it's good enough for you. Isn't than right, partner?"

"What can I say, Jake. I owe you one," Matt replied more cynically than usual.

"Do you seriously want us to search the creek in all this rain?" Jake needlessly asked.

"You're damned right I do. There won't be much use in doing it later on if the rain keeps up at the rate it's coming down now. Listen to how fast the creek is moving already. We had better get down there before it starts rising again."

"If you ask me, we're wasting our time."

"Spare me the gory details, Jake. I've heard it all a hundred times before. We've got a job to do and the sooner we get started, the sooner we can get out of this rain. Did you bring any tools?"

"Yeah. I put some shovels and metal detectors in the trunk of my car."

"Let's get them out of there and pass them around. The main thing right now is to get started before the creek bed gets too murky to see anything on the bottom. It's moving so fast now that we may have missed our chance."

Matt put his slicker and hip boots on while Jake dispensed the metal detectors to the rest of the officers in the detail. The officers had waited patiently for the most part, but Jake detected a strong undercurrent of unrest. A couple of them grumbled about having to stand in the downpour, and the rest looked ready to abandon ship at a moment's notice. Jake couldn't blame them either. It was raining torrents . Water poured off the men's slickers, creating puddles on the already sodden, muddy ground around their feet. Jake's disgust was evident as he silently concluded that Matt couldn't have picked a worse day to search the creek if he had tried.

Ignoring the weather, Matt briefly explained what they were searching for and how he wanted them to go about it. Then, they found the path that wound down the sloping embankment to the creek bed below.

The steep path down to Rock Creek was narrow, over-grown, and slanted at an angle that made it nearly impossible to plant your feet on solid ground, if there had been any. Rain had reduced the path to a slimy obstacle course as it snaked its way down the wooded bank. The officers went down one-by-one, holding onto anything they could grab, including each other. Matt was the last to go down. His progress down was far slower than he had expected. His rubber hip boots gave little traction on the slippery mud, and he was forced to use the shovel he carried to stay on his feet.

Once down, he was pleased to see that the bank flattened out to level ground some distance before it reached the creek. The creek itself was relatively shallow for some distance in both directions. It was filled with fallen tree limbs, rocks, pebbles, and debris. From where Matt stood, the rocks looked treacherous as fast-moving water swirled over and around them. He guessed that the creek bed itself would be hell to navigate on foot, but he quickly assigned half the contingent of men to the creek with the shovels and the other half on the bank with metal detectors. He and Jake took the creek detail.

It was very slow going at first. The rocks were even worse

than they looked, and everyone got baptized before they got their footing. Jake bitched like a wet hen. Most of the men stayed close to the bank until they felt secure enough to venture farther out into the creek. Icy water rushed past their feet and legs and poured off their backs. They used their shovels more for support than their intended purpose of sifting through the rocks and silt on the creek bed. Getting murkier by the moment, the creek moved fast stirring up driftwood, silt, small pebbles, and anything else that was loose enough to be moved by the current. Matt quickly realized that the rapidly rising water left them precious little time for the search. He urged the men in the creek to search more vigorously. He alternated the men on the bank with those in the creek, and they searched the creek bed and the embankment in shifts for two solid hours without finding Walter Bowman's gun. After two hours of useless searching, everyone began to complain about the cold. Jake complained the loudest. Before calling the search off, Matt put all the men into the creek and ordered them to search for thirty minutes more. A chorus of protest drowned out the sound of the rushing creek, but he held firm. They searched and complained for the next thirty minutes, after which time Matt called a halt to the search, satisfied that they had done their best.

"How the hell are we going to get back up that bank?" Jake asked, disgust oozing from every pore.

"That's your problem, man," Matt answered as he started up the slippery path, using his shovel for leverage.

It took him seven minutes to climb the bank to Seventeenth Street. It had taken at least five to go down, a total of twelve minutes in all. From the Bowman house, a round trip to the creek bed after a heavy rain would take at least fifteen minutes...too much time for someone racing against a clock. Of course, everything hinged on when Waterson was killed. Matt knew he could probably pin down the time the victim left the Martins' party from the other guests. He didn't have to take the

Martins' word on that. On the other hand, Angela or her parents could have shot Waterson immediately after he was admitted into the house, in which case there would have been time to run down to the creek and back again before calling the dispatcher at ten-thirty.

Everything depended on what happened between ten and ten-thirty. Angela couldn't have had enough time to let Waterson into the house, kill him, get rid of the gun, and spend ten minutes in Claudia Martin's kitchen. That was cutting it too close. Matt thought it more likely that Angela went over to Claudia's to establish an alibi for herself while her father got rid of the gun for her...if she killed Waterson. That would explain why both Tom and Claudia denied that someone from their party had called her for ice. Either way, he was certain that they wouldn't find the Bowman gun. The case would have to be built without it.

Jake was the last one to come up the path. He emerged from the woods puffing like an old engine. He took a few minutes to catch his breath before he went over to Matt to smooth things over. He didn't actually apologize, he never did. But, he did fumble around for the right words long enough to let his partner know that he wanted to apologize. Matt didn't say anything. He had guessed that Jake was in one of his funky moods when he pushed the slicker and hip boots through the window earlier. Matt's time-tested strategy for dealing with Jake's tantrums was to ignore them. ìWhat do you want me to do when I get back?" Jake asked in a contrite mood.

"I need that information on prior arrests and gun registration that I asked you for yesterday, man."

"I put the computer requests in last night, but the print-outs hadn't come back when I was at the office this morning, I'll check first thing when I return."

"Make sure you do. I needed that information yesterday," he replied giving Jake his slicker and boots. "Lloyd wants a report on the investigation this afternoon. I'm going over to the Watersons' when I leave here. Tell Lloyd where I am if he starts to get antsy. If anything important comes up, call me over there. Make sure that the priors and gun registration information are on my desk by one even if you have to go down to central processing to run them. Make sure the secretary gets my work done, too. I have a meeting with Lloyd at three and I promised to give him copies of everything at the meeting. Light a fire under Sam Johnson as soon as you get back, Jake. I need the results from the print and powder tests before I meet with Lloyd."

"Is that all?" Jake sarcastically asked.

"That'll do for starters," Matt replied just as sarcastically.

"I'll be damned if I go all the way downtown to central processing," Jake muttered to himself after his partner drove away. "That terminal had better cough up those print-outs or tell me why not."

The other officers waited for Jake to open his trunk. Some had already removed their slickers, but the smart ones waited until Matt drove off to remove theirs. They threw their gear in the trunk helter-skelter. Jake would have complained under normal circumstances, but he was as relieved as the men to have the creek ordeal behind them.

Two somberly-dressed men came out of the Waterson house as Matt drove up. From the look of compassion and sympathy on their faces, Matt surmised that they had to be those indispensable, temporary family members whose expertise and understanding eased the dearly departed's transition from this world to the next. Their black Cadillac Coup de Ville was parked behind a red Porshe Targa. Matt waited for them to leave before he parked behind the sports car, giving the Porshe an envious once-over before ringing the doorbell to the Waterson residence.

The door was opened by a nervous middle-aged house-keeper who started when he identified himself and asked to see

Felicia Waterson. She looked confused before mumbling that Mrs. Waterson was asleep and couldn't be disturbed. Matt politely but firmly insisted that the housekeeper wake her up. The housekeeper looked even more bewildered at that, but she declined just as firmly saying that Mrs. Waterson's son had left strict orders that she wasn't to be disturbed under any circumstances. Matt had no intention of forcing his way into Felicia Waterson's bedroom, so he asked to see the son instead. Visibly relieved, the housekeeper went upstairs to get William Waterson. She was gone several minutes before the young man appeared downstairs. Matt decided that he didn't like Harold Waterson's son any better despite his break-down at the morgue. Young Waterson obviously didn't feel any warmer toward him. The atmosphere between the two men was icy. William Waterson wore a white crew neck sweater, chino slacks, and a heavy scowl. Matt ignored the scowl and got to the point of his visit.

"I have to talk to your mother, but your housekeeper refused to wake her up on your orders, I understand."

"That's right. I told Mrs. Crawford that she wasn't to bother my mother for any reason. Her doctor said she needs all the rest she can get."

"I understand that your mother has had a shock, but I have to question her all the same. I could have done it last night, but I waited until today to give her a chance to recover. I don't want to resort to a subpoena Waterson, but I will if you refuse to cooperate."

"Why do you have to talk to her anyway? I can answer any questions you need to know about my father."

"I intend to question you as well, but your mother will have to speak for herself. That's the way we do things in the homicide division, Waterson. Last night, you insisted on knowing who killed your father. You can help me find his murderer by cooperating with my investigation. I can postpone talking to your mother until after I question you, but I have to speak to her before I leave here."

"What do you want to know from me?"

"When did you last see your father alive?"

"I saw him leave with the old lady around ten on Saturday morning. That was the last time I saw him."

"What type of car was he driving?"

"His white Mercedes."

"What did you do after they left?"

"I talked to my mother for a while, and then I went over to my gym to work out."

"Where is your gym?"

"The Health Club on MacArthur Boulevard and Forty-Eighth Street."

"How long were you there?"

"I stayed two hours, from eleven to one o'clock."

"Where did you go after that?"

"I drove over to Georgetown University Library to do some studying."

"How long were you there?"

"I stayed at the library until six o'clock. We're having mid-terms and I had a lot of studying to do."

"Where did you go after you left the library?"

"I came home."

"Did you go out after that?"

"No. I was home all evening."

"Sounds as if you spent a boring Saturday night, Waterson."

"To you, maybe, but it suited me just fine."

"Do you spend most of your Saturdays like that?"

"How I spend my Saturdays is none of your business, Lieutenant. You asked about this past Saturday and that's what I did. If you're not thrilled, that's your problem."

"So it is, Waterson, so it is. You deny leaving your house after you returned home at six o'clock Saturday evening?"

William Waterson looked trapped for a moment, but he stuck to his story.

"I told you I was home all evening."

"Did you see your father's car when you returned?"

"No, I didn't see his car because he wasn't home. The old lady was the only person in the house when I got back. Both of my parents' cars were gone."

"What kind of man was your father, Waterson?"

"What's that supposed to mean?"

"Just what I said. I didn't know your father personally, so I'm asking you to describe his character and personality for me. That shouldn't be difficult for you, considering the fact that he was your father."

"I don't see what his character and personality have to do with his murder."

"They have everything to do with why he was killed. Your father's homicide wasn't a random event. Whoever killed him did it for a reason. Knowing what kind of man he was and how he behaved could help me hone in on the killer's motive."

Young Waterson thought he could finesse his way through the question. However, as soon as he opened his mouth, his real feelings spilled out.

"My father was cruel and selfish. He ran around on my mother for years. I couldn't stand the way he treated her. I had absolutely no respect for him."

"How did he treat you, Waterson?"

"I told you he was cruel and selfish."

"You described his relationship with your mother. I want to know how he treated you, his son."

"How many times do I have to tell you that he wasn't concerned about anyone but himself," the young man insisted.

"How was he cruel and selfish toward you? What cruel things did he do to you, personally?"

"He was cruel to my mother; and whatever he did to her, he

did to me."

"Did he ever do anything cruel to you that he didn't do to her?"

"He was always on my back about something, grades, money, drugs...it didn't matter to him as long as he could beat me over the head with it."

"It sounds like he was concerned about you, Waterson."

"Don't make me laugh. He didn't give a damn about anyone but himself and the old lady. He couldn't care less about me or my mother."

"Do you have a job, Waterson?"

"No, I don't."

"Does your mother work?"

"No, she doesn't. Why should she?"

"Is that your red Porshe out front?"

"Yes, that's my car."

"Who paid for it?" It took a minute for the question to sink in, but when its implications became clear, William Waterson became furious.

"What business is it of yours who bought my car!? My car is my business, and I don't have to explain anything about it to the likes of you!"

Matt ignored William Waterson's hostile outburst.

"I understand that your father and mother had a fight Friday night."

"I don't know anything about a fight. So what if they did?"

"Do you know what they fought about?"

"Even if I did know, I wouldn't tell you. Why do you have to pry into their personal affairs, anyway?"

"Personal or not, your father had a violent fight with his wife less than twenty-four hours before he was killed, and I want to know what they fought about."

"I told you that I don't know what they fought about."

"Did your parents fight often?"

"He made my mother miserable. He was never home. He claimed his business kept him away, but he didn't fool her. She knew it was his women."

"Why didn't she leave him if she was that miserable?"

"He refused to give her a divorce," young Waterson naively replied.

"Maybe she loved him," Matt suggested.

"She did not love him! She despised him! How could she love someone who treated her the way he did?"

"It happens, Waterson, more often than you'd think. Let's talk about how you felt about your father."

"I had no respect for him. I stayed here because of my mother; otherwise, I would have left long ago."

"Did you hate your father?"

"What if I did?" the young man stammered close to tears. "He deserved it. He cheated on my mother...he deserved it."

"Do you know anything about the Anacostia Riverfront Development Project your father's firm was constructing?"

"No. Why should I know anything about that?"

"Your father never mentioned it to you?"

"No, he didn't. He never discussed his business with me."

"How much do you know about your father's firm?"

"Nothing!, and that's more that I want to know."

"What will happen to your father's firm, now?"

"I have no idea. I suppose the other partners will buy it."

"I understand that it's a very lucrative partnership, Waterson."

"I couldn't care less," William Waterson smugly replied.

"Spoken like a real ass-hole," Matt thought. "Anyone with half a brain would kill for that partnership. I can't believe this guy is as dumb as he seems."

"Do you own a gun, Waterson?"

"No."

"Did your father own a gun?"

After a moment's hesitation, the young man replied: "I think he did, but you'll have to ask my mother to be certain."

"I don't have any more questions for you. I'd like to talk to your mother now."

"She's still asleep."

"You'll have to wake her up, Waterson. I'll come up to her bedroom if she wants me to, but I'm not leaving this house until I speak to her."

"I'll see if she feels up to it," William Waterson reluctantly agreed before he rose to go upstairs.

"Have you made the arrangements for your father's funeral?"

"Yes. The funeral directors were here earlier. The service will be tomorrow in the mortuary chapel. I decided to make the service short and simple for my mother's sake. The old lady had a fit when she found out that the funeral isn't going to be held in her church, but that's her problem. She's not running things around here anymore. I don't want my mother to go through a long, drawn out service the way they do it. What difference does it make anyway? Funerals are for the living. What do the dead care how they're buried? I wanted to have his body cremated, but the old lady went berserk when I told her...did a total freakout number on me. I was afraid that she might keel over herself, so I decided against cremation. She wanted to take his body to Warren for burial, but my mother wouldn't go along with that."

"What time is the service?"

"One o'clock, tomorrow."

"What mortuary?"

"Burton's on Wisconsin Avenue."

Matt thought about Aunt Martha after the young man left. He wondered whether William Waterson had been intentionally cruel or whether he simply didn't know how much his father had meant to her. Asking her to cremate his body was like asking her to throw her life's work in a fire and watch it burn to ashes. The bond between them was nurtured on suffering, loss, and selfless devotion. He was everything to her...the son she didn't conceive, the husband she never married, the love she never consummated, the only man in her life. It should have been obvious to anyone that her nephew's death had been a devastating blow to her.

Matt wondered how Felicia Waterson was handling her grief. He waited downstairs for five minutes before William Waterson motioned for him upstairs to come upstairs to his mother's bedroom.

Felicia Waterson sat in her bed supported by pillows. She was calm...too calm. She looked like she had taken more tranquilizers than she needed Matt thought, but better passive than hysterical. She seemed unaware of his presence in the room as she watched the rain fall through her bedroom windows and listened to its steady drumming against the window panes. She turned as he approached her bed, and Matt recognized what it was about her that had eluded him the night before—her eyes. She had sad, troubled eyes. It was ironic that a woman could have so much and so little at the same time.

Felicia Waterson had been unhappy with her husband, but that wasn't a problem for her any longer. His killer had eliminated her miserable marriage with two well-placed gun shots. There would be no more fights between them, no more harsh words, no more hostile recriminations. He would never hurt her again. But, as Aunt Martha had said, Felicia wasn't satisfied with him, and she wasn't satisfied without him. She was miserable while he lived, but she was absolutely devastated by his death. Her problem hadn't been solved. It had been altered from what was to what might have been if they had loved each other more, or understood each other better. She didn't think about the infidelity or the women anymore. They weren't important...now that it was over. She thought about the promise of a love not realized, a chance for happiness lost, squandered by hard hearts and narrow minds. They had treated each other as if their feelings didn't matter, as if their love for each other wasn't important when it was the only real thing they had. They destroyed their chance for a life together, and they destroyed their son with it. Felicia Waterson sat in her bed gathering the fragments of what might have been, sifting through the ruins of her tortured marriage; and she saw the waste, now that it was too late to change it.

Matt sat in a chair near her bed. He offered condolences and other commonplaces before getting to the point of his visit.

"I know you've had a terrible shock, Mrs. Waterson, but I have to ask you some questions related to your husband's death."

She gave him a cold stare before replying, "My husband is dead, Lieutenant Alexander. Will any of your questions change that?"

"No, they won't, but they will help me find out who killed him."

"I don't want to know who killed him! I couldn't bear to know!" she cried out. "Why are you torturing me like this?"

"I told you my mother wasn't well!" William Waterson shouted. "Get out of here and leave us alone!"

"I'm not trying to upset you, Mrs. Waterson," Matt insisted, ignoring her son's hostile outburst. "But I want to know who killed your husband even if you don't. No one had the right to take his life. He deserved to live as much as you and me. You can help me find his killer by telling me anything you know about what happened Saturday night."

"She doesn't know anything about it!" young Waterson shouted. "I want you out of our house right now!"

"Will you please ask your son to leave the room! I can't question you if he continues to interfere!"

"It's all right, William. Leave us alone, so I can answer his questions and get this over with."

"He has no right to bother you with his stupid questions, Mother."

"I said I'll be fine, William. Now, leave us alone so he can ask his questions and leave."

William Waterson left the bedroom grudgingly, but he remained in the hallway outside the door.

"What do you want to know, Lieutenant?"

"What did you and your husband fight about Friday night?"

"Who told you we had a fight?" she demanded.

"That's not important, Mrs. Waterson. What did you fight about?"

"There's no point in hiding it, now. Hal was having an affair. I found out about it and I told him he had to stop seeing her. He promised that he would, but he didn't."

"How do you know that he didn't?"

"I hired a private investigator. He followed Hal and saw the two of them together after Hal assured me he had stopped seeing her."

"Who was the other woman, Mrs. Waterson?"

"Angela Bowman."

"Did you know your husband was killed in her house?"

"Yes, William told me after he read the article in the paper today. It seems Hal went to see his lover once too often."

"How long had they been seeing each other?"

"I don't know. Hal wouldn't tell me, but I guessed that the affair had been going on for some time before I found out about it."

"How did you find out?"

"I got an anonymous letter in the mail about five weeks ago. The letter didn't say who the woman was, but it did say she was black."

"Do you still have the letter?"

"No. I threw it away. It was so spiteful, I couldn't bear to keep it."

"What, exactly, did it say?"

"It said that Hal was having an affair with a black woman."

"Was that all it said?"

"No that wasn't all. There were some other nasty comments about the fact that I couldn't satisfy my husband. It was a vulgar, hateful letter, Lieutenant."

"Did you keep the envelope it came in?"

"No, I didn't. I threw both the letter and the envelope away."

"Do you have any idea who sent it?"

"No, I don't."

"Have you made any enemies lately, Mrs. Waterson?"

"Not intentionally. I try to get along with everyone, but I can't control how they feel about me. I tried to figure out who might have sent it, but it wasn't worth the effort. I began to suspect all my friends, so I tore that hateful letter up and threw it in the trash where it belonged."

"Maybe the letter was sent by someone who wanted to hurt your husband, not you."

"No. If you had read it, you wouldn't say that. There was no doubt in my mind that the letter was intended for me."

"If you got the letter five weeks ago, why the fight on Friday night?"

"Things had been going badly between us since I confronted him with what I learned from the letter. I guess I had been brooding about it all that time. After the private detective told me that Hal was still seeing her, I became furious because I knew then that he had no intention of giving her up. I couldn't hold my feelings in any longer, so I confronted him Friday night."

"Did you fight often?"

"No. Normally, we didn't fight, but we had several arguments over the past five weeks...Friday night was the worst. I told him he'd have to give her up or else."

"What did you intend to do if he refused?"

"Divorce him, I suppose."

"When did you hire the private detective?"

"A week after I got the letter."

"Who did you hire?"

"Richard Langford."

"I know Dick Langford. Why him? Was he recommended?"

"No. I selected his name from the yellow pages."

"When did you learn who your husband was seeing?"

"Several days after I hired Mr. Langford."

"Is he still working for you?"

"No. I paid him for a week's worth of his time. I found out what I wanted to know, and I didn't see any point in keeping him on."

"Did your husband admit he was seeing Angela Bowman?"

"No, he never did."

"Did he know that you were having him followed?"

"No. I'm positive he didn't know. He would have been furious if he had found out."

"Did your son know about the affair, Mrs. Waterson?"

"No. He couldn't have known. I didn't tell him, and I know his father would never have mentioned it to him."

"Is it possible that he overheard you fighting?"

"No, it isn't. The only person who snoops around here is that aunt of his."

"Are you referring to your husband's Aunt Martha?"

"Who else? She creeps through the house snooping and spying all the time. She told you about the fight Friday night, didn't she?"

Matt ignored Felicia Waterson's question.

"How long has she lived with you, Mrs. Waterson?"

"Since the beginning, Lieutenant Alexander. She was part of the nuptials. I didn't know that when I married Hal, but he was already married to Aunt Martha. He gave her the run of my house. We had the guest house built especially for her, but she refused to move out there, claimed she was afraid to live alone.

Hal didn't have the guts to put her out there anyway. She had him wrapped around her little finger. She tried to do the same thing with my son, but I wouldn't stand for it. William's wise to her, so she can't get him to do her bidding the way Hal did. She had Hal right where she wanted him, though. I would have thrown her out of my house years ago it hadn't been for him. He adored her, if you can believe that."

"How long were you married, Mrs. Waterson?" Her eyes filled with tears.

"For twenty-five years. I gave up everything to marry Hal. My family turned against me. My friends ostracized me too, but I didn't care because I loved him. I gave up everything for him, and he always put her needs before mine, always. They were so close, it made me sick. She was always there between us, catering to him, spoiling him, cooking special dishes for him, washing for him, ironing for him. It got to the point where I couldn't stand the sight of her. But, all that's changed now. I'm going to send her back to Warren on the first bus."

Matt almost advised Felicia Waterson to postpone her plans for Aunt Martha until after the will was read, but he held his tongue. He was surprised to see how much animosity existed between the two women. Felicia Waterson was so cool and composed otherwise, that it seemed out of character for her to harbor such strong feelings against Aunt Martha or to share them with him for that matter. Matt wondered if she had harbored equally strong feelings against her husband.

"When did you last see your husband alive, Mrs. Waterson?"

She gave him a questioning look before replying, "Friday night was the last time I saw Hal. He left before I got up Saturday morning."

"What did you do on Saturday?"

"I was home most of the day. I went shopping with some friends around three, and I didn't get back until seven-thirty."

"Did you go out Saturday night."

She quickly replied: "No. I was home Saturday evening. I went to bed early, around nine o'clock, and I slept until Aunt Martha woke me up when you arrived to tell us about Hal."

"Weren't you supposed to attend a cocktail party at Tom and Claudia Martin's Saturday night?"

"Yes. I was supposed to be there. But, Hal wasn't home and I was tired, so I decided to skip it. I wasn't in a cocktail party mood, and Claudia Martin isn't one of my favorite people."

"Did you know that your husband went to the party without you?"

"No! I didn't know. That was a strange thing for him to do. Hal always fussed about going to fundraisers with me."

"Why do you think he went without you, Mrs. Waterson?"

"I have no idea. He never did it before."

"So, you didn't ask him to go in your place because you weren't feeling well?"

"No, I didn't. I mentioned it to him last week so he could put the date on his calendar, but I don't know why he went without me. It's a strange thing for him to do."

"Do you know the Martins well?"

"Hardly. Claudia sits on the board of Youth Shelter with me. I know her only through board work. We don't associate otherwise."

"What did you mean when you said that Claudia Martin wasn't one of your favorite people?"

"Claudia has been a member of the Youth Shelter Board for five years. She expected to be elected president of the board. I've been on the board for just two years; and when they elected me president, Claudia didn't like it. She's very arrogant, and she can be very difficult to work with. We've managed to iron out most of our difficulties, but she still gets testy at times."

"How long have you known the Martins?"

"Only since I joined the board of Youth Shelter."

"Did your husband know them before that?"

"I'm almost certain that he didn't. He never mentioned either one of them to me."

"Did your husband own a gun, Mrs. Waterson?"

"Yes, he owned a pistol."

"Do you mind if I take a look at it?"

"Not at all. It's in the nightstand drawer."

Matt opened the drawer and found a fancy thirty-eight caliber revolver with exquisite tooling and an inlaid butt of pink mother of pearl. He didn't get excited. If Felicia Waterson was offering it to him, it couldn't possibly be the murder weapon.

"I'll have to take this revolver back to Headquarters with me, Mrs. Waterson. Do you know whether your husband registered it downtown?"

"Yes, he did. The registration papers are in Hal's things, but I don't know where they are. I'm very tired, Lieutenant."

"I'm almost finished, just a few more questions. How did your son get along with his father?"

"Not very well, I'm afraid. William has always been very close to me, so I understand him better than Hal did. William is an only child, and Hal expected too much from him. He wanted him to make good grades, to be out-going and well-liked, to excel in sports...all the usual ambitions fathers have for their sons, I suppose. He wanted William to go into his firm, too, but William couldn't be everything his father wanted him to be. He's always been a sensitive child. He couldn't meet all of his father's expectations. Hal simply didn't understand our son the way I do."

"Your son has some very strong feelings about the way your husband treated you, Mrs. Waterson."

"I know that I wasn't the best wife I could have been, but I never tried to turn my son against his father. I often defended Hal to William in spite of the way he treated me. Maybe I should have pretended that everything was wonderful between us for William's sake, but I couldn't. I hated Hal for seeing other women behind my back. I simply couldn't pretend that he was a perfect husband when I was so miserable."

"Did your husband ever discuss his business with you, Mrs. Waterson?"

"Very rarely, but he talked to Aunt Martha about it every morning over breakfast. They had a lot more in common than the two of us."

Matt concluded that Aunt Martha had long been a thorn in Felicia Waterson's side. He suspected that part of it boiled down to jealousy, and part to indignation at having to knuckle under to an old black woman. Felicia Waterson compromised her social status to marry Harold Waterson in a society where race is everything. The least she expected was appreciation of her sacrifice from him, but Aunt Martha had become a chronic obstacle in her relationship with her husband. An obstacle that Felicia couldn't fight, because Harold Waterson refused to concede his wife's point of view in the matter of Aunt Martha. Matt saw justification on both sides. Aunt Martha had given Hal Waterson a home and taken care of him from infancy, so he felt he owed her. On the other hand, Felicia Waterson had a right to ask that she find other accommodations if they couldn't work things out with her living with them. It was obvious that Aunt Martha held the trump card, and she played it selfishly, he thought. The old lady was Felicia's nemesis. She stole her husband's affections and his loyalty, and Felicia wasn't able to touch her until now.

Matt finished questioning Felicia Waterson, who appeared to be asleep when he left her bedroom. William Waterson was nowhere in sight, but the Matt guessed that he was close at hand. He met Aunt Martha at the bottom of the stairs. The old lady had a curiously cunning look about her, like a cat on the prowl.

"I overheard William tell you that he didn't know his parents had a fight Friday night."

"Yes, that's right."

"Well, he lied. He heard every word of it from where I'm standing now. I saw him down here Friday night. I don't know why he lied about it, but since he did, I figured that you ought to know he did."

"Thanks, I appreciate the information."

"What did Felicia tell you she did Saturday night?"

"She said that she was home all evening, and that she went to bed early."

"Well, she lied too. She left here at nine o'clock and she didn't get back until ten forty-five. I saw her leave and come back with my own eyes."

"Why didn't you tell me this last night, Aunt Martha?"

"I was too upset last night, but I remembered it after I came to myself. It's like this, young man. When your head is in the lion's mouth, you have to ease it out because there's no telling which way he'll jump. I'm living in a snake pit, but I don't aim to get bitten, indeed I don't."

Aunt Martha walked back into the kitchen before he could ask her what she meant. He followed her into the kitchen and sat down beside her at the kitchen table.

"Do you understand what you've just told me, Aunt Martha?"

"I only told you the truth, young man. The Lord works in mysterious ways, yes He does. I understand everything now. It's as clear as day."

"What's clear, Aunt Martha? What do you understand?"

"I'm talking about Hal. He told me what happened at breakfast this morning before he went to work. He told me what they did to him." Matt concluded that the shock had been too much for the old lady. He felt sorry for her, but all the same, he was intrigued by what she said.

"What did he tell you this morning, Aunt Martha?"

"He told me who killed him," she replied matter-of-factly.

"How could he tell you that? He's dead!"

"I know he's dead, young man! I'm not crazy! The Lord sent him to me," she sobbed. "He saw an old woman's misery and He sent my child to ease my suffering. He's a wonderful God, indeed He is. Hal had breakfast with me this morning just like we always do. I fixed him scrambled eggs and bacon, just the way he likes them. He loves my scrambled eggs. He always said nobody makes scrambled eggs like his Aunt Martha."

Then she smiled, closed her eyes, and started to hum a gospel tune very softly. Matt looked around the kitchen for the remains of a scrambled egg and bacon breakfast for two. He found what he was looking for in the kitchen sink, two of everything from coffee cups to cutlery. The old lady was beginning to spook him.

"Who did he say shot him, Aunt Martha?"

"I can't tell you that. He made me promise not to tell, but it's as clear as day, Lord knows it is." She closed her eyes and started humming again.

Matt sat for a while trying to decipher what he had heard she said, "I want to take his body home, so I can lay him to rest next to his mother; but they won't let me. They're cruel and heartless, the two of them. They didn't love him. Why won't they let me bury him among his own people instead of among strangers like they plan to do? Why must they be so heartless?" she cried.

Matt didn't know how to answer her question, so he didn't try. He left her sitting at the kitchen table crying and shaking her head in defeat. The housekeeper was dusting in the foyer when he walked out of the kitchen. He asked her who had eaten breakfast from the dishes in the kitchen sink. She replied that Aunt Martha was the only one who had cooked anything since she arrived.

"Didn't Mrs. Waterson or her son eat any breakfast, this morning?"

"No sir, they didn't. Mrs. Waterson didn't want anything but juice, and William said he wasn't hungry. When I got here this morning, I washed up all the dishes left over from last night. Miss Martha must have used all the dishes out there now because Mrs. Waterson's juice glass is still sitting on the night stand in her room."

Matt considered what she told him, thanked her, and left.

The rain had stopped while he was inside. He felt uneasy as he drove away from the Waterson house. Talking to them had raised more questions than they answered, especially Aunt Martha. He was too hardened a skeptic to put any credence in her story about Hal Waterson having breakfast with her, but it was obvious that she believed it. It was also obvious that she was very frightened. That bothered him. There was no love lost between her, Felicia and William Waterson. He was less concerned about Felicia Waterson hurting her, but the son was another matter altogether. He was as unstable as hell and might easily resort to violence, if he hadn't already. On the other hand, if what Aunt Martha told him about their whereabouts was true, he had two more suspects for his investigation. The old lady could be lying, but he doubted it. He believed her when she said Felicia went out Saturday night. It made sense, somehow. She had been expected at the Martins' cocktail party. As board president of Youth Shelter, she probably felt obliged to go, but she hadn't shown up at the Martins' after all. Matt wondered why Aunt Martha had withheld telling him that Felicia was out Saturday night. The gun in the nightstand was too convenient...a red herring, most likely. He didn't know what to make of it falling into his lap so easily, but Sam could tell him whether or not it was the murder weapon.

The ride across town to Fourth District Headquarters took forty minutes. It was one o'clock before Matt arrived at his office, where he found most of the information he requested from Jake on his desk. The crime report and statements had been typed. The computer print-out was also there along with a note from Sam Johnson telling him to kiss off as politely as Sam could say it, which wasn't polite at all. Jake was out of the office, so he welcomed the time alone to read the report and statements before his meeting with Lloyd. When he got to the print-out, he realized that the information on prior arrests was missing. He silently cursed Jake for his incompetence and promised to jack him up as soon as he returned to the office.

The handgun registration information merely confirmed what he already knew: only Walter Bowman and the deceased were listed as owners of registered handguns, both thirty-eight caliber revolvers. He threw the print-out aside, frustrated at how little it actually told him. It didn't tell how many suspects owned guns but intentionally failed to register them. It didn't tell him whether the owners of registered handguns also owned unregistered handguns. It was a crime to own an unregistered handgun in the District of Columbia. Even so, police statistics showed that there were five times as many unregistered as registered handguns in the city. It hadn't taken long for District residents to appreciate the fact that people who registered their guns weren't criminals, or that criminals weren't registering their guns. Matt briefly considered the possibility of search warrants for the other suspects, but he knew Lloyd wouldn't go for it. There wasn't enough time left anyway. A homicide that wasn't solved within forty-eight hours after the crime was committed wasn't likely to be solved. Knowing Lloyd, the arrest warrant would probably come down on Tuesday.

He looked at the Waterson gun lying on top of his desk in a plastic bag. It was a beautiful weapon, expertly tooled and perfectly balanced. The mother of pearl handle was too fancy for his taste. It made the gun look ornamental rather than practical. Its ostentation was deceptive, though. The weapon's precision and expert craftsmanship identified it for what it was, an instrument of death. He toyed with the gun for a few minutes more before placing an internal call to the forensics lab downstairs.

Matt generally regarded Sam Johnson as a prick, and the smart-assed note Sam left on his desk only confirmed his opinion. Sam answered the lab's telephone. When he heard Matt's voice, he read him the riot act. Matt listened without interrupting, thinking all the while what a pleasure it would be to go downstairs and kick Sam Johnson's ass from one end of the lab to the other. Not that Sam wouldn't be ready for him. He was a spunky little bastard who gave as good as he got. Sam had incredible staying power, too. He was well-known for his ability to out-curse several shiploads of sailors without taking a breath. Sam could lace your shoes up for you, no doubt about it. Matt allowed Sam to finish his sabre rattling before he got to the point of his call.

"Did you finish analyzing the prints you lifted at the Bowman house, Sam?"

"Hell no! I just this minute finished the goddamned powder tests, for all the good it did."

"What do you mean?" he asked bracing himself for bad news.

"None of the Bowmans had powder on their hands, man. I just wasted the better part of the day for nothing."

"You couldn't be mistaken could you, Sam?"

"Is the Pope Catholic? Does a chicken have lips? Hell no, I'm not mistaken. Man, I could do this test in my sleep, and I'm telling you that none of the Bowmans had gunpowder on their hands. The father didn't have any, the mother didn't have any, and the daughter didn't nave any. What more can I say?"

"Damn!" Matt said curiously relieved and confused.

"And you're perfectly sure about that, Sam?"

"What do I have to do to convince you that I know what I'm talking about. That's what I'm paid for, Lieutenant, to know what I'm talking about? By the way, the medical examiner's office sent the slugs they took out of Waterson's chest over today. I don't see much point in rushing the ballistics tests if you haven't found the Bowman gun yet. You haven't found it, have you?"

"No, we haven't found it, and I don't think we're going to find it. I picked up another thirty-eight at the Waterson house today, Sam. I'll bring it down in a minute, although I'm almost certain it isn't the murder weapon. It won't hurt to test it against the slugs, though. When are you going to be finish the prints you lifted at the Bowman residence?"

"If you leave me alone long enough, Alexander, I can finish them, today. How do you expect me to get any work done when you pester the hell out of me? I keep telling you clowns that I need more help down here, but it doesn't do a goddamned bit of good."

Matt hung up before Sam could launch another of his tirades against the division bureaucracy. After he rang off, Jake walked in and gave him another computer print-out.

"The prior arrest information didn't come up on the terminal this morning," he explained. "I had to go downtown to central processing and raise hell until they agreed to run the request from there."

"Thanks, Jake. I owe you one," Matt replied, conveniently forgetting his vow to berate his partner's incompetence.

"What did you found out at the Watersons' man?"

"Too much, but I'll have to fill you in later. I have a meeting with Lloyd in ten minutes." He leafed through the print-out, quickly noting several old bench warrants for moving violations, none of them outstanding.

"There's nothing in there we don't already know," Jake commented.

"I know," Matt replied as he gathered the papers on his desk. "I've got to stop at the copy machine and the forensics lab before my meeting, Jake. If Lloyd calls, tell him I'm on my way."

# (HAPTER XII

Matt wasn't surprised to find Ed Davenport, the District Prosecutor, waiting in Lloyd's office when he arrived. Wearing a three-piece suit, button-down shirt, striped tie, and winged-tip shoes, Ed Davenport looked more like a corporate general counsel than a prosecuting attorney. A tough adversary in the courtroom, Ed was aggressive, industrious, clever, and ambitious to a fault. He prosecuted anything that moved and won convictions in the majority of his cases. Ed didn't have a compassionate bone in his body. He'd gladly prosecute his own mother if he thought there was a percentage in it for him, which explained why he had amassed such an impressive conviction record over the years. Recognizing a hot case when he saw one, Ed was virtually straining at the leash at the prospect of prose- cuting the Waterson homicide. Matt sensed the District Prosecutor's eagerness to move in on his investigation. He knew that Lloyd was anxious for an indictment, too; but after their talk with Chief Carter, he hoped that Lloyd wouldn't let Ed goad him into a premature arrest. Ed's presence at the meeting meant that his predatory instincts were already on the prowl.

Lloyd looked strained. The pressure was beginning to get next to him. He seemed ready to hand the case over to the District Attorney's office just to be rid of it, but being as astute as he was, he was reluctant to let it go without exhausting every productive lead. The first meeting with Chief Carter hadn't been reassuring.

"It's about time you got her, Alexander. Lately it seems that I spend most of my time waiting for you to show up."

"Sorry, I'm late, Lloyd; but I had a lot to do today."

"That's no excuse for keeping me waiting."

"I understand you have an interesting case for us, Lieutenant," Ed said, a little too smugly.

"You might say that, Davenport," Matt cooly replied.

"Well, what have you learned since we talked yesterday?" Lloyd demanded.

Matt refused to be rushed. He gave Lloyd each suspect's typed statement one at a time, carefully pointing out where the suspect claimed to be and what they claimed to be doing during the time Harold Waterson was killed. Lloyd gave the statements little more than a cursory glance, having heard it all before. Ed Davenport eagerly pounced on the statements, reading each one with unabashed interest. Next came the homicide report and the computer print-outs. Lloyd read the report carefully. When he finished, he passed it to Ed Davenport and handed Matt a copy of the interim post mortem, which had just arrived from the medical examiner's office. Matt noted the medical examiner's confirmation of the fact that Waterson had more than enough alcohol in his system to qualify him as legally intoxicated. The time and cause of death remained the same as in the preliminary post mortem.

"Have you found the weapon yet?" Ed asked Matt as he finished reading the homicide report.

"No, we haven't found the Bowman thirty-eight. Felicia Waterson surrendered a thirty-eight when I questioned her this morning. I'm certain it's not the murder weapon. But I told Sam to match it against the slugs from Waterson's chest anyway."

"Has the medical examiner's office sent the bullets over yet?" Lloyd asked.

"Sam got them this morning. He's working on the prints he lifted from the Bowman house and Waterson's Mercedes. He finished the powder tests on the Bowmans."

"What were the results?" Ed immediately asked, taking the words out of Lloyd's mouth in the process. Not one to take turf intrusion lightly, Lloyd gave Ed a long, hard stare before repeating the same question himself.

"Sam says that none of the Bowmans had powder on their hands."

"Is he sure about that?" Lloyd asked with obvious skepticism.

"He says he's positive."

"The killer wore gloves," Ed suggested. "That fits into a pattern of pre-meditated homicide. It also explains why you haven't found the murder weapon. They got rid of it after they killed him."

"Who are they?" Matt asked Ed.

"The Bowmans, of course, who else?"

"Do you have any one in particular in mind, or are you willing to indict all three?" Lloyd asked.

"That all depends on the circumstances, and their motives. I could prosecute this case from either angle and still win," Ed confidently boasted. "A conspiracy is harder to prosecute, but I can get one of them to turn state's evidence against the other two, I guarantee it."

"You'll still have two Bowmans left," Matt insisted. "Harold Waterson was shot twice, but even you have to admit that it's not likely that he was shot by two different people."

"I agree, Lieutenant. However, one could be indicted for murder while the other two could be prosecuted as accomplices.

I've won similar cases before."

"The Bowmans are a close family, Davenport. It won't be easy to get them to testify against the other. Helen Bowman can legitimately balk at testifying against her husband, and I guarantee you that she'll never testify against her daughter," Matt warned. "The same goes for Walter Bowman. He'll never implicate his daughter in the homicide. I know these people."

"You'd be surprised at what people will do with the proper motivation, Lieutenant. I've prosecuted cases where family members swore they'd die before they turned state's evidence, but they eventually gave us what we wanted after we made them an offer they couldn't refuse. The instinct for self-preservation is stronger than the urge to protect family members. When it comes to serving hard time in the slammer, it's usually every man for himself. They'll confess, all right."

"I wish I shared your optimism, Davenport," Lloyd said.

"Leave it to me, Lloyd. I know I can build a solid case against Angela Bowman with or without her parents' cooperation. From what I gather, she had the clearest motive and the best opportunity to kill Waterson."

"There's something about his case that bothers me," Lloyd insisted. "For instance, Angela Bowman admits that she was having an affair with Waterson and wanted to break it off. Her estranged husband and Claudia Martin both corroborate the fact that she told him she wanted out of the affair, but that Waterson didn't want to let her go. So, it looks like that part of her story is probably true. She admitted letting him into her house Saturday night, but where's her motive for killing him? It seems more likely that he would have tried to kill her under the circumstances. Why the hell would she shoot him in her own house?"

"Maybe he attacked her, or maybe she lied about who wanted to drop whom," Ed suggested. "He may have been the one who wanted out of the affair, and she might have lured him into the basement and killed him out of spite. She could have easily planted her version of who wanted out of the affair with the Martin woman and her husband."

"Where's the evidence for that scenario?" Matt asked Ed.

"Let's, for the moment, concede that he attacked her and she shot him in self-defense," Lloyd said. "Why wouldn't she admit it? She admitted having the affair with him and letting him into the house. The fact that two people knew she wanted out of the affair would have strengthened her story if she admitted shooting him in self-defense. Even if she murdered him in cold blood, she could still claim self-defense with the same corroborating evidence. That's why I don't believe she planted the story about who wanted to end the affair, Ed. If she had deliberately planted lies, it seems to me that she would have used them by now. But, she claims that she didn't kill him under any circumstances. Where's the percentage in that?"

"Maybe she didn't shoot him, Lloyd. Either one of her parents could have come to her defense and killed him," Ed countered.

"In that case, why won't they admit that they shot him to protect their daughter? Both of them deny that they shot him, too. If Hal Waterson was shot in self-defense or accidentally, the Bowmans are damned fools not to admit it. Even if they deliberately killed him, it would still be to their advantage to claim self-defense. Something's not right about this case," Lloyd concluded.

"It depends on whether they felt they had a better chance to beat the rap by stonewalling, Lloyd. It's been tried before," Ed insisted. "Even if they confessed to self-defense or accidental manslaughter, they might still have been indicted for murder. They ran a substantial risk either way."

Lloyd wasn't convinced. "Getting rid of the gun was dumb," he said. "It practically guarantees that they'll be charged with murder."

"They had to get rid of it if it was the murder weapon," Ed reasoned.

"Not if they claimed self-defense."

"Maybe it would have made better sense to claim self-defense and keep the gun, Lloyd, but the facts remain. The gun is missing, none of the Bowmans had powder on their hands, Hal Waterson was having an affair with the daughter, and he was killed in their basement. All that adds up to murder in my book," Ed insisted.

"What about Gary Washington?" Lloyd asked looking at Lieutenant Alexander. "He had a damned good motive to kill Waterson, and he admitted following Angela Bowman home Saturday night."

"That's true," Matt replied. "But we can't place him in the house at the time Waterson was shot, unless Sam finds his prints among those he lifted Saturday night. Gary Washington said he was driving back to Southeast from ten to ten-thirty Saturday night. It's possible Angela Bowman may be protecting him, but it would be at considerable risk to herself and her parents. I don't believe she cares that much about him."

"Maybe she put him up to it," Lloyd suggested. "She may have slipped Washington her father's gun. That would explain why the Bowmans' powder tests are negative and why the gun disappeared."

"It's plausible," Ed admitted. "But I prefer going with one of the suspects who admit being in the house during the time Waterson was shot. Indicting Gary Washington means that we have to prove that he couldn't have been anywhere else during the time in question." Lloyd was more open-minded with respect to Gary's complicity.

"Have Washington tested for powder, Alexander. Have you substantiated his alibi, yet?"

"Not yet, Lloyd. I haven't had time. By the way, Davenport, Angela Bowman claims that Waterson was shot after she left to take ice over to the Martins' cocktail party. She says she went over there shortly after ten o'clock, and Claudia Martin confirms the fact that Angela was over there until approximately ten-fifteen Saturday night. Then she left and went back home."

"Doesn't mean a thing," Ed insisted. "She probably shot him before leaving for the Martins' and then went over there to establish an alibi for herself. Didn't your report mention that both of the Martins denied asking someone to call her for ice, Lieutenant?"

"Yes, that's right. Claudia Martin insists that Angela is lying about the call."

"I agree with the Martin woman. Lying about the call fits into a pattern of pre-meditation, or at the very least complicity in covering up the homicide."

"If the Bowmans killed him, when did they have time to get rid of the gun?" Lloyd asked Ed. "We searched every inch of that house and the surrounding area with metal detectors and didn't find a damned thing. Where could they have hidden it between the time he was killed and the time Walter Bowman called the station?"

"That's a good question," Ed conceded. "It's practically impossible to search a large house without missing something, Lloyd. In my experience, the best way to get that kind of infor-mation is to arrest the lot and interrogate the hell out of them until they break."

"I would agree with you under normal circumstances, Ed, but my instincts tell me to go slow. I don't think this case is as open and shut as it seems, so I'm going to hold off on an arrest until we complete the preliminary investigation."

Turning to Matt Lloyd asked, "Did you talk to the Watersons today?"

"Yes, I just returned from there."

"Did you learn anything useful?"

"There are some strained relations between Waterson's wife

and son and his aunt, but I don't think it directly affects our case. Felicia Waterson knew her husband was having an affair with Angela Bowman, and she admits putting pressure on him to end the relationship."

"That fits my scenario," Ed chimed.

"Let me finish," Matt cautioned. "The Watersons had a big fight Friday night. Apparently, she discovered that he was still seeing Angela Bowman, so she blew her top and issued him an ultimatum. Either he end the affair or else."

"Or else what?" Lloyd asked.

"Or else she'd divorce him and name Angela co-respondent. The interesting thing about all this is how she discovered they were having an affair. She claims that someone sent her an anonymous letter informing her of the affair and that the woman was black."

"That she was black!" Lloyd exclaimed. "What the hell does that have to do with anything? He was black, wasn't he?"

"Yes, he was black, but his wife is white, Lloyd."

It took a moment for Lloyd to get accustomed to the idea.

"You mean Waterson was married to a white woman? I thought she was...well, you know...I though she only looked white like him."

Matt smiled.

"Unfortunately, Lloyd, she's a bona fide Caucasian. The letter didn't reveal the woman's identity, so Felicia Waterson hired Dick Langford to follow her husband for a week. That's how she found out who he was seeing."

Lloyd became incensed at the mere mention of his former nemesis and fellow traveller from the land of Dixie.

"Dick Langford! That ass-hole couldn't find a goddamned needle in a haystack if he sat on it. How the hell did she got hooked up with him?"

"Selected him from the yellow pages, so she claims."

"I'd as soon hire my dog to tail someone as Dick Langford.

My dog's a hell of a lot cheaper and he doesn't drink. We're running around in circles, Alexander. The question is, did Angela Bowman kill Waterson simply because she wanted out of their affair? It seems to me that she had other options short of killing him, like telling his wife about them, or filing a harassment complaint against him."

Ed didn't agree with Lloyd's conclusions.

"You're over-looking the fact that she may have sent the anonymous letter herself, Lloyd. That certainly brought his wife into it."

"Why go to the trouble of sending an anonymous letter when a telephone call would have done just as well?" Lloyd asked Ed.

"Some women have a flair for the dramatic, Lloyd. They like to do things the hard way just for effect."

"Maybe you're right, Ed. The only thing I'm certain about is that the more I know about this case, the more uncertain I am as to why Harold Waterson was killed. Neither of you has given me what I consider to be a credible motive as far as Angela Bowman is concerned. So what if she was going with him? What sense does it make for her to kill him in her house and then claim that she didn't do it?"

"I agree with Lloyd," Matt insisted. "There are some other possibilities, but I haven't had time to pursue them yet. I found a connection between Walter Bowman and Harold Waterson other than Angela Bowman. Do either of you remember the stink that occurred when the District government awarded the Anacostia Riverfront Development contract to Waterson's firm?"

"Yes, I remember that another firm protested the award. The losing firm filed suit, didn't they?" Ed asked.

"Yes, that's right. The Waterson firm's bid was ten million dollars higher than the losing bid. The losing firm was shot down on some technicalities in their bid. The dispute went to arbitration where the original award to Waterson's firm was upheld."

"How is that connected to this case?" Lloyd asked.

"Walter Bowman manages the District Reclamation Land Office. He supervised the awards process for that contract."

"That's very interesting," Lloyd commented. "Did you ask Walter Bowman about the contract dispute?"

"Yes, I did. He swears that everything was handled strictly by-the-book. He even offered to show me his records. Bowman's no slouch, though. If there was some graft involved in the award, it's going to be damned hard to prove."

"You're barking up the wrong tree, Lieutenant," Ed cautioned. "Bribery and graft cases are the worst. It takes months, sometimes years to compile the necessary evidence to prosecute a case like that. I'd never agree to ask for an indictment on the basis of that sort of evidence, not when we've got something as good as the affair between Angela Bowman and the deceased. Looking for evidence of graft in this case is like flying to New York by way of Tokyo when you can get a direct flight from D.C. You reach the same destination with a fraction of the effort."

"I'd like to pursue it anyway," Matt argued. "You never know what may turn up. The other possibilities concerns some information I learned at the Waterson place today, which may or may not amount to anything. When I asked Felicia Waterson what she did Saturday night, she claimed that she went to bed early and was home all night. Harold Waterson's aunt lives in the house, and she claims that Mrs. Waterson left the house at nine o'clock Saturday night and didn't return until approximately eleven o'clock. The question is who do you believe because one of them is lying. There's no love lost between the two of them either."

"Who do you think is lying?" Lloyd asked Matt.

"My instincts tell me that it's Felicia Waterson. She was expected at the Martins' cocktail party, so she had a legitimate reason for going out. She didn't show up there, but her husband did and he wasn't expected at the party without her. If she went out, the question is where did she go and what did she do?"

"What makes you think that Waterson's aunt is telling the truth?" Ed asked.

"I'm not totally convinced that she is," Matt conceded. "She was devastated by her nephew's death, so she may be pointing the finger of suspicion at Felicia Waterson out of spite. But, she doesn't strike me as the kind of person who'd plant a deliberate lie like that. She's very religious, but that could be a smoke-screen. She also told me that the Watersons' son, William, overheard the fight between his father and mother Friday night. When I questioned him about that fight, he denied knowing anything about it."

"It seems that anyone who had a grudge against Harold Waterson was on the prowl Saturday night," Lloyd pessimistically concluded.

"It does look that way," Matt agreed. "William Waterson claims that he was home Saturday evening; but he doesn't have any witnesses. He says he was alone all night, claimed to be studying for mid-term exams."

"You aren't seriously suggesting that his wife or son killed him are you, Lieutenant?" Ed asked a little incredulously.

"I'm not suggesting anything, Davenport. I'm simply trying to account for the facts as they were presented to me."

"If you ask me, his wife had a stronger motive for killing him than Angela Bowman," Lloyd stated. "She probably stands to inherit his estate and she admitted issuing him an ultimatum."

"None of the evidence places her at the scene, Lloyd," Ed cautioned. "It's her word against the aunt's as to whether she left the house Saturday night. Even the Lieutenant here admits that the aunt has an ax to grind."

"So where are we?" Lloyd asked.

"We're as far as we're going to go without an arrest," Ed confidently asserted. "I'll wager the Bowmans know where the murder weapon is, but you won't get it out of them until you put them on the hot seat one-by-one. I don't know why you've waited this long."

"The word came down from on high," Lloyd replied. "Chief Carter doesn't want any foul-ups with this case, Ed, so I'm not going to rush into anything. One false move could cost me a hell of a lot more than I'm willing to pay."

"The longer you wait to make a move, the more time they'll have to cover their tracks, Lloyd. You have to strike while the iron is hot. Chief Carter is trying to keep the heat off him. If you wait too long, you'll lose all your momentum. Arrest them now and answer to the downtown brass later. He can't fire you for doing your job can he?"

"The hell he can't," Lloyd insisted. "Give all the advice you want, Ed, but I'm the one who'll get it in the neck if this case blows up in my face."

"Lloyd's right," Matt said. "I'll need at least one more day to follow up on some obvious leads like Gary Washington, Dick Langford, and the maid and bartender who served the Martins' party. We need to know what these people have to say before we arrest anyone."

"You're wasting your time, Lieutenant. You can run around ten barns and you'll still come back to the Bowmans. You'll save yourself a lot of time and effort if you arrest them now. There's no getting around the fact that Waterson was killed in their basement while all three of them were in the house. I don't need the gun to convict them. They're sitting ducks, just waiting to be indicted."

"You're probably right, Ed, but I'm going to give Alexander another day to complete his investigation anyway. I'll set up a meeting with Chief Carter for Wednesday morning. I want every piece of information you have on this case typed and on my desk first thing Wednesday, Alexander. We'll present what we have to the Chief at the meeting and let him decide who to arrest."

"Suit yourself, Lloyd," Ed Davenport admonished as he prepared to leave. "I gave you the best legal advice around for free. That consultation would have cost you a thousand dollars if I was charging."

"Only if I was dumb enough to pay for it," Lloyd laughed. "Look here, Ed. You're lucky I didn't charge you for listening to that spiel. People have been arrested for less."

Ed laughed too.

"You can lead a horse to water, Lloyd, but you can't tell him a damned thing once he drinks his fill. Don't say I didn't warn you, buddy. Strike while the iron is hot, that's my advice."

Matt got up to leave, too, but Lloyd motioned for him to stay.

"Do you think you can get all that done by tomorrow, Alexander?"

"Yes. It'll be a tight squeeze, but I can do it." Lloyd thought for a moment before asking: "Who do you think killed him, Lieutenant?"

"Unless we find some concrete evidence to the contrary, I'd say that Ed is right. Angela Bowman is the most obvious suspect. On the basis of the evidence we've uncovered so far, it would be hard to develop a sound case for charging anyone else."

"It looks that way," Lloyd agreed. "Keep digging. You may find something we can use. In the meantime, I'm going to read these statements and the homicide report again. I can't shake the feeling that there's a missing link somewhere...something we've overlooked that might explain a lot we don't know yet."

Matt doubted that Lloyd would find his magic bullet. There weren't any glaring inconsistencies in the statements, just a pattern that didn't reasonably add up to murder. Manslaughter, yes, but not murder. He left Lloyd's office at a quarter past four. The evening shift had arrived, so there was plenty of noise and traffic on the stairs. Jake was waiting for him in the office.

"How'd it go, man?"

"Not too bad, all things considered. Ed Davenport was there.

He advised Lloyd to arrest all the Bowmans and interrogate the hell out of them until they tell us what they did with the gun."

"Did Lloyd go along with that?"

"No, he didn't. I expected him to jump at the bait, Jake, but our Commander actually showed some restraint."

"That's not like Cullison, man. What's come over him?"

"It's not what's come over him as much as what's going to come down on him if he fucks this case up."

"What's that?"

"Chief Carter, like a ton of bricks. Lloyd is running scared, man, and I don't blame him one bit. His career is riding on this case."

"It looks like an open and shut case to me. One of the Bowmans must have killed him. Who else had the chance?"

"You're probably right, Jake, but there are still some loose ends that haven't been investigated."

"Like what, man?"

"Like Waterson's secretary. He made two appointments for Saturday afternoon. I want to know who came to see him on the day he died. I also need to question the Martins' bartender and maid. They may be able to tell us whether Angela Bowman really got that call for ice as she like she says."

"Is that all?"

"No, I have to talk to Dick Langford, too."

"He's private, now. Why do you need to talk to him?"

"Mrs. Waterson hired him to follow her husband. That's how she found out he was having an affair with Angela Bowman."

"So, she knew all about them, huh?"

"Looks like it. She was squeezing him to stop seeing Angela. That's why he wanted Angela to move to New York City. The Watersons had one helluva fight last Friday night, Jake. Felicia Waterson says that she threatened to divorce Hal Waterson if he didn't stop seeing Angela Bowman."

"Old Waterson didn't want to give her up, did he?"

"Looks like he was between a rock and a hard place."

"Too bad, the rock landed on him when it did," Jake mused. But I can't blame him for holding onto her, Matt. She's a knockout."

"Nobody's worth the price he paid, including Angela."

"What's next on the agenda?" Jake asked.

"The maid and bartender and Gary Washington's apartment building. He says he was back home in Southeast by ten-thirty Saturday night. I want to see if anyone in his building can place him there at that time. He also says he stopped at the service station on the corner of Columbia Road and Eighteenth Street to gas up on his way back to Southeast. We can check that out on the way over there."

"Where do the maid and bartender live?"

"The bartender lives in Oxon Hill, Maryland. The maid lives in Anacostia."

"You ready to go?"

"Not yet. I have to do some work on the Waterson statements before I leave. Why don't you get yourself something to eat while I finish them. I should be ready at five-thirty."

"Do you want me to bring you something back?"

"No thanks, man. I'll get something later."

After Jake left, Matt called Carla to tell her he wouldn't be home for dinner. She was a good deal more understanding than he expected. After he rang off, it occurred to him that her replies had been distant, as if she had something more important on her mind. Then he remembered that her Thanksgiving dinner party was just two days away. Carla had invited his mother, her parents, her sisters, and Jake and Florence. It promised to be quite a production number for her. He was confident that she could pull it off, but she didn't share his optimism. Either way, it promised to be an interesting dinner.

Jake got back at five-thirty P.M. on the nose. It took Matt

fifteen minutes more to finish what he was working on. Jake was tired of waiting for his partner when, at six-thirty, Matt finally put all the information on the Waterson homicide in his brief case, intending to read it thoroughly after he got home.

So far the case was still fragmented for Matt. The major clues weren't contradictory, but they refused to coalesce to form a cohesive picture of what had occurred Saturday night and why. The evidence remained diffuse. The signs were there, but their significance eluded him. Harold Waterson's character was still shrouded in mystery. Like a chameleon, his personality depended on who described him. He was a hero to Aunt Martha, a villain to his son, an adulterer to his wife, and a nuisance to Angela Bowman. It was hard to isolate a clear picture of the deceased from so much difference of opinion, but it had to be done. A lot was riding on why Waterson attended the Martins' party alone. Was he lured there? Angela Bowman hadn't attended the party, but she may have intentionally waylaid him once he left.

Matt still didn't know what Waterson had done between the time he dropped Aunt Martha off at his house on Reservoir Road Saturday morning and the time he arrived at the Martins' party. Those hours were shaping up to be crucial. If someone lured him to the cocktail party, they probably did so during that time. It was reasonable to assume that his wife asked him to go in her place, but she denied it. Felicia Waterson had appeared genuinely surprised when she learned that her husband had attended the fundraiser without her. She may have been pretending, but Matt didn't think so. And, if she didn't ask him to attend for her, what possessed him to go alone?

"We'd better get a move on if you want to get out to Southeast before dark, man. Addresses out there aren't easy to find in the dark."

"I have everything I need. Let's go."

As they walked across the lot to Matt's car, Jake asked,

"When do you think Lloyd will go for an arrest?"

"Wednesday, for sure. He gave me one more day to complete the investigation. We meet with Chief Carter first thing Wednesday morning. Somebody will be in custody by quitting time Wednesday afternoon, Jake. You can count on it."

"I'll be relieved when it's all over," Jake said, as if he were the one who had been working around the clock.

"You won't be half as relieved as I will, Jake. This case is kicking my butt, man."

The service station was on the northwest corner at the intersection of Columbia Road and Eighteenth Street. There were two attendants at the station when they arrived. Matt passed the picture of Gary Washington around. None of the station attendants recognized him. Both of the attendants were on duty Saturday night, but they both swore they had never seen Gary Washington before. Being old, the gas station didn't have any credit-card pumps, so one of them must have taken Gary's money if he really stopped there for gas. Of course, there was always the possibility that he stopped and they simply didn't remember him. Matt left the station by way of the Duke Ellington Memorial Bridge, which he took to Calvert Street. From there he drove south on Rock Creek Parkway toward Southeast.

Driving into Anacostia, his old stomping grounds, Matt thought about how isolated the far southeast community was from the rest of the District. When he was growing up there, living in Anacostia was much like living west of the park in a pejorative sense. It wasn't unusual to hear long-time District residents insist that they had never been to Southeast across the river, particularly Anacostia — a community that appeared to be more densely populated per square mile than any other area of the city. Matt knew that Anacostia's rolling hills had the best panoramas in the entire city, but hardly anyone seemed to know or care. He blamed the lack of interest on the fact that

Anacostia's hills were smothered in low-cost, multi-unit, subsidized apartment dwellings whose form, function, and density had long since eclipsed the natural beauty of the community.

There wasn't much sense of an Anacostia community in touch with its natural terrain with the exception of the spectacular vistas provided by Cedar Hill, the ancestral home of Frederick Douglass Washington's namesake. Matt knew the streets in Anacostia weren't laid out like they were in better planned sectors of the District. The disorganization created an unexpected charm, but it was common to search in vain for a street address that ought to be where it should be but wasn't.

Their progress across the Southwest Freeway slowed perceptibly as traffic approached the Anacostia Bridge. Matt looked south down the bank of the Anacostia River and saw the area that had been targeted for the city's Riverfront Development Project. Huge signs denoting the firm Waterson, Sullivan, & Loew as general contractor were posted at the boundaries of the project. Seeing the signs made him wonder again whether there was a connection between the project and Waterson's homicide. He wouldn't have time to follow that lead before the Wednesday morning meeting with Chief Carter; but he promised himself to investigate it regardless of who was arrested. Traffic inched across the Anacostia Bridge onto Good Hope Road. Matt drove east on Good Hope through what had been the tiny Anacostia business district until he arrived at Gary Washington's apartment building at the corner of Good Hope and Naylor Roads.

The building superintendent was cooperative. She knew Gary Washington by sight, but she hadn't been on duty Saturday night. She introduced them to the building security guard who was on duty that night. The guard refused to commit himself one way or the other. It would be almost impossible for him to pinpoint a particular person at a specific time. He wouldn't swear to it either way. They struck out with Gary's story twice.

Ed Davenport was right. They couldn't prove that Gary wasn't where he said he was.

"Where do we go from here?" Jake asked as they left the building.

"Oxon Hill. The bartender lives on Cold Spring Drive. That's only a couple of miles from here," Matt replied.

Frank Sawyer, the bartender, was parking his car in his driveway when they drove up. Sawyer walked over to their car when he saw them park in front of his house. A dark, solidly built man, Frank Sawyer was big...at least two hundred and eighty well-distributed pounds on a six-foot-four-inch frame. He could easily have been a Redskins defensive tackle. He hadn't run to fat yet, but the potential was definitely there. Sawyer walked to the end of his driveway and waited for the two officers to get out of their car. Matt was the first to speak. He told Frank Sawyer why they wanted to talk to him after introducing himself and Jake. Sawyer looked uneasy at the mention of the homicide, but he readily identified the picture of Harold Waterson Matt showed him. All three men sat in Matt's car while Sawyer was questioned.

"So, you remember seeing Waterson at the Martins' party?"

"Yeah, Lieutenant. I saw him there, but I took him for a white dude. There were quite a few of them there, and I thought he was one, too."

"Do you remember what time he arrived at the party, Mr. Sawyer?"

"No. I wasn't paying much attention to when people arrived. When you're tending bar for a large party, you don't have much time to notice when people are coming and going."

"Do you tend bar for a living, Mr. Sawyer?"

"No. I only do that on the side to make extra money. My regular job is at the government printing office on North Capitol Street. I've tended bar part-time for ten years. I started doing it regularly the year I bought this house. The Martins are my best customers, so I make a special point of working their parties whenever they ask me to. They pay good money and give large tips too."

"Did you see much of Harold Waterson while he was there Saturday night?"

"I'll say I did. He was drinking like a fish. When I saw that he was loaded, I started cutting back on the liquor I put in his drinks. He was drinking Scotch and soda, mainly soda after I saw how many drinks he had put under his belt."

"Did you mention his condition to the Martins?"

"Never said a word, Lieutenant. I just do my job. I don't try to tell people how to run their parties. But, I don't like to see anyone get loaded on my drinks and drive themselves home. I have nightmares about being hit by a drunk from a party I served."

"You don't drink do you, Mr. Sawyer?"

"Never touch the stuff. It's poison, pure and simple."

"How many drinks would you estimate you served Waterson Saturday night?"

"At least four that I can remember, and he wasn't there that long. That's why I started to hold back on the Scotch."

"Now, this is important, Mr. Sawyer. Do you remember anything unusual about Waterson, like him arguing or having a heated conversation with another guest?"

"That's a tough question for a bartender, Lieutenant. When people drink they ordinarily get a little rambunctious. Man, you wouldn't believe some of the things I've seen serving parties. So, unless someone is really making a fool out out themselves, I don't pay much attention."

"Did you see him talking to any one person in particular?"

"No, I didn't. He was always alone when he came to the bar to refresh his drinks."

"Who stocked the Martins' bar Saturday night?"

"Doc Martin. He always buys what he needs for his parties.

The only thing I bring is my uniform."

"This is important too, Mr. Sawyer. Did you run out of ice at any time during the party?"

"No, indeed. Doc Martin bought more ice than I could use. He always does. There were two full bags left when the party was over."

"Are you sure about that?"

"I'm positive. I put them in the basement freezer myself. Who says we ran out of ice?"

"No one, Mr. Sawyer. I was simply curious. So, you didn't tell anyone that you needed more ice?"

"That would have been stupid, considering how much we had on hand, Lieutenant."

"Did you happen to see Waterson leave the party?"

"No, I didn't. You can't see the front door from the bar in the family room."

"What time did you finish tending bar, Mr. Sawyer?"

"Around ten o'clock. It took me a while longer to clean up around the bar. I was hired to stay from seven to ten, so I packed it in at ten o'clock. I left at ten twenty-five."

"Did you notice anyone hanging around outside when you left at ten twenty-five?"

"There was someone walking toward the house on Floribunda. They seemed to be in a hurry."

"Did you get a good look at the person in your headlights?"

"No, I didn't. My headlights were pointed east, the same direction they were walking. I didn't think there was anything unusual about it at the time."

"Could you tell whether the person walking toward you was a man or a woman, Mr. Sawyer?"

"It was too dark, and they were too far away, Lieutenant. I couldn't say for certain."

"I guess that's all for now, Mr. Sawyer. By the way, do you know the maid who helped you serve on Saturday night?"

"Yeah. I've known Thelma Wallace a long time. She's one of my church members. I recommended her to the Martins."

"How long has she known the Martins?"

"She just met them on Saturday. Thelma's new to the party circuit, so I had to show her the ropes. She's a hard worker and she catches on fast. She and I are going to team up. You get more work that way, especially if you're good." Matt looked at his watch.

"Thanks for your time, Mr. Sawyer. You'll have to sign a written statement detailing what you've told me; but it's strictly routine procedure. We'll call you when it's ready." They left after Frank Sawyer got out of the car.

Sawyer hadn't expected the visit, so he took a minute to mull over what had transpired. He watched the car drive away with more than a little apprehension. He hoped the Martins weren't involved in the homicide more for his sake than theirs. His primary consideration was financial rather than legal or moral. He didn't know where they stood on murder, but they paid good money plus tips. And, he had made a good piece of change off them over the years. Without the extra income he made from tending bar, Frank Sawyer knew he would quickly sink into debt and eventually lose his house. He definitely couldn't afford to lose good customers like the Martins.

Matt drove back to Anacostia via Suitland Parkway. He was intrigued by Frank Sawyer's account of someone walking toward the Bowman house at ten twenty-five because that person was also walking away from the creek.

"Who do you think that was walking east on Floribunda?" Jake asked his partner.

"It could have been anybody."

"It might have been one of the Bowmans. Maybe they did throw the gun in the creek after all, Matt."

"Could be, but it seems more likely that they would have used the service alley behind the house instead of the street to keep from being seen."

"Yeah, that's true. But, when you're running scared you aren't always as careful as you ought to be."

Thelma Wallace lived on Bowen Road. Matt directed Jake to her house with ease. Jake was always amazed at how well Matt knew the most obscure streets in Anacostia, streets that he himself had never heard of, let alone visited. Thelma Wallace's house was the only single family residence on Bowen Road. It stood out like an oasis in the middle of a desert of down-at-heel garden-side apartments. It had to be a precarious way to live at best, but obviously worth it to Thelma Wallace and her family. The front of the house was as neat as could be considering the amount of foot traffic that moved up and down Bowen Road. It was quite dark when they parked in front of her house. Matt's watch said eight-thirty which wasn't bad considering the amount of time they had spent in traffic and the stops they had made before they arrived at Thelma Wallace's front door.

They knocked on the front door. All the lower level windows were protected by burglar bars. Thelma Wallace looked through her peephole, saw them standing on her stoop and refused to let them in. Matt tried to convince her that they were police officers, but she wouldn't be moved by their badges or identification cards.

"Tell her to call Frank Sawyer," Jake suggested. "He can vouch for us."

It took Thelma a few minutes to place the call. She let them in after that, but she was still wary all the same. Thelma's house was scrupulously clean. It even smelled clean, like she disinfected it regularly. Her living room was bursting at the seams with furniture, what-nots, and dubiously arranged bric-a-brac as unique as its owner. All the stuffed furniture was draped in plastic slip covers. The living room walls were covered with religious paintings from the Old and New Testaments. Thelma looked as religious as her paintings and as straight-laced as a corset. Thelma quickly informed them that she wasn't alone, claiming to share the house with her invalid mother. She listened intently as Matt explained the purpose of their visit. After he finished, she vigorously denied knowing anything about the homicide. When he informed her that the news of Waterson's death had been in all the papers and on radio and television, too, she didn't recant. Thelma emphatically pointed out that she read only Christian material and that her radio and television time was restricted to religious programming. According to Thelma Wallace anything else was the work of the devil and she refused to succumb to his evil influence. She said that most of the programs on radio and television were an affront to God and that she, for one, wasn't about to be corrupted by them. Both detectives stood patiently while Thelma read them the religious riot act. She reluctantly offered them seats when she saw that they didn't intend to challenge her version of what she knew. She chose the most uncomfortable looking chair in the living room for herself.

Thelma was attractive in a quiet sort of way. Matt guessed her age to be forty, but her nondescript dress and sensible black shoes made her look at least fifty. She wore a loose fitting button-down-the-front brown dress with a nigh neck and long sleeves. Devoid of make-up, Thelma's face was as clean as her house. She wore her hair pulled away from her heart-shaped face and twisted into a bun on the nape of her neck. Her large brown eyes were wary, and her full, beautifully-formed lips were pursed.

In Matt's opinion, Thelma Wallace suffered from too much religion. Women like her snuffed the candle out on life too soon. They extinguished the fire before it got hot enough to give them an appetite for loving. He decided that Thelma would do well to loosen her corset, shorten her dress, let her hair down, and save the religion for when she really needed it. She had the rest of her life to be prim and matronly; but there she sat, as proper as a

Sunday school teacher, which she probably was. He correctly guessed that Thelma wouldn't know a good time from a cold shower. He was certain that repressed sensuality smoldered somewhere beneath that religious armor, but it would take a good deal of time and patience to stoke it into a flame, time that could probably be put to more productive use. Thelma Wallace appeared to be a terminal case. Matt showed her the photograph of Harold Waterson.

"Do you remember seeing this man at the Martins' cocktail party Miss Wallace?"

"Yes, I remember him. He was drunk the whole time he was there. He must have been drinking before he came because he didn't stay that long."

"Do you remember what time he arrived at the party?"

"No, I didn't see him come in, but I know he wasn't there when the party started."

"Do you remember when he left?"

"Yes. He left just as Frank started cleaning up around the bar. I was collecting empty glasses from the living room when the Martins said goodbye to him at the door."

"How long have you known the Martins, Miss Wallace?"

"I only met them on Saturday before the party started. Frank Sawyer recommended me to them. Are they mixed up in this killing?" she warily asked.

"Not as far as we know, but they were some of the last people to see the deceased alive the night he was killed."

"Who killed him?"

"That's what we're trying to find out. Did you notice anything strange or out of the ordinary about him while he was at the party?"

"I saw that he was drunk," she replied with a full measure of disgust.

"Do you drink, Miss Wallace?" Matt needlessly asked, knowing full well that she didn't.

"I've been saved, Lieutenant Alexander. When you're filled with the spirit of our Lord and Savior, Jesus Christ, you don't need artificial stimulation. I get high just by singing His praises. Alcohol is an abomination before the Almighty. It's what the devil uses to lure us into hell fire and damnation. It's bottled sin."

"If you feel that strongly about drinking, why would you served a cocktail party, Miss Wallace?"

"I don't like it, Lieutenant, but I have to make a living. My mother is bedridden and I have to hire someone to look after her while I'm at work during the day. I don't make much money working as a nurses' aide at the hospital. I need that extra money, Lord knows I do."

"Did you notice the deceased arguing with anyone at the party Saturday night, Miss Wallace?"

"Well, I was moving around a lot, but I saw him talking to Dr. Martin for a while...I think. I know I saw him talking to Mrs. Martin just before he left. They weren't arguing, though. They were just talking, as far as I could tell."

"Did you notice him talking to anyone else, Miss Wallace?"

"Well, there was a man who acted kind of funny when he...the man who was killed I mean, walked into the family room. I was in there serving some snacks on a tray. I walked up to this man and offered him some. Well, he reached for the food and his eye caught the man who was killed. Then he got nervous and spilled his drink all over the tray, so I had to go back to the kitchen and fix another snack tray."

Matt was definitely interested.

"Who was the man that spilled his drink?"

"Mrs. Martin called him Walter. I don't know his last name, but I do remember that his wife was named Helen."

"I know exactly who you're referring to, Miss Wallace. Did the man named Walter say anything to the deceased?"

"I don't know. You see, I left right after he spilled his drink into the tray."

"Did you see Waterson talking to either Walter or his wife, later on?"

"No, I didn't."

"Now, I have something very important to ask you Miss Wallace, and I want you to think very carefully before you answer. Did either Tom or Claudia Martin ask you to call next door to borrow some ice?"

"Borrow some ice? No, they didn't ask me to do any such thing."

"Did you hear anyone place a call like that?"

"No, I didn't. When did they run out of ice? It looked like they had plenty to me."

"So it seems," Matt replied. "What time did you leave the Martins', Miss Wallace?"

"I left at eleven-thirty."

"Did you notice anything unusual when you left?"

"There were several police cars parked out front."

"Weren't you curious about that?"

"No, I wasn't. I like to steer clear of trouble, Lieutenant, so I don't pry into things that don't concern me. Whatever was wrong, I figured the police could handle it a lot better than me."

"Do you recall seeing a woman named Angela Bowman in the Martins' kitchen Saturday night?"

"Yes. She was helping Mrs. Martin with the food."

"Do you recall what time she got there?"

"Not exactly, but I do remember that it was after the man who was killed left."

"Did you let her in the back door?"

"No, I didn't. Did she say I let her in?"

"No, she didn't. Were you in the kitchen when she left?"

"No. I took the food Mrs. Martin had fixed out to the dining room table. I didn't see her leave, but I do know that she wasn't in the kitchen when I went back in there a little while later."

"Can you think of anything else you'd like to tell us, Miss Wallace?"

"No, I can't, Lieutenant. I've answered your questions the best I can, but I don't know anything about that man being killed Saturday night."

Matt thanked Thelma Wallace for her cooperation and left. Thelma locked at least three dead-bolt locks inside her front door after she let them out. She watched them through the burglar bars of her living room window.

Matt made a U-turn on Bowen Road and drove the short distance to Howard Road, which led to the interstate. They left Anacostia via the interstate. Their next stop was Jake's house on Ridge Road north of Fort Dupont Park. He dropped Jake off at nine-thirty and headed for LeDroit Park.

When he got home, he found Carla at the kitchen table pouring over recipe books. She made some polite inquiries about the case, but it was clear that she had other things on her mind.

"Why are you looking through cookbooks, Carla? I thought you had already decided on a menu."

"I had, but it was so humdrum. The same Thanksgiving dinner I've eaten all my life. I wanted to have something different this year."

"Don't get fancy, Carla. When you have people over, it's best to stick to things that you know will work. You shouldn't serve anything you haven't fixed before."

"I won't do anything far out, honey, but I did want to do something a little special."

"I like your regular Thanksgiving dinner. I think you ought to keep the menu you already selected. It sounded fine to me."

"Let's compromise. I'll fix everything on that menu plus a couple of new dishes. If they don't work out, I'll dump them before the meal, and no one will know. How's that?"

"I'll buy that. Did I get any calls today?"

"Yes, you did. I left the messages on your desk. You seem to be very popular these days."

"Not by choice, Carla. If I were smart, I would have quit the force along time ago."

"Who are you trying to kid, Matthew? You know you love your work. Sometimes I think you love your work more than you love me."

"You know better than that, Baby. Everything I do is for you and the kids."

"I have a newsflash for you, honey. The kids and I would rather have you at home with us. Do you love us enough to take a job that won't keep you away so much? We simply love having you around the house...in one piece. You don't have the safest job around either, you know."

"You knew the demands of my job when you married me, Carla. It hasn't been that bad, has it?"

Carla instantly felt guilty for putting him on the spot. He had that effect on her. She replied, "Of course not. It's just that I would like to see more of my husband while I'm still young enough to enjoy his company."

"You can enjoy my company right now. Let's go to bed."

"I wasn't fishing for a roll in the hay, so I'll pass if you don't mind."

"I do mind very much, but have it your own way. I'm going downstairs to work, and I don't want you down there bothering me later on. Remember, you had your chance and you blew it."

"You may not believe it, Detective Lieutenant Alexander, but I'll survive the night."

"You'll live to regret those words," he laughed.

"Why did you bring work home? Haven't you worked on the case all day?"

"This investigation hasn't clicked yet, Carla, so I'm going to spend some time tonight just thinking about it; maybe it'll begin to make more sense."

"Everyone thinks Angela Bowman shot him, Matthew. You ought to arrest her and be done with it."

"I wish I could be as certain as you are, Carla. But there are minor matters to clear up first, like evidence."

"You'll never convince me she didn't kill him."

"I hope you're not called for jury duty if she is arrested. She wouldn't stand a chance."

"It would serve her right, too. I don't have a bit of sympathy for her. The only reason you haven't arrested her is because you feel sorry for her."

"That's not true. We haven't made an arrest because the investigation isn't complete."

"You're a soft touch, honey, but that's why I married you. If I ever kill someone, I'm going to insist that you handle my case."

"That would be a conflict of interest, Carla. Besides, if you ever kill someone, you're on your own."

"That's gratitude for you. You work your fingers to the bone for Angela Bowman and throw me to the wolves."

"I'll bring the children to see you on visitors' day," he laughed. You can't ask for much more than that."

"Thanks, for nothing, Matthew."

Matt left Carla at the kitchen table with her cookbooks. His basement study was damp as usual, so he reluctantly flipped the on-switch on the little electric heater near his desk. He began work immediately, reading through everything once. It took an hour and a half, but no clear pattern emerged. On the second read-through, a faint glimmer of intuition stirred somewhere in the back of his mind. The third time through, it almost jumped off the page. He still didn't know who had killed Harold Waterson, but he was certain that he knew who sent Felicia Waterson the anonymous letter.

# (HAPTER XIII

Dick Langford's office was in the Madison Building on the corner of Thirteenth and "G" Streets in downtown Washington. When Matt and Jake arrived at the fifth floor office, they found Dick sitting at his desk drinking his morning coffee and reading his morning paper. He was expecting them. Short, stocky, and past his prime, Dick Langford barely eked out a living as a private investigator. His one-room office screamed for a good cleaning, and the closest he came to a secretary was the answering machine on his secondhand desk.

Dick Langford had taken early retirement from the District police force ten years before. He had worked his way up to the rank of Detective-Sergeant when it occurred to him that he was taking the easy way out. The police force had never been his ultimate ambition, but the job security and steady paycheck had a strangle hold on him. Most of his dreams had died on the vine from want of courage to risk the financial security of the DCPD against his long-deferred ambition to run his own detective agency. During his fifteen years on the force, Dick never relented in his determination to get out of the system before it used him up and put him out to pasture. So, ten years earlier, he had finally summoned the courage to risk job security and a regular paycheck to follow his dream of starting his own detective agency.

Regular confrontations with the homicide division captain at that time, Lloyd Cullison, hastened his decision to take early retirement. He had started the Langford Detective Agency immediately after he left the DCPD and never once regretted his decision. Full capacity was a staff of two, Dick and an office temporary who was usually forced to spend a day cleaning before any office work could be done. Dick made very little money from the agency, but it satisfied him to be his own boss.

Sunlight streaming through the window behind his desk wasn't kind to Dick. It danced over his sparse blond crew cut and bounced off his bald spot. Not that Dick cared one way or the other. He had long since abandoned any pretense to vanity. Content with his paunches and jowls, Dick Langford enjoyed his food, cigars, liquor, and women, in that order. A two-fisted bourbon man, Dick could drink his friends under the table and walk away under his own steam. A born and bred southerner from Valdosta, Georgia, he had called the District of Columbia home for twenty-five years and two wives. He loved marriage but, marriage didn't love him. Recently divorced from his second wife, he was temporarily living in a downtown residential hotel and hating every minute of it. He got depressed thinking about the fact that he owned two houses, but was legally excluded from living in either one of them. He tried not to think about it.

Dick loved home cooked meals southern style. During the week, he could likely be found at the Florida Avenue Grill wolfing down collard greens, fried chicken, and corn bread. It was home cooking to him, one of the last remaining vestiges of a way of life he had eagerly abandoned three decades ago. He rarely went back to Valdosta, now that his parents were dead and most of his family had moved away. But, he didn't need to go back because the Valdosta he knew was no longer there; and the values he learned from that way of life were still with him...at least the ones he cared to keep alive.

"Well, well, what have we here? I figured you for Monday at the latest, Lieutenant. What took you so long?" Dick asked in a resonant drawl.

"We were waiting for you to come to us, Langford. Whatever happened to your loyalty to the force, man?" Matt cynically inquired.

"I got rid of that load of horseshit the same day I retired. Flushed it down the toilet with my last crap as I recall. It's every man for himself out here in the real world, Alexander. I'm loyal to myself and my clients in that order."

"That's obvious, man. Just wait until you need another favor from me, Langford. I wouldn't lift a finger to help you out again."

"I run a confidential business here, Alexander. My clients trust my discretion; otherwise, they wouldn't give me their business. You don't seriously expect me to ruin my reputation for the DCPD do you? I haven't been on the city's payroll for ten years."

"It wouldn't have hurt you to drop a dime on me, Langford."

"Give me a break, Lieutenant. If I blabbed my clients' confidential affairs to every Tom, Dick, and Harry who wanted to know, I would be out of business in no time flat. Besides, there's no harm done. You found out what you needed to know from Felicia Waterson. She must have told you about the tail, otherwise you wouldn't be here."

"She told me yesterday, not that you give a damn, Langford."

"You judge me too harshly, Lieutenant. Now that you're here, I'll show you just how cooperative I can be. This is the Waterson file," Dick stated pointing to a scruffy manila folder that had to be as old as his agency. "It's a confidential file, of course, but I'm offering it to you in the spirit of cooperation and mutual advantage. Here, read it."

Matt took the file rather suspiciously and began to read it while Jake spoke for the first time.

"Man, this place smells like an armpit. Open the window and let some fresh air in here," Jake insisted.

The stagnant air reeked of stale cigar smoke and discarded sandwich wrappings in the waste basket.

"The air is part of the decor, Jackson. It gives the room ambience."

"Ambience, nothing. It stinks in here. Open the windows, Langford."

"You call that stew of pollution out there fresh air? It's nothing but gasoline fumes and particulate matter. I'd rather smell stale cigar smoke than ruin my lungs with that poison. I have to breathe it when I go out, but I don't have to breathe it in here."

"That's a load of crap, man. Some fresh air would do this place a world of good."

"Shows how much you know, Jackson. My clients pay good money for this decor. Once they get a load of the ambience, they figure I'm either very good at what I do or very lousy. If they stay long enough to hear me out, they're hooked. So, breathe deep, this air is money in the bank," Dick laughed.

"You're full of it, Langford."

"See anything interesting, Lieutenant?"

"Hell no. Is this the complete file?"

"I only tailed him for a week. I tried to drag it out; but Felicia Waterson wouldn't go for it. She's a shrewd lady. I should have gotten at least two weeks out of the case before I told her who he was seeing. I'm too honest for my own good."

"Honest! Don't make me laugh, Langford. Who else did you see him with besides Angela Bowman?"

"What makes you think I saw him with someone else, Alexander? That file there tells the whole story. Angela Bowman was the only person Harold Waterson met while I was tailing him, aside from the usual business lunches, of course. They're noted in there by the way."

"Give me a break, Langford. What I want to know is did you see him with anyone else connected to the homicide case?"

"Everything I saw is in the file, Lieutenant."

"When donkeys fly. Save that song and dance for your suckers, Langford. You know something you're not telling us."

"I may or I may not. What's in it for me?"

"Let's talk about what's not in it for you, Langford. If you tell me what you know, I won't arrest you for withholding evidence; and you won't lose your private investigator's license."

"Come off it, Alexander. You can't scare me with that kind of talk. I've been there, remember. The fact is that I have some information you want. You don't know it yet, but you have some information I want. I suggest we trade off. How about it?"

"Why should I trade with you? If you don't tell me what you know, I'm going to arrest your ass for withholding evidence. It's as simple as that, Langford."

"I like to think of myself as a diplomat, Lieutenant. Diplomacy is an art, you know. You need finesse to negotiate a sensitive situation like the one we have here into a satisfactory conclusion for everybody concerned. I've always believed that it's to my advantage to leave my customers satisfied. I don't like to leave a bad taste in anybody's mouth if I can help it. You never know when that person will cross your path again. Now, take the solution you're proposing to our little dilemma here, Alexander. Arresting me would leave a very bad taste in my mouth; and you still wouldn't have the information you need. That may not bother you, but it concerns me a lot. Fraternizing with the criminal element in close quarters doesn't make my list of things to do before I die. Frankly speaking, arresting me ought to be a last resort for both of us. Now, I have a counterproposal that'll give both of us what we need and keep me out of the slammer at the same time."

"I'm listening," Matt replied.

"It's like this, Alexander. I'm working on a case that's got me stumped, and I've researched it as far back as I can go on my own."

"So what do you want from me?"

"I need to use the computer at central processing."

"That's out of the question, Langford. You know I can't authorize anyone outside the department to use the system."

"I know that, but you could get the information for me. I've already got the routine written up. All you have to do is enter it into the computer. The instructions in the routine will let you access the city's back tax file. It's easy," Dick alleged as he gave the computer routine to Matt.

"And what if I'm caught? You know we have to pay central processing for all the computer time we use. If Lloyd catches a charge that doesn't look kosher, he'll be on my ass like a bulldog on a bone."

"Does Cullison still have his nose to the grind? Some people never learn do they?"

"How far back do you need to go?"

"Just four years. The city keeps six years of records available for public use. After that, they're stored on tape in central processing. I need ten years of tax information for my case, and I've only managed to get six so far."

"Can't you buy the tapes from the city, Langford?"

"I could, and they're not expensive either, only about twenty-five dollars each. But computer time is going to cost me an arm and a leg because of the search routines. There are four tapes for each year of tax information. You can get around the charge at Headquarters by entering the requests one year at a time. Lloyd won't know the difference. How about it, Alexander?"

"I'll think about it. Now, tell me what you found out when

you followed Waterson."

"There was the woman, Angela Bowman. They had a standing rendezvous at the Summit Condominium on Friday afternoons when he left work. They both drove their own cars. To make a long story short, Waterson also met two other people connected with the case while I was tailing him."

"Who were they?"

"Be patient, Lieutenant. I'll get to that. I started tailing him on Friday morning four weeks ago. The first day I started following him, he met Angela Bowman around five that afternoon. But I also saw him with Dr. Thomas Martin earlier the same day."

Both Matt and Jake were surprised.

"Where did you see them together?" Matt asked.

"At a bar close to the Summit, a small joint called DeNiro's. Dr. Martin was already there when Waterson arrived. I followed Waterson into the bar, where I spotted the two of them sitting in a booth at the rear of the bar having a heated discussion. Dr. Martin looked like he was getting the worst of it. Waterson was furious."

"Was anyone else with them?"

"No. It was just the two of them."

"Did you overhear anything they said?"

"No. I couldn't get close enough. All the seats at the back of the bar were taken."

"How long did they talk?"

"About thirty minutes. After that, Waterson got up and left. Tom Martin left soon after Harold Waterson left."

"Who was the other person you saw him with, Langford?"

"Gary Washington."

"I'm not surprised," Matt replied. "When did you see them together?"

"It was the following Friday, the last day I tailed Waterson, actually. I was parked in front of his office building in Foggy

Bottom waiting for him to come out for lunch. While I was sitting there, this young black man drives up in a maroon 280Z. He parked in front of the entrance to the building about five or six cars in front of me. Waterson came out at twelve-fifteen. He was alone. When he saw Waterson come out, Gary Washington got out of his car, ran over to him, and started shouting in his face and pushing him around. The building security guard saw what was happening so he ran out to help Waterson. Gary Washington ran back to his car and drove off, but I got his license number before he got away. The guard wanted to call the police, but Waterson wouldn't let him, for obvious reasons of course. That's it, Alexander. Now, are you going to help me out or not?"

"Did Gary Washington have a weapon on him?"

"None that I saw. Well, will you do it?"

"Yes, I'll do it; but I can't start until this case is closed."

"What about you, Jackson? Do you have time to run the routine for me?"

"He's on the case too, Langford. We're both tied up for the time being. If you need the information right away, you'll have to find someone else to run it for you."

"I can wait. I've been working on this case for weeks. A few more days won't hurt. Have you figured out who killed Waterson, yet?"

"We wouldn't be here if we had."

"It looks like an open and shut case, but it isn't. Everything's a little too pat, if you know what I mean. It's the kind of case where the obvious circumstances can lead you down the garden path, Alexander. You've been burning the midnight oil haven't you?"

"You said it, man. Everybody connected with this case had a motive for the homicide; and most of them had opportunity."

"I've sweated this type of case before. You think you have it all worked out until another piece of evidence comes across your desk, and then you're back to square one. Good luck."

They left Dick Langford's office at nine-thirty A.M.

"What about that Gary Washington, Matt. He didn't impress me as having enough guts to jump Waterson."

"He was jealous, probably couldn't stand to think about her screwing another man. Since he didn't bring a weapon, he was just trying to scare Waterson off. He still took a chance, though. Waterson and the guard together might have subdued him and called the police. He was lucky to get away from there the way he did."

"Where to now?" Jake asked.

"Waterson's office building in Foggy Bottom."

Fifteen minutes later, Matt parked at a meter in front of the building. He ignored the time limit on the meter, deciding that he would rather deal with the tickets that the nuisance of feeding the meter every half hour. They were in luck. The security guard who had come to Waterson's rescue three weeks ago was on duty in the building lobby. Matt asked him about the fracas between Waterson and Gary Washington. The middle-aged guard said that he hadn't heard most of what went on between them, but that he did hear Gary threaten to kill Waterson as he ran off. Matt wondered which was worse, Gary's bark or his bite. He thanked the guard before he and Jake took the elevator up to the tenth floor to the suite of offices occupied by Waterson's firm. The receptionist showed them to Waterson's office, where they found his secretary packing his personal effects.

"I knew you'd be here sooner or later, Lieutenant Alexander. I'm Rosalind Peters, Mr. Waterson's Administrative Assistant; or rather, I was his administrative assistant. I should have started packing his things yesterday, but I couldn't bring myself to do it. I still can't believe he's dead, and his funeral is at one o'clock today."

"Are the firm's other partners in the office, Mrs. Peters?"

"Yes. All of them are here for the funeral. One of the

partners, Mr. Loew, runs the New York office. Mr. Waterson and Mr. Sullivan took care of the business here in the District. They went over to see Mrs. Waterson after we left the funeral parlor last night. Do you want to see them now?"

"After I talk to you, Mrs. Peters," Matt replied.

Rosalind Peters was attractive in a competent, no-nonsense way. She wore a gray suit, a white silk blouse, and pearls. Her long black hair was peppered with gray and styled into an upswept chignon. She offered them seats on a plush white leather sofa, which sat in front of a wall of glass windows. From the look of Waterson's expensively furnished office, his firm was doing well. They both sat on the sofa while Mrs. Peters took one of the matching leather chairs.

"How long have you worked here, Mrs. Peters?" Matt asked.

"For twenty years. I've worked for Mr. Waterson since I started here. He hired me, Lieutenant. Losing him is like losing a member of my own family. He was such a considerate man to work for. I don't understand why anyone would kill him. It was such a brutal, senseless thing to do."

"Homicides usually are. Had you noticed any changes in him lately, things like late hours, strange visitors, anything out of his usual routine?"

"Mr. Waterson usually worked late. We have a staff of seventy-five people at this location, and he was always swamped with work. To be perfectly honest, I don't recall him acting any differently than he usually did, but he wasn't the kind of boss who took his frustrations out on me. He was very business-like in the office. He rarely mentioned his personal life to me, but I understand that there were problems between him and Mrs. Waterson."

"Who do you understand that from, Mrs. Peters?"

"Just office gossip, really. I don't encourage that sort of thing, but people talk just the same."

"How well did you know Mrs. Waterson?"

"Not well at all, I'm afraid. I only saw her once or twice a year. She almost never came to the office. She called more frequently, but she didn't chat. She always stated her business and rang off. She was like that...not friendly at all."

"What's your impression of her as a wife, Mrs. Peters?"

"Well, it's only my opinion you understand, but she seemed to be unhappy. I don't know whether you've met her; but she's a beautiful woman, well-preserved if you know what I mean. Their home is simply gorgeous and her clothes are the best that money can buy. They have a fine son, and no apparent money worries, but she wasn't happy and neither was he."

"Why do you say that, Mrs. Peters?"

"Rumors again, I suppose because he never told me as much. I shouldn't say this, but there have been calls from strange women over the years. He got one of those calls Friday, as a matter of fact."

"Did he take the call?"

"Yes, he did."

"Did the woman identify herself?"

"No, she didn't, Lieutenant."

"Did her ever mention any of those women to you, Mrs. Peters?" She was shocked.

"No, never! He wasn't that type of man."

"Did he normally work on Saturdays?"

"Almost always."

"Did he work this past Saturday?"

"Yes, he did. I was here too until three in the afternoon. He was still here when I left."

"Was anyone else here?"

"Not on this floor. We rent the floor below this one, too. The engineers and architects work down there. I'm sure some of them were here because it's not unusual for them to work weekends. However, I know for a fact that Mr. Waterson was the only person left on the tenth floor when I went home Saturday afternoon."

Matt gave her Harold Waterson's pocket appointment book.

"We took this off Waterson's body Saturday night, Mrs. Peters. He listed two appointments for Saturday afternoon, one at twelve o'clock noon and the other one at four o'clock. Can you tell us who he was scheduled to meet at those times?"

"He had a meeting with the architects at twelve o'clock. That meeting lasted for two hours. They had lunch brought in. I didn't know he had a four o'clock appointment. Let me check his calendar." She walked over to his desk and looked at his appointment schedule. "He noted the time here too, but he didn't write a name beside it."

"That's interesting. What time did he usually leave on Saturday?"

"No set time. I usually work until noon on Saturdays, but we had a lot of work to do this past Saturday. That's why I stayed until three."

"Where are the other partners, Mrs. Peters?"

" Mr. Sullivan's office is next door, and Mr. Lowe's office is next to his."

They spent the next two hours talking to the firm's executives. They learned a lot about the firm, but very little about the homicide. The New York partner confirmed the fact that Hal Waterson had arranged for someone to take a position in the New York office. He assumed the person was a transfer from the Washington office. Each partner denied knowing Angela Bowman or anyone else connected with the case outside Harold Waterson's immediate family. All in all, the two hours could have been put to better use. He didn't ask them about the Anacostia Riverfront Development Project, for fear of putting them on their guard in case there was a connection.

Matt finished questioning the partners at twelve o'clock. When he and Jake left the office, all of the staff were getting ready to attend the funeral, which was at one o'clock in Georgetown. On the way out of the building, Matt asked the guard if he had seen anyone take the elevator to the tenth floor around four o'clock the previous Saturday. According to the guard, the building was always locked on Saturdays. To gain admittance, you had to have a key or be admitted by someone inside the building since there was no guard on duty during weekends. Matt collected three parking tickets off his windshield before leaving Foggy Bottom by way of Virginia AVenue.

"I'm hungry, Matt. You gonna stop for lunch?"

"No."

"Why not?"

"I don't want to be late for the funeral."

"The funeral! Who said I wanted to go to Waterson's funeral?"

"You don't have any choice, Jake. You're with me, and I'm going to the funeral."

"The hell you say! Let me out. I'll get a cab back to Headquarters. He wasn't any kin to me. Why should I have to go to his funeral."

"Why shouldn't you go? You're working on the case just like me. We might learn something there."

"What do you plan to do, question the goddamned corpse?"

"You can get the hell out at the next light, Jake."

"All right, all right, I'll go. Man you sure know how to ruin a person's day. I was all set to enjoy my lunch."

"You can eat anytime, man. Waterson is only going to be buried once, and I don't intend to miss it."

"You take your work too damned seriously, man. It's bad enough to go to a funeral when you have to. Why would anybody go when they don't have to? I hate funerals."

"What's to hate. It's only a ritual. You have to get rid of the body, and a funeral and burial is as good a way as any."

"I don't care what you say, I hate funerals."

"You look on the down side of everything, Jake. Stop

thinking about how much you hate funerals. It'll only last an hour at the most."

Georgetown traffic was congested as usual, but it flowed evenly past the U.S. Naval Observatory, the Washington Cathedral, and the Sidwell Friends School before Matt arrived in front of Burton's Funeral Home on the corner of Chesapeake and Wisconsin Avenues. They sat in the car and watched as the string of mourners entered the chapel. Harold Waterson's office contingent was the first to arrive. Mrs. Peters had already begun to cry. She wiped her eyes with a white handkerchief as she walked into the mortuary chapel.

At least fifty people showed up over the next thirty minutes, including several well-known Washington dignitaries. The family arrived last, led by a black hearse which overflowed with flowers. Felicia Waterson's family arrived in the first three limousines. Harold Waterson's side of the family came in the next seven. At least ten cars followed the limousines. Matt and Jake waited until everyone entered the chapel before they went in and sat on the very last pew.

The service was subdued and sterile as chapel services go. The minister did the best he could, but even Aunt Martha's side of the family was controlled. Aunt Martha herself was stoic. Unlike her nephew's wife, she wore no veil and she didn't cry. She stared at the bronze coffin with her black-gloved hands folded in her lap as she faintly rocked herself back and forth. She looked very old and very frail. William Waterson sat between his mother and Aunt Martha. He was dry-eyed and expressionless. Felicia Waterson's family sat in front of Aunt Martha's family and the immediate family sat on the front pew.

The ultra-modern chapel was filled with mourners. Its cathedral ceiling echoed to the strains of organ music as the organist played something somber by Brahms. Aunt Martha's minister might have done a better job if his congregation had been there to urge him on with their "Amens" and "yes, Lords."

As it was, he did the best he could with an over-refined contingent of mourners and an unresponsive family. The service lasted exactly one hour. After it was over, the mourners filed out behind the family. Everyone found their cars, and the procession left for the cemetery with the occupied hearse in front.

"Do we have to go to the cemetery, too?" Jake asked.

"No, I think that we can pass that up."

"That's a relief. Let's go, man. This place is depressing." They stopped for lunch at the Hamburger Haven and ate their carryout in the car. They arrived back at Headquarters at three o'clock Tuesday afternoon. Matt made a decision as they walked into the building.

"Jake, take a couple of men over to Gary Washington's house and pick him up."

"You want me to arrest him? What's the charge?"

"No, I don't want you to arrest him, but I want him picked up for more questioning. I have a bone to pick with Mr. Washington."

"So, you think he's involved in the homicide after all?"

"Maybe...probably. I'm going to come down on him hard this time. I should have done it on Sunday. He lied about Harold Waterson, told me he'd never met him."

"You want me to leave now?"

"Yes. We don't have much time left."

Matt left Jake with the duty officer and continued up to his office. He pressed the secretary into overtime despite her protests. The forensic lab results were on his desk, including the disappointing powder tests results from the Bowmans. Nearly all the prints Sam found matched the Bowmans'. There were four unidentified prints from the basement powder room, but they were partially smudged and Sam doubted that they could be successfully matched. The only prints Sam found in the Mercedes were Waterson's-not very encouraging results taken as a whole. He put the forensic lab tests aside and worked uninterrupted for two and a half hours. Jake returned at five forty-five.

"We got him, but he wasn't as cooperative this time. He was scared shitless, man, thought we were arresting him."

"Where did you put him?"

"In the same interrogation room. Isn't that where you wanted him?"

"Yes. That's fine. See if Sam is in the lab, Jake. If he's still around, tell him to do a powder test on Gary Washington."

"Okay. You gonna need me downstairs."

"Yes. We have to really put the squeeze on Washington, this time. After that, I want you to go along with me while I pay a surprise visit to the Martins later on. I don't expect any trouble, but you never know. It'll take me thirty minutes to finish what I'm working on, but it won't hurt to let Gary Washington sweat for a while."

"Why do I have to ask Sam to do the test? Can't you call down there?"

"What's the matter, Jake? You scared of Sam?"

"Hell no, but I hate to be bothered with Sam. You know what a prick he is, man, always bitching or yelling about something."

"I know exactly what you mean," Matt replied. "Some people have a perpetual ax to grind."

Jake didn't get the implied association, so he left the office grumbling, as usual. Matt completed the statements he took at Waterson's firm. He gave the draft copies to the secretary, who did some bitching of her own. He soothed her ruffled feathers by promising to put a good word in for her at her next evaluation. She looked skeptical, told him he was full of it, and started typing again.

When Matt entered the interrogation room, Gary Washington was wiping his hands with his handkerchief. Apparently Sam had come and gone. Gary jumped when the door slammed. What little self-control he had possessed during his initial interrogation had disappeared, replaced by outright fear as he squirmed in his seat like a cornered animal with no place to run. He avoided making direct eye contact with Matt.

"Why have you arrested me, man? I told you on Sunday that I didn't kill that dude. You're trying to set me up to take the rap. You know you don't have any evidence on me."

"I've got plenty on you, Washington," Matt insisted as he paced behind Gary Washington's chair. "For starters, you told me that you had never met Waterson, but that was a damned lie and you know it. You jumped him on the street in front of his office building. We've got two eyewitnesses who'll testify that you attacked him without provocation. Deny that if you can."

"Okay, okay, I admit it. I lost my head, that's all. I didn't mean him any harm. I just wanted him to leave Angela alone. I wasn't trying to hurt him, man. You've got to believe me."

"Why did you threaten to kill him if you didn't mean him any harm?"

"That was my temper talking, man. I didn't mean it. You know you've said things you didn't mean when you were mad at somebody. Give me a break, Lieutenant. I didn't kill the dude. I don't even own a gun."

"We've been over who owned the gun before, Washington. All I want to know is what you did with the gun after you shot Waterson on Saturday night?"

Gary began to sweat bullets.

"How many times do I have to tell you! I didn't shoot him! You're trying to railroad me, man! I couldn't have shot the dude in Northwest when I was in my apartment in Southeast at ten-thirty Saturday night."

"We checked that lie out, too, Washington. The security guard in your building says that he didn't see you come into the building after ten o'clock. Admit you killed him, you ass-hole. If you cop a plea, the District Prosecutor will drop the charge from murder one to manslaughter. If you don't admit you killed him, you lying son-of-a-bitch, I'll nail your ass for murder one!" Matt shouted into Gary Washington's face while he held him in the collar.

Gary was too frightened to move, and his voice quivered with fear when he replied, "I told you I didn't kill him. Why won't you believe me. I never had Walter Bowman's gun."

"You're a liar, Washington. You know Angela gave you her father's gun. You killed Hal Waterson with it and then you got rid of it. Admit it you creep, you know you killed him."

"I didn't kill him, I didn't! You'll never make me admit that I killed him!" Gary screamed.

"You did it all right. Angela put you up to it. You killed him for her."

"That's a lie! I didn't kill him for her, I swear I didn't! How many times do I have to tell you that I didn't?!"

"You'll tell me as many times as I want to hear it, you jive chump. I'm going to throw your pretty butt in jail until you confess; and believe me, Washington, before I'm through with you, you'll be glad to confess."

"I'll never confess to killing Waterson. I know my rights, man. You can't hold me without charging me, and you can't charge me without evidence. You can't have any evidence on me because I'm innocent. I want to call my lawyer right now."

"You don't have any damned rights until I give them to you, Washington. You haven't been arrested. We can hold you for forty-eight hours without charging you. And I'll let you call a lawyer when I get good and damned ready to. How do you like those rights?"

"You don't scare me, Lieutenant."

Matt released Gary's collar, but continued to pace behind his chair. Gary nervously lit a cigarette and tried to recoup some of the leverage he had lost since the interrogation started.

"I know my rights, man. You can't harass me like this, man. it's against the law. This is a free country. You have to arrest me or let me go."

"I am going to arrest you, Washington. I just wanted to give you the opportunity to come clean before we bang you up in the slammer. We already have a confession from the person who helped you kill Waterson."

"That's a lie. Nobody helped me kill him because I didn't do it."

"The hell you didn't! We know for a fact that Angela lured Waterson into her house so you could kill him. After you killed him, you drove back to Southeast and got rid of the gun."

"Man, you ought to quit lying on me. I didn't kill Waterson, and I didn't get rid of that gun. I want to call my lawyer."

"What can a lawyer do for a jive chump like you, Washington? There's no way you can beat this rap. Your best bet is to cop a plea before it's too late."

It was Gary's turn to get angry.

"I'm not copping shit! I can't stop you from charging me, but I'll never admit that I killed him, never!"

"We'll see about that. Do you know what happens to pretty boys like you in the slammer, Washington?"

Gary recoiled like he'd been slapped in the face.

"I see I don't have to spell it out for you. My advice to you is to cop a plea right now and we'll see what we can do for you. If you don't cooperate, I'm going to personally see to it that we sock your ass with a charge of capital murder."

Matt interrogated Gary Washington for an hour and a half without success.

"Have it your way, Washington, but don't say I didn't give you a chance. You can make your call now." Gary practically jumped out of his chair. Matt told the officer on duty outside the cell blocks to allow Gary to place one call and put him back into the interrogation room. He returned to his office, where he found Jake reading the afternoon paper for lack of anything else to do.

"Carla called. She wanted to know when you would be home."

"What did you tell her?"

"I told her I didn't know. She wants you to call her. Did you get anything out of Washington?"

"Hell no! He's sticking to his story tighter than white on rice. I couldn't shake him. I want you to go down there and mess with him for a while, Jake, but I don't believe he'll crack."

"Man, I can't believe you didn't get anything out of him. He was ready to cry when we picked him up."

"He didn't admit anything to me."

Jake left the office as Matt called home. Carla listened to his excuses and hung up hot. He knew he'd have to make it up to her, but he put his domestic troubles on the back burner for the time being. He had other worries more serious than a cold dinner and a pouting wife. Gary Washington didn't look like he was going to break, so it was back to the Bowmans. Gary's test might come back positive, but he doubted it. It would have made his life too easy, and he seemed to be batting three hundred in the opposite direction. He felt that he was learning more, but that it was adding up to less. He turned the lights off in his office and went downstairs to see how Jake was doing with Gary Washington. Jake hadn't made any progress with Gary either, so Matt decided to hold Gary overnight to see if a sleep-over in the slammer would soften him up. He completed the necessary paperwork and escorted Gary to his cell. Gary cursed everyone within earshot for all the good it did. They locked him in and left.

"What do you expect to get from the Martins?" Jake asked as they walked to Matt's car.

"They've got some explaining to do, especially Tom. Half of what they told me wasn't true, and the other half was lies."

They arrived at the Martins' at seven-thirty P.M. They heard piano music from inside the house. Jake peeked through the living room windows and saw Claudia Martin playing the piano.

It was obvious that she didn't intend to stop playing to open the door for them. Matt had to ring several times before Tom Martin came to the door. Unhappy to find them on his doorstep, Tom stammered something incomprehensible as he let them in.

"Hello, Tom. We need to talk," Matt said.

Tom stammered again as he backed into the foyer like he was being mugged. Jake closed the front door. Claudia continued to play, although she had to know that they were there. Tom looked like a child who'd been caught in a transgression, a child who knew that his punishment was imminent with or without admitting his guilt.

Tom recovered his voice and his nerve to the point of stammering, "We told you everything we had to say on Sunday, Matthew."

"That's a lie, Tom. Both of you know a damned sight more than you told me."

Tom briefly struggled for a comeback before he bolted into the living room and rushed over to the piano, where Claudia played as if she were alone with her music. Tom frantically explained what was going on while Claudia calmly continued to play with her eyes closed.

She finished her piece, opened her eyes, closed her piano cover and said, "So what if he has come back, Tom. We don't have anything to hide."

After that she turned her spite on Matt and Jake. "Do you have a damned search warrant?"

"No, we don't, " Matt replied.

"In that case, I want you to get the hell out right now."

"You've got a hell of a nerve, Claudia. I know both of you lied about knowing Harold Waterson when I questioned you on Sunday. You're both in this up to your necks, and jumping bad on me isn't going to make it any easier for you. Your best bet is to admit your involvement in Waterson's homicide before it's too late."

"Save your breath, Matthew. We aren't admitting anything."

"Speak for yourself, Claudia. Tom is the one who's going to prison."

Tom shouted, "I didn't have anything to do with Hal Waterson's death!"

"We have an eyewitness who'll testify that he saw you and Waterson in DeNiro's bar four weeks ago, Tom."

"That's a lie!" Claudia shouted as she rose from the piano bench. "Tom wasn't seen anywhere with Hal Waterson!"

"Not only were they seen together, Claudia, but our witness will also testify that they were having a heated argument. Isn't that so, Tom?"

"Don't admit anything, Tom. He's bluffing."

"Shut up, Claudia. I'm sick and tired of all these lies. Matthew's right. I did meet Hal Waterson at DeNiro's."

"So what if you did. That was four weeks ago, Tom; and it didn't have anything to do with his murder last Saturday night in Walter Bowman's basement. This is a free country. You can meet anyone you like. It doesn't mean a damned thing."

"If it doesn't mean anything, why were the two of you trying to cover it up, Claudia?"

"Did you come here to arrest us? If you didn't, we don't have anything else to say about Hal Waterson; and I want you to leave my house immediately!"

"It wouldn't take much to make me arrest you and Tom. I'm trying to give you the benefit of the doubt, Claudia; but if you say another goddamned word, I'll arrest both of you and take you to jail in handcuffs."

"I told you to shut up, Claudia! You're only making things worse for us. Come sit down, Matthew; and I'll tell you what happened at DeNiro's."

Tom sat down on the sofa as Claudia stormed over to the fireplace,where she paced back and forth like a cat. She wore a sleek, form-fitting, white silk jumpsuit and Jake could hardly keep his eyes off her.

"I did meet Hal Waterson at DeNiro's, but it's not what you think, Matthew. We were business partners. Hal and I had an arrangement where he used me as a minority contractor. His firm couldn't qualify for the city's minority set-aside because his other partners are white, so we formed a minority corporation and he threw a lot of business my way."

"Are you saying that you were a minority front for Waterson's construction firm, Tom?"

"No, nothing like that, I swear! It was a legitimate business," Tom weakly protested.

"But you're not a contractor, Tom. I thought you were into residential property and apartment buildings."

"Most of my business interests are residential. But, I'm also a licensed minority contractor supplying heating and cooling systems. Not many people know that side of my business because I've intentionally kept it quiet. Hal helped me start the business. He showed me the basics of the construction game and taught me how to bid on contracts. He was a silent business partner, but we owned equal shares of the company."

"So, what was the meeting at DeNiro's about?"

"Hal accused me of stealing from the firm, but it was a dirty lie. I never cheated him out of a dime."

"What proof did he give you?"

"He said his records showed a hundred thousand dollar discrepancy across three contracts. I told him he was mistaken, but he swore that I'd stolen the money. He said he was going to buy out my interest in the company and pick up another partner."

"I thought you said you were equal partners."

"Financially, we were; but the way the corporation was set up, Hal had final decision on a lot of things. I wouldn't have gone into the business if I had known that at the time."

"Did he buy you out?"

"No, he didn't."

"He can't buy you out now, can he?"

Tom didn't reply.

"How long had you and Waterson been in business together, Tom?"

"For ten years."

"How much money were you making?"

"My cut was about five hundred thousand dollars last year. It hasn't always been that much, though."

"Now that's the best motive for murder I've heard since we started this case, partner," Jake insisted.

"I though you were doing well with your own business interests, Tom. Why did you get involved with Waterson?"

"My properties were doing okay, but they aren't half as lucrative as the deal Hal offered me. He picked me because I was already in real estate and I could secure the financial backing to branch out into contracting. He arranged for me to get the bank loan, and he channeled some contracts to the corporation. It was all legal, though. I don't know where he got the idea that I was stealing from the corporation. I swear I wasn't stealing from him."

"Did he show you any records to back up his claim?"

"No, he didn't. He simply called me out of the blue four weeks ago and told me to meet him at DeNiro's. He said he had something important to discuss with me. I assumed he was going to discuss new business he was arranging for the company. Well, I was shocked when he accused me of stealing a hundred thousand dollars from the corporation. I told him to look at his books again, because I knew that I hadn't taken a dime above my cut."

"Did you meet with him again after DeNiro's?"

"Not until Saturday night. Before then, he wouldn't return my calls or answer my messages. I couldn't believe it when he showed up at the party Saturday night. When he left the meeting at DeNiro's, he said that some people are too smart for their own good, and that they should keep their noses out of other people's affairs."

"What did he mean by that?" Matt asked, although he had a good idea what Hal Waterson had meant.

"I'm damned if I know, Matthew. I asked him what he meant; but he wouldn't explain. After he left the bar, I didn't see him again until Saturday night."

"Why did he show up here on Saturday, Tom?"

"He said that he reconsidered and that he wanted to make a deal with me. He told me that he'd allow me to keep my partnership in the corporation if I paid the hundred thousand dollars back. Some deal that was. I couldn't believe his nerve. First he accuses me of stealing money I didn't take, then he offers me a chance to pay it back."

"Did you accept his offer?"

"No way....but I told him that I would think it over."

"How much time did he give you to decide?"

"Two weeks."

"Could you have raised that kind of money in two weeks?"

Tom looked at Claudia who was still pacing in front of the fireplace. He looked trapped before he answered: "Yes, I could have gotten the money, but I didn't intend to pay him a dime. I would be a fool to hand over a hundred thousand dollars of my own money to Hal Waterson just on his say so."

"If you were making five hundred thousand dollars a year from doing business with him, you would have been a fool not to pay him," Matt asserted. "What happens to the business now that Waterson is dead, Tom?"

"There's a clause in our contract that says that the business reverts to the remaining partner if the other one dies."

"Do you realize what that means?"

"I didn't kill him, Matthew. I swear I didn't."

"He was blackmailing us," Claudia insisted breaking her

silence. "He knew Tom didn't steal that money."

"Why would Waterson blackmail Tom, Claudia? He didn't need the money."

"How do you know he didn't need it? You don't know what condition his finances were in, Matthew."

"Maybe not, Claudia, but it won't be hard to find out. His will ought to be filed in probate court any day now, if it hasn't been filed already. Waterson probably was extorting money out of Tom, but it wasn't because he needed it."

"Why do you think he did it?" Claudia cynically asked.

"He did it because you sent Felicia Waterson an anonymous letter telling her about his affair with Angela Bowman."

"That's a damned lie!" Claudia shouted.

Tom stared at Claudia as if he couldn't believe what he was hearing, "An anonymous letter! Claudia, did you do that?"

"Of course not, Tom. You know me better than that. Why would I do something like that to Angela? She's one of my best friends."

"Maybe so, Claudia. but, you hate Felicia Waterson more than you like Angela Bowman. That's why you sent her the letter. You didn't mention Angela's name in the letter; but you may as well have. Felicia Waterson hired a detective to follow her husband. That's how she found out who he was seeing, and that's why Wateson was putting pressure on Angela to move to New York City."

"You don't have a shred of proof, Matthew. I would never do anything as underhanded as that."

"You did it to get even with Felicia Waterson, Claudia. You wanted to bring her down a peg or two. That's why you pointed out the fact that Waterson was having an affair with a black woman in the letter. Hal Waterson knew that he hadn't told anyone about his affair with Angela, so he naturally asked her who she told after his wife got the letter. That's when he put two and two together and came up with you."

Jake was fascinated. He knew that Claudia Martin was an audacious woman, but the extent of her daring surprised even him. Tom was speechless. He stared from Claudia to Matt as the conversation bounced back and forth between them.

"That's pure speculation, Matthew Alexander. You can't prove I sent Felicia Waterson an anonymous letter. You're wasting your time trying to pin that on me."

"Oh, you sent it all right, Claudia. but you weren't aware of Tom's business arrangement with Hal Waterson when you did it. You had no idea that your poison pen letter would come home to roost the way it did. She didn't know about your partnership with Waterson, did she, Tom?"

"No, she didn't." Tom wearily replied. "I didn't tell her about it until last week."

"Just whose side are you on Tom Martin?! He can't prove I wrote that letter."

"After you realized the fall-out your letter had created for Tom, you went to see Waterson to try to patch things up with him. You called him last Friday and set up an appointment for four o'clock the following Saturday afternoon. That's when you tried to talk him out of dropping Tom from the corporation, and that's when Waterson came up with the idea of letting Tom pay him back. Isn't that so, Claudia?"

"You're crazy, Matthew. I don't know when I've heard a more vicious, absurd pack of lies. You must make them up as you go along."

"Was Claudia home at four o'clock on Saturday, Tom?" Tom was about to answer when he was interrupted by a shrill harangue from Claudia.

"It's none of your damned business where I was on Saturday afternoon, Matthew Alexander."

Tom made a moaning sound and put his head between his hands.

"The only thing I have to figure out, Claudia is whether you lured Waterson to your party to talk him into giving Tom a second chance or to kill him."

Tom shook his head out of desperation. Claudia screeched a string of curses that made Jake wince. Matt wasn't impressed.

"Curse all you want, Claudia. It won't change the facts. You and Tom are in serious trouble. My advice to you is to get the best lawyer you can find."

"Facts! You call that string of lies and fairy tales facts. You don't have a shred of solid evidence against us, otherwise you would have arrested us by now. You're bluffing, Matthew."

"You're the one who's selling woof tickets, Claudia. All I have to do is show your picture to enough people in the vicinity of Hal Waterson's office building and someone is bound to recognize you. You may as well tell the truth now and save me the trouble."

"I don't have to tell you anything. We didn't kill Hal Waterson, although he deserved it, that's for damned sure."

"But you went to see him at his office on Saturday, didn't you?"

"So what if I did. I didn't break any law by going to his office."

"How long were you there?"

"About an hour. It was a complete waste of my time. He laughed in my face, the smug SOB. He thought he was so high and might sitting behind that desk all haughty and smug like he owned the world. He talked to me like I was dirt. He admitted that Tom hadn't stolen any money from him. He said he made that up to punish me and Tom because I sent that anonymous letter to Felicia. I told him I didn't send the damned letter, but he didn't believe me either. When he told me how much money he wanted, I told him it was blackmail; but he only laughed and said I could call it what I wanted but his price wasn't negotiable."

"Why did he show up at your party, Claudia?"

"How do I know why he came? I guess he came to watch me and Tom squirm after he gave Tom the terms of his deal."

"What did he say to you at the party?"

"More of the same. He told Tom he had two weeks to pay him the money."

Claudia was scared, but unlike Tom, she was determined to make the best of a bad situation.

Matt finished questioning them at nine o'clock. He and Jake were about to leave Floriubunda Lane when Matt had a brainstorm. He walked over to the Bowman residence and rang the doorbell. Walter Bowman answered the door. Matt remained on the front porch as he talked to Bowman for several minutes. When he returned to the car, Jake asked:

"What was that all about?"

"Some information I needed from Walter Bowman."

"What did you want to know?"

"Whether the Martins have keys to his house."

"Well, do they?"

"Yes, a full set. They keep an eye on each other's homes when one of them is out of town.

# (HAPTER XIV

The Wednesday morning meeting with Chief Carter was at ten o'clock. Lloyd used the time before leaving for the downtown meeting in Chief Carter' office to go through the Waterson case file one more time. He had lingering doubts about Angela Bowman's motives, but she remained their strongest suspect anyway.

Matt sat upstairs in his office thinking. He couldn't decide what to do about Tom and Claudia Martin. They had the strongest motive for killing Hal Waterson he had uncovered so far, but how they might have killed him wasn't clear. He could reasonably construct a scenario depicting how Tom Martin might have slipped out of his basement door while Angela Bowman was in the kitchen with Claudia. The question was, would it fly? He wasn't optimistic that it would. Being the hard-headed pragmatist that he was, Ed Davenport would probably insist on arresting his bird in the hand, Angela Bowman. Angela's arrest and indictment were a near certainty. Introducing the Martins as probable suspects might raise suspicions about them; but since he couldn't place either Claudia or

Tom in the Bowman's basement, it wasn't likely to change any minds about Angela Bowman's guilt.

"I'll be in a meeting in Chief Carter's office for the rest of the morning, Jake," he said as he left for the meeting.

"Have fun."

"I have to ride downtown with Lloyd. How much fun can that be?"

"You have my sympathies, man. Tell him I want my goddamned promotion. He ought to get a real good laugh out of that."

The ride to Chief Carter's office was uncomfortable for both men. Lloyd said very little. He asked a couple of banal questions that were too obvious to be taken seriously. Matt tried to ease the tension by talking about the Redskins. Both men were relieved when they finally arrived at the Municipal Building where they parked in the lot under the building and took the elevator to the Chief's second floor offices. Marge Smith greeted them with her usual flair, a potent combination of business and boudoir that worked wonders on tired policemen. Matt guessed that Ed Davenport would already be there. He was. The meeting began without the familiar banter that usually accompanied Chief Carter's meetings. Lloyd was the first to take the floor.

He gave the Chief a copy of the Waterson case file. He had also brought copies for Ed Davenport and himself. Matt had his own copy. Lloyd walked the Chief through the file one document at a time. When he finished, Lloyd asked Matt to summarize the case.

Chief Carter listened without comment, taking notes periodically. When Matt finished, the Chief asked them several pointed questions that zeroed in on the weak spots in their evidence. After that he asked Ed Davenport to give his assessment of the case. Ed abandoned any reticence he may have had and launched into a full-blown dissertation of who was prosecutable, who wasn't, and why. He presented the arguments skillfully and concluded by saying that Angela Bowman was the most probable suspect on the basis of the evidence gathered so far. Chief Carter didn't dispute Ed's contention, but he didn't agree with him either.

"What's her motive, Ed?" the Chief asked.

"She wanted him out of her hair, Chief."

"She could have done that without killing him, couldn't she?"

"She could have, but it's obvious that she didn't."

"What did she do with the gun after she shot him?"

"Who knows? I suggest that we arrest her and find out what she did with it."

"Why did her powder test come up negative?"

"She probably wore gloves."

"Where are the gloves?"

"Hidden away with the gun."

"Very convenient for her, isn't it?"

"She can be made to talk, Chief. She should have been brought in for interrogation before now."

"Just suppose she doesn't tell you where the gloves and the gun are, Ed?"

"She'll talk, but even if she doesn't, I can still convict her."

Chief Carter addressed his next question to Matt, "Do either one of her parents have a motive for killing Waterson, Lieutenant?"

Matt explained what Thelma Wallace had said about Walter Bowman's spilling his drink into the food tray she was serving when he caught sight of the murder victim at the Martins' cocktail party. He also explained the circumstances surrounding the Anacostia Riverfront Development Project contract process. When he finished, the Chief asked, "What have you uncovered about that so far, Lieutenant?"

"Almost nothing, sir. I didn't want to put the other partners in Waterson's firm on their guard by questioning them before I was ready to move on it. They can destroy a lot of records before we serve a search warrant on them. Walter Bowman offered to let me inspect his books, but we'd need a subpoena to see the books at Waterson's firm. Commander Cullison told me to put that line of investigation on hold for the time being."

Ed Davenport eagerly added his two cents worth to the discussion, "That contract was contested at the time it was awarded, Chief. An impartial review board vindicated the selection of Waterson's firm, so that's a long shot at best."

The Chief looked skeptical before replying, "Even so, Ed, it may be more than mere coincidence. I wouldn't rule out that line of investigation altogether."

"I still say it's a waste of time, Chief. Angela Bowman can be convicted, I guarantee it."

"But what if she's not guilty?" Matt asked.

"I think she is guilty, Lieutenant," Ed replied in his most patronizing tone. "All of your evidence supports the fact that someone inside the house killed Hal Waterson. I didn't see a shred of evidence indicating that an intruder was anywhere near the scene when he was shot. You yourself didn't find any evidence that Gary Washington was inside the house. None of the fingerprints matched his, and his powder test was negative. He denies being there. And none of the Bowman family have implicated him, so the murderer has to be one of them. I contend that Angela Bowman is the most likely one of the three since she had the strongest involvement with the deceased and, from where I stand, the clearest motive."

Chief Carter finally agreed with Ed Davenport, "He's right, Lieutenant. The case against Angela Bowman is the strongest we've got. Neither of her parents is tied to Waterson as tightly as she is. She had probable cause for wanting him dead. She had the opportunity to kill him. She let him into the house, and he died there."

Lloyd agreed with the Chief's conclusions. "She must have

know that she would be suspected. I still can't understand why she didn't claim self-defense and keep the weapon."

"Well, she didn't claim self-defense, Lloyd, so that sets her up for a murder charge. I personally think we ought to stop second-guessing what she should have done and go with the facts we have on hand," Ed insisted.

Matt listened quietly. He didn't want to appear to be dragging his feet on arresting Angela Bowman, but any way he looked at it, Tom and Claudia had a stronger motive for killing Hal Waterson.

"What do you think, Lieutenant?" Chief Carter asked.

"Tom and Claudia Martin had a stronger motive than Angela Bowman for killing Waterson."

"The Martins! Since when?" Ed demanded.

"Since I talked to them last night."

Matt recounted his visit to Tom and Claudia in detail. When he finished, Ed was the first to respond.

"That's all very well, Alexander, but when and how did they do it?"

"Walter Bowman told me Tom Martin has a full set of keys to his house, so it wouldn't have been difficult for them to take Bowman's revolver before the night of the murder. All they had to do was wait for a time when all three of them were out of the house."

"When did they kill him?" Ed asked, the exasperation apparent in his voice.

"There's the call Angela Bowman said she received. That got her out of the house. Claudia kept her in the kitchen for ten minutes pretending she needed help with the party food. Tom Martin admitted that he went downstairs to his basement bar to get more liquor immediately after Harold Waterson left their party. They could have gotten someone to place the call to get Angela out of the house. Tom could have used his basement door to go over to the Bowmans', shoot the victim while Angela was away and then back again to his house before Angela Bowman left his kitchen.

"How did they know he was in the Bowman basement, Lieutenant?"

"The maid who served the party said both Tom and Claudia were at the front door when Waterson left. Angela Bowman admits meeting Waterson on the sidewalk immediately after he left the Martins' house. If they were watching, they would have seen him meet Angela, and they also would have seen her take him around back to the basement entrance."

"There are entirely too many 'ifs' in that scenario, Alexander. There's no way I'd go into court on a string of circumstantial 'ifs' like that. You have to give me some hard evidence linking the Martins to the homicide. I don't care what their motives were, the evidence you've pulled together makes them unlikely suspects. It doesn't matter how you cut it, Angela Bowman is our prime suspect."

Chief Carter agreed with Ed again, "Do you have any evidence placing Tom Martin in the Bowman house during the time Waterson was killed, Lieutenant?"

"No, I don't. Sam Johnson found some smudged fingerprints in the basement bathroom, but he says it will be next to impossible to match them."

"What about the telephone call to Angela Bowman?"

"Both Tom and Claudia Martin deny making the call or asking anyone else to make it. Both the maid and bartender claim not to know anything about the call either. But that doesn't rule out the possibility that the Martins could have asked one of their other guests to call. However, I did substantiate the fact that they had plenty of ice. If the call was made, its sole purpose was to get Angela Bowman out of the house."

"They had no guarantee she would leave," Ed replied.

"They took a chance," Matt insisted.

Chief Carter frowned.

"Even if we agreed to let you question all the Martins' guests you still might come up empty-handed, and that would take at least another week. That's too much time, Lieutenant."

The Chief looked at Lloyd. "What should we do, Commander?"

Lloyd expected the question, so he was ready for it, replying, "It's obvious that we have to decide whether we should continue the investigation, arrest Angela Bowman or do both."

"That's a very diplomatic answer, Commander, but it doesn't tell me which option you recommend."

"There are consequences for all three, Chief. You have to decide which consequences you can live with."

"Diplomacy again. What do you think we should do, Ed?"

"Arrest Angela Bowman, today, and spend all of our time and effort building a strong case against her."

"What do think we should do, Lieutenant?"

"I think we should continue the investigation and hold off on arresting anyone until we get more evidence."

Chief Carter took a moment to consider the differing points of view before making his decision known, "Arrest Angela Bowman and continue the investigation, Cullison. I want the Lieutenant kept on the case. Give him two more detectives, full-time. Get Judge Rankin to sign the arrest warrant this morning. He's usually in chambers until three o'clock. Pick her up as soon as the warrant is signed. I'll schedule a press conference for five to coincide with the evening news. I can't tell you how to charge her, Ed, but you had damned well better make the charge stick. I won't have this shit blowing up in my face. If I get burned, we all go down."

"We've got you covered, Chief," Ed smugly replied.

"I can live with that," Lloyd stated as he got up to leave. "Will that be all, Chief?"

"I want you at the press conference, Cullison. It's going to be in the conference room next door at five o'clock. Get down here by four-thirty."

Ed Davenport didn't look pleased at being overlooked, but for once he kept his opinion to himself. Lloyd was pleased with the outcome of the meeting and the invitation to the press conference. He spent several minutes talking to Marge Smith before they left. They walked across the quadrangle to the Judicial Building, where they found Judge Rankin in his chambers on the fifth floor. He signed the arrest warrant.

"When are you going to pick her up?" Lloyd asked on the ride back.

"As soon as I can get Jake and two other officers to go with me."

"Take another squad car over there when you go, Alexander. You may run into some trouble."

Matt didn't look forward to the arrest, but it had to be done. Jake was leaving for lunch when he got back.

"How'd it go?"

"Angela Bowman all the way."

"That figures. Did you get the warrant yet?"

"It's right here," Matt replied, taking the document out of his breast pocket.

"When do you want to pick her up?"

"As soon as possible. Go downstairs and ask Bryant to assign us two more men and an extra squad car before he leaves for lunch, Jake."

"Are you sure you want to go, partner? I can make the arrest for you if you want me to."

"Thanks for the offer, Jake, but I can handle it. I'm responsible for the investigation, that includes making the arrest. It's no big deal."

"Whatever you say, man. It's your call," Jake answered before going downstairs to see Captain Henry Bryant.

Matt checked his pistol. It was fully loaded and ready to fire. He didn't anticipate any problems, but better safe than sorry. The two cars left fourth District Headquarters at one-thirty P.M. They arrived in front of the Bowman house twenty minutes later. Matt noted the unmarked patrol car parked a safe distance away with two plainclothes detectives in it. The Bowmans had been under surveillance since the homicide Saturday night.

The sun had been shining all morning, but as soon as they parked in front of 1637 Floribunda Lane, it disappeared behind a dark cloud leaving an overcast sky and a distinct chill in the air. Jake swore it was an omen, but Jake was inclined to be superstitious. Walter Bowman opened the front door for them. From the look on his face, they didn't need to tell him why they were there. He stood aside as the four officers walked into the foyer. Matt was the first to speak.

"We have a warrant for Angela's arrest Mr. Bowman."

"Arrest! You can't arrest her! What's the charge!?"

"First degree murder."

Walter Bowman's knees buckled when he heard the charge. He had to lean against the door for support. When he finally spoke his voice sounded strained and distant.

"She didn't kill him, Matthew! Angela couldn't kill anybody! My God...first degree murder!"

"I suggest you get her a good lawyer as soon as possible, Mr. Bowman. She's going to need all the help she can get."

Hearing voices in the foyer, Helen Bowman came downstairs to see what was going on. When Walter Bowman saw her, he excitedly blurted the news.

"They've charged Angela with first degree murder, Helen. They've come to arrest her."

"They were bound to come, Walter. Any fool could see that," Helen Bowman replied from where she stood on the bottom step of the staircase. "Why are you arresting Angela, Matthew?"

"It boils down to the fact that one of you had to kill him, Mrs. Bowman. We didn't find any evidence that an outsider had been in here Saturday night. Angela had the strongest motive."

"You haven't found Walter's gun. What did she shoot him with?"

"No, we didn't find the gun yet, Mrs. Bowman. We may never find it, but that doesn't change the fact that Harold Waterson was shot and killed in your basement. If what the three of you have told me is true, you were the only people in the house when Waterson was killed. I warned all of you that you were facing serious charges. Angela is going to need a damned good lawyer." "I shot him!" Walter Bowman insisted. "Angela didn't kill him, I did."

"Where's the gun, Mr. Bowman?" Matt asked.

"Wait a minute, let me think. Yes, I remember now. I hid it in the attic until the police left. Then I took it down to the creek and threw it in."

"You've been watched since Saturday night, Mr. Bowman. You haven't been down to the creek."

"I sneaked out, Matthew. I swear I did."

"If you want to add something to your statement, I suggest that you come to Fourth District Headquarters later this afternoon, Mr. Bowman. Right now, I have to serve an arrest warrant on your daughter. I hope you won't make this any harder than it already is."

"You can't arrest her!" Walter Bowman shouted. "She didn't kill him, I did!"

"Walter, please! You're not making this any easier." Helen Bowman started crying. "I'll get her ready to go. Will she need any clothes, Matthew?"

"Not right away, Mrs. Bowman. You can bring them down later."

"I'm going with her," her father insisted close to tears himself.

"Both of you are welcome to come," Matt said anxious to get Angela in the car and leave. Helen Bowman went upstairs. A moment later, they all heard Angela scream that she didn't kill Harold Waterson. Walter Bowman rushed upstairs when he heard her scream. Matt sent the two officers who came with them upstairs after him to keep things under control.

"They took it better than I though they would," Jake said.

"I agree. It could have been a lot worse."

"The father was close to losing it, Matt. I expected him to go off the deep right here in the foyer."

They didn't hear any more screams, so Matt guessed that Angela had gotten herself under control. They eventually came down. Angela looked dazed. Matt read her her rights and informed her that she was being charged with first degree murder in the death of Harold Willian Waterson, Sr. He also advised her to secure an attorney as quickly as possible. She left the house without incident, too upset to respond to what was happening. Jake frisked Walter Bowman and searched Helen Bowman's handbag before they left the house. Jake sat in the back of Matt's car with Angela Bowman. The Bowmans rode in the back of the second squad car.

They drove downtown in silence. Matt parked in the lot under the municipal jail. They took Angela upstairs in a nonstop elevator. Jake stayed with her while Matt tried to expedite her processing. Walter and Helen Bowman arrived five minutes later. She was calm, he was frantic. He pressed Jake for information, pacing all the while, between the bench where they sat and the desk where Matt stood. Helen Bowman held her daughter's hand and looked straight ahead with an unwavering stare that made Jake uneasy. Matt finally finished the required paperwork. He went over to Angela and her parents and tried to sum up what the next few days would be like for them. Angela held up as well as could be expected under the circumstances, but her father was fast coming apart at the seams. The two detectives had to restrain him from interfering when the matron came to take Angela away. Helen Bowman held her daughter a long time. She stroked her face, kissed her several times, and assured her everything would be all right. She left before the matron took Angela deeper into the jail. Walter Bowman collapsed when he saw his only child taken away. Matt helped him to the bench. He also went after Mrs. Bowman to offer her a ride home, but he couldn't find her. Water Bowman accepted the offer. He was too exhausted to refuse.

On the ride back to Floribunda, Matt again advised Walter Bowman to call a lawyer as soon as possible. He informed him that Angela wouldn't be released until she was arraigned, but that the judge would set bail at the arraignment. They arrived at the Bowman residence at two-thirty. They both accompanied Walter Bowman inside the house. Helen Bowman had already arrived. Her purse was lying on the table in the foyer. They left Walter Bowman standing in his foyer.

They arrived back at Headquarters at three o'clock. Matt briefed Lloyd on the arrest. Lloyd's misgivings still lingered, but he had resigned himself to the fact that the time for doubt was past. Never one to second guess his decisions, Lloyd tenaciously defended his positions once they were taken. Now that Angela Bowman had been arrested, he intended to put all of the department's resources behind the District Attorney's efforts to convict her. He didn't believe in straddling the fence or changing horses in midstream. Misgivings aside, if Chief Carter wanted Angela Bowman, then Angela Bowman he would get.

"Did you have any trouble?" Lloyd asked.

"None that we couldn't handle. It could have been a lot worse."

"We need to have a meeting about where to go from here, Alexander."

"Can it wait until tomorrow, Lloyd?"

"Tomorrow's Thanksgiving. I don't plan to come in. Why don't we do it first thing Friday morning?"

"That's fine with me. It'll give me a chance to think about how to deal with the other leads in the case."

When Matt got back to his office, he found Carl Davis sitting on his desk.

"Get off my desk, Davis."

"Excuse me for living, Alexander. Is your desk solid gold or what?"

"No, it's not gold; but it's mine and I don't want you sitting on it. That's what that chair over there is for."

"Looks like your case is grating on your nerves, Lieutenant...kicking your natural behind to be more precise. I understand you arrested your girlfriend this afternoon."

"Just what the hell do you mean by that, Davis?"

"Nothing personal, man; but I heard on the grapevine that she used to be your main squeeze. It must have been a real emotional struggle for you to clamp the leg irons on her and drag her down to the city jail."

"My case is none of your business, Davis. I don't have to defend myself to you. Anyway, knowing someone doesn't stop me from doing my job if they break the law."

"Your sense of duty makes me sick, Alexander. There's no way I would send a fox like Angela Bowman to the slammer. If she wasted Waterson, he probably had it coming. You're a rate buster, Alexander, a goddamned boy scout."

"Are you finished, Davis?" Matt asked trying to keep his temper.

"You said it, blood. The sanctimonious atmosphere in here is more that I can stand."

"Then, get the hell out of here!"

"Hey, man. There's no need to get up tight. I don't stay anywhere I'm not welcome."

Carl Davis left as smoothly and unobtrusively as he came. Charming when he wanted to be, Davis was as deadly as a snake if you crossed him. Matt knew from experience that Davis could break bread with you one minute and cut you down the next.

"Don't let Davis get next to you, Matt. You know how he is, always pretending to be Billy Bad Ass. He would have arrested her too if Lloyd told him to. He was just selling woof tickets to try to rattle your cage, man."

"Davis doesn't bother me, Jake. It's the Bowmans. I feel sorry for them. Maybe I should have let you make the arrest without me. They all looked so desperate."

Jake was more objective in his assessment.

"All I can say is that she had better get the best damned lawyer money can buy, because Ed Davenport is going to throw her to the dogs."

"I know he is, but there's not much that we can do about it, now."

"What's to do, Matt? She's probably guilty."

Jake was interrupted by the telephone, which Matt answered. The party on the other end of the line did most of the talking. Matt's replies were terse and noncommittal.

"Who was that?" Jake asked after Matt rang off.

"A lawyer from the Public Defender's Office. He's representing Gary Washington and he wants him released."

"There's not much point in holding him now, is there?"

"No. I'll process his release papers before I leave, today."

"Do you believe he had anything at all to do with the homicide?"

"No, I don't, but it's not because of anything he said. I don't believe that Angela Bowman would jeopardize herself to protect him. If he were involved, she would have admitted it by now."

"He's a convenient scapegoat," Jake suggested. "I'm surprised they didn't blame him anyway."

"You're right, he would have been an easy way out for them if they killed him."

"So, you still have doubts?"

"Yes, I do. But, what I think doesn't matter anymore. The arrest has been made."

"What about the other leads, Matt?"

"They're all circumstantial, Jake. I'd have to build a much stronger case against Walter Bowman or the Martins before Ed

Davenport would consider prosecuting either one of them. I can't do it on the evidence I have so far."

"Look, man. If I were you, I wouldn't lose any sleep over her because I think she's guilty. It's almost quitting time anyway. Let's forget this case, Matt, and go out for a drink."

"Sounds good to me, Jake. Where to?"

"Lacey's, where else?"

Matt processed Gary Washington's release papers before they left Headquarters. They drove the short distance down Georgia Avenue to Lacey's Bar and Grill. They arrived just before the influx of the after-work, pre-holiday crowd.

The bar was nearly empty if you didn't count the bartender, Tiny, and a trio of down-and-out drinkers who usually stood outside the bar waiting for it to open at five o'clock. Tiny sat behind the undulating wraparound bar polishing glasses. At five-feet- seven- inches tall, Tiny weighed over three hundred pounds, so he sat down every chance he got. Tiny's feet and legs had turned against him years ago, worn out from the strain of supporting his excess bulk for well over fifty years. He suffered from a small army of complaints...water on the knees, flat feet, bunions, corns, and varicose veins. Above the knee, he was subject to a spastic colon, high blood pressure, double vision, and ringing in his ears. Most of the bar's regulars knew Tiny's health problems as well as they knew their own. If you sat at his bar, you heard his complaints. As a matter of fact, Tiny received a good deal more sympathy than he dispensed to his customers. An hour with Tiny and his health problems was enough to make a depressed man count his blessings.

In Tiny's former life he had been head chef at one of the better District hotels before he got too big to stand on his feet all day. He retired with twenty years of service and moved uptown to tend bar in his brother's establishment. Bill Lacey was fifteen years younger than Tiny and about a third his size. Unlike Tiny, Bill was very conscious of his weight. One of the high points in his life was the time he made the Olympic Trials as an amateur boxer. He didn't win any medals, but you'd never know it from the pictures of Bill in varied boxing stances that papered the walls of his bar. Bill Lacey talked about his brief stint as an amateur boxer with as much enthusiasm as Tiny gave his assorted health problems. If you went to Lacey's bar more than once, you quickly learned that you didn't discuss boxing with Bill and you never but never asked Tiny how he was feeling.

"What's the word, Tiny?" Jake asked after he placed their order.

"Oh man, I've been sick as a dog. I caught that flu bug that was going around about a month ago. Man, I just knew that I wasn't long for this world," Tiny replied in a gravelly voice slightly above a whisper, the result of too much oven heat from his former career and too much cigarette smoke from his current one.

"Looks like you pulled through it okay, man."

"I might look all right on the outside, Sergeant, but I'm still a sick man. That bug hit me so hard, I'm lucky to be alive."

"What's on the menu, today, Tiny?" Jake asked.

"Man, you're in luck. I've got some gumbo back there that'll make you smack your mama. I spent damned near half the day making it, but it was worth every minute. It's delicious."

"It has to be if you cooked it, Tiny. You know how to put a hurting on some food, man. I'll be sure to order some of that gumbo before I leave."

Jake joined his partner at a table near the front of the club strategically selected for its proximity to the bar, the men's room and the front door. They had been there about ten minutes when the after-work crowd began to collect. Lacey's was a popular watering hole for both in-towners and suburbanites who usually mixed it up pretty good on Friday nights in anticipation of a weekend of boredom in the suburbs. Conveniently situated on a main thoroughfare, Lacey's had enticed many a desk-weary bureaucrat to stop on his way home. Known for its good food, generous drinks, and fine jazz, Lacey's held its own while more trendy night spots came and went. Bill Lacey took a lot of pride in his place. He didn't tolerate violence, profanity, or soliciting of any kind. His firm management paid off. Lacey's customers were loyal, and Bill did a brisk business most evenings and weekends. By six o'clock there wasn't a vacant seat in the house.

"Can you believe this crowd, Matt? I'm glad we got here early."

"It's always like this before a holiday, Jake. What did Tiny have to say?"

"Complaining about his health as usual. He recommended the gumbo. I think I'll order some. Do you want any?"

"No thanks, I'll stick to Maker's Mark."

Matt signalled for their waitress, Sonja, over the sound of Sarah Vaughn in one of her mellower moods. Sonja saw him wave for her, but she waited on three more tables before she got to theirs.

"You took your own sweet time, Sonja. Isn't our money good enough for you anymore?"

"Did you expect me to jump over three tables to wait on you, Matthew Alexander? You don't know me that well, baby."

Jake laughed.

"Hey, Jake, what's happening?"

"You're what's happening, Sonja. Listen sugar, I've got a bad jones for you. All you have to do is say the word."

"You never give up do you, Jake? I don't waste my time with detectives. They're too poor to show me a good time. When you get to be a captain, we can talk business."

"Come off it, Sonja. You'd go out with Matt tonight, and he isn't a captain."

"There's an exception to every rule, Jake," Sonja replied as she lightly stroked the side of Matt's cheek with her finger, "and you ain't it."

"Give it a rest, Sonja. You act like your stuff is gold. It ain't no better than nobody else's," Jake insisted.

"Maybe it is and maybe it isn't; but you'll never know one way or the other, Detective Sergeant Jackson."

"You've been after Matt a long time, Sonja, and you haven't gotten him, yet. Maybe, your stuff isn't so hot after all."

"You mustn't believe everything you're told, Jake. Isn't that right, Lieutenant Alexander?"

"All we want to order are drinks, Sonja. Save the other merchandise for the customers who don't know any better."

"Suit yourself, sweet thing, but you don't know what you're missing."

Jake's eyes followed Sonja's gyrating hips under her short hostess skirt from their table to the bar.

"Didn't you tell me you had never messed with Sonja, Matt?"

"Give me a break, man! I don't want Sonja."

"You're crazy man. That stuff is hot. She won't give me the time of day, otherwise I'd be dead on her case. Sonja's a stone fox."

"You don't know when you're well off, Jake. You have about as much as you can handle anyway," Matt replied, alluding to Jake's long standing affair with Yvonne, his outside woman who called Jake at Fourth District Headquarters with such spousal regularity that officers who didn't know any better left messages that Jake's wife Yvonne had called.

"Sonja would take me for every cent I've got, Matt, but it would be worth the ride while the money lasted. She looks like she could make it worth my while, man."

"You give her too much credit, Jake. Forget about Sonja. Are you and Flo still coming over for dinner tomorrow?"`

"You bet we are. What time should we get there?"

"Around four. I think Carla wants to serve dinner at five. She's worked herself into a frazzle over Thanksgiving dinner. I'll be relieved when it's over."

Sonja returned with their drinks.

"That'll be five dollars a piece, please."

"Are you referring to the drinks or your other merchandise?" Matt asked.

"And just what are you insinuating by that remark?" Sonja screeched.

"Don't get excited, Sonja. I just want to know what we're paying for, that's all."

"Just what the hell do you expect five dollars to buy besides drinks?"

"It depends on who's selling, Sonja. Five dollars goes a long way with some people."

"It buys exactly one drink from me, so pay up!" Sonja snarled as she angrily snatched the money from Matt's hand and stomped off without waiting for a tip.

"Mind if I join you?" Carl Davis asked. "It looks like you have the only empty chair in the joint."

"Sure, sit down, Davis," Jake offered.

"Don't I remember you saying you didn't want to be anywhere you weren't welcome, Davis?"

"That was back in your office, Alexander. This is Bill Lacey's place. Are you claiming dibs on this chair, too?"

Matt was preparing to force Davis to leave when he saw Sam Johnson walk into the bar. He motioned for Sam to come over to their table.

"Sit down, Sam. We saved you a seat, man."

Carl Davis was angry enough to spit bullets, but he left without creating a scene.

"What do you want from me now, Lieutenant?"

"Nothing more than the pleasure of your company, Sam."

"You're being too nice to me. You must have something up your sleeve."

"Don't look a gift horse in the mouth, Sam. I appreciate the job you did for me on the forensic tests, so I'm going to buy you a drink. Name your poison."

"I may be a skeptic, but I know a good offer when I hear one, Lieutenant. My drink is Jack Daniels Black on the rocks."

Jake wasn't impressed. He said: "You've got expensive tastes, Sam," he wryly commented.

"Why not, Sergeant? You only live once. Why settle for coach when you can go first class."

Matt ordered another round of drinks.

"It must be nice," Jake replied. "Most of us working stiffs are happy if we meet our bills every month. Tell us how you do it, Sam."

"It's like this, Sergeant. You join the FBI, then you work like hell for five years to become a forensic specialist. You retire after twenty years of service with the FBI and start working full-time for the District of Columbia Police Force. In the meantime, you buy property and catch pure hell trying to get your rents on time and keeping the tenants from wrecking it or burning it to the ground. After you retire, you sell off your real estate and invest the money in high-yield mutual funds, and treasury bonds, and you stay married to the same women for thirty years. You should give it a shot, Sergeant."

"There are easier ways to make money," Jake suggested.

"Sure there are, but most of them are illegal. Take this bar for instance. Bill Lacey makes a good piece of change in here, but his overhead eats it up. I count five people working in here right now and that doesn't include the entertainment. It costs a small fortune to keep this place going...liquor, food, entertainment, salaries, bennies, taxes, and whatever other payoffs he has to make. If I were in Lacey's shoes, I'd sell this place tomorrow, invest my money in high-yield mutual funds or treasury notes and hire myself out to manage someone else's bar for a salary. As a sole investment, this place is a sinkhole."

"Maybe Bill likes being a proprietor," Matt suggested.

"He must love it to keep this place open. There's very little net rate of return in an investment like this. Over in Georgetown maybe, but not on Georgia Avenue."

Matt didn't agree with Sam's assessment.

"I'm glad Bill hasn't sold out, Sam. Lacey's is a nice bar, and the food is good."

"He'd make more money if it was a hole-in-the-wall, Lieutenant. Nice means more overhead to keep the place up and provide good service. I still say it's a sinkhole."

"What brings you to Lacey's, Sam? I've never seen you in here before?" Jake asked.

"Don't I deserve a break once in a while, Sergeant?"

"Just curious, Sam."

"I heard you arrested the daughter today, Lieutenant. You sure she killed him?"

"Not really. But, it wasn't my decision. Do you think she's guilty, Sam?"

"Probably, but where's the gun?"

"Who knows, but you can't say we didn't look for it."

"This investigation reminds me of a case I worked on a while back." Sam said. "It was over fifteen years ago. That particular case had more twists and turns than this one. It nearly drove the chief investigator crazy. It was a unbelievably tough case...had everybody running around in circles."

"So, what's the point?" Jake wanted to know.

"The point is that the murderer was someone we didn't remotely suspect. That's why we couldn't make any sense out of what went down. There wasn't any reason to it. We were trying to impose reason and logic on a set of circumstances that were altogether unreasonable and illogical."

"How did you find out who the murderer was?" Matt asked.

"That's just it, Alexander. We didn't find out until the killer simply up and confessed out of left field. There was nothing in the evidence that could have led us to him."

"That's crazy," Jake insisted.

"You've got it, Sergeant. It's just a suggestion, Alexander, but if I were you, I'd start looking for someone who isn't wrapped too tight. It wouldn't surprise me a bit if the person who killed Waterson isn't all there."

"None of the homicide suspects have a history of mental illness, Sam."

"Oh, don't get me wrong, Lieutenant. The person you want hasn't been diagnosed. And they've probably never seen a psychiatrist either; but that doesn't mean a damned thing. Some of the sickest people I've met have never been near a psychiatric hospital."

"How can you second guess someone like that when they don't show any outward signs?" the Lieutenant asked.

"It's a shot in the dark, Lieutenant, a crap shoot with a blindfold."

Matt didn't attach much significance to Sam's theory, but it was an interesting angle.

"Did you finish the ballistics test on the Waterson gun, Sam?"

"Yes. That was the last thing I did today. The markings were very similar, but they didn't match perfectly. That thirty-eight you gave me isn't manufactured any more. It's a collector's item. Do you think Mrs. Waterson would be interested in selling it?"

"I doubt it. She made a point of telling me to be sure it was returned to her. Besides, she doesn't need the money."

"What happened to the other gun?"

"What other gun?!"

"I thought you knew that thirty-eight was originally manufactured as one of a pair. You can get a good price for one, but together they're worth a small fortune."

"Why didn't you tell me this before now, Sam?"

"What the hell! I thought you already knew!"

"How the hell was I supposed to know! Felicia Waterson gave me one gun, not two!"

"Maybe she only has one. It's unusual for an expensive pair of matched revolvers to be sold separately, but it happens. All I know is what you gave me, Lieutenant. I'm not paid to second guess the evidence."

"How similar were the markings?"

"Very similar."

"Similar enough to lead you to believe that the other gun would match the slug perfectly?"

"It might or it might not. Guns are funny that way."

"Do you think she has the other gun, Matt?" Jake asked.

"If she has it, she'll never give it up, Jake. That explains why she gave me the first gun so easily."

"She didn't have much choice since Waterson registered it downtown. It's odd that he didn't register both of them, Alexander, unless he didn't own both guns." Sam reasoned.

Matt disagreed. "He owned both of them all right, Sam. Registering just one gun was his way of outsmarting the system, since they were matched weapons. He thought he was putting one over on us."

"Where would you buy a set of guns like that, Sam?"

"Only one place here in the District, Lowery's Gun Shop. If Waterson bought them in town, that's where they came from."

"Are you going to get a warrant to search the Waterson house, Matt?" Jake asked.

"It depends on what I find out from Lowery's, Jake. Damn! Tomorrow's Thanksgiving. The shop won't be open."

"Can't it wait until Friday, man?"

"Not if I can get the information from Lowery's tomorrow." Sonja refused to take Matt's order for their next round of drinks, so Jake had to go over to the bar to get them.

"How close were Gary Washington's prints to the prints you found in the bathroom, Sam. Are you sure they couldn't have been his?"

"No, I'm not sure because those prints are too smudged to

tell me anything. I may as well throw them out. His powder test was a complete waste of time, too. I should have never let you talk me into that."

"I guess that leaves Gary Washington in the clear unless he confesses and leads us to the gun."

"He didn't strike me as being retarded, Alexander. He'd have to be a total idiot to turn himself in since you don't have a shred of evidence linking him to the crime."

Jake maneuvered three drinks through the crowd without spilling them. The club's regular jazz trio launched into their first number as Sam prepared to leave, insisting that two drinks were as much as he could stand before falling asleep at the wheel. Matt and Jake stayed long enough to hear the trio play several of its best numbers before calling it a night. Lacey's was jumping when they left. The jazz vocalist warmed her vocal cords on some groovy blue notes that said what you wanted to say only so much better than you ever could. The drums, bass and piano backed her up with some funky rhythms and chords that palpitated through the bar, touched the patrons where it mattered most, and came on back home. Jake caught a glimpse of Sonja out of the corner of his eye. He was tempted to stay; but the thought of Flo waiting up for him spurred him on. He wanted to stay on his good foot now that he was out of the dog house.

Carla was fit to be tied when her husband walked through the back door. She smelled the bourbon and refused to speak to him for an hour. Matt played with the children while he waited for her to cool off. After he put the children to bed and waited a safe interval, he went down to the kitchen. Carla sat at the kitchen table smoking.

"I wish you wouldn't smoke, Carla. You know it's bad for your health."

"You're bad for my health, Matthew Alexander. I'm stuck here with the children and everything else that needs to be done in this damned house while you're out all day doing God knows what. I'm sick and tired of it."

"You know I've been swamped with work on the Waterson homicide, Carla. It's a tough investigation, baby. I told you on Sunday that I would be tied up most of the week. I know it isn't easy on you and the kids, but I promise to make it up to you."

"Do you know how much work it is to prepare Thanksgiving dinner for twelve? I've been working like a dog, not that you are."

"The dinner was your idea, Carla. You can't blame that on me. Why are you so upset, you seem to have everything under control."

"Under control! Look at this place! I'm on my second bottle of wine! You call that control! I'm a nervous wreck!"

"Calm down, honey. What can I do to help you?"

"Everything is a mess! The damned turkey is too big for the roaster! The ham is too fat! The cornbread I made for the stuffing didn't rise; and the rolls fell while they were cooking!"

Matt began to laugh, which was a mistake. Once he started he couldn't stop.

"If you don't stop laughing at me, I'll hit you over the head with that skillet of cornbread. It's so heavy, it'll probably kill you instantly." Then she started to laugh. They laughed together, Matt until he cried.

"Fix me a drink, Matthew. I need it." He made drinks for both of them.

"You've let this dinner get the best of you, Carla," he said still smiling. "It's just a dinner, baby. Nobody expects it to be perfect. Here, drink this and calm yourself down." Carla took the drink and lit another cigarette.

"I had everything planned down to the letter, honey, but the minute I started cooking, everything fell apart."

"You're suffering from a case of anxiety, Carla. You know you can cook Thanksgiving dinner with one hand tied behind your back. You have to think positive. Now, where's that big-breasted turkey?"

"It's in the refrigerator. I dressed it before I realized I didn't have anything big enough to cook it in." He took the turkey out of the refrigerator.

"Good grief, Carla. This turkey must weight twenty-five pounds. Why did you buy the biggest turkey in the District?"

"I wanted to get one big enough to feed a dozen people."

"This bad boy will feed the entire block." He found a shallow casserole dish big enough to hold the turkey's wingspan and long enough to accommodate its length. Then he cut most of the fat off the ham. After that, he placed the ham and turkey in the oven. The bread came next. The cornbread could be salvaged by adding eggs to the stuffing; but the rolls were too far gone to resuscitate. He dumped them into the trash.

"Everything's squared away but the rolls, Carla. You'll have to make a fresh batch."

"Why don't you make the rolls, honey?"

"You must be kidding. I can't make rolls. but, I will go to the grocery store to buy some before it closes. That's my best offer."

"I have some store bought rolls in the freezer. I was looking forward to having home-made rolls. They're so much better than the store rolls."

"Forget the home-made rolls, Carla. I think you're putting too much pressure on yourself."

"You're right, scratch the home-made rolls. How was your day?"

"The worst. I had to arrest Angela Bowman this afternoon." Carla almost choked on her drink.

"You're kidding. Did you really put her in jail, matthew?!"

"Yes. I didn't have any choice, Carla. Chief Carter ordered the arrest."

"So, she really killed him?"

"I'm not convinced she did, but she had the most obvious

motive and the best opportunity."

"Angela Bowman behind bars, I can't believe it. What did she do when you arrested her? What did she say?"

"Nothing much. She was scared and crying, but she didn't resist."

"Her father must have freaked out. What did he do?"

"He put up the most resistance, but he didn't' cause us any real trouble. They were pretty cooperative, all things considered."

"What did you charge her with?"

"First degree murder."

"Murder! Good grief! They'll put her in prison forever, Matthew."

"Probably."

"Angela in prison. It sounds like a bona fide nightmare."

"I'm sure it will be for her. There's a chance that she may not be guilty; but the other possible leads are too circumstantial to be seriously considered for prosecution. Chief Carter authorized me to continue the investigation. It could take weeks to find a solid lead, though. Meanwhile, Ed Davenport isn't going to waste any time moving against Angela."

"He usually goes for the jugular doesn't he?"

"That's putting it mildly, Carla."

"You shouldn't blame yourself, honey. You did the best you could for her."

"I know I did, but that doesn't make me feel any better."

"You've been working too hard, matthew. You need some time off."

"That's easier said than done, Carla. Ed's going to push this case through the court docket. He can't wait to get her into court."

"You can't stop him, so what's the point in worrying about it?"

"I worry that she may be innocent, Carla."

"If she's innocent, won't it come out in the trial?"

"Not necessarily. Somebody killed Harold Waterson; and Ed is going to pull out all the stops to prove that Angela Bowman did it."

"That doesn't mean she'll be convicted, Matthew."

"You've never seen Ed Davenport work, Carla. He's good, damned good. He has the best conviction rate in the District Prosecutor's office."

"Angela needs a good lawyer."

"I'm sure her father will get one for her; but Ed is still going to throw the book at her in court."

"You didn't find the gun did you?"

"No, but Ed says he can convict her without it."

"She probably did kill him, you know."

"I know there's a good possibility that she did; but the case against her has too many holes in it to suit me. Harold Waterson had a stronger motive for killing her than she had for killing him. The gun is missing; but there's no evidence that she fired it. The Martins had a damned strong motive for wanting him dead; and they had keys to the Bowmans' house. One of them could have taken the gun from Walter Bowman's desk...shit, I'm tired to talking about the case, Carla. What else is new?"

"Phyllis and Roger bought a new Lexus today. She couldn't wait to call me to gloat about it."

"Your sister has a Lexus already. Why did they buy another one?"

"Phyllis traded it in on the new model. It must be nice to have money to burn like that."

"I don't know, Carla. It seems to me that they work hard for their money just like we do."

"But, why do they have to have so much more than we do. Phyllis is such a cat about it too. She's constantly finding ways to throw it up to me. I hate to go shopping with her because she never worries about what things cost. Why couldn't you be an actuary like Roger, Matthew?"

"I love my work, Carla; and even if I didn't, an actuary is the last thing I'd want to be. Look at it this way, Phyllis can't have Roger's money without Roger. They're a package deal."

Carla laughed. "You're right honey. Roger is such a jerk. Phyllis wouldn't have given him the time of day if he didn't make so much money."

"Phyllis isn't that mercenary, Carla."

"You don't know her like I do, Matthew. When we were growing up all Phyllis talked about was marrying somebody with money. She used to say you could learn to love anybody if they had enough money."

Matt laughed. "I guess Roger is a prime example of that philosophy. But, what the hell, if Phyllis likes her life with Roger, I love it. The way I see it, Carla, they're simply two people trying to make it like everybody else."

"I only wish they didn't have so much money. It seems unfair, somehow."

"So what if they do have more money. They don't love each other any more than we do. They can't love their children any more than we love ours. Their love making couldn't be as satisfying as ours. The sun shines as brightly on us as it does on them. Money can't buy the most important things we need, Carla."

"That's all well and good, honey, but it won't make me feel any better when Phyllis drives up in her new Lexus tomorrow wearing her full length mink coat."

"Now, you're the one who's being a cat."

"I know I am, but Phyllis always got the pick of everything when we were growing up. Daddy used to say it was because she was the oldest, but I know better. It was because he liked her the best."

"Please, Carla, not that again."

"Why not, it's true. She is his favorite. I'll bet he gives her money all the time, and he never gives me a dime."

"Maybe he would if you were nicer to him. Phyllis pets him

up, and you cut him up—every chance you get."

"That's not true, Matthew. I love my father. I simply can't stand his old-fashioned, snobbish ideas."

"He's had those ideas all his life, Carla; and he's too old to change now. You should accept him for who he is and try to get along with him."

"I will not knuckle under to Daddy! Nothing would please him more than to say `I told you so' to me. He's living for the day when I tell him he was right about everything and I was wrong. Well, I won't give him the satisfaction."

"You can't have it both ways, Carla. If you're not willing to cater to your father you ought to stop worrying about what he thinks of you. If you're concerned about what he thinks of you, you ought to try to be nicer to him. You're playing both sides against the middle and losing."

I really don't like it when you talk to me like that, Matthew. I know how to handle my own father."

"Have it your own way, then. I'm going to bed."

"Are you going to leave me up with all this food cooking?"

"Yes. I'm so tired, anything I watched would burn to a crisp. Set the timer on the stove in case you go to sleep. I'll see you, the ham, and the turkey in the morning." He kissed her before going up to bed.

# CHAPTER XV

"Man, I don't remember the last time I laughed so hard," Jake insisted as he wiped tears from the corners of his eyes. "This was the best Thanksgiving I've had in years. I thought I'd die when Carla called her father a stuffed turkey. Man, he looked mad enough to bust a gut when she told him two stuffed turkeys for Thanksgiving was one too many.'" Jake roared with laughter as he drove south on Seventh Street to Lowery's Gun Shop.

"Don't laugh, Jake. Dinner was a disaster. I've never seen Arthur Channing so mad. He would have left if Portia hadn't talked him out of it."

"Lighten up, partner. I don't know about everyone else, but I had a ball. The food was delicious, and Carla was in rare form today, especially when your mother kept saying she didn't believe a nice girl like Angela would kill anyone. Did you see your mother's face when Carla told her that nice girls don't have affairs with married men in the basement of their parents' house. She almost choked on her turkey."

Jake was laughing so hard he almost ran through a stop signal. Matt laughed in spite of himself.

"Carla will say anything when she's angry. Mom knows that Carla can't stand Angela. She should have left well enough alone."

"What about when she told you that you wouldn't believe Angela was guilty unless she had killed old Waterson on the Capitol steps at high noon in full view of both houses of Congress and a Nigerian trade delegation."

Matt wasn't amused, but Jake laughed until his sides hurt and tears streamed down his face.

"What did Carla say to her father when he told her that her language was so foul he wasted good money sending her to private schools, Matt?"

"She told him she had learned most of what she knew from private schools including her vulgar language, and he hadn't heard anything yet. That's when Arthur asked for something to settle his stomach." Jake was enjoying himself too much to stop.

"Then her sister, Phyllis, said that Gary Washington probably killed Waterson because Gary grew up in public housing. Man, it was all I could do to keep from laughing out loud when Carla told her that was the kind of logic she expected from someone who flunked kindergarten."

"That wasn't funny, Jake. Phyllis lost her appetite after that. It wouldn't have been so bad if Roger hadn't said that Phyllis was as smart as anybody at the table. Then Carla had to say if that`s so why is she the only one at the table married to you?'

Jake howled.

"Its not funny, Jake. We'll have to mend fences in Carla's family until next Thanksgiving. The only people she didn't zing were her sister Cassie, you and Flo and her mother. Carla's crazy about her family, but when she's upset she loses control and feels terrible afterwards."

"Her mother wasn't upset, Matt. I saw Portia splitting her sides behind her husband's back after she talked him out of leaving. She was doubled up laughing out in the foyer after

Arthur came back to the table. She straightened up when she caught me looking at her."

"Portia is a good sport, but Arthur Channing is as dry as an old bone and as straight as an arrow. He and Portia are a strange pair, but they're devoted to each other. I'll bet he's never looked at another woman, and they've been married thirty-five years."

They arrived at Lowery's Gun Shop on the corner of Seventh and "H" Streets in Northwest at seven-forty-five in the evening. Sid Ross, the proprietor, was waiting inside the shop. He looked thoroughly disgusted when he opened the door for them. Matt was the first to speak.

"Thanks for coming out, Mr. Ross. I apologize for taking you away from you family on Thanksgiving, but we need whatever information you have as quickly as possible."

"It's a damned nuisance, Lieutenant Alexander. I still don't see why it couldn't have waited until tomorrow."

"A man was shot to death last Saturday night, Mr. Ross. We've arrested a young woman who's been charged with his murder. Your information could be vital to the case."

"If I have any information. I've been going through my records, and I haven't found a bill of sale to Harold Waterson, so far. There's a good chance that he didn't buy the gun from me, Lieutenant."

Sid Ross went back to his ledgers. He adjusted his bifocals as he read through his sales ledgers, one precise handwritten entry at a time. He was painstakingly slow and thorough about it, but neither officer dared ask him to speed it up. After forty-five minutes and three more ledgers, he gave up.

"I can't find a record of a sale to Harold Waterson, Lieutenant."

"What about Felicia Waterson?"

"There's no record of a sale to anybody named Waterson. I'm afraid you're out of luck."

"Do you remember selling this gun to anyone? Maybe Hal

Waterson bought it from someone else." He showed Sid Ross the Waterson gun.

"You should have shown me the pistol earlier. It would have saved me the time and effort of going through five ledgers of sales records. I never sold this gun to anybody."

"Are you certain of that?"

"I'm positive, but I wish I had. A pair of pistols like this bring a damned good price in today's market. Where's the matching gun?"

"That's what we're trying to find out. We hoped you could tell us."

"Sorry to disappoint you, Lieutenant, but I would remember if I had sold this gun. However, it may have been sold before I started running the shop. I bought the store from Zack Lowery five years ago. He owned it for fifty years before that."

"Where can we find Mr. Lowery?"

"Six feet under. He died three years ago in Florida."

"Damn! What happened to his records?"

"Those he left in the store are in the supply room out back."

"Can we take a look at them?" Matt asked.

Sid Ross frowned and looked at his watch.

"Only if you promise to make it brief. I don't intend to be here all night."

Then he grudgingly led them back to his supply room, where Zack Lowery's records were stored in three large boxes neatly stacked in one corner of the room. Jake was dismayed at the size of the boxes.

"It'll take us all night to go through this stuff, Matt." Sid Ross was alarmed at the prospect of staying in his shop the rest of the evening.

"I'm not going to stay here all night, Lieutenant Alexander."

"You won't have to if you let us take the boxes with us. I'll give you a receipt and return them as soon as we finish going through the contents."

Sid Ross looked skeptical, but his resistance faded when he considered the alternative of staying in his shop until they searched the boxes. The two detectives loaded the boxes in their car and were back at Matt's house by nine o'clock. Jake helped carry the boxes into the house, but quickly left before he was asked to help search them. He had no intention of wasting the rest of his evening sorting through musty old boxes. He waited for Flo in the car. Matt sensed that Jake was in one of his uncooperative moods, so he didn't press him to stay. He decided that he'd rather do all the work himself than listen to his partner's complaining all night. He put all three boxes in the kitchen and went upstairs to check on Carla, who was in bed nursing a sick headache. He sat down on the bed beside her.

"How do you feel?"

"My head feels like it's going to split in two. This is the worst headache I've ever had."

"Did you take anything for it?"

"Yes, but it doesn't seem to be helping much."

"You worked overtime for your migraine, Carla. I warned you to take it easy. You put too much pressure on yourself. I'm surprised you didn't get it sooner. Would you like a drink?"

"No. I had one while you were gone. Flo did all of the washing up and she put the children to bed, too."

"Flo's nice when she wants to be, which isn't often."

"You're too hard on her, Matthew. Cassie wanted to stay, but Daddy wouldn't let her. He's very angry with me. I don't blame him. I ruined everybody's dinner, didn't I?"

"Of course not. Jake said it was the best Thanksgiving dinner he's had in years, but you didn't zing him." Matt laughed, Carla smiled faintly.

"It was a fiasco and you know it. You're just trying to make me feel better."

"You're being to hard on yourself, Carla. The dinner was fine. Everyone said the food was delicious."

"Your mother didn't even say good-bye when she left. I wouldn't be surprised if she never spoke to me again."

"Don't be silly, Carla. Mom isn't like that. She's a good sport."

"Be honest, Matthew. You know she doesn't like me, she never has."

"That's not true, Carla, but I'm not going to argue about that tonight."

"The hostess was a witch. You know it, even if you won't admit it to me."

"A beautiful, sexy witch in my opinion." He leaned over and kissed the soft spot in her throat.

"Forget about the dinner. You'll feel better after a good night's sleep. I have a lot of work to do tonight, so I'll be in the kitchen if you need anything."

After Matt left Carla, he went down to the kitchen and fortified himself for the tedious work of sorting through Zack Lowery's boxes. He poured himself a drink, put one of his favorite jazz CDs, "Mo Better Blues," on the stereo and sat down to reflect on the day's events, including Carla's feelings about Jake's wife, Florine, which were far different from his feelings about her.

Sticking with Florine would have been understandable if she and Jake had children, but their thirty-year union was childless. It would also have been understandable if she were attractive or loving or well-heeled, but she lacked any obvious assets. Matt concluded that Jake's apparent devotion to his wife had to be grounded in an emotional bond not readily perceptible to an outsider because, on the surface, Florine Jackson was an incredible shrew who left a lot to be desired as a wife and lover.

But when it came to his wife, Jake didn't care what anyone thought. He and Florine were living examples of how to survive the hard way. They had come through bad times together that he couldn't have endured without her. Florine stood by him when he had no prospects and couldn't produce two dimes to rub together, and never complained until she lost two babies in succession early in their marriage and most of her capacity to love with them.

Florine Jackson fought her way up from insignificance and back-breaking poverty and never lost her will to survive. But when she lost her children, something shriveled and died inside...the same something that gives love, affection, and a kind word. She was as good as gold, but few knew except her husband, Jake, and others like Carla Alexander who could see that the biting tongue and indifferent attitude were a smoke-screen Florine used to mask her own bitter disappointment. Jake endured his wife's tantrums and bad moods because he was a witness to the trauma that battered a resilient spirit into the alternately bitter and depressed woman he lived with every day. So his commitment to her was strong, even after thirty stormy years of marriage. Jake Jackson didn't take his emotional attachments lightly.

When Matt finally got around to opening the first box, he was relieved to see that it wasn't as bad as he expected. Inside, he found seven large ledgers and three times as many bundles of loose receipts separated by thick, rotting rubber bands. The sales receipts were dog-eared and yellowed from age. Repair invoices, sales receipts, shipping and receiving invoices were interspersed in most of the bundles. The ledgers were filled with Zack Lowery's accounts, figures which had very little meaning for Matt. He tackled the ledgers first, inspecting each one in detail and finding nothing of interest. He searched the bundles for an hour and a half without stopping. At eleven o'clock, he went upstairs to check on Carla and the children. Everyone was asleep. Back in the kitchen, he made himself a strong Maker's Mark and changed the jazz CD on the stereo to his all time favorite, "Sarah Vaughan's Finest Hour," before he opened the second box.

The second box was more chaotic than the first. Sales receipts were scattered loosely throughout the box. Old stock invoices and correspondence were mixed in with the receipts. It took him an hour to sort the disarray before it could reasonably be inspected. He finished the second box at one o'clock. By two o'clock he was exhausted and discouraged by the pointless searching. His eyes ached from the strain of reading so much faint writing on the old receipts and ledgers, but he refused to give up. He made himself another drink and opened the third box. The third box wasn't as messy as the second one or as well ordered as the first. It contained at least twenty ledgers and about half as many piles of old receipts. Half of the ledgers listed stock records while the other half held accounts. He went through the ledgers quickly, but even so, it was four o'clock A.M. before he finished them. By then, he was so sleepy he could barely keep his eyes open. He went over to the kitchen sink and washed his face in cold tap water. It helped. He changed the CD againñthis time to a classic Ella Fitzgerald-Louis Armstrong compilation including a beautiful rendition of "Isn't This a Lovely Day."

He didn't hold out much hope for finding a bill of sale to Harold Waterson in the third box, the odds were against him. But since he had come so far, he decided to see it through. About half way through the bundle of sales receipts, he found it...a small green slip of paper with Harold Waterson's name in the upper left hand corner. The address listed wasn't current, but it was Waterson's name, no doubt about that. The date on the sales receipt indicated that Harold Waterson had purchased a gun from Lowery's twenty years before.

Matt was elated until he realized that the receipt didn't indicate how many guns had been sold. It suddenly occurred to him that it might be possible to match the stock number on the receipt to the lists of stock numbers in the ledgers. He started searching the ledgers at four-thirty. He didn't find what he was looking for until six o'clock A.M. He was so elated at finding it he shouted out loud and kissed the ledger. Harold Waterson had bought a pair of matched revolvers from Zack Lowery twenty years earlier. The stock ledger indicated as much and even included the serial numbers for both guns. Matt was jubilant. He felt his case connect for the first time since the investigation started. It was a good feeling, so he took a while to savour his victory before going upstairs to shower and get ready for another day.

Matt felt miserable Friday morning from too little sleep and too much bourbon. He was supposed to be in Lloyd's office at seven-thirty, but he didn't get to Headquarters until eight. Lloyd was furious when he finally showed up for the meeting.

"You're late again, Alexander. You're supposed to set an example for the rest of the men by coming in on time. What are they supposed to think when they see you coming in any goddamned time you please? You seem to enjoy seeing just how far you can push me."

"Give me a break, Lloyd. I was up until seven o'clock this morning working on the Waterson investigation."

"What's to work on, Angela Bowman's been arrested."

"Maybe she shouldn't have been. Look at this." He gave Lloyd the sales receipt and stock ledger.

"What the hell is this?"

Matt explained what he'd learned about the ballistics test from Sam Johnson and how that information led him to Zack Lowery's records.

"How close were the markings?"

"I haven't seen them yet, but Sam says they're very close."

"So, you think the Watersons have the other gun?"

"I think they had it. If it was used to kill Harold Waterson, they've probably gotten rid of it by now; but to be on the safe side, I'd like to get a search warrant just in case it's still on the premises."

"I won't authorize it unless Chief Carter agrees, Alexander. I don't see much point in putting my ass in a sling now that Angela Bowman has been arrested."

"Damn it, Lloyd. This is the best lead we've found in this investigation. All I'm asking for is a search warrant. Who can that hurt?"

"It can hurt me if the Chief doesn't want you to search Felicia Waterson's house. Don't push me, Alexander. You're damned lucky I've agreed to call the Chief."

Matt was dangerously close to telling Lloyd how he really felt. He held back because he didn't want to give Lloyd a pretext for refusing to call the Chief. He silently cursed both Lloyd and Chief Carter for their willingness to cave in to special interests and self-serving priorities. Matt and Lloyd spent the next thirty minutes reviewing the case. Lloyd agreed to give him two more men, part-time, and to allow him to work on the case for the next five days after which time he reserved the right to re-assess depending on Matt's progress.

"Chief Carter said I was to have two men full-time, Lloyd."

"I run the Homicide Division, Alexander, not Chief Carter. You'll take what I give you or nothing at all."

Lloyd returned the sales receipt and the ledger. After Matt left Lloyd's office, he went downstairs to the forensics lab and got the Waterson ballistic test results from Sam, who was more amenable than normal. He attributed it to the two drinks he bought Sam at Lacey's Wednesday night. He made a note to buy Sam drinks more often. Jake was on the telephone when he walked into their office.

"Hang up, Jake. I"m expecting a call from Lloyd as soon as he talks to Chief Carter."

"What the hell! Can't I use the damned telephone without being ordered around? I only make one call a week anyway!"

"Sorry, man. I just got out of a meeting with Lloyd and he really pissed me off. He can be a real SOB when he wants to."

"Lloyd Cullison is an SOB all the time. So, what else is new?"

"I found what I was looking for in Zack Lowery's records, Jake."

"Hey man! That's great! What did Lloyd have to say about it?"

"He wasn't impressed. As a matter of fact, he said he wouldn't authorize a search warrant for the Waterson house unless Chief Carter approved it."

"I'm not surprised, partner. Cullison is always looking to cover his butt. He doesn't want to blow his chances to become Chief of Police when Carter retires. What are you going to do if they don't authorize the search?"

"They've got to authorize it, Jake. This sales receipt is the best lead I've uncovered in this entire investigation. Harold Waterson's Aunt Martha swears that Felicia Waterson wasn't home during the time her husband was killed."

"But you haven't placed her at the scene, man."

"I know it, Jake; but I've got a feeling I'm onto something this time."

"Don't build your hopes up, Matt. Neither Cullison or Chief Carter will risk anything when it comes to covering their butts, especially with a broad like Felicia Waterson. Don't be disappointed if they leave you hanging, man. I'll be surprised if they don't."

"Angela Bowman's been arrested for first degree murder, Jake. The department owes it to her to follow through on this lead, man. All they have to do is authorize a search warrant. They have to give me a chance to find that other gun."

"You know better than that, partner. They'll let you do it if it doesn't put a cramp in their style. That's the way the game is played, man. You ought to know that by now. You're setting yourself up for a fall."

"The game isn't always played that way, Jake. If I believed the system was that heartless, I wouldn't be here."

"You can believe what you want to, partner; but I know better. You do too, but you don't want to admit it."

Matt spent the better part of the morning clearing out paper-work and correspondence in his in-box. The call from Lloyd came shortly before noon. Matt answered the telephone.

"He wants to see me in his office."

"He wants to let you down easy, man."

"You're a born pessimist, Jake. You look on the down side of everything."

"Have it your own way, then, but you'll be singing a different tune after Cullison lays the bad news on you."

Lloyd's attitude had changed from testy to tolerant between Matt's first and second visit.

"Sit down, Alexander. I spoke to the Chief about the search warrant a little while ago."

"What did he say?"

"He didn't think it was a good idea. We don't have any evidence suggesting that Mrs. Waterson was anywhere near the scene when her husband was killed. There's no reason to suspect she shot him. To make a long story short, we're not going to authorize the search of her premises."

"Damn it, Lloyd. The fact that the other gun exists is reason to suspect Felicia Waterson. She doesn't have any witnesses for her alibi. As a matter of fact, the old lady says she lied about it. There was no love lost between her and her husband. She admits threatening him when they fought last Friday night. You've got to let me look for that other gun, Lloyd. If I find it, the entire focus of the investigation may shift."

"Shift to what, Lieutenant?"

"To Felicia Waterson."

"I haven't mentioned this before, Alexander, but it occurs to me that your interest in this case may just be a little too personal, if you know what I mean."

"No, I don't know what you mean, Lloyd. Why don't you

spell it out for me?"

"The word is that you're partial to Angela Bowman. They say you used to go with her a while back."

"You know me better than that, Lloyd. There are some selfish interests being served around here, but they aren't mine."

"Just what the hell do you mean by that?"

"You know I have a damned good lead. You could have persuaded Chief Carter to go along with me if you wanted to."

"Maybe I could have, but why should I? All you ever give me is grief, with your smart-ass back talk and know-it-all attitude. You even call me by my first name in front of the men even though I've told you I don't like it. Why the hell should I help you out? You don't do a damned thing to make my job any easier."

"There's nothing personal in this...uh, Commander. The search warrant has nothing to do with you or me. I asked for it based on the evidence I showed you this morning. Your decision should have been based on the evidence, not how you feel about me."

"Spare me the lecture, Lieutenant. My decision was based on the evidence, and what you showed me this morning doesn't support a search of the Waterson residence, case closed."

"Why do you have to be so goddamned close-minded abut this, Lloyd?"

"Close-minded! I've bent over backward for you on this case, Alexander! I gave you extra time when you said you needed it, and I've given you two extra men which, in my opinion, is a total waste of time and manpower. Your problem is that you don't know when to quit. We've made an arrest in this case, and everybody is satisfied but you. Give it a rest, Lieutenant. Climb down out of your ivory tower and admit that you may be wrong...for once."

"Maybe I am fighting windmills, Lloyd. But, I'll be damned if I give up until I'm satisfied that I've exhausted every possible lead in this case. I don't care if everyone else is satisfied that

BARBARA FLEMING

Angela Bowman is guilty. I'm not satisfied, and I won't go along with the program simply to keep from stepping on everyone else's toes. I'm not afraid to make waves, Lloyd. I still have some principles left."

"He who makes waves often gets wet, Lieutenant. Principles and politics mix about as well as oil and water. Go along with the program this time and forget about the search warrant."

"I don't have any choice, do I?"

"Now you're getting the picture, Alexander. You do what you can do and what you can't do you blame on the system. It's a time-tested recipe for survival, and you save yourself a lot of grief in the process."

Matt could see that there was no point in continuing his conversation with Lloyd. His mind was made up, and once Lloyd took a stand, it was almost impossible to move him off center. Jake saw that the meeting hadn't gone well when Matt returned to their office.

"Did he authorize the warrant?"

"Hell no!"

"I told you he wouldn't, man. The way Lloyd sees it, she's guilty because she's been arrested. He won't deal with the possibility that she may be innocent at this stage of the game. What reason did he give you for refusing to authorize the search?"

"He said the new evidence didn't justify a search of the Waterson house."

"That's just an excuse, man. He could have authorized it if he had wanted to. Lloyd has a one-track mind. He's putting his money on Angela Bowman. You know how stubborn he is once he makes up his mind."

"You don't have to tell me, Jake."

"What are you going to do, now?"

"I don't know. I hate to blow such a good lead, but it looks like I don't have much choice."

"You did the best you could, partner."

"I haven't given up yet, Jake. I'm going after that second gun. I just haven't figured out how."

"Where you want to go for lunch?"

"I'm staying in. Have you got those statements signed yet?"

"Most of them. I'll get the ones from Southeast signed today."

After Jake left, Matt couldn't work for thinking about the second Waterson revolver. It didn't make sense for Felicia Waterson to hold the gun back unless she had a damned good reason for keeping it out of his reach. Murdering her husband with it was the best reason of all. She had probably gotten rid of it by now, but if she didn't think she was a suspect, she might still have it. Either way, the powers that be conspired to keep him from searching her house. If he couldn't go to the gun, maybe he could get the gun to come to him. He though about a con he learned a long time ago. It was an old one, but it just might work. Jake returned an hour later.

"Man, did you see this?" Jake said holding up a computer print-out that had been recently delivered to his in-box. "I can't believe they had the nerve to send this up here five days after I requested it. This is the print-out of the request for priors that I submitted five days ago, and they're just getting around to sending it up."

"Better late than never, Jake."

"That's bullshit, man. They left me holding the bag on Monday. I'd be in a world of trouble if I hadn't gone down to central processing on Monday to light a fire under their butts. This is a damned shame. Five days late, I'm going to file a complaint with Cullison about this."

"When did the computer print it?"

"It has today's date on it; but I turned the request in on Monday."

"If it has today's date on it, that means it didn't run until today. I'll bet the computer went down on Monday. They probably saved the on-line requests and ran them today."

Jake leafed through the print-out for lack of anything better to do.

"We already have this information...hey! What's this?!"

"What's what?"

"I don't remember an outstanding bench warrant on that other print-out."

"That's because there wasn't one."

"Somebody has one now."

"Who?" Matt went over to Jake's desk to inspect the print-out first hand. He searched through most of the entries listed before he got to the name with the outstanding bench warrant. It was the last one on the list, Harold William Waterson, Jr.

"It looks like William Waterson didn't show up in court Wednesday morning for a moving violation."

"When did he get the ticket?" Matt asked. Jake ran his finger along the computerized entry until he reached the date and time the ticket was written. Both men spoke at the same time.

"Saturday night!"

"Ten-twenty P.M. Saturday night! I'll be damned, Jake. I think we've hooked a live one this time!"

"But it doesn't say where he got the ticket, Matt."

"I'll give you a hundred to one that he got it on Sixteenth Street. Are you game?"

"I never bet against a sure thing."

"Who do you know at the traffic bureau, Jake? I want to trace that ticket, fast."

"Let me make the call. They know me down there."

Jake swore, bluffed, begged, and cursed for ten minutes before he got the information he wanted. After he rang off, he grinned like a Cheshire cat.

"So, where did he get the ticket?"

"Sixteenth and Colorado."

"Hot damn! I knew this case would break sooner or later."

Matt on his way out of the office. "Come on, Jake, let's go. Bring that print-out with you."

"Where are we going?"

"To see Chief Carter."

"Are you sure you want to do that, man?"

"Hell yes, I'm sure. I'm sick and tired of beating around the bush with Lloyd. I'm getting this search warrant authorized at the top so Lloyd won't have any excuse for dragging his feet this time."

"Cullison is going to be furious when he finds out, Matt."

"That's his problem," Matt replied with far more bravado than he actually felt.

They arrived at Chief Carter office at two o'clock. Marge Smith didn't want to announce them without an appointment, but Matt raised such a stink, she was afraid not to. Chief Carter wasn't pleased with the unexpected visit. But, he agreed to see them as much out of curiosity as anything else.

"This had better be important, Lieutenant. I'm a busy man, and I don't like unexpected interruptions."

"I'm sorry to barge in on you like this, Chief, but what I have to say is important. Commander Cullison told me you didn't want the Waterson house searched."

"That's right. the Commander and I both agreed that there wasn't enough evidence to justify a search warrant."

"I came down here to show you the new evidence firsthand sir. I'm convinced that we've uncovered a substantial lead in the Waterson case."

Matt gave Chief Carter the ballistics test, the sales receipt, the ledger, and the computer print-out with William Waterson's outstanding bench warrant underlined. Chief Carter listened while he explained how he felt the evidence fit together.

"What does Commander Cullison think about this, Lieutenant?"

"Lloyd told me his decision was final this morning, sir."

"I see you don't mind rocking the boat."

"No sir, I don't, especially when a person's life is on the line."

"I like team players, myself. You can count on them not to rock the boat. That means a lot when you're sitting where I am. But, I also like a man who won't quit when the odds are against him. You took a big chance coming down here. What kind of alibi did William Waterson give you for Saturday night?"

"He said he was home all evening, but he doesn't have any witnesses. The ticket he got at Sixteenth and Colorado at ten-twenty proves he lied."

"Have you talked to the officer who wrote the ticket?"

"Not yet. He's in traffic court this afternoon. I'm going over there after we leave here."

"What if you don't find the other gun, Lieutenant? Sixteenth and Colorado isn't Sixteenth and Floribunda. You still can't place him at the scene."

"We've put him in the vicinity, and that's a hell of a lot more then we had before, Chief."

"I'll go ahead and authorize the search warrant, Lieutenant. You may as well bring him in for questioning while you're at it, but don't get any ideas about charging him. If you don't find the gun and if he doesn't break, you're out of luck. Angela Bowman stays where she is, and we proceed as planned. Do I make myself clear?"

"Yes sir, you do. Thanks for hearing me out, Chief."

"Call before you come next time, Lieutenant. I like things done by the book."

Matt was on cloud nine when he left the Chief's office. Traffic Court lay across the quadrangle in the Judicial Building. They found the officer who wrote the ticket waiting to testify in another traffic case. He confirmed what they already knew about the time, location, and type of violation on the ticket. According to the officer, William Waterson was flying down Sixteenth in his red Porsche doing at least eighty-five miles an hour. The officer picked him up on radar at Sixteenth and Jonquil. He followed the Porsche south on Sixteenth for several miles. He didn't catch him until he crossed Colorado just south of the Carter-Barron Amphitheater. The breath-alyzer test indicated that William Waterson hadn't been drinking. He passed his sobriety test easily. The officer gave him a body search, and he didn't have a weapon on his person. Since he assumed it was a case of simple speeding, he didn't search the car. William Waterson had been scheduled for traffic court at eight o'clock the previous Wednesday. He didn't show up, so the court computer automatically issued the outstanding bench warrant for his arrest.

After they left traffic court, they got Judge Rankin to sign the search warrant and were back at Headquarters by three-thirty P.M. Matt sent Jake to round up Foster and Coleman, the two officers Lloyd had assigned to him part-time. He took four metal detectors from the supply room, and they left for the Waterson residence at four o'clock with Coleman and Foster following.

"Man, you should have told Lloyd about the search warrant," Jake warned. "He's going to pitch a roaring bitch when he finds out that you went over his head to the Chief."`

"The damage has already been done, Jake. I'm in too deep to turn back now; so, I may as well go all the way and give Lloyd some real ammunition for my disciplinary hearing."

"I hope you don't get burned, Matt."

"Don't sweat it, man. I can live without the DCPD any day."

"You'd be a damned site better off if you did. Look at me. I gave the department the best years of my life, and they treat me like dirt."

Matt quickly changed the subject. "We have to be careful with William Waterson, Jake. He's got a volatile temper, and he still may have the other gun."

"Maybe we should restrain him while we search the house."

"Either that or put a man on him." Thirty minutes later, they arrived in front of the Waterson residence on Reservoir road. The house looked deserted. The drapes were drawn, and there weren't any cars parked in the driveway out front. Matt rang the doorbell several times before Aunt Martha answered it. She looked very feeble until he told her why they were there. Then she took on a cunning look and acted a good deal more sprightly as she walked up the stairs to get Felicia Waterson, who stormed down the stairs in a rage when she found out why they were there.

"What right do you have to search my home, Lieutenant Alexander?"

"I have a warrant to search the premises, Mrs. Waterson."

"A warrant to search my house! This is incredible! What do you expect to find?"

"The other gun."

"What other gun?"

"I'm sure you know exactly what I mean, Mrs. Waterson, but let's pretend for the sake of argument you don't. The gun you gave me on Monday belongs to a matched set of revolvers your husband bought from Lowery's Gun Shop twenty years ago. We have proof that he bought two guns, not one as you tried to make me believe. Our forensic lab compared the markings on the bullets taken from your husband's body to the markings made by the gun you gave me. They were very close, Mrs. Waterson, so close that we think the other gun will match the markings on the bullets that killed your husband perfectly."

"Are you accusing me of killing my husband, Lieutenant?"

"I'm not accusing you of anything, Mrs. Waterson, but I want that other gun."

"You have no right to invade the privacy of my home with these men, Lieutenant Alexander. I won't stand for this intrusion. I demand that all of you get out right now!"

Aunt Martha sat in one of the vestibule chairs and watched contemptuously.

"We have a warrant to search this house, Mrs. Waterson, and that's what I intend to do."

"I forbid you to search my house."

"I'm trying to be patient, Mrs. Waterson, but if you don't calm down, I'll have to restrain you. We are going to search your house, so you may as well get used to the idea."

While Matt and Felicia Waterson were arguing, Aunt Martha had quietly slipped upstairs. Felicia Waterson could see that she wasn't getting anywhere with Matt, so she angrily marched out to the kitchen to call her attorney. While she was gone, Aunt Martha came back downstairs and gave Matt a square-shaped polished mahogany box. The box had a small brass name plate on the lid with an engraved inscription that read LOWERY'S GUN SHOP, WASHINGTON D.C. The box wasn't heavy, and when he opened it Matt understood why. Inside, there were two gaping impressions where a matched pair of revolvers normally rested. Felicia Waterson was livid when she returned from the kitchen and found Matt holding the gun box. She turned her fury on Aunt Martha this time.

"How dare you give my husband's gun box to these men. You'd do anything to hurt me and my son. I wish it had been you who died instead of him."

Aunt Martha didn't say a word. She simply resumed her seat and waited. Felicia Waterson looked angry enough to spit fire. Apparently her attorney hadn't given her any consolation from the onslaught of determined policemen who had invaded her home. She climbed the stairs in a huff and disappeared into her room. She was incensed when they decided to search her bedroom first. She made no attempt to conceal her contempt as they searched her personal effects and clothing. She cursed them soundly when they finished and slammed the bedroom door after they left.

It took all four men over two hours to search the second floor of the house. They had to go through five large bedrooms with as many walk-in closets and baths, a large mahogany-paneled study which must have been Waterson's home office, in addition to two sitting rooms in the largest bedroom suites, and still failed to find the matching revolver on the second floor of the house. At six o'clock, Matt sent Coleman and Foster up to the attic while he and Jake went downstairs to start on the first floor. Aunt Martha hadn't moved for the past two hours. She sat as still as a statue, her eyes focused beyond them on a time and place they couldn't comprehend. They didn't disturb her.

For the next three hours, they searched the immense first floor and and equally large basement. They finished shortly before nine o'clock without finding the second gun. Aunt Martha made them a pot of freshly brewed coffee. She was unnaturally quiet as she served them at the kitchen table, nodding "yes" or "no" to Matt's questions, but refusing to be drawn into conversation. They finished their coffee quickly and went outside to start on the guesthouse and garage, which occupied the south side of the property along with a beautifully landscaped patio and pool. In addition to the semi-circular drive in front, the residence also had a long driveway which ran along the west side of the property beginning at Reservoir Road and ending in front of the three-car garage in the rear of the house. They searched the garage first. The only car parked inside was a white Cadillac Seville that apparently belonged to Felicia Waterson. Harold Waterson's white Mercedes was still in the impound lot and William Waterson must have been driving his red Porsche because it wasn't parked out front. They came up empty-handed in the garage, and Matt didn't hold out much hope for the guest cottage either because William Waterson would have to be crazy to leave the gun in the guest cottage where he lived. Suddenly he thought back to the conversation he had with Sam Johnson in Lacey's bar Wednesday night. It occurred to him that Sam may have been right on the money. Maybe young Waterson really wasn't wrapped too tight.

Matt found the guest cottage to be an odd mixture of traditional and modern furniture, probably cast-offs from the main residence. It was surprisingly neat and clean. Matt surmised that whatever else William Waterson happened to be, he wasn't a slob. The cottage was the size of a small two-story house. It had a living room, dining room, powder room, and kitchen downstairs in addition to two bedrooms and a bathroom upstairs. He was relieved to find that the cottage didn't have a basement or an attic.

All four officers searched upstairs without success. At nine o'clock P.M. they started searching the first floor. Everyone was tired and discouraged. Matt had long since abandoned any hope of finding the gun, but he refused to admit that fact to the other men. The officers divided the first floor rooms. Matt got the kitchen. He was down on his hands and knees going through some of the kitchen drawers when he found a box of bullets tucked into the back of the bottom drawer. The box looked new, the price still stuck on the side. When full, the box held thirty, thirty-eight caliber cartridges. Six were missing. He counted twenty-four bullets still in the box. He called the other men into the kitchen.

"Look what I just found."

Jake got excited, "We're getting close, Matt. I'll bet the gun is in here, too."

"I hope so, Jake. Let's take this place apart."

They literally tore the kitchen apart, but the errant gun still failed to materialize. Matt's frustration got the best of him as he kicked the refrigerator.

"Damn it! He's gotten rid if it!"

"Looks that way, man. We've searched this place from top to bottom. If the gun was hidden in here, we would have found it by now."

"Damn it to hell! Why did we have to get so close?"

Jake was about to answer when they heard a car pull into the driveway from Reservoir Road. William Waterson was back. The four officers snapped to attention when they heard the low whine of the Porsche's expensive engine.

"Get the lights, quick!" Matt shouted.

All four officers made a mad scramble throughout the first floor in a frenzied attempt to put the lights out before William Waterson drove into the garage. Jake hit the living room switch just as the Porsche made the turn around the corner of the house. Young Waterson drove slowly, as if he sensed their presence. They waited for him inside the dark guest cottage to search his car. They could see his face clearly from the patio lights as he prepared to park in the garage. He made a wide arc over the pavement behind the house and as he did so, his headlights hit Coleman full in the face before he could duck behind the dining room curtains. William Waterson knew instantly that they were waiting for him. He hit the Porsche's accelerator and made a screeching two-wheeled U-turn in front of the garage and sped down the driveway toward Reservoir Road. The four officers were just seconds behind him running on foot. They ran around the corner of the house just as William Waterson drove his car out of the driveway into oncoming traffic on Reservoir Road. They were all stopped short by the awful sound of colliding metal and screeching tires from the street.

Matt's blood ran cold when he saw that the red Porsche had been hit broad-side by a panel truck that was, in turn, hit in the rear by a city bus that subsequently swerved into opposing lanes of traffic to avoid creaming the panel truck. Then all hell broke loose on Reservoir Road. Traffic was stopped in both directions as the bus straddled the street. Bedlam erupted on the bus as passengers climbed over each other trying to get off.

"Keep those people on the bus under control, Jake!" Matt shouted on the run toward the red Porsche and William Waterson.

When he reached the wrecked Porsche, Matt felt a hot flash

of anxiety rush through his entire body as he experienced the intense fear that William Waterson had been killed. He breathed easier when he saw that young Waterson hadn't been killed, but he was seriously injured, maybe fatally. He was unconscious and bleeding from his nose and mouth. All the Porsche's windows were completely shattered. Glass was all over the car, young Waterson, and the street in front of his house. The impact of the crash had caved the driver's side of the car in and threw it into a spin, forcing it into the far right lane facing south on Reservoir Road. The Porshe was leaking gasoline and smoking from the impact. Matt sized up the situation quickly. William Waterson was seriously injured, probably fatally.

"Coleman! Use the car radio to get an ambulance over here, quick, man! Get a fire truck over here, too. This car looks like it might blow any minute!"

The driver of the panel truck rushed over to the Porsche. When he saw the young man lying unconscious in the wreck, blood all over his face, he broke down.

"My God! Is he dead?!"

"No. He's still alive," Matt assured him, although he didn't want to guess as to how much longer how much longer William Waterson would live.

"It wasn't my fault, I swear it!" the truck driver insisted. The driver was young, probably no older than William Waterson. He was extremely agitated and the longer he stared at William Waterson pinned inside the wreckage, the more upset he got.

"He drove out in front of me! I didn't see him until I hit him! He came out of nowhere! It wasn't my fault!"

"Look man, I know it wasn't your fault," Matt replied. "I saw him pull out in front of you without stopping. Right now, I'm more concerned about getting this man out of this wrecked car. He's in bad shape. "

"Is he dying?"

"God! I hope not!"

Sergeant Coleman ran over to tell him that the ambulance and the fire truck were on the way. In the meantime, Jake managed to calm the bus passengers and to assist the drive in maneuvering the bus back into the southbound lane. That done, he and Sergeant Foster directed traffic around the accident. Matt told Coleman to start the accident report.

William Waterson was in shock. He was very pale and continued to lose blood. Matt got a blanket out of the trunk of his car and spread it over the young man, who was making low moaning sounds and jerking movements with his arms and legs. Matt checked his pulse. It was weak. His breathing was shallow and he wouldn't stop bleeding. Matt looked around and walked over to where Jake was directing traffic.

"I think he's dying, Jake." Jake looked scared.

"You'd better get his mother out here, man. Did you call for an ambulance yet?"

"Yes, it's on the way. Did you see how tightly he's wedged into the front seat?"

"Yeah. It's going to be a bitch getting him out of there in one piece."

"The driver's door won't budge. Man, we have to do something. He's sitting in that goddamned car bleeding to death. The car is leaking gas like a sieve and smoking like a chimney."

"You know there's nothing we can do until the paramedics gets here, Matt. You shouldn't try to move him until the paramedics get here."

"I worked my way through college as a paramedic, Jake, and I keep my certifications current."

"You're asking for trouble, man. Don't try it."

"He's dying, Jake. If we wait for the paramedics, it'll take them ten or fifteen minutes to get him out and he'll be that much worse off. If we take him out now, he'll be ready to go when they get here. Besides that, the damned car may blow. I'm taking him out."

"It looks like they'll have to cut him out of there to me."

"It's not as bad as it looks. I'm pretty sure I can get him out."

"I'm not going to touch him, Matt. It's too much of a risk, man. Don't do it."

"Fine, Jake. I'll do it myself. I can't stand around and wait for that car to blow."

Matt walked over to the panel truck driver. "What are you carrying in that truck?"

"Lumber and plaster board."

"Do you have something I can use for a stretcher?"

"Yes, I think so. Do you want me to get it out?"

"Yes, bring it over to the car quick. I'm going to take him out."

Getting William Waterson out of his damaged car wasn't an easy job. Because there was so little room inside the caved-in hull of the Porshe Targa, Matt had to virtually fold himself in half to get inside the car. He pushed the back of the passenger seat as far back as it would go. The back of the driver's seat wouldn't budge. He then used his left knee to pivot his weight after he climbed into the car while he planted his right foot on the street for leverage. Matt, Officers Coleman and Foster and the panel truck dirver gingerly moved him out of the wrecked Porsche and onto the improvised plywood stretcher. The rescue squad ambulance arrived seconds later.

The paramedics started an IV and oxygen on the street after they checked his vital signs. Both his blood pressure and pulse were critically low. Matt wanted the paramedics to wait for William Waterson's mother, but they refused.

"He's dying, Lieutenant. Every second counts from here on out," the driver shouted as they drove off.

"Where are you taking him?" Matt shouted after the ambulance.

"D.C. General Emergency Trauma Unit," the driver shouted back over the ambulance's blaring siren.

The fire truck arrived immediately after the ambulance left. The firemen doused the wrecked Porsche with fire retardant. After the car stopped smoking, the detectives helped the firemen push the wreckage into the driveway in front of the Waterson house. The panel truck driver pulled into the driveway too, as Sergeant Coleman began to clear southbound traffic lanes on Reservoir Road. Matt left Jake and Sergeant Foster to complete the accident report as he very reluctantly walked up to the house to inform Felicia Waterson about her son's accident. Aunt Martha opened the door again. When he told her what had happened, she seemed to have been expecting it.

"I'm not surprised," she replied. "The Lord works in mysterious ways, indeed He does." Then she went upstairs to tell Felicia Waterson. Matt dreaded another hysterical confrontation with Mrs. Waterson. He decided not to tell her how badly her son had been hurt. The doctors at D.C. General could do a better job of that than he could, anyway. Felicia Waterson was down the stairs in a flash, demanding to know how he had been hurt. When he explained what had happened, she vented the full fury of her maternal wrath on his head. She cursed him up one side and down the other and accused him of deliberately trying to kill her son. When she finished, he offered to drive her to the hospital. She told him she wouldn't be caught dead in his car and slammed her front door in his face.

Foster and Coleman finished the accident report and Jake sent the bus on its way. The panel truck driver looked like he had gotten a reprieve when they let him go. Matt sent Foster and Coleman home. He and Jake drove over to D.C. General's Emergency Trauma Unit to get an update on William Waterson's condition. They parked close to Felicia Waterson's car, but she was nowhere in sight when they walked into the emergency waiting room. The admitting clerk knew that young Waterson was in surgery, but she couldn't give them any information about his condition. She paged the emergency room resident doctor who didn't show up until forty-five minutes later. The doctor told Matt exactly what he didn't want to hear...William Waterson was in critical condition. He had lost several pints of blood and had sustained extensive internal injuries, including a ruptured spleen, and a punctured lung. They rushed him into surgery, but they didn't hold out much hope for his survival. His prognosis was bleak. The doctor also said that Felicia Waterson had collapsed when she learned about her son's critical condition. He had given her a sedative and put her into a hospital room to rest until she recovered sufficiently to go home. He told them that he didn't know how long William Waterson would be in surgery since they didn't know the full extent of his injuries. He advised them not to wait for him to come out of surgery and went back to the emergency room.

For his part, Jake wasn't thrilled at the prospect of staying at the hospital all night. He said: "I think the doctor's right, Matt. There's no point in staying over here if we don't know how long he'll be in surgery."

"You're right, Jake. I'll call later on to see how he's doing."

"Why did he have to go and get himself half-killed like that?" Jake asked as he drove out of the hospital parking lot. "The stuff is going to hit the fan all over the Fourth when Cullison finds out what happened, man."

"Don't remind me, Jake. Of all the terrible, rotten luck!"

"If he dies, you'll have to tell Cullison; so you may as well tell him now. There'll be hell to pay either way."

"If he dies, I'm finished; so there won't be any reason to tell Lloyd anything, Jake."

"Hell, Matt! It wasn't your fault he drove out in front of that truck without looking!"

"Lloyd won't see it that way. If William Waterson dies, Lloyd won't rest until he drums me off the DCPD."

"Chief Carter approved the search warrant. He'll support you, man."

"No he won't. He'll run for cover like everyone else, and leave me to take the spear alone. And, that's okay too. I stirred the mess up, and now I have to live with the consequences."

"It's not that bad, Matt."

"It's worse than that, Jake. I'm going to resign if he dies."

"You're over-reacting, man. Nobody's going to ask for your resignation. You were right about him, partner. He must have killed his father, otherwise why did he run like that when he spotted us?"

"The gun wasn't in the car, Jake, and without the gun, we can't prove he killed his father."

"You have the gun case and the box of bullets. Won't that be enough evidence?"

It's all circumstantial. Ed Davenport isn't going to drop the case against Angela Bowman to prosecute a circumstantial case against William Waterson. He already told me that."

"William Waterson lied about being home last Saturday night. That speeding ticket proves he was on Sixteenth and Colorado at nine-twenty, right after his father was killed."

"It doesn't prove he was in the Bowman's basement shooting his father."

"Don't' you believe that he did it?"

"Yes, I believe he did it, but I can't prove that he did it and Ed Davenport won't prosecute him without hard evidence."

"He'll change his mind once he sees what you have against William Waterson."

"No, he won't, Jake. The best I can do is to pray like hell for William Waterson to live. If he dies, it's all over for me."

Jake tried to be optimistic, but he could see the handwriting on the wall, too. His young partner was a born risk-taker. He jumped in when everyone else stood back cautiously testing the water. Jake had warned him time and again to go slow and consider the consequences before he made a move, but he was young. He was still naive enough to think that he could make a difference. He still contemplated the possibilities of what life had to offer. Jake, on the other hand, was too old and ill-used to harbor such illusions. Jake's optimism had withered and dried up from years of bitter disappointments and unfulfilled expectations. Time eroded his resilience in the face of too many failures and missed chances. Jake's youthful optimism had disappeared so long ago, he couldn't remember what it felt like when he had it. Now, all he had left was a brittle pessimism tempered by a steadfast belief in God.

Matt was different from Jake. Where Jake saw a half-empty glass, he saw one that was half-full. Where Jake saw discrimination and hopelessness, he saw opportunity and a chance to survive on his own terms. Where Jake saw the past, he saw the future and he went after it with everything he had. Jake had chided him more than once for being too cocky and thinking he could beat the system. But at the same time, he admired him for his audacity and courage. He envied his young partner's self-assurance and took vicarious pleasure in his success. Jake wished all the good things for his partner that life had denied him, but maybe they weren't to be his after all. Life had a cruel way of slapping you down in spite of your best efforts. It looked like the system had finally caught up with Lieutenant Matthew Alexander. He had taken one chance too many. Jake wished it weren't so, but he didn't hold out much chance for William Waterson's survival either.

Jake let Matt out in front of his house at twelve o'clock. He tried to cheer him up, but there really wasn't much that could be said under the circumstances. Matt went straight up to his bedroom and got ready to run. He ran whenever things began to close in on him. Jogging helped to rid him of his pent-up frustrations. Tonight, he ran out of desperation, because jogging was powerless to alter the course of events that was set in motion with William Waterson's accident. When he told Carla he was going out to run, she was surprised.

"Out to jog! You never jog at midnight, honey! What's going on?"

"Nothing's going on, Carla. I feel tight and I want to run it off without an inquisition, if you don't mind."

"Are you seeing another woman? Because, if you are all you have to do is tell me."

"Don't be an idiot, Carla! I'm not seeing anybody. Why is it so hard for you to understand that I simply need to run tonight."

"I don't know what to believe when you get home at midnight, jump into your running clothes, and tear out the door like the house is on fire. Something`s wrong isn't it?"

"Yes. Something happened tonight, but I can't talk about it right now." Then she saw how upset he was.

"It's serious isn't it?"

"Yes. It's very serious. I'll tell you about it when I get back."

She had never seen him so strung out before. She got a queasy feeling in the pit of her stomach after he left. Then she realized that she was afraid, too. She couldn't imagine what had happened to affect him so intensely. It botherd her because he was her touchstone. She depended on him for support and reassurance when she couldn't trust her own resources to see her through. She needed him to take the edge off her anxieties, to complete her in a way no one else could. His distress was her distress because she couldn't imagine her life without him.

Matt rarely ran at night. The streets were dark and the automobile headlights were a glaring nuisance as they reflected off his glasses, but he had to run this night. The Waterson case pressed him from all sides. All of the frustrations of the past week came to a head with the accident. He couldn't imagine a more disastrous outcome to his investigation. Had he pressed too hard as Lloyd suggested? Had he been too arrogant to admit the possibility that Angela Bowman might be guilty? Was he too personally involved to exercise good judgement? Yesterday, he would have confidently answered all those questions with a resounding NO. Tonight, he didn't know how to answer them.

He ran hard, each footfall slamming the pavement in a steady rhythm as he shifted his weight from one foot to the other. He ran fast, pushing himself to the limit of his physical tolerance until his heart beat like a hammer and sweat poured out of his body. He ran until he thought he would drop from exhaustion, and then he ran some more. When he could no longer run, he walked. He didn't know where he was until he looked up and saw Fourth District Headquarters towering over him. He crossed the street to the Catholic school that faced Headquarters from the other side of Georgia Avenue. He rested on the school steps in the shadows created by the street light on the corner.

He sat there and thought about William Waterson fighting for his life at D.C. General Hospital. He thought about Harold Waterson cheated out of his life by a killer's bullets. He thought about Angela Bowman in a jail cell, her life on the line for first degree murder. He thought about Carla and his children and how badly he wanted to do what was best for them. He thought about his career on the force and how hard he had fought for it and how easily it could be snatched away from him. But most of all, he thought about Matthew Alexander and the demons that drove him to make the choices that he made.

He felt vulnerable and exposed and weak. His defenses were down, and anxiety crept up on him. He was more frightened than he'd ever been...afraid for his career, his family, William Waterson, Angela Bowman, himself. He did what he thought was best; but maybe he didn't know what was best after all, so he sat there and sorted through his confusion. He didn't know how long he had been there when he finally got up to leave. He took one last look at Fourth District Headquarters across the street. It looked so solid and reassuring, so invulnerable. He wished he was as strong. He ran home slowly and deliberately. It was well after three o'clock when he got back. Carla was waiting up for him when he opened the door, and he needed her more than ever.

# CHAPTER XVI

Saturday was not promising as days went. It arrived cold, glum, and dreary. The prediction was for rain possibly mixed with light snow and sleet. The weather hung over the District like a chronic depression, cheerless in its aspect and mood. Matt arrived at his office earlier than usual. He had been there two hours when Jake showed up at nine.

"Any word on William Waterson yet, partner?"

"I went over to D.C. General before I came to work, Jake. He's alive, but he's still in critical condition. He's in the intensive care unit."

"That's good news, man. I expected him to die last night."

"The doctor said his chances are no better than fifty-fifty."

"He hasn't died yet. Doctors don't know as much as they think they do. I put my trust in God, Matt. He's the one who decides who lives and who dies. If it's not his time to go, he won't die; it doesn't matter what the doctor says."

Matt's skepticism ran a good deal deeper than Jake's, but the didn't argue the point. Arguing religion with Jake was like arguing politics with a member of the opposition, a no-win proposition.

"I hope you're right, Jake."

"Trust in God, Matt. He'll see you through this mess. He's seen me through worse." Jake looked up to see Sam Johnson storm into the office looking as disagreeable as forty miles of bad road.

"What the hell do you have to show me that can't wait until Monday?" Sam barked his question at Matt.

"Give me a break, Sam. It'll only take you a few minutes to compare some bullets we found at the Waterson house to the ones that killed Hal Waterson."

"Give you a break! You've got one hell of a nerve, Lieutenant! Give you a break! Do you know how long it's been since I've had a whole weekend off? Do you care how long it's been since I've had a whole weekend off? Of course you don't care. Otherwise, you wouldn't have gotten me out of bed to come all the way over here to look at some freaking bullets. It's been a year, Lieutenant...twelve months, fifty-two weeks, three hundred and sixty five days since I've had a whole weekend off. You can see as well as I can. Why didn't you compare the damned bullets?"

"I'm not a forensic specialist, Sam."

"And I'm not at your beck and call any time of the day or night, Alexander. In case you don't know it, I have a life outside the District of Columbia police force. Anway, where's the gun? That's what I should be comparing to the slugs taken out of Waterson's chest."

"We didn't find the damned gun, so you'll have to look at what we did find."

"Well, give me the bullets, so I can look at them and get the hell out of here." Matt took the box of bullets from his desk and gave them to Sam who left in a huff. Jake was glad to see him go.

"That Sam Johnson is a real pain in the butt. Why do you put up with his mouth, Matt?"

"Because he's the best forensic man on the force, Jake. We're lucky to have him."

"Lucky! It's more like a curse if you ask me. The only thing I like better than seeing Sam leave is not seeing Sam at all. He gets on my last nerve with all his hell raising."

"Sam is hard to take first thing in the morning, but he gets the job done in good time; and you can't ask for much more than that."

"Why does he have to be such a smart-ass all the time. You'd think he could do his job without raising hell every time someone asks him to do something."

Matt thought about someone else who regularly raised hell about work assignments and concluded that it was ironic that Jake could recognize characteristics in Sam Johnson that he didn't see in himself.

The office telephone rang. It jarred both men. Jake usually jumped to answer the phone, but this time he hung back. He was afraid it would be D.C. General Hospital on the other end calling to say that William Waterson had died. Both men hesitated to answer it out of fear. Matt finally swallowed the lump of fear in his throat and got up enough courage to answer on the sixth ring. The voice at the other end of the line was barely audible. He thought he had a bad connection.

"Hello! Hello! Who is this?!" The voice didn't get any louder. "Who is this?" he kept asking. He was about to hang up when his mind made some sense of what was being said. He heard a woman's voice whispering:

"I did it...I shot him," over and over. Her speech was slurred and sounded like a recording being played too slowly.

"I did it...I killed him," she softly insisted. The voice was so soft and distorted that Matt thought he might be mistaken about what he heard, so he let Jake listen to it. Jake heard it too.

"I did it...I killed him." Jake returned the receiver to Matt.

"Who the hell is that, partner?"

"I don't know! Who is this?!" Matt demanded several times.

The voice didn't respond. it kept on repeating its message like a broken record. "I did it...I shot him."

Then, it hit Matt like a flash that whoever it was on the other end of the line had taken an overdose of drugs.

"Somebody's OD'd, Jake. Get to another telephone and call Felicia Waterson's number quick! We have to get a rescue squad over there on the double!"

Jake ran out to the secretary's desk to place the call. She looked at him as if he had lost his mind when he grabbed her telephone out of her hand.

"Hurry!" he screamed at the operator. "This is a matter of life and death!" The operator finally placed the call, and he was floored when Felicia Waterson answered her own telephone.

"Is this Felicia Waterson?" He rang off the minute she said ëyes', and ran back into the office.

"It's not Felicia Waterson, Matt! She just answered the phone at her house when I called."

"I know who it is, Jake. I just recognized her voice. I've got to get a rescue squad over to Floribunda Lane, quick! Get the secretary in here, Jake! Somebody has to keep her on the line as long as possible!" Matt shouted his instructions to the secretary on the run. He grabbed both of their coats on the way out of the office and met Jake, who was rolling up to the entrance of Headquarters as Matt ran out the front door. Jake hit the siren as they pulled away from the curb. They arrived at Floribunda Lane twenty minutes later. The rescue squad was already there.

Jake had jumped out of the car and was running for Claudia Martin's front door before he realized that his partner wasn't behind him. He turned around and was shocked to see Matt race up the Bowman's front steps and through the double doors, which showed several sizeable gashes from the rescue squad's axes. Taking the stairs three at a time, Matt was in Helen Bowman's bedroom before Jake entered the house.

Helen Bowman was lying on the floor fully dressed. Two of the paramedics were giving her cardiopulmonary resuscitation. The third was talking on the bedroom telephone. He hung up as Matt walked into the room.

"How is she?" he asked, expecting to hear the worst.

"Her heart had stopped by the time we got here. We started to work on her immediately, but it's too late."

"How long have you been giving her CPR?"

"For five minutes, but she hasn't responded so far. I gave her an injection right into the muscle, but that didn't kick it off either. She took an overdose of these."

The paramedic gave Matt an empty bottle of sleeping pills.

"I don't know how many were in there, Lieutenant, but she had to take at least two dozen pills at that dosage to stop her heart and respiration."

When Jake saw the two paramedics working on Helen Bowman, he wouldn't go into the bedroom. He felt death stalking the room, calmly waiting to claim its latest victim. He knew she was dead the minute he saw her lying there. Death knew it too, so it patiently waited for foolish men to abandon useless attempts to save her. Jake understood when he saw her dressed as if she were going to church, all in white. He could smell death, feel its presence, the same feeling he experienced when he saw Harold Waterson in the basement last Saturday night. Clearly, death had never left the house. The others tried to pretend it wasn't there, but Jake knew better, so he wouldn't go into the bedroom. Thirty minutes after they arrived, the paramedics working on Helen Bowman gave up. Death was not to be cheated after all. The two men accepted their defeat reluctantly. They cleaned the smeared make-up from her face and placed her body in the center of her bed. Helen Bowman was serene, having accepted the inevitable long before the men surrounding her bed that Saturday morning dared to admit they had failed.

Jake turned around when he heard footsteps running up the stairs. It was Walter Bowman. He looked at Jake standing outside his bedroom door and knew that something was terribly wrong. He rushed past Jake over to the bed, where it took just seconds for him to realize that his wife was dead. He issued an agonized scream that seemed to come from the depths of his soul, dropped to his knees beside the bed and cried bitter, useless tears. He held her hand and cried her name over and over. His agony wasn't an easy thing to witness. Matt and the chief paramedic joined Jake in the hall.

"She took a large overdose of these sleeping pills, Lieutenant. There was very little we could do for her once the drugs had been in her system for so long. She was dead when we got here. Some people are more susceptible to barbiturate poisoning than others. Once it reaches the brain stem and suppresses the respiration and heart function, there's not much we can do. She died shortly before we got here."

Matt accepted the chief paramdeic's explanation; he had no other choice. He walked over to the alcove, to the same spot where he stood the previous Sunday and looked out of the window. He felt defeated, angry, and helpless. He knew he couldn't have saved her, but it didn't ease the anguish that tore him apart. He looked at the suicide note he found on the nightstand for the first time. It was handwritten on blue personalized stationery. He didn't doubt that she had written it herself. The note read:

My daughter didn't kill Harold Waterson, I did. I shot him in my basement last Saturday night with Walter's pistol. I saw her take him around back. I knew he was trying to make her to move to New York. She didn't want to go, but he would have forced her to move anyway. He was determined to have his way, to make her do what he wanted. She would have gone, because she's weak like me, and he was strong like Walter. He would have used Angela until he got tired of her and then she would have come home again to me and her father. I got Walter's gun out of the desk drawer while he was in the bathroom. Then I went to the basement and I shot him. I went outside after that and dropped the gun down the storm drain. I can't continue living knowing that my daughter is being punished for something I did. I killed Harold Waterson, and I can't go on knowing the pain I've caused his family and mine.

She signed her name at the bottom of the page and neatly folded it in half before she placed it on her nightstand. Matt read the note through several times. Helen Bowman's confession hit him like a bolt from nowhere. He didn't know what to make of it. It was totally unexpected, the last thing he would have predicted. Her confession meant that he was completely off base with the evidence against William Waterson. Could he have been so wrong? He was convinced that the case against William Waterson was strong enough to stand on its own, but if he took Helen Bowman's confession at face value, the evidence was meaningless, little more than a red herring.

"What have you got there?" Jake asked.

Matt gave him the note to read. Jake couldn't believe it either.

"I'll be damned! Who would have thought that she killed him? She was the last person I would have suspected, Matt."

"I still find it hard to believe, Jake."

"It's all written down here in black and white. I guess this note solves your case for you, partner."

"I suppose it does, Jake."

It was an unsettling solution, though. One that went

against the grain and strained the limits of Matt's reason. He knew the case against William Waterson was solid, but Helen Bowman's confession made it seem trivial. It was a confusing turn of events to say the least. He went back into the bedroom, where he found Walter Bowman just as he had left him, kneeling beside the bed sobbing and holding his wife's hand. Matt stood on the other side of the bed and looked at Helen Bowman's body lying there so still and motionless. There was an aura of peace and serenity about her as if death had delivered her from a life more anguished and tormented than anyone knew. Death suited her somehow in a way that life never had. Matt looked around the bedroom where Helen Bowman took her life. It was a beautiful room, too beautiful to be a tomb. But, maybe that's all it had ever been for her. Maybe that's why she chose to die there. He looked at her lying there in her white dress and shoes, and he wasn't sorry for her anymore. She gave death dignity and grace.

"Why did she do it, Matthew? Why did she kill herself?" Walter Bowman asked between sobs.

Matt read him the note his wife had left. When he finished reading it, Walter Bowman cried out as if had been stabbed in the heart.

"Oh my God! She didn't kill Hal Waterson. She couldn't have killed him, she was afraid of guns!"

"Somebody got rid of your gun. If she didn't do it then who did?"

Walter Bowman started to speak, but he caught himself and stopped short of saying what was on his lips. He buried his face in the coverlet of the bed instead. He didn't have to finish what he started to say, because Matt was almost certain he knew what it was. Helen Bowman knew that they hadn't found the gun. She said as much when they came to arrest Angela. If she knew that they hadn't found the gun, then she probably knew what had happened to it even if she didn't get rid of it herself. Had the Bowmans gotten rid of the gun because they assumed that Angela had actually killed Waterson? Had Helen Bowman confessed to murder and committed suicide because she believed that Angela was guilty? If only they had told him the truth. What they told him amounted to half-truths, distortions of the facts, feeble attempts to conceal what really happened behind assumptions that just may have cost Helen Bowman her life. He didn't know whether she was guilty or not, but he knew he was tired, very tired. The chief paramedic called him into the hallway.

"What do you want us to do about the body, Lieutenant?"

"It has to be taken to the city morgue at D.C. General Hospital."

"We can't wait around here indefinitely, Lieutenant. We're still on call. If you want us to deliver the body to the morgue, it'll have to be soon."

"What are you going to do about Walter Bowman, Matt?" Jake asked.

"I don't know, Jake."

As it turned out, the only person Walter Bowman would agree to see was Tom Martin. Matt convinced him to go over to Tom's house before they moved the body. He wanted to spare him the anguish of seeing his wife leave the house in a body bag. Jake escorted Walter Bowman next door. Matt instructed the two officers on duty outside the house to secure the perimeter of the property while they waited for the forensics team. He watched the rescue squad ambulance leave from the foyer. He didn't leave immediately. He wanted to take a final look at the house that produced two bodies in seven days.

The house that Walter Bowman made was still, almost solemn. Matt could hear himself think as he wandered about the first floor. The house that Walter Bowman made was impressive, too. He walked through the living room, where the trappings of wealth and status were so tastefully assembled. He walked across the foyer to the dining room. The crystal chandelier was as beautiful as before, but it all seemed hollow somehow. The house that Walter Bowman made had never been a home. It was never intended to be a haven for the comfort and companionship of its residents. Certainly, Helen Bowman didn't find respite there when she needed it most. It was a shrine, really. A repository for its maker's pretensions and insecurities. There was very little love in the house that Walter Bowman made. It was expensive, and tasteful, and beautiful. It was also cold and shallow and distant. The house that Walter Bowman made stood while the marriage that it was meant to shelter lay in ruins, destroyed by desperation, loneliness, and finally suicide. Matt lingered a while longer, then he left the house that Walter Bowman made for the last time. He closed the doors and it suddenly occurred to him that the gashes were fitting, a symbol of the emotional and physical destruction that had taken place within the house. Jake waited for him in the car. Matt took one last look at 1637 Floribunda Lane before he got into the car. While he was standing there, the sun came out for the first time that morning. He left Floribunda Lane more reassured than he'd been at any time since the investigation started.

"I guess that's that," Jake said as they drove away. "What's next on the agenda, Matt?"

"I'll have to call Lloyd as soon as we get back to the office, Jake. Then I'll make out a crime report and wait for Lloyd to figure out what to do with Helen Bowman's confession."

"What do you think he'll say, Matt?"

"He'll call Chief Carter, for starters." They got back to Headquarters at eleven o'clock. There was a note waiting on Matt's desk. He read it and breathed a huge sigh of relief. Then he passed it on to Jake.

"He's going to be all right, Jake. His vital signs have stabilized and he's conscious. There doesn't seem to be any neurological damage either. He's damned lucky if you ask me."

"You probably saved his life by taking him out of that car, partner. But, the way I see it, it wasn't his time to go. Man! This is great news! You're the one who's damned lucky. Somebody up there is looking out for you, Matt."

"Tell them to keep their fingers crossed, Jake. I'm not out of the woods yet."

"You don't have to worry about Cullison. He's going to be busy figuring out how to gloss over the fact that he arrested the wrong woman."

"Chief Carter sanctioned the arrest before we made it."

"Doesn't make a damned bit of difference, man. Cullison will have to take the fallout because we made the pinch, and he had better not mention the Chief's name if he knows what's good for him. Serves him right, for once." They both laughed.

"I think Lloyd has this one coming, Jake."

Matt called Lloyd at home to fill him in on the suicide.

"How did he take it, man?"

"He didn't like it, that's for sure. But, what could he say? He wants to see the note, of course, so he's coming into Headquarters PDQ."

"I'm glad to see the great Commander Cullison on the spot for a change," Jake insisted. "He deserves a good dose of his own medicine."

Matt worked fast to finish the suicide crime report before Lloyd arrived. Jake went to lunch alone. At one o'clock, he got the summons to the Commander's office. Lloyd looked grim. He read the handwritten confession and the preliminary crime report without comment.

"Is there any question about her death being a suicide, Alexander?"

"None that I can see, Lloyd. Of course, we won't know for sure until the autopsy, but I'd say there's very little chance that it wasn't a suicide. She took an overdose of prescription sleeping pills. The medical examiner has the pills that were left in the bottle."

Lloyd inspected the container warily before replying, "I called Chief Carter, Lieutenant. He and Ed Davenport are going to meet us here in my office. Where was the husband while she was swallowing the pills?"

"He was out of the house. The rescue squad had to force the front doors open to get inside. They couldn't revive her. The chief paramedic said she probably died a few minutes before they got there."

Chief Carter and Ed Davenport arrived within a few minutes of each other. Ed Davenport was obviously distressed by the confession. He had looked forward to prosecuting Angela Bowman and he didn't welcome the news that her mother had confessed to the crime in a suicide note. He was extremely reluctant to relinquish his chance to shine in court one more time. Chief Carter had mixed emotions. He was obviously concerned about the fallout from Angela Bowman's, as it now appeared, premature arrest; but he welcomed the opportunity to close the case without a public trial and its consequent publicity. Lloyd was noncommittal. He had gone along with the Chief's decision to arrest Angela Bowman against his instincts, now it was the Chief's turn to salvage the mess they found themselves in.

They talked for nearly an hour before Matt told them about William Waterson's accident. Lloyd hit the ceiling. He was furious when he found out that Matt had gone over his head to get the search warrant from Chief Carter. He dressed him down royally in front of the Chief and Ed Davenport. He also accused him of causing the accident through hot pursuit. Matt explained that the Porsche was hit as it left the Waterson driveway because William Waterson failed to give on-coming traffic on Reservoir Road the right of way. But that didn't make any difference to Lloyd. Matt laid low because he knew he had it coming. Chief Carter waited for Lloyd to cool off before he told him, as diplomatically as possible, to back off. Lloyd agreed to overlook Matt's assault on the chain of command in front of the Chief in order to stay on the Chief's good side, but he strongly resented the insubordination and he wasn't going to take it lying down in spite of what the Chief said. Matt knew he hadn't heard the last of this from Lloyd.

Chief Carter wasn't impressed with either the gun box or the box of bullets found in William Waterson's kitchen. The Lieutenant hadn't found the gun; and as far as the Chief was concerned, that was the end of that. The meeting lasted two hours. Lloyd gave Helen Bowman's confession to Ed Davenport. The District's chief prosecuting attorney's office agreed to verify its authenticity and make whatever adjustments were required in the case based on what they found and results of the autopsy. Matt was relieved to be rid of the responsibility. No one seemed particularly concerned about the fact that Helen Bowman didn't have any gunpowder residue on her hands when Sam checked them the night of the murder. It was as if they didn't want to look a gift horse in the mouth. Both Lloyd and Chief Carter saw Helen Bowman's confession as a convenient escape from a messy trial and potentially bad publicity for the department if Angela Bowman was acquitted. Ed Davenport wasn't entirely convinced, but he went along with the others in spite of his disappointment. The meeting was over at three, and Matt went back to his office.

"You got a call from Sam Johnson while you were gone, Matt."

"What did he want?"

"He said the slugs taken from Waterson's chest are the same type of bullets in the box you gave him."

"I knew they would be."

"How did you know?"

"It was a reasonable assumption considering the other

evidence against William Waterson."

"How did the meeting go?"

"The suicide investigation has been turned over to the District Prosecutor's office. They have to verify the confession's authenticity. Once they do that, they're going to drop the charges against Angela Bowman."

"What did Lloyd say when you told him about the accident, Matt?"

"I've never seen him so angry, Jake. He was furious. The Chief put in a good word for me to Lloyd, so I don't think he'll demand a disciplinary hearing."

"The Chief did that for you? I told you somebody up there was looking out for you, Matt. You've got nine lives, man."

"Lloyd won't forget that I went over his head, Jake. He'll pay me back. The only question is where and when."

"Don't sweat it, man. You can handle Cullison. If worse comes to worse, you can always transfer to another District."

"I like the Fourth, Jake. Lloyd is a good Commander. I'd rather work for him than any of the other three."

"You must be crazy, Matt. I'd transfer out of here today if I could. Cullison is a goddamned racist!"

Matt listened patiently as Jake raked Commander Lloyd Cullison over the coals one more time. He put Jake in neutral after a couple of minutes and cleared the top of his desk. Jake finished his tirade and looked at his watch.

"Let's go over to Lacey's for a drink, Matt. We should do something to celebrate the end of your investigation, man."

"I don't think it calls for a celebration, Jake."

"It's over. That ought to be worth at least one drink."

"You're right, Jake. It's funny how the Waterson case began with a letter and ended with one."

"How did it start with a letter?" Jake asked as they walked out of the office.

"The anonymous letter Claudia Martin sent to Felicia

Waterson out of spite set the wheels in motion. Everything that happened in this case can be traced back to that letter."

"I'll bet Claudia regrets the day she ever sent that letter, Matt."

"I'll bet a month's pay that she couldn't care less."

THE END